KU-591-316

ONE MORE CHANCE

LUCY AYRTON

dialogue
books

DIALOGUE BOOKS

First published in Great Britain in 2018 by Dialogue Books
This paperback published in 2018 by Dialogue Books

10 9 8 7 6 5 4 3 2 1

Copyright © Lucy Ayrton 2018

The moral right of the author has been asserted.

*All characters and events in this publication, other than those
clearly in the public domain, are fictitious and any resemblance
to real persons, living or dead, is purely coincidental.*

All rights reserved.
No part of this publication may be reproduced, stored in a
retrieval system, or transmitted, in any form or by any means, without
the prior permission in writing of the publisher, nor be otherwise circulated
in any form of binding or cover other than that in which it is published
and without a similar condition including this condition
being imposed on the subsequent purchaser.

A CIP catalogue record for this book
is available from the British Library.

ISBN 978-0-3497-0020-5

Typeset in Berling by M Rules
Printed and bound in Great Britain by
Clays Ltd, Elcograf S.p.A

Papers used by Dialogue Books are from well-managed forests
and other responsible sources.

Dialogue Books
An imprint of
Little, Brown Book Group
50 Victoria Embankment
London EC4Y 0DZ

An Hachette UK Company
www.hachette.co.uk

www.littlebrown.co.uk

To Paul,
who promised to support me
in all my endeavours,
and did.

Lucy Ayrton is the communications manager of a prisons charity, and much of *One More Chance* is informed by the people she has met and the time she has spent in prisons. She has an MA in Creative Writing from Warwick University, and is also a performance poet.

All of a sudden, the pain stopped.

There was a second when everything was quiet. After the sweat and screaming and 'come on now love, little pushes now, come on', there was a moment of nothing. Just the midwives whispering, shuffling around just out of my sight. I lifted my head up off the pillows, straining to see, but they were all huddling around this little bundle on the table. Panic gripped at the heart of me, squeezing tight. It was so quiet. I thought of all the reasons she might not be okay, all the things I know I didn't do, and all the things I did. I went,

'Is she alright?'

And my voice came out just a croak. And in that moment, I knew that I wanted her more than anything. For her to be safe, for her to be well, for her to be with me, in my arms. I shuffled up the bed, wincing. Where was she? Please let her be okay, please please please . . .

Then, a cry. And all I remember thinking is, stupid of me, but, that this was like on telly. She sounded just like a baby on telly.

'Decent pair of lungs on her.'

The nurse smiled down at me and I smiled back. The kind of smile that you can't help, that hurts your face after you're done.

'It is a girl then?'

She nodded.

'*A healthy little girl.*'

And I felt this rush, this massive bang of happiness and guilt and worry and love. This little scrap of a thing was mine to love and protect now. I'd been so sure that I'd lose her, and I might still, I knew that. But it was hard to think of it just then, of the social workers and forms and meetings in the future. My head and heart were so full of this feeling – I know it's stupid, because it was just a hospital bed, wasn't it? But for the first time in forever I felt like I belonged, like I was exactly where I needed to be. Like I was finally home.

'*Can I hold her?*'

The nurse laughed.

'*Of course you can, Dani. She's yours.*'

Mine, I thought. She's mine.

And she laid my little girl, so gently, into my arms. I curled myself around her, feeling her weight laying on me, just exactly right. I thought of my own mamma. Had she held me this way, all torn and bloody and euphoric on a hospital bed? She must have. Funny to think of her, feeling exactly the same as me. We never were much alike.

The nurse smiled down.

'*Well done, love. Anyone you'd like me to call for you? Family, maybe, a friend?*'

I shook my head, hard, not letting my eyes leave the baby's little face. It was just her and me now, wasn't it? It didn't matter if we didn't have anyone else. The nurse sighed, disappointed.

'*Lovely little thing, anyway. Do you have a name for her yet?*'

And I looked into her tiny pink scrunch of a face and I made her a promise. A promise that, whatever happened, I'd always do my best for her. I'd always protect her, I'd always try to do what was right, I'd always keep her safe. I've fucked up a lot in my life, but I swore, not this. She'd get the very best of me.

Out loud, I said,

'Bethany. Her name's Bethany.'

And I stared into her little face and, despite everything, I didn't think in all my life I'd ever felt as good as that before. I was so peaceful, you know? I was complete.

Chapter One

Extract from PSI 54/2011 – Mother and Baby Units

1.4   MBUs cater for mothers with babies up to either
9 or 18 months. Timescales are a guideline only
and separations should be influenced by the best
interests of the child concerned.

Lisa picks up a T-shirt from the end of my bed and waddles across the cell.

'Oi, Dani! This one's mine.'

I give her a bit of a glare. I've only got two T-shirts other than that one. She's got, like, five. Her family's always sending in stuff.

'It don't fit you, though.'

'It will soon,' she says, shaking it out and laying it over her bump. Like she needs the support to fold up a crappy little T-shirt. But she fucking loves being pregnant, does Lisa, and she'll remind you about it any chance she gets.

'You said I could borrow it, didn't you?'

'I'll get this weight off before you know it. I'm going to do breastfeeding, aren't I? The nurse says it's good for the baby, and it helps you get the weight off.'

I shrug. I wouldn't know about that. And she starts talking about something else, but if I'm honest I'm not listening. I'm thinking about being pregnant. And babies, the soft, milky smell of them. The feel of a newborn that trusts you that much it's gone to sleep in your arms. I let my eyes drift up to the pictures I have of Bethany, stuck to the wall with dried toothpaste. Four of them, neat in a row, one every six months. I smile up at her, feeling that hollow in my chest I always get when I remember where she is – not with me.

'Dani. Are you listening?'

She's glaring at me, holding the folded T-shirt in her hand. I really did like that one.

'Yeah. Course I am.'

'Yeah? What was I saying then?'

I give her a grin, one of my good ones.

'I *was* listening, Lise. What was that last bit, though?'

She rolls her eyes at me.

'I *said*, I heard they've got some really nice stuff. Up there on the unit.'

I nod and pull her a face, like, *I am well interested in what they've got up the mother and baby unit.*

'Yeah?'

Lisa lays the T-shirt in a bag, all neat and prim as if it was a Louis Vuitton suitcase rather than a manky old Tesco carrier bag she only got in the first place because Miss Green felt sorry for her.

'Yeah. Like, they say it's not the babies who are in prison, right? It's just the mums. So the babies get everything they'd get on the outside. A cot and blankets and clothes and stuff. Even toys.'

I'd wanted to get Lisa a toy, as it goes. For the little one. You're allowed to save up for stuff and get it sent in from Argos, they always say that. I'd saved up my canteen money and gone last week to see what I could pick up. Just something little, you know? To remember me by, when she's up on the unit.

'Yeah. That's well good.'

'Because the experts say, it doesn't matter to the baby. They don't care about their, like, wider environment. It's just being in decent surroundings and being with their mum, that's all they need.'

Hearing that gives me this sharp pain in my belly. I don't like it when people go on and on about how good it is for babies to stay with their mums. I go,

'Yeah, not always, though. Like, they can have a good life if they're adopted as well. Looked after or whatever.'

I think of Bethany, staying with the foster parents. But it's okay. It's not for long, is it? I'll get her back. And Lisa don't suddenly know everything, just because she's knocked up. She's not the first one to ever have a kid, and you can bet she won't be the last.

'Well, yeah, if their birth mum's shit, maybe. But I'm going to be a good mum, aren't I? It's staying with me that'll be best for my baby, isn't it?'

The stabbing pain is back again, but I shrug. I don't want to be a bitch to Lisa. She's been a good mate to me over the last few months.

'Yeah. That's right. You'll be alright.'

She looks around the cell, then gives her carrier a little pat and sits down on the bed.

'Will you come and visit me, when I've had it? Come and see the baby?'

I shift on my bed, like, uneasy.

'They won't let me, will they? I'll be in here.'

Lisa gives me a frown.

'You'll be out in a few months, though. I'm in for another year. Promise you'll come and visit as soon as you get out.'

I sit up, feeling the springs creaking beneath me.

'Yeah ... I'll try.'

'You'll try, or you will?'

She looks well pissed off, now.

'You'll be proper busy with the baby by then, though, won't you, Lise? You won't want me getting in the way.'

'I will, though.'

I feel proper bad about it, but there's no point lying.

'I dunno. It's not that easy, is it? Like, coming back to the prison and that.'

Lisa folds her arms. They look ridiculous, perched on top of her swollen boobs.

'What's difficult about just coming, like, a mile down the road to come and see me and the baby?'

I swallow, all awkward.

'It's just ... I might not be able to. You know how it is.'

I can't generally be trusted, outside, is the problem. I always mean well, I swear, it's just ...

'You know what, Dani? Whatever. I thought we were mates, that's all. But if you don't give a fuck, fine. Neither do I.'

And I think to myself, it's really not that I don't give a fuck! It's not. But I can't promise you. It's hard out there, isn't it? Promises get broken.

I say,

'Yeah. Fine.'

And that's the last thing we say to each other.

The day the princess died, was when I first met him. That's why I remember it so well.

I'd woken up early, like every Sunday, and tiptoed downstairs in my pink Minnie Mouse pyjamas to watch cartoons. I snuck into the kitchen, quiet quiet, and got a box of Crunchy Nut Cornflakes out of the cupboard. All through the week I had to have boring Weetabix for breakfast, which doesn't damage your teeth or make you fat. But on the weekend, I was allowed whatever I wanted.

Saturday mornings were too busy for cartoons – we had to get up at seven so I could be ready and have dance class at nine, then do the big shop together at Tesco which was boooooooring but I got to pick some sweets at the checkout. Then home for lunch, which was always pasta on Saturdays, with proper sauce made from fresh tomatoes, not out of a jar. Mamma says that my nonna would turn in her grave, if we ever ate sauce from a jar. Mamma would go out with her friends in the evening and Mrs Fowler from down the road would come over and look after me. But on Sundays, Mamma liked to sleep in and I got to watch cartoons for ages. She'd be up in a bit, and then we'd clean the house up and maybe go into town to do shopping. On Sunday nights we always watched a Disney film together and had a cuddle on the sofa, and that was maybe my favourite bit of the whole entire week.

I jumped up onto the sofa, holding my cereal bowl carefully so it didn't spill. I wasn't really meant to have food in here because we kept the living room nice, in case of guests, but I was five now, I knew how to be careful. I nestled back into the brown leather of the sofa seats, and stirred at my bowl of cereal, making sure all of them were properly covered in the milk. Mamma sometimes asked me why I always picked these for my weekend cereal, and if I was sure I wouldn't like to try something else? I said that I just liked them best, but that wasn't true, not really.

It was actually because of Daddy. Daddy had a red jumper that he used to wear all the time and we used to dance in the kitchen together to David Bowie and his eyes went all crinkly at the edges when he smiled. And his favourite cereal was Crunchy Nut Cornflakes.

I clicked on the TV, but instead of cartoons there was just the blank screen with the BBC logo on it. The announcer said,

'Normal programming has been suspended and we now join Martyn Lewis in the news studio.'

I frowned at the TV. I didn't want to watch the news. It was Sunday. There were always cartoons in the morning on Sunday. A man wearing glasses replaced the blank screen. He looked sad.

'This is BBC Television from London. Diana, Princess of Wales, has died after a car crash in Paris.'

I scooted forward to get a better look. Milk slopped over the edge of the bowl and onto my lap, soaking through my pyjamas and onto my legs.

That was how I knew he was gone, the cornflakes. I came down one morning and I found the box in the bin, even though it was nearly full and Mamma hates wasting food. That's when I knew it was real.

'The French government announced her death just before five o'clock this morning. Buckingham Palace confirmed the news shortly afterwards. Normal programmes have been suspended while we bring you the latest developments throughout the morning.'

I stared at the screen as it changed to a picture of the Union Jack, but only flying halfway up the pole, and 'God Save the Queen' started playing.

I stared, my legs all cold from the spilt milk.

'MA!' I shouted. 'Mamma!'

I jumped off the sofa, and a wave of milk and soggy flakes flew over the edge and landed on the carpet. I'd get in trouble for that later, Mamma was fussy about things being tidy, but she'd understand. This was a proper emergency – the princess was dead! That wasn't meant to happen. I knew all about princesses, and I knew that they lived happily ever after. They didn't get killed in car crashes. Maybe it was a mistake. Mamma would know.

I scrambled up the stairs and flung Mamma's bedroom door open.

'Mamma! I was watching the news because there were no cartoons. The man on the TV said . . .'

The curtains were still drawn, the duvet all bumpy on the bed with her underneath it. I went over. I didn't know why, exactly, but I was a little bit scared.

'Mamma?'

And from underneath the lumpiness of the duvet, a figure emerged. Dark wiry hair, a stubbly face, and glaring brown eyes. A broad, hairy chest.

I screamed. And screamed and screamed and screamed and screamed and . . .

'Daniella. Honey. It's okay, I'm here, shhh.'

Mamma stuck her head out from under the duvet. She was smiling, even laughing a little bit, and I don't know why because it WASN'T funny.

Unless ... I frowned at the man. She'd said he wasn't coming back. The taste of my cereal was still in my mouth, milky and sweet.

'Papa?'

Mamma screwed her face up at me, like, sorry, bella.

'No. Not Papa, bella. This is Richard. He's Mamma's friend, and we had a sleepover last night. Okay? Say hello to Richard.'

Richard gave me a tight little smile and I swallowed down the funny feeling in my throat and tried to be a big girl. Of course it wasn't him. I'd known that, really.

'Hello, Daniella. Shouldn't you be still asleep? It's very early.'

And then I remembered. Tears brimmed over my eyes, because everything was wrong today.

'Princess Diana died! In a car crash. She's dead.'

Mamma looked shocked at that. She ran a hand through her tangled-up hair. It was going to take her ages to brush those knots out.

'Oh. Oh no, that's so sad. Those poor little boys.'

Richard sat up, stretching. I could see the hairs underneath his armpits and it was gross.

'I don't see what's sad about it. Less of my tax money she gets to use up now, isn't it?'

I stared at him, open-mouthed. I couldn't believe anyone could ever be so mean.

'Mamma!'

But instead of telling him off, or telling him to get out, that this was our house, not his, she just smiled at me.

'Richard was just joking Daniella, don't worry. Weren't you, Richard?'

A look flashed between them, just for a second, and then Richard smiled at me. But there was something about his face I didn't like, even when it was smiling.

'Yes. Sorry. Bad joke.'

'Aren't you going to say hello to Richard?'

I stared at Richard and clamped my lips shut. I didn't want to say hello to the strange man with his chest hair and his jokes that weren't funny.

She laughed and gave me a one-armed hug, clutching the duvet over her chest with the other hand. She smelled odd – not like her normal mix of perfume and a little hint of fried onions. This morning she smelled a bit sour – like the smell you get in pet shops when you go in to look at the hamsters.

'Awww. She's shy. You're shy, aren't you, Daniella? Don't worry. You're going to get to know Richard and we're all going to be the best of friends.'

And me and Richard looked at each other, me tucked under Mamma's armpit, him glaring over from the other side of the bed. And I could have told you right then, I knew that we absolutely weren't.

'The question is,' Emma says, 'are you going to use your time here to better yourself? Or are you just going to coast along, to take the easy way? Hmmm? Which will it be, Daniella?'

I stare at her and say nothing. She gives me one of her looks, the ones she always gives me, like, *I'm being very patient, but you're getting on my nerves.*

'Well?'

I give her the look I always give her, like, *you're getting on MY fucking nerves, actually, Miss.*

'I dunno, Miss.'

'You don't know. What do you mean, you don't know? You have to make a choice.'

I turn and stare out the barred window. The sky outside's so blue it doesn't look real.

'Yeah, Miss.'

Emma gives me a little sigh and pats at her braids, which is a thing she does sometimes when she's thinking. Thinking how to piss me off, probably. Emma's been my probation officer for three years, and so far her hair's the only thing I've found to like about her. It's beautiful, a proper mane of box braids, that she catches back in this fat French plait. Plaits in plaits, makes you want to keep looking at it. It doesn't go with her boring trouser suits and her thick-soled flat shoes and her fucking aggravating do-goody little face.

'Daniella, you need to make some kind of effort. Show that you're doing something to engage with the process, to try to help yourself, you see? If you don't change what you're doing, you won't change what happens to you, and you'll end up straight back inside. You know you will.'

A line of sweat drips straight down my back under my T-shirt and I shift in my seat. This time's coming straight out of my association. I want to get back on the wing.

'Yeah, Miss.'

'When you have the parole hearing, they won't automatically

knock you back, you know. There *is* a chance to turn it around.'

And I roll my eyes because that just goes to show Emma doesn't know shit. There isn't a chance for me to turn it around. I'm a junkie, that's my problem, and I can never stay out of trouble or off the smack for long. I haven't been out of prison for more than a couple of months at a time since I was eighteen. And if I could change that I would, no question, but it's who I am, you see?

Emma's looking at me like she expects me to say something. I shrug, and go, 'Mmmm', which is as close to answering as I reckon she deserves.

She leans in to me, all matey.

'Come on, Daniella. Don't you want to get Bethany back?'

I glare at her. That's like a punch to the gut, and she knows it.

'Course I do.'

A week with her, was all I had. One week, and a handful of visits when I've been out. And she's still my world, even though we had so little time. I ache for her.

'Well then. Sign up to a course and we'll get you back together sooner.'

I scowl down into the corner. I've done courses, is the problem. Again and again. Back in the early days, my first and second times inside without her, I'd do whatever they said, anything at all, to try and get her back. But there's only so many times you can keep hoping for something, you know? When you fuck it up, every single time, and end up back inside again. The courses don't work.

'Can't pass them, though, can I?'

She looks at me, all earnest.

'You can, Daniella.'

I give her a look, like, *well, we'll have to agree to disagree on that, won't we, Miss?* She goes on.

'It's not just the parole hearing you should be thinking of. The courses are there for a reason. You could learn a trade, if you wanted. Make this your last time inside. If you just used this as an opportunity, you could really make some changes.'

I roll my eyes at her. That's the thing about probation officers. Don't listen, do they? Won't take it in, when you say their way isn't going to work, that you need to do something different.

'Come on, Daniella. You can do this. Remember, you only need to do six months without offending and we can start proceedings for getting Bethany back. Three months to a first visit, if you did well. I know you want that. You could get out by the end of August if you just showed some sign that you were trying. If you worked with me.'

But I'm never, not fucking ever, going to work with Emma. She's proper shafted me in her time, and I have one rule in life – you only get to fuck me over *once*. The fucking cheek of her, even saying Bethany's name ...

I match the little smile, mine just as goopy as hers.

'Work with *you*? You're alright. I'd rather rot.'

Emma sighs a cross little sigh, blowing the air out through pursed lips. I smile myself a little secret smile. She only does that when something's really pissed her off.

'Well, you will then. If you don't cooperate, you'll never get out of here.'

I get this tingle of anger round my forearms. It always starts in the arms with me, anger.

'What? You threatening me or something?'

She raises her hands, palms facing me, like she's surrendering, or telling me to stop.

'Daniella . . .'

I stand up. The chair clangs on the floor behind me. I half say, half shout,

'Are you saying you'll keep me in? If I don't play along, you won't release me when you're meant to?'

Emma keeps her eyes locked on mine. They always do that. It's supposed to calm you down, I think.

'No, of course not. All I meant was—'

But I don't want to calm down. I let myself remember that day two years ago, her shuffling all those papers and the look on her face like she was pretending she was sorry and I let the anger take me, the hotness of it filling me up.

'Cos you can't be fucking doing that! I know my rights, and you're full of shit, you can't fucking threaten me, you fucking bitch, I'll fucking—'

And the officers come in. They plough their way through the door, filling up the tiny room with their uniforms and batons and arms as big as your thighs. Emma must have pressed the alarm before I even started saying anything. She proper provoked me for this. On purpose. Fucking bitch. Fucking Emma. Fucking Lisa, with her baby she gets to keep.

'Keep still, Grove.'

The officers grab me. Their massive hands grip tight around my arms and twist them back and I let myself go limp. It hurts less if you go with it. They lift me, just by the arms, and the sockets in my shoulders pop and groan. My arms always feel like they're going to be dislocated, at this bit, or just pulled clean off, but it's okay. They never do.

'Calm down, alright?'

But like I said, I'm already still. I know how it works, you can say that about me. I know when to stop fighting.

As I get hauled through the door, I catch Emma's eye. A normal probation officer would look a bit startled, a bit of argy-bargy like this going on, or worried, because it doesn't reflect that well on them. But Emma just looks sort of ... knackered, and, like, resigned to it. Like she doesn't expect anything else from me.

I use my last second in the room to stare at Emma. I take all my anger and all the hurting in my arms, all the humiliation of being picked up, carried about like an animal or a kid, and I throw it into one poisoned look and mouth *bitch* at her, because she really fucking is.

The officers who're holding me let go of my arms and shove me away, proper rough. I stagger a bit, getting used to having my feet on the ground again. One of the officers gives me a real bitch-face look.

'You pull any of that crap again, you'll get a week in solitary.'

I stare at the floor and do my best to look sorry.

'Yeah, Miss. Sorry, Miss.'

There's a proper din on in the wing, the way there always is during association. And at any time, come to that. The sound of hundreds of girls, chatting, shouting, fighting and singing along to the radio, it bounces all around this old building. The air's full of sweat and cheap perfume and toast, the smell of hundreds of women living too close together.

'Keep your nose clean, Grove, yeah?'

And they leave me there. I give it a couple of seconds still staring at the floor, 'til I'm dead sure they've gone, then I look up. I grin at the girls all hanging round the landing. Everyone's staring at me, all curious, like, *whatcha done now, Dani?* Chris raises an eyebrow at me.

'What you done now, Dani?'

She's stretched out on a stained blue sofa thing. There aren't enough seats round here – a lot of the girls are standing, or sitting on the grubby floor, but Chris is taking up enough space for two. She's got shoulder-length, mousy brown hair, always pulled back in a tight little ponytail at the top of her neck, and she always wears this tatty grey tracksuit. Despite that, something about the way Chris holds herself makes her look as put together as some of the lawyers that come in. No one except Chris could get away with that. On me, it'd just look shit – I need my highlights, even if I do have a forest of roots showing half the time.

Chris waits, giving me a look, like, *go on then*. For a second, I think about maybe making her up a better story than what's just happened. A little bit of gossip to brighten a dull day. Tempting. It's probably not that clever though, so I go,

'I called Emma a fucking bitch.'

Chris laughs, and a second later the girls hanging round her do as well. Pathetic, the way they all suck up to her like that. Not that I want to cross her, you understand, but you don't want to kiss up too much either. In here being fake is almost worse than being arsey with someone. So I put a smile on for her, too, just a little one. If you toe the line, Chris is fine – I've

even done a bit of work for her before now, it's just, as I say,
you don't fuck with her. She goes,

'Yeah? Why'd you say that?'

I get a bit angry again, just at the memory of it.

'She proper fucking slagged me off. She was saying all sorts
of stuff about me. About how I was never going to get out of
prison, shit like that. Like, threatening me, that if I didn't do
what she said, she'd keep me inside.'

Kerry, who's been here a fair while and tends to know her
shit a bit, cranes up from her seat on the floor and squints at
me.

'She can't say stuff like that. You should get her written
up, get compensation or something.'

'Oh, yeah.' I hadn't thought of that. You always hear about
people getting compensation for shit, happens all the time.
Everyone talks about it. Kerry raises her skinny eyebrows.

'Set you up nice for release, wouldn't it? I know a girl got
five grand once.'

I let myself imagine it. Five grand. That'd be enough to live
on for . . . I don't even know. Months and months. You could
go on holiday, even. I've always wanted to go to Tenerife.
Somewhere hot and sunny, where they bring you drinks in
coconuts and you can always see the sea. It's been five years
since I saw the sea.

Chris makes a noise, like half laugh half phlegm-hock, and
goes,

'I applied for compensation last year. Never got it, though.
Whole system's fucking stacked against you. I wouldn't
bother, Dani.'

And she looks down at Kerry, like, menacing. Kerry sort of

shrinks back a bit, but she still meets Chris's eyes and goes,

'I knew a girl who did, though. Just cos you didn't get it, doesn't mean no one can, does it?'

And Chris leans down to her and grabs her middle finger, making a fist around it. She says, all quiet,

'You calling me a liar?'

And starts to bend it back.

The normal din of the landing goes on in the background, but in our group no one says anything. Kerry gasps out,

'No! I'm not, no.'

Chris lets go and looks back up at me. She gives me a bright little smile.

'I wouldn't bother, Dani. If I were you.'

Kerry's still sitting next to her, jaw set and looking hard at nothing. I swallow and look sort of nonchalant, like, and I go,

'Yeah. Right.'

And that's the end of that.

Back in my cell on lockup, the radio's on. It's one of those phone-in type shows that I normally love, but I'm not listening. I'm staring over at the empty bunk across from me, its neat green sheets all tucked up and waiting to be filled. I used to hate that prison-sheet green when I first got here, but now I'm not that bothered. It's the kind of green a kid would use to colour a tree. It's okay. I stare around the rest of the cell, taking in the extra cabinet, all empty of Lisa's stuff now, the table and chair that always had her hoodie on the back of it. The loo. However many times you've had to do it, shitting in front of someone new is always a bit weird.

I kneel up on my bed, and have a stare at my pictures.

They come every six months, from the foster mum, on her birthday and halfway through the year as well. My Bethany, as a little pink six-month-old, a sturdy one-year-old, turning into a cute blonde toddler. I sit back on my heels and wipe at my eyes where they've gone watery. It's shit to be missing the baby bit of her, but her foster mum seems nice enough and, anyway, I'll get her back soon. Surely I will.

There's a swell of noise from out on the landing. Calls and shouting, louder than just the normal prison baseline throb. Something's happening. The springs twang under me as I get up. I step over to the door and press my face against the tiny little window and swivel my eye about, trying to see. They're a nightmare, these little cell door windows, if you're as nosy as I am.

There's three women making their way down the landing, flanked by a gang of officers. The one on the left is black and tall, with long braids hanging down her back, a bit like Emma's. The left-hand one is white and blonde and small – wiry, though. I can see from here she's got some serious muscles going on under her grey prison sweatshirt. The middle girl is white as well, and bigger than the other two – chubby, I'd almost say.

Someone shouts,

'Oi, you. I said, OI! Alright?'

The women in the cells they're walking past call out to them, just a couple at first, then more, then everyone. The two newbies on either side are handling it the way you're meant to, look up, eye contact, quick nod and that, but the middle one's doing nothing. She's got her eyes on the floor, long dark hair swinging across her face, but you can tell from her shoulders, and the way she's got her hands in her pockets, that she's not crying, like a normal first-timer would. She's just . . . looking down. Strolling along as casual as if she's going for a walk in the park or something.

Someone goes,

'Fucking look at Rapunzel over there!'

And she looks up. She isn't looking up in a normal way, like, a paying-her-respects kind of way. Her eyes rove around, not settling on anything, like she's taking in the whole place and finding it lacking for her. For a second they look straight into mine and the way she looks at me, it's like she's worked me out and she thinks I'm fucking scum.

Someone calls out,

'Oi, new bitches!'

I scowl at her through my tiny little window. That was such a big mistake on her part – pure stupid. The best thing to do, when you first get in prison, is to look everyone dead in the face, so they can see that you're okay. Looking scared isn't great, doesn't exactly show your best side or whatever, but it's understandable. People will get it. Smacked off your face or bricking it with a comedown (my own normal state on arrival, if I'm honest) is the same – not brilliant, but we've all been there, we all know. Then you get your foreigners, the ones who don't speak English and don't know what the fuck's going on because no one's bothered getting them a translator. That's okay too. But the one thing you want to avoid like the plague, the thing that'll fucking sink you, is looking like you think you're better than everyone else. Being snotty carries zero weight around here; it just makes you a target. On the inside, respect has to be earned, nod by nod and slap by punch, and there's no way around that, nor should there be.

Someone goes,

'Hey, you! Alright, yeah?'

I stare out as the three of them come closer, my three maybe-cellmates, and I proper pray for one of the other two. The one on the left, she's nodding like she's meant to, and I really like her braids. Maybe she'd let me redo a couple of them for her. Lisa used to let me do her hair. Not that you can keep it going in prison, a style like that, for long. Can't get the hair on the canteen, can you? Can't get anything on the canteen.

Someone goes,

'You going to look up or what, new bitch?'

The thing is, round here, your cellmate's important. Whoever ends up in your cell, it's like you're responsible for them, a bit. Unless you have a proper out-and-out feud with them, it's sort of assumed that you're mates. Anything they do, it's obviously not as bad as if you'd done it yourself, but, still, you didn't stop them, did you? You obviously didn't think it was that out of order, then. And I really don't want anyone to think that I reckon disrespecting people isn't that out of order. If you're sharing with a target, you kind of become one yourself. Bad reputations rub off on you – that's why we have to be locked up in here, I suppose. So we can't taint the decent folks outside.

Someone goes,

'What, you not calling back, Rapunzel?'

They stop outside my cell door. I meet her eye again, the one in the middle.

Someone goes,

'You think you're better than us or something?'

Come on. Left-hand one. Let's go. Come on.

Someone goes,

'Snotty fucking new bitch.'

And no. Just my fucking luck. To cap off the end of my fucking perfect day, my door clangs open, nearly hitting me dead in the face. I launch myself back onto my bunk, which creaks at me like it's bitching about being sat on too hard, and the bloody snotty one gets shoved into my cell. She staggers a couple of steps, then comes to a stop in the middle of the room just a foot or two away from my face. She brings with her a cloud of hot, stale air from the landing, and, very faint, the petrol fume and fried chicken smell of the outside. An officer goes,

'Alright, Duchess. Enjoy your suite!'

And then there's sarky laughing, and the door slams shut behind her. I hate that sound, of doors slamming. Sets your teeth on edge, particularly if your day wasn't going that great to start with. I look the new cellie up and down. She just stands there in front of me, staring at my abandoned flip-flop on the floor, not saying hi. Very bloody rude. So I say to her,

'Alright?'

But not in a friendly way.

Chapter Two

Extract from PSI 74/2011 – Early Days in Custody

3.31   *New prisoners must be issued with a pack
     (variously known as a reception pack, comfort
     pack or first night pack) containing items such
     as tea, milk, sugar and sweets ...* Prisoners
     should be told that the cost of the pack will
     be recovered from their future earnings in the
     establishment, and they may therefore choose
     to refuse to accept it.

The new bitch looks up. Even though her long, tangled hair
is so dark it's nearly black, her eyes are a clear bright blue.

She gives me this frightened little half-smile and for a
second that really makes me hate her, the weakness of it.
You've got to be tough to survive in here, and if you can't hack
it you shouldn't rob stuff or whatever, should you? I give her
my best tough-bitch stare.

I say,

'What's your name?'

And she says, in this thick Scottish accent,

'Martha.'

And that's all. Bloody weird, if you ask me, being all quiet like this. I've never understood people who don't want to have a bit of a chat – you've got to do something to pass the day. She's standing there looking at me, just holding her ground and staring. But not wincing or looking away. And that's, not impressive exactly, but alright. We were all new once, even if most of us were teens back then, rather than, like, twenty-five, like she is. And there's no point in making an enemy in here unless you have to, especially a cellie. That'd be knack-ering, watching your back and that all the time. I'm sure as long as she'll play along, we'll do just fine.

I ramp up my scowl a notch and I go,

'You get your first night pack?'

Which is a bit of a risky thing for me to say, to be fair. If she gives me a flat no, I've either got to accept that she's the one calling the shots, or I've got to thump her. Neither's that appealing at the moment. The C&R and aggro for kicking off at Emma was one thing – I'm already on basic, there's nothing for them to take. If I start a fight and it escalates, though, that'd probably land me in the seg, which I can do the fuck without. But I need to get the measure of her fast if we're going to be living eighteen inches away from each other for the next however long.

I lean in towards her, threatening, like. This is a nice quick way of working out how much I can get away with. The whole pack's a hell of a lot, but if she gives me, like, her teabags or whatever, then we shouldn't have a problem.

But she nods and holds out a plain brown cardboard box to

me, no fuss at all. I wasn't expecting that. But I take off my scowl and give her a nod, like, *yes, of course you gave me your whole pack, that is the proper thing to happen.*

'Err . . . Ta.'

I grab the box, pull the top off and count out the stuff in there – three Dairy Milks, a pack of custard creams, two apples, a jar of coffee, a bag of sugar, a toothbrush, toothpaste, and soap. I look up at Martha. She's sitting on her bed now, sort of wary, like it might break beneath her. But it won't. They're shitty beds, but she's not *that* big.

'You don't smoke then?'

She shakes her head, looks out at me from under her hair and goes,

'Sorry.'

And her voice is quite nice, actually. Gentle. You could get used to a voice like that, I reckon.

'It's okay,' I say.

I shove the toiletries back in the box and hand it back to her. She looks at me like I've given her a million quid or something.

'Thank you.'

It's pretty shit toothpaste and soap to be honest, and she did say sorry. I always like to respect good manners if I can. I smile, all gracious about it.

'You're alright.'

Back in the day, they'd always give you a Mars bar in the first night packs. I bloody love a Mars bar. Now, they don't even have them in the canteen, they only have Cadbury's stuff. I asked about it, and they said it was because of the contracts. They said if I was that bothered I could get a Mars bar sent in, by my family or whatever, but I ain't got no family, not that stay in touch. No one out there gives a shit if I'm not getting my favourite snacks, or any food at all come to that. I suppose that's one thing to look forward to when I'm out. Better chocolate range. Silver linings.

Martha gives me a tight little smile.

'It's . . . nice to meet you.'

I open my cupboard and stash the food there, laying it out next to my deodorant and my toothbrush and an empty packet of bourbon biscuits I'd been trying to make myself save for a really bad day.

One of the Dairy Milks I keep in my hand. There's nothing wrong with Cadbury's, not really.

I nod at Martha.

'Yeah. Likewise.'

I lie back on the bunk, and stare up at the ceiling. I unwrap the Dairy Milk, shiny purple foil scrumpling under my fingers, and I drink in the smell. It's always the best bit of anything, the moment just before. I wish I had the patience, more often, to make it last. But I don't. I bite a chunk off the chocolate and feel it spread, smooth and sweet around my mouth, and I'm happy enough, considering.

A few days later, me and Martha are lying around the cell, listening to the radio. It's proper roasting in here. Prison gets like this a lot in summer, close hot stale air right in your face all the time. The tiny windows open but barely any breeze gets through the bars, cos even the air don't want to be in here. The sweat off my back's pooling on the plasticky coating of the mattress. I think about shifting positions a bit, but it's too hot to move, and, anyway, if every bit of me's sweating, there's no point in moving.

'Who's this song by?' Martha says.

It's too hot to even tilt my head over to give her a *what the fuck?* look.

'Taylor Swift.'

'Oh.'

'You not heard of Taylor Swift?'

There's a pause from Martha's side of the room, longer than you'd need for a question like that.

'No.'

I peel myself off the mattress, prop up on an elbow and look at her.

'What? How can you have not heard of Taylor Swift? She's *everywhere.*'

Martha's staring straight up at the ceiling.

'I just listened to what my mum listened to.'

She looks a bit upset. I let myself flop back down on the bed.

'I don't think she's that great either.'

There's a silence, except for Taylor, and the clang-shout-chatter of the wing beyond our door. Martha goes,

'What kind of music do you like?'

I stare at the ceiling. There's a crack above my bed. I try to work out if it's getting bigger or not.

'Hip hop.'

'Why?'

Christ. I don't know. It's not just any hip hop that I like, it's the proper old-school swagger stuff. I suppose I like the beats, and the don't-give-a-fuck attitude of it. No one's ashamed of themselves, when they sing songs like that. They're just the person they are, and they glory in it.

I shrug, my sweat-soaked T-shirt sliding moist against my skin.

'I dunno. I just like it.'

The song's stopped and the news comes on.

'But there must be a reason. Why do you like it?'

'Shut up,' I go, but not in a mean way. 'It's the news.'

There's a little snort from Martha that sounds suspiciously like a laugh. I'm forced to roll over and give her one of my *looks*. Her smile drops.

'I like the news,' I say, and the two of us listen.

'*The BBC understands that Prince George will undertake his first royal engagement next month.*

'*Clarence House has confirmed that the prince will open a Prince's Trust outdoor play area for children his age in London.*'

Despite the heat, I sit up again at that. I like the little prince.

'*At two and a half, the future king of England is several years younger than his father, the Duke of Cambridge, was when he made his first official appearance, making a visit to Cardiff on St David's Day at the age of eight. Prince William will accompany his son, along with the Duchess of Cambridge, on the day.*'

I like the whole family, as it goes. I like Kate Middleton's hair, and the new baby. The little prince is my favourite, though. He was born about the same time as Bethany, and he's such a little treasure. His little cheeks are amazing when he smiles, I've seen him on the telly. I look up to my Bethany pictures. I don't know exactly what she looks like now, cos I'm due another photo, but I bet she's got lovely fat little cheeks.

I imagine myself squeezing one of them. Her skin, so soft under my fingers.

'*Our royal correspondent, Corrina Jones, has more.*

'*I'm here in Brockwell Park where the play area is nearly complete—*'

I turn to Martha, all excited.

'Brockwell Park! I know that park. I used to go there all the time.'

Brockwell Park is dead close to Justin's place. Justin was my sort-of-dealer-sort-of-mate-sort-of-boyfriend, on the outside. I never quite worked it out. We used to go up there in summer, and drink cans under a tree, really chilled, just watch the world go by. Like an advert, or something. I've got a lot of happy memories of that place. Martha gives me a timid little smile.

'You should go and see the opening.'

I shrug and lean back against the cell wall. The painted bricks are cool on my back.

'Nah. I'll still be inside then, won't I?'

'Not if you get parole.'

I shrug.

'Yeah. Maybe.'

The thing is, if I'm honest, even on the out I'd have missed the opening anyway. No way I'd go that near Brixton without dropping by Justin's, and no way I'd go somewhere with so many police hanging about after I'd been round there.

Martha shifts, creaking her mattress springs.

'What are you in for, Dani?'

I stretch my arms up, crack my knuckles and consider. I'm a bit torn on this. On the one hand, I like a chat. There's arse-all to do in here, so you have to take your entertainment where you can. On the other hand, this is *not* on.

I give her one of my looks.

'You're not meant to ask people that.'

Not ask direct, that is. You find out in the end, of course, through gossip from the girls and the officers, but you're not meant to ask anyone *outright* like that. It's rude. Martha shifts on her bunk.

'Sorry.'

And she does look sorry. And like I said, it's fucking boring in here.

'It was possession and intent. *This* time.'

And I look over to her, to see if that's had any effect. But she's just looking back, blank, like she doesn't know what I'm on about. I roll my eyes. Bloody newbies know nothing. It's up to me to explain.

'Possession of heroin. Intent to supply. Dealing, you know? Not that I was, wasn't even my gear . . . But that was just this time. I've been in nine other times, for this and that.'

Her eyes go big.

'Nine? What kind of things did you do?'

I smile to myself. I do love to tell a story, and she's as good an audience as any.

'A fair few for robbery, that kind of thing. Fighting, attacking people. A couple for ABH. You know, normal stuff.'

Her eyes have gone massive now. She's looking at me like I'm in a film. I prop myself up, wanting to do the attention justice.

'Once there was this guy, proper evil fucker. He was hassling me all the time, wanting me to do some work for him. You know. *Work.*'

I look over to her to check. She obviously doesn't know.

'Like, on the game, you know? Work? But with him taking half the cash. Fucker. Anyway, he comes at me one night, won't take no for an answer about it. He's pawing all over me, says if I won't do it nice, then he'll make me. I manage to get an arm out, and I grab the first thing I can get. It's this vodka bottle, sitting next to me. I smashed it right into the side of his stupid fucking face. He got ten stitches, I got ten months.'

She doesn't look impressed, quite. Just concentrating. Her eyes bore into me.

'What else?'

I hesitate. There were one or two that was just shoplifting, picking up leather jackets to sell on for smack, and not checking the tags right. Not that impressive. Once, two winters ago, I smashed the window of a Dorothy Perkins and just sat there 'til the police arrived because I was so fucking cold that I couldn't think what else to do. When it's boiling hot, like now, I can't remember what that felt like. It must have been pretty bad, for me to have chosen this.

'It's all that kind of stuff, really.'

I look up at the crack. It really is getting bigger.

And I wouldn't normally, but as we're on the subject and she started it, I can't resist. I go,

'What *you* in for, Martha?'

And she looks at me, all huge blue eyes and dirty brown hair, and she says,

'Grievous bodily harm' in her soft little voice. 'I'm in for five years.'

I just look at her, and, fair play, she's proper surprised me with that one. Because five years is a LOT, especially for a woman, and most especially for a white girl with a soft little voice. Like, I've never done more than eighteen months, and there've been a couple of times I've really fucked people up. You can fight really hard when you're on the best painkiller in the world, you can just keep coming. When you're smacked up and you get into trouble, it's like there's two of you. The drug's got your back and you're never alone.

Anyway.

Martha's just sitting there watching, waiting for me to say something. I got nothing, though. I just have to let the radio babble on for a bit. More news. Nice safe real life happening to other people.

To get five years she must have pretty much killed them.

There's heavy footsteps and Miss Green clangs open the door and comes into the cell. With her she brings in a waft of hot, stale air from the wing. It's probably not much worse than our cell, but there's something about a bad smell you're used to – it's not as horrible, somehow. The new smell's worse just for being new, you know?

Miss Green stands, blocking the doorway, pen and notepad held up ready. She's wider than ever and frowning down her nose at us two, which is nice, hear me out, because most of the officers don't pull proper faces. Whether they're happy or angry or whatever, they just keep, like, a mask up in front of you and give you this professional front, which I don't like. Take Emma, for example, who you can't get a proper rise out of no matter what you say. The good thing about Miss Green is, she won't hide what she's thinking from you, even if she's in a bit of an arse. Like now.

'Alright there, ladies. Dani. Back again? How many times is that now?'

'Ten, Miss. And this one'll be my last.'

This is the first time I've seen Miss Green on this sentence, because she's been off on maternity. Last time I saw her she was barely showing, and now she must have a proper big six-month-old at home. I give her a smile, bit cheeky, and go,

'But I always say that, don't I, Miss?'

She's still frowning, but it kind of softens, to, like, a caring frown. One of my theories about people is that it takes a certain kind of person to frown in a nice way – you've got to be pretty nice yourself.

'If you meant it, Dani, it could be. You know that, don't you?'

And I roll my eyes, because they say this kind of thing a lot to you in here and I had quite enough *bettering yourself* this and *turning your life around* that to keep me going with Emma the other day. To distract her and save myself a lecture, I give her a grin and go,

'You got a picture of the baby, Miss?'

And she stops frowning and goes,

'Oh, I'm not meant to show you . . .'

But she's already reaching into her jacket.

I take the photo off Miss Green and hold it by the fresh, clean edges, and for a second it feels like I've been punched, a vicious jab right to the heart of me. I drink in the kid's little face. He's got chubby little cheeks, perfectly smooth brown skin and bright black button eyes. There's a dog in the picture as well, but I do my best to ignore that, just sort of blank it out in my mind. I bloody love babies, even though looking at them makes my chest feel all tight and hard. They're worth the hurt, even an ugly one, but Miss Green's kid's a little stunner. Not as gorgeous as my Bethany, mind.

'What's his name?'

She smiles, all fond. It's weird to see a smile like that, in here.

'Charlie.'

I nod. Fair play, that's a nice name.

'Anyway. Grove. Clark, is it? What's your choices today, ladies? You can have gym, outside, pool, or wing time.'

I give her a good-little-prisoner smile and go,

'Pool please, Miss.'

Martha laughs, like, *what?* and Miss Green gives her an arsey-face look.

'And you, Clark?'

I butt in.

'She'll do swimming too, Miss.'

And Martha looks at me, like *what the fuck*, but she knows to keep her mouth shut. She's a smart one, is Martha. So she just flashes Miss Green this frightened little smile and goes,

'Yes please, Miss, swimming.'

Miss Green nods and makes a couple of marks on her notepad.

'Alright, girls. I'll be back in an hour.'

I give her a respectful little nod and she fucks off. Martha shifts on her bed, and I can see she's all hot and bothered. I'm alright now. Even the idea of the pool's cooled me down. She goes,

'I can't even swim.'

I just smile at her. I like this, this feeling of being the old hand, the one that knows what's going on. I say,

'Trust me, mate. A day like this, you want swimming.'

'Come on, Daniella. Hurry up.'

I scowled at Mamma and slipped on my new swimming costume, which wasn't the one I'd wanted.

'I'm going as fast as I can.'

I'd wanted the pink one, with the little skirt bit on it. It was really pretty, like the kind of swimming costume a princess might wear.

Mamma rolled her eyes at me.

'You're not. Come on, Richard and Jamie will be waiting for us.'

But Mamma had said, don't you think that's a bit babyish, Daniella? *And I hadn't done, actually, I'd thought it was great, but Jamie was there. And he'd swung round at me, jeering, going,* awwww, pretty little swimming costume for a baby, is it? Awwwwww, little baby *and he'd kept doing that, on and on, until I'd kicked him. And then he'd made a massive fuss about it and got me told off, so who was the baby then?*

'I don't care if they're waiting,' I said, which was true.

But after Jamie had said that, I'd looked at the pink swimming costume, and it didn't seem right, somehow. He'd spoilt it for me. So I'd just got a plain purple one. If Jamie and Richard weren't always hanging around with us, I could have got the one that I wanted. Nothing would have been ruined.

Mamma gave me one of her looks, and said,

'Don't be cheeky. Why do you always have to make things so difficult, Daniella?'

I gave her a glare back, like, I'm not the one who makes things difficult, it's Jamie and Richard, everything was great before they came along. *But I didn't say it. I'd just been told not to be cheeky, hadn't I?*

We walked out together into the bright and shouty swimming pool. The air was spiky with the smell of the water and the ridges of the tiles prickled the soles of my feet. Standing there waiting for us were Richard and Jamie. I scowled at Jamie. We were enemies, which was a shame because we spent every single Saturday together. The days that used to be just Mamma and me time were Mamma and me and Jamie and Richard time. No more making pasta sauce together – we went out for lunches by then. Richard smiled at us.

'Finally ready, you two?'

Mamma smiled back and leaned over to kiss him, which was disgusting.

'Sorry about that. Daniella was having a bit of a slow day. Weren't you, Daniella?'

Jamie gave me a mean little grin with his stupid round freckly face.

'You shouldn't be so slow, Daniella. I got dressed in, like, two seconds, didn't I Dad? I was so fast.'

I glared at Jamie. He was such a little goody-goody.

'Bet you weren't.'

He smirked at me.

'You were so slow, though. Connie said.'

And he flashed this simpering little face at my mamma. And I hated it, how much she liked him. It made my brains feel itchy when I thought about it, so I shouted out,

'At least I'm not a . . . Stupid poo!'

Richard gave me this little sigh, like, I am not angry at you Daniella, I'm just disappointed.

'You two are going to have to learn to get along, you know. When we live together—'

I felt cold then, not just only-wearing-a-swimming-costume cold, but proper cold inside my bones.

'What do you mean, when we live together?'

Mamma gave Richard this soppy little smile and shook her head at him, like oh, you're so naughty but I love you. She went,

'Well, this isn't exactly how we wanted to tell you, Daniella.'

'What? What are you telling me?'

Jamie did this big sigh, like he was making a point about how stupid I am.

'They're moving in together. They told me ages ago.'

And he threw me this smug little smile. I turned to Mamma, outraged.

'MAMMA! That's not fair, why did you tell him first?'

Mamma took a deep breath and then blew it out, all slow.

'Well, he is older . . . '

'By a year! Only a year older, I'm eight soon anyway.'

Jamie rolled his eyes at me. I tugged down the bottom of my swimming costume where it was riding up my bum. I wished I was wearing real clothes for this.

'You're eight in nine months. That's ages.'

I stuck my tongue out at him. Mamma went,

'Don't be rude, Daniella. And we also told him first because it's his and Richard's house that we're going to be moving in to.'

I swallowed. My house. My room, my telly, my sofa, my

garden ... I'd only ever been to Richard's house once, and it had been too cold and everything had smelled of dog.

'Why can't we stay at ours?'

'Well, his is bigger. And it's closer to Richard's work, and then there's the dog to consider ...'

The cold turned to this hotness, starting in my arms and going all over me.

'What about me? What about me to consider?'

My voice was all high and my breathing was getting faster and faster, running away from me.

Richard crouched down next to me and looked at me, all serious-faced.

'Look, I'm sorry this is upsetting you, Daniella. But the decision has been made. This is what's happening.'

And I looked at Mamma, hoping – I don't know. Hoping she'd say something. Hoping she'd reach out and give me a cuddle. Hoping she'd tell him that she'd changed her mind, and she just wanted it to be her and me forever like it used to be.

But she didn't. She just smiled at Richard, like he was the prince and she was the princess and nothing was ever going to keep them apart, especially not an ugly little stepdaughter.

And I didn't know what to do. I could feel my eyes burning, not just with the swimming-pool air but with the idea of having to move out of our house, which had only ever just had the two of us in it, and moving in to Jamie and Richard's. They'd be there all the time and I'd never get any time on my own with Mamma, ever again. Richard went,

'Maybe we can talk about it more over pizza tonight. What do you say to that then, Daniella?'

But I couldn't say anything. So I went,

'Can I go swimming now?'

And I jumped right into the pool and put my head under the water, so that at least Jamie wouldn't get to see me cry.

We walk into the swimming pool and the noise of screeching and shouting hits us, solid as a fist. Because of the tiles and that, on busy days the pool is noisier even than the wings, and this is the most packed I've ever seen it.

Not a lot of people know that Holloway prison has a swimming pool, but, then, there's loads that happens in here that outside people have no idea about. Most people like to think it's gruel and hard labour and that, proper punishment. It's not like I disagree. Thing is, the pool's not even used that much. It's kept really hot, too hot to swim in properly, do lengths or whatever, so that the babies up on the unit can use it. Of course, they never do, because, would you take your baby swimming in a prison pool? Exactly. So it's empty. A day like today, though, you can't be picky. It's so hot you'd swim in a cup of tea, if that was all there was going.

Me and Martha stand on the prickly poolside tiles in our prison-issue swimming cossies. That's the other bad thing about swimming here – the suits are communal, which means you don't get your own. You get some old, saggy, worn-out one that's been going around the prison for years. The one I've got on today is so knackered it's practically see-through over the tits. It's worth it for the water, though, and, besides, you have to count your blessings a bit when you're in prison. Back in the days I was first inside, you weren't allowed your own clothes unless you were on Enhanced for good behaviour, and that includes knickers. I was never on Enhanced. Every

Monday you'd get your week's supply of prison pants, all washed in a big stack together so you'd get a different pair each time, never the right size and normally stained a bit with shit or period. You never think of getting to wear your own knickers as a luxury normally, but I'm grateful for a clean pair. They only changed it for women from what I've heard, the men still share their boxers.

It seems like the whole prison's turned out to the pool today. The place is a parade of knackered black swimming costumes and hairy legs. I look down at mine. They're not bad as legs go, apart from the deep grids of scars around the top of the thighs. That's nothing compared with my proper scar, though, which is a massive one, sitting puckered and pink all round the top of my shoulder. Also, my limbs are ghost-white, especially compared to the colour of some of the other legs around. But they keep me up and they'll do. I turn to Martha, and it's that noisy I have to put my face up to her ear to be heard.

'Follow me.'

I lead her over to a dead good spot, nearly at the deep end, and sit down on the edge and stick my feet in. Even though the water's too hot to swim, if you keep still it's just enough to cool you down, to make you feel less mental for a bit.

She sits down next to me, all awkward. She's got a fair bit of tits and arse, has Martha, and she carries it embarrassed, like she wishes she took up less space. I wish I had a bit more flesh going on in the boobs and bum areas to be honest. I'm skinny as a little boy most of the time. The only time I put any weight on at all is when I'm inside – outside, there's plenty more interesting stuff to spend your money on than food.

I spot Chris, walking over with her normal gang. She's proper swaggering along the poolside, like she's got on a designer bikini rather than a black Lycra all-in-one that's gone loose about the crotch. She sits down next to Martha, legs wide and hands on knees. The rest of her gang just stand there, sort of watching her, waiting for her to tell them what to do. To be fair, I'm waiting too. I can feel Martha, rigid beside me.

Chris turns to me and gives me a quick, hard smile.

'Alright?' she says, and I nod back at her and shout,

'Alright, Chris', all respectful. She nods back at me, then leans in to Martha. I can feel her breathing quicken next to me, like she's a fucking bunny or something, a little frightened thing waiting to get pounced. Chris nudges her.

'Alright, new bitch?'

And even over the bustle and yelling of the pool, there's this silence between them. Martha won't look up. In my head I'm going *come on come on come on just say 'alright'* but I know she won't. I know Martha a bit now and I can see she's shit scared, so she's frozen right up.

Chris leans even closer in to her now, her side pressed against Martha's, and she goes,

'I SAID, alright. New. Bitch?'

And there's this long, long pause where Martha says nothing and Chris does nothing and it's like the whole prison holds its breath. After a forever, Chris moves. She turns around, looks at her little gang and she smirks. They all grin back at her, showing their teeth. Then Chris spins round and shoves Martha into the pool. She hits the water with a splash, and sinks straight down, like a brick. I hold my breath along with her, and wait for her to surface.

Martha thrashes around and bobs back up, but Chris, cool as anything, reaches down and holds her head under the water. Martha flails, bubbles streaming out of her mouth, limbs churning up the water, faster and more frantic by the second, pure panic in every twitch of her.

Chris turns and looks up, grinning round at us all, and I make myself laugh along. She'll be fine. It's been ten seconds, if that. No one ever drowned in ten seconds, or even twenty. She'll be fine, and, I think I've already mentioned this, but you *really* don't want to piss Chris off. So I hold my face up in a smile and I watch as the seconds drag on and on. And on.

I look at Chris. She's still got her hand pushing down on Martha's face and she's laughing, finding it all just as funny as she did at the beginning. She's not getting bored. All her gang are cackling and the officers haven't seen and it's been more than twenty seconds now, for sure. Maybe thirty.

I don't know if I'm imagining it but I reckon Martha's struggling's getting slower. I look around. The officers still haven't noticed. It's like a mad house in here, there's that many people and that much noise, it's no wonder they haven't clocked us. I try to keep it together, stay calm, but I look down at Martha under the water like that and I panic. She trusted me. With my last little bit of control I make myself smile at Chris and I go,

'Lay off her, Chris, yeah?'

In what's meant to be a real friendly sort of way. Chris looks back with this sort of mad glee in her eye and she goes,

'Fuck off, junkie, you're next. I'll drown you like a fucking kitten.'

And I know that she means it. I look down at Martha, not

struggling at all now, and I just snap. I'm all for a quiet life, but I'm not just letting her kill my cellie right in front of me.

I put all my force behind my hand and I square my weight on both my bum cheeks and I fucking wallop Chris, right in the mouth. I feel the jolt all up my arms as it connects and Chris loses her balance, falling in the pool. She lets go of Martha, who bobs back up to the surface, gasping. Chris's gang are all standing there gawping at me, like, *whaaat?* and I let myself have a little grin. I've always thrown a good punch.

I reach a hand into the water and I fish Martha out. She scrambles up over the side of the pool all awkward, flopping up like a stranded sea thing, me hauling on her hand. You can tell she's never been swimming before. Right behind her Chris hops out, proper fast, all muscle under shining wet skin, and she flings herself at the two of us, roaring,

'You fucking bitch, I'll fucking . . .'

And without the surprise, I'm no match for her. I curl myself up into a ball and just take her punches as they fall on me. You don't get away with something for nothing when you're in here – you've got to expect a bit of retribution. It's like gravity – things that go up, fall. But I only count four little warm-up jabs before they stop. I jerk my head up, and see Chris getting C&R'd. Fucking lucky the officers finally noticed something was up.

The whole pool is quiet now, everyone's stopped dead to stare at Chris getting dragged away. She's fighting it, though, big time. The officers have to hold her tight as she writhes and pulls away, making them fight for every step. Before they've got her more than ten feet, she gets her head free from under the officer's arm, and she shouts,

'I'll fucking kill the pair of you for this! You fucking WAIT, Dani Grove, I'll fucking KILL YOU.'

And I just about manage to keep it together enough to shrug, and give her a look, like, *yeah? You and whose army?* I give that same sharp stare round all Chris's gang, like daring them to start something. I shove my chin out, and pull my hardest face.

But it's all front. Inside, there's this cold little feeling in my stomach saying *massive fucking mistake, Dani. Massive mistake.*

Chapter Three

Extract from PSI 47/2011 – Prisoner Discipline Procedures

1.27   A fight involves two or more persons assaulting
       each other by inflicting unlawful force. But the
       force will not be unlawful if the accused only
       acted in self-defence in response to an assault.

Back in the cell, I'm all shaken up and clammy and cold
now, despite the day still being so hot. I hug my legs to my
chest and put my head down on my knees. The room stinks
of chlorine from our skin and Martha's hair. That, and the
memory of the punch, is making me feel sick. There's this
very specific feeling I get when I've had to hit someone –
sort of thrilled and lightheaded and like I might throw up,
all at once. I've never been able to work out whether or not
I like it.

There's this quiet little voice over from Martha's bunk.

'Thank you, Dani.'

But I don't look round. I'm fucking furious with myself, to

be honest. I know better than to mess with people like Chris. Anyone'd think I was a dozy teenager who just got nicked for her first punch-up, but I'm not. I'm pretty much an old hand now, and I don't do stupid shit like this any more. I don't even bother lifting my head as I go,

'She's going to kill us both now. You know she meant that, right? She can't let something like this just slide.'

I can hear Martha turning over to look at me, but I'm too miserable to move. I just sit there, head buried in my knees. I wish I could squeeze myself up so hard I'd disappear. I can still feel her eyes on me, so I say,

'People like Chris, their reputation's all they've got. She's never getting out of here, so how people see her inside's more important than anything. She really would kill us. No reason not to.'

'Why's she never getting out of here?'

Martha doesn't seem that scared, even, which is really stupid of her. She should be fucking shitting herself. I give her a hard, *you want to listen to what I've got to say and watch yourself, new bitch* kind of look.

'She's a serial killer, Martha. You must have seen her on the news. She's killed seven men. All boyfriends. All strangled.'

I turn to look at Martha and she's just staring at me blankly, which is typical. Martha never knows shit like this, it's always me explaining it, looking after her. But who's going to look after me?

'I didn't know.'

'Well, she did. She got full life. Really rare, to get full life. But that means, she kills us, it's no odds. She can't get any more time inside, no matter what she does.'

Martha's staring at me, her lips pursed up in this little cat bum of surprise.

'Oh.'

She's quiet for a bit. Then,

'Fuck.'

And there's something about the way she says that. To hear her swearing, in her soft little Scottish voice, just strikes me as proper funny. I burst out laughing, and she looks at me, all startled, like, *what, are you mental?* and that just makes me laugh even harder. I let out this big snort and that sets her off, so she's laughing at me laughing and then I'm laughing at her laughing until we're both, like, hysterical. We look at each other and I start to think that maybe, just maybe, everything'll be okay.

Martha comes over and sits on the other end of the bed. That'd normally be a bit familiar for me, to be honest, but whatever. I really don't feel like starting an argument. The smell of chlorine gets stronger, but somehow I don't mind it so much now. She says,

'You know why I never learnt to swim?'

I shrug. I mean, a lot of people in here didn't have the kind of childhoods that were all Saturday-morning swimming lessons and a tube of Smarties on the way home. Half the girls in here can't read; you think nothing of not knowing how to swim.

'It's because my mum's scared of water. She never goes in it, not ever.'

I nod politely. Why's she telling me this? Doesn't she want to talk about, like, the serial killer we just massively pissed off? I'm not sure how much I care that her mum don't like swimming, compared to that.

'Yeah?'

And Martha's looking at me, big blue eyes held open extra wide, like I'm meant to be getting something from this, something more than what she's saying. But I haven't got a clue.

'She's . . . taught me some things. You know?'

I shrug. I mean, good for her. Mammas teach you loads of stuff, don't they? How to make pasta sauce not out of a jar and do French plaits. Not swimming, though, if you're Martha, obviously. Hang on, why are we talking about this? What is she getting at? I say, in a nice way,

'Martha. What the fuck you on about?'

She wriggles a bit on my bed and the springs creak under her bum. She looks half shifty, half really bloody pleased with herself.

'The thing is, my mum had a lot of . . . skills. She could make things happen. You know, protect people. Find things out. Bring luck. Good, or bad.'

I sit there, silent. I mean: *WHAT*?

Martha gives me this little smile, tight and bright.

'And I'd like to say thank you for today. So if you've got something, like . . . a wish. Something you'd like? Or someone you'd like to see? Maybe I could help.'

My eyes snap up to my photos on the wall. My Bethany, my baby, the only good thing I've done. I think of the day she was born, the feeling of rightness when I held her, like she'd made me who I was meant to be. God, what I wouldn't give to have her in my arms again. Even for a moment.

I look back at Martha. She's perched on the end of my bed, dark hair drying around her shoulders in waves, and sitting bolt upright, like it's a throne she's on, not a ratty prison mattress. I look deep into her eyes and she looks right back and there's this moment where I really want to believe her. I want to think that there's such a thing as wishes, that things can change. But despite that moment of totally shitty decision-making at the pool, I'm not actually a proper nutter, so I say,

'What are you, a leprechaun? Fuck off, you!'

And I shove her off my bed. But not in a mean way, because I feel like we've been through something, her and me. We're mates now, and even though she's mental, she's mine.

I gaze around the office, which is just a glorified cell, really, but with a desk and a fake pot plant in it. They're not allowed real ones. Something about us trying to hide stuff in the soil. Or smoke it, I suppose.

'Daniella. Have you had any thoughts about our chat the other day?'

I'm back with bloody Emma, again, missing time off my association, again, and hearing her patronising bullshit, again.

I give her a look, like, *what the fuck do you think?*

'Not really, Miss.'

She gives me one of her fake-matey little smiles, and goes,

'I know you don't like to take risks and try things. But can you really say that strategy's working for you, at the moment?'

I blink at her. Working for me? What? I mean, I just punched a serial killer – which was, to be fair, a new thing and pretty fucking risky – so I go,

'You what?'

Emma smiles her *I really am very patient* smile.

'Do you think it's the best way to live, to not try new things? Or do you think life would get better if you did?'

I laugh, so suddenly that I hear it before I even know I'm laughing. It sounds like a bark. Do I always sound like that?

'That's not really a fair question, is it, Miss?'

She looks at me, like, clueless, so I go on,

'I mean, things never get better, do they? That's just stories. So why does it matter what you do?'

'But you think things can get worse. So why wouldn't they get better?'

I narrow my eyes, and say nothing. Feels like a trap, that kind of thinking. You don't want to go trusting probation officers. Emma shuffles her papers, then goes,

'You're a capable young woman, Daniella. Don't be afraid to put effort into things. You might be surprised by the results.'

Capable young woman?

'I don't think so, Miss.'

She tilts her head and stares at me.

'About being capable? Or about being surprised?'

I think *both* and say nothing.

Emma goes,

'I heard about the . . . incident. In the swimming pool.'

Of course she fucking has. Gossip goes round like wildfire, places like this. I roll my eyes and brace for a bollocking.

'Yeah, Miss?'

She gives me this look, like, proper intense.

'Yes. It was very good of you not to fight back. That would have spoilt your chances at probation. Well done for keeping your head.'

I lean back in my chair, balancing on the back two legs. Fair play to Emma, she's proper surprised me there.

'Erm. Thanks.'

She gives me this little smile, and pats at the braids.

'Have a think, Daniella. You can do it. Really. It's not too late to sign up for the courses.'

And maybe it's because Martha made me think about seeing her again, and maybe it's because it's on my mind because of Lisa, but I go,

'Six months on the out then they start visits again, yeah? They let me see her.'

Emma looks well surprised, but she goes,

'No, sooner than that. The visits can start a lot sooner, maybe at three months, but if you prove you can keep out for six months, we can start the procedures for you to get her back permanently. If everything goes well, and your housing and employment are adequate, you could have her back a year after that with the proper support.'

I chew at my lip. Eighteen months without offending. Adequate housing and employment. And three months to even see her, to hold her in my arms again? Three weeks is all I manage, sometimes ... There has to be another way to get her back.

Emma's still looking at me, all bright hopeful face. It's hard to remember to hate her when she looks like that.

'So you'll consider a course?'

I give her a shrug. I dunno. I'm not going to pass any courses, am I? I never do. But no point having a fight about it.

'Yeah. Right. Can I go now, Miss?'

And Emma sighs, 'I wish you took me more seriously, Daniella, but yes,' she nods. 'You can go.'

Walking back onto the landing, I put a bit of swagger in my walk. That wasn't a bad meeting, for me and Emma. Not bad at all. I head up the steps back to my cell, clanging my feet on the metal stairs, making them sing out. She's clearly cracked if she thinks that I can pass a bloody course. But that motivational shit is a lot better than the hassle I normally get. I get to the top of the stairs, jumping hard onto the last step.

'Alright?'

Fuck. Speaking of hassle ... Chris smiles at me. Not a nice smile. Slow and, like, predatory. Like if a cat could smile, you know? My mouth's suddenly full of spit. I swallow and go,

'Alright, Chris?'

And I wait. All her gang's just standing there, staring at me, with Chris in the middle, staring the hardest. I hold myself dead still. Every bit of me wants to leg it, but that'd be fucking stupid. You want to never show you're scared in here, even though you'd be an idiot not to be, most of the time. Chris goes,

'Where you off to, Dani?'

I point down the corridor, like a dick.

'My cell.'

Chris nods, like, thoughtful.

'Yes. Good idea. Nice and safe in there. We wouldn't want anyone to come and fuck you up, would we?'

And, like, blatantly, that's a threat, isn't it? By rights, I shouldn't let her get away with that. And I look at her, and I can tell she's gagging to fight me, to have another go at me. And this won't be the end of it, will it? She'll keep doing this every time she's bored, or wants to look tough, or just fancies something to punch. And Emma being, like, *well done for not fighting back* swims through my head. And I just think, *Nah. Not today*. So I smile and go,

'Yeah. Cheers, then.'

And I make myself walk past them, slow, slow, slow, not running or cringing even though I'm expecting something any second. She threw a girl off the balcony once, for owing her teabags for too long. I mean, there's nets strung up on every level, she didn't die or anything, but imagine that – the feeling of someone lifting you, chucking you over the edge and into space, and you, plunging, wondering if the nets will hold ... She's that close to me now, she could touch me. She could reach out, push, punch, scratch me. Or stab. There's plenty of room for a little shiv, in those baggy tracksuit pockets of hers. As I step past her, I can't help holding my breath.

I take a step. Then another. And another. They do nothing.

As soon as I'm past them they burst out laughing, cackling like a load of fucking hyenas. The laughing follows me all the way along the landing, but I don't look back. I hold my head up and walk, all calm, back to my cell. I even manage to put my swagger back in.

Don't get me wrong, that could have gone better. But it could have gone worse. She basically didn't do anything to me, did she? Just a bit of laughing, little bit of threatening. Maybe I can get away with that little incident at the pool, if I keep my nose clean.

I've only got to last, like, six months, and then I'm out. It might be alright.

You never know.

*

The next day is as boiling hot as the last one, and by 9 a.m. I'm already sweating through my T-shirt. I ran out of deodorant about three days ago, and we only get showers a couple of times a week, which isn't really enough in this weather. It's surprising how soon you get used to your own smell, though. A couple of weeks and you barely notice; a couple of months and you barely care. One nice thing about prison is you're all in the same boat. There's no point in pretending you're different to anyone else. We're all as bad as each other, underneath.

Still, today's canteen day, which means I can get myself more deodorant, as well as toothpaste and as many Dairy Milks as I can out of whatever's left out of my weekly £7. Really fucking thrilling, the shopping you can do in prison – it's like Bond Street in here.

I lie on the bed, looking up at the crack in the cell ceiling. It's not, like, a tiny thin little thing, it's pretty big. I'm sure it's bigger than yesterday. Maybe I should try measuring it. I narrow my eyes at the ceiling. What would I use?

Martha's off getting her canteen, so I'm alone in the cell with no distraction apart from the crack. I'm waiting for her to get back before I go, to see what I still need to buy. The question is, how much of her stash am I going to be able to get her to give up when she gets back? I reckon about half's fair. After all, I'm her protector now, aren't I, as well as her, like, mentor or whatever. I proper risked my life to save her – the odd KitKat's the least she can do. I squint up at the crack again. Maybe a bit of bog roll, stuck to the ceiling with water then marked with a pen?

I mean, Chris was okay yesterday, as it goes. A lot better

than I would have expected her to be. Martha doesn't know that, though. Half seems about right.

This crack's definitely getting bigger. I don't even need to do the bog roll thing, I just know. Also, there's not a lot of point in it. Even if I proved the ceiling was about to fall down on me, there'd be nothing I could do about it.

There's the groan-squeak-clang of the cell door and Martha comes bursting back in. She's beaming all over her face; by the looks of it she's in a bloody great mood. I smile back, and open my mouth to deliver my careful, fair little speech about the importance of paying your dues and sharing your chocolate digestives and that. But before I can say anything, she reaches deep into her pockets and pulls out six Mars bars. She dumps them all on the bed in front of me. Their glossy black wrappers glint bright under the fluorescent cell lights. I look up at Martha, like, *what*? Her smile gets even more massive.

'They're to say thanks, for the other day. I know they're your favourite.'

I look down at the Mars bars again. I reach out. I rip one of them open and the rich sticky smell of it blasts out at me, like a big sugary hug. I stuff as much of the bar as I can into my mouth and bite, feeling the crack of the chocolate, the give of the nougat, the caramel oozing over my tongue. Mars bars are so bloody brilliant. I used to have this art teacher in school, and I loved her. Art was the only subject I wasn't completely shit at. And at the end of every term, she used to pick out her favourite pictures we'd painted, and hold them up, and any that she really liked would get a Mars bar as a prize. And I'm not completely stupid, I did notice that every single kid in the class would get one, but there was still something about it, about her holding up something that you'd done, and just going, 'yeah, this is good' that always made me feel bloody great. The taste always reminds me of her, and the smell of the paints and having the splashes of colour all around me, and of a place where I didn't feel like I always fucked everything up.

I hold out the rest of it, offering a bite, and Martha shakes her head. I give her a look, like, *seriously?* Because come on, who doesn't like Mars bars? But she just keeps smiling and, whatever, more for me. Gob still stuffed full of chocolate, I go,

'I can't believe the canteen had them! They never bloody have them. I wrote a *letter.*'

Martha gives me this modest little shrug-smile and sits on the end of my bed. That's the second time, but I can hardly have a go, still with a mouthful of her chocolate. I go on,

'I don't remember telling you I liked them, even.'

Martha's been grinning this whole time, but when I say that, her smile goes, like, supernova. It changes her face, makes her into a different girl. You'd never think, looking at her now, that she was the same person who came shuffling down the hall to me just a week ago. This Martha in front of me isn't scared, or snotty. She's all lit up inside. She takes a deep breath, leans in towards me and says,

'You didn't.'

The only noise in the cell is the distant shouts and the tinny buzz of radios and the clatter of the landing as what she says sinks in. It's like everything real's far away, and all that's left is the two of us, sitting next to each other on this bed.

Shit. No, I didn't.

I turn to her, and face her dead on. She's got my attention now, fair and square.

She leans in and says in this quiet, coaxing little way,

'Come on. What harm can it do? Isn't there anyone you'd like to see?'

And I stop chewing.

Of course there really is.

I look up to the pictures, and despite the sugar in my mouth I feel this massive hollowness inside. Because, don't get me wrong, it's nice of them to send me the pictures, but four photos, compared to how much I want to see her, is nothing. She's my baby girl and I want every little piece of her. It drives me mad, the idea of some other woman being the one to cuddle her while she's watching telly, to make her dinner and to brush her hair. I'm so hungry for her, for any little crumb I can get. I let myself imagine, just one proper hug . . .

I swallow the mouthful of half-chewed chocolate and give Martha one of my *don't fuck with me, yeah?* looks.

'What you talking about?'

She gives me a little smile.

'I told you. I can do things.'

The taste of the chocolate's still heavy and thick on my tongue.

'What *kind* of things, though?'

Her smiles grows. It's like someone's turning the brightness up on her.

'Just little things. A nudge of fate. A bit of protection. A peek through the veil.' She bites her lip. 'Nothing bad. Just a peek. Wouldn't you like that?'

I look at Martha, and she looks so excited. So genuine. I

mean, if it doesn't work, it doesn't work, and if it's a trick, it's a pretty shit one. I think, *fuck it. What harm'll it do? It's not like anyone'll believe her, if she tells.*

Also, I'm her only friend. Who's she going to tell?

And what if it's real? *Bethany* . . .

I swallow. My head's all full of chocolate. So sweet you can't think straight.

Because the thing is, right, I'm not saying this kind of stuff is common, but you do see it, don't you? On the TV and that, and the phone lines. I always used to like watching the psychics on telly, when it was on. Justin always said it was just bullshit for idiots and I'd laugh along with him, and change the channel, but he doesn't know as much as he thinks. There's some stuff the psychics tell you that you can't explain. And they wouldn't show it on the TV, would they, if there was nothing to it at all?

I nod.

I mean. Just a peek would do. What I wouldn't give, for just a look at her. Just for a second.

Martha goes,

'Oh, great!'

And for a second she looks that happy I think she's going to try to give me a hug or something. I just sit there, eating the rest of my Mars bar, confused. Because she's acting like she's won something, but that doesn't make sense. Because aren't I the one who's meant to be getting thanked?

But I eat the rest of my chocolate and I keep quiet and I let myself think, just for a minute, about seeing Bethany again.

Chapter Four

Extract from PSO 4800 – Women Prisoners

2.2   Two-thirds of women prisoners are mothers.
      Only one quarter of children of women prisoners
      live with their biological or current fathers. Only
      5% of children stay in their own homes after
      mother's imprisonment.

It's evening; that beautiful sweet spot of the day when the heat is just bearable. This boiling hot bit of summer, you're either sweltering, lying in a puddle and dreaming of autumn, or you're waking up at three, with your feet sticking out from the flimsy duvet, wondering if they've dropped off, it's so cold. But right now, in this little pocket of time, half an hour after bang up, I'm comfortable.

The prison din is worse than ever. As soon as the doors lock, the yelling of the day changes into something else. The day-yelling was just about telling people stuff, not quietly, no, but it had a point. When you're caged like this you stop making noise to get any particular message across – you just

want to show, *I'm here, I exist, I'm still fucking here.* The only
quiet time, in a prison, is really early in the morning. That
feeling you get, walking out of a club and it's already light,
but the world hasn't quite woken up yet? You get that feeling
even here, if you get up early, or stay up late enough.

Me and Martha are sitting together on the floor. I wasn't
keen, but she got some loo roll and spit-scrubbed it a bit, I
suppose it's as clean down here as it is anywhere else in the
prison. We've turned the light off, even though we never turn
the light off, and we're holding hands. Hers is pale and feels
as soft as a kid's, but her nails are long and sharp.

It's funny touching people in prison. The officers'll touch
you, whether that's in a nice, hand-on-the-shoulder sort of
way, or a not nice, twist-your-arm-round-up-your-back kind
of a way. Then there's the medical exams . . . and the searches.
With the other girls there's the occasional scuffle. But it's
mainly quick, or it hurts, and it's all for a reason. This is the
first time in a long while I've just touched someone. No purpose, just laid their hand on mine, and had it not be about sex
or hurting. Maybe that's not even a prison thing, maybe it's
just a life thing. Either way, it's pretty nice, just this touching
and sitting still like this in the din and the nearly dark. I go,

'What happens now, then? You going to get out your crys-
tal ball and show me Bethany?'

And I give her a grin to show that I'm joking but I'm actually kind of not. How do I know what she's going to do? It'd
be easier, in a way, if it was just like on TV. Martha looks at
me, big eyes and serious face. She's so close to me I can see
flecks of green in her eyes, sparkling in the light that filters
through the cell door.

'No. It doesn't work like that. I don't do flashy tricks, or puffs of smoke. This is all working with the goddess … Nature work.'

I give her a look, like, *goddess*?

Martha leans in, a little closer to me and there's a faint smell of spaghetti hoops on her breath.

'I can reveal what's already there, or give a nudge towards something that might have happened anyway. If there's something you were always meant to see, I can show it to you early. If there's a thing that someone was maybe going to do, I can make it be earlier, or bigger. I can make people believe things, but only if the thing was already believable to start with. I can't force it or change people's nature. All I can do is give them a tiny little push.'

She looks off to the side, like she's remembering something.

'But a tiny little push is all it takes to roll a boulder down a mountain.'

I don't think I've heard Martha say this many words before all together, let alone at the same time. There's something about her face and the way she's holding herself that makes her different tonight. She looks like she's doing what she was made to do. Like she belongs. I swallow, and remind myself that I don't necessarily believe her, that it's probably all bollocks. I'm just going along with this for a laugh, for something to do.

Martha holds up a twist of paper and a bright pink lighter.

'When I light this, you stare right into the heart of the flame. Don't think of anything else. Just the flame. Then, as soon as it goes out, shut your eyes tight and say her name in your head, over and over again. I'll tell you when to stop.'

There's something about sitting here on the floor and the hand-holding and Martha's soft talking and serious face that makes me not want to take the piss. I want to listen to her, to really try. So I stare into the flame, as hard as I can, and I try to think of nothing.

As soon as I start, I immediately think *this is fucking stupid.* I nearly give up, but something in me manages to push the thought away. I last about a second of no thoughts, then my brain goes, *great, I'm doing it! This is easy!* and I have to start doing it again from the beginning. I can't remember trying this hard at anything before, but ... I don't know. The not ever trying hard at anything hasn't been working out that great for me, has it? Like Emma said. Maybe I should give this a proper go.

Before I know it, the flame reaches her fingers and gutters out. I don't hang about, I just slam my eyes shut tight and I think *Bethany, Bethany, Bethany.* I feel Martha take my hand again, and hold it soft in hers. *Bethany, Bethany, Bethany,* I say to myself, over and over again, until the thought of her is all that's in me. It's like I have her inside me again, she's filled me up that much. *Bethany, Bethany, Bethany,* again and again with my eyes tight shut, and, before I know it, I'm crying, and the *Bethany, Bethany, Bethany* turns into *Bethany I'm sorry, I'm sorry, I'm sorry.* The tears are flowing hot down my cheeks and my chest's tight and hard and it's all I can do not to sob out loud. Martha's gripping my hands, hard. She goes,

'Just keep your breathing deep and smooth. Deep and smooth. Don't worry, it's okay. Just let the thought of her into you.'

I do what she says and try to keep my breaths slow. I

breathe in for two *Bethany*s and then out for two, and the juddery, gasp-and-sob feeling of crying leaves me bit by bit and I calm down. My face is still wet, but my cheeks are cool. *Bethany, Bethany, Bethany,* but I'm not upset at all now, all I am is peaceful because it's like she's with me again. I sit there for what might be hours or half a minute, Bethany with me inside my head and Martha with me outside it, her hands cool and strong and holding mine. Eventually, Martha goes,

'Keep your eyes shut. Here, we're standing up, but don't open them. We're nearly done.'

And I'd never, not ever, normally let someone do this, but I do what she says and keep my eyes tight shut as she lifts me to my feet and sits me down on the bed. It's just . . . I don't want to ruin it. Just in case. She spins me so my legs are up on the bed and gently lays my top half down. She lets go of my hands, and mine feel weird and empty now without hers in them, they've been holding each other that long.

Martha gets the duvet and covers me over. Normally this duvet's crackly with static, thin and rough, but tonight I swear the cotton feels as soft as something a duchess would sleep on. I let her lay my arms and legs where she likes. They feel as heavy as stones, nothing to do with me any more.

When she's got me still, everything feels warm and calm and peaceful. There's still the noises of the prison, the cat-calls and radios blaring out in the background, but it doesn't matter. It's like me and Martha and Bethany are in this bubble of peace, and nothing can touch us. Martha leans so close I can smell her skin. She's still very slightly chloriney. She presses a finger, so gentle, in the middle of my forehead and whispers,

'Sleep.'

And, just like that, I do.

That night, I dream of Kate Middleton. Her teeth bright, her hair bouncy, and a perfect baby boy in her arms. She's wearing a lemon-coloured dress, the kind of thing no real person could ever wear with a two-year-old on their hip, but she's not all covered in snot and grime like a normal mum. She's so clean that in the dream-light the dress seems to glow. She's shining.

She turns my way and waves and smiles. I have to squint to see her against the harsh bright white of the sun. It's hot out here, boiling, and everyone around me's wearing summer dresses and flip flops. There are blokes with their tops off and girls in those shorts where you can see the bottom of their bum cheeks, not that appropriate to meet royalty, I'd have thought. I look down at myself. I'm still in my faded prison joggers and a ratty green T-shirt. Even though it's high summer and roasting hot, there's a hoodie tied around my waist.

The crowd's swarming, pushing around me, but the press of bodies parts for a second, and through that gap I see her. *Bethany, Bethany, Bethany*. A little girl, about two and a half years old and with a head full of messy blonde curls. She's got a pink spotty sundress on and her face is all smeared with ice cream. *Bethany, Bethany, Bethany*. She's beautiful, exactly as I imagined. I head over, shoving people out of the way, wanting to get up close, to take her in my arms and squeeze her and know that she's real. She's standing under this big, spreading tree, an oak or something, and I realise I know that tree, I know where we are. We're in Brockwell Park. I'd know it anywhere. I always thought I'd bring Bethany here, give her a go on the swings and maybe take her to McDonald's. I mean, I will. One day I will. *Bethany, I'm sorry*. Finally, I get through the worst of the crowd and she sees me. I swear, the look on her face, it's as if she knows me, she knows who I am. She looks up and gives me this massive, happy, gap-tooth smile, like a little angel.

I smile back, so full up with the sight of her. It's like I'm glowing inside.

Bethany.

It's then that I see the dog.

A big nasty brute of a thing, the kind of dog you normally see with lads who need people to think they're hard. It's growling, somewhere deep down in its chest, and baring its teeth. The dog's crouching, and you can see the massive muscles of its shoulders, tight and tense under mangy brindled fur. Ropes of drool hang off its fangs and glint in the sunlight. Bethany doesn't look bothered, she's only a baby still and she doesn't know to be scared, but I'm in a cold sweat all over despite the sun blazing down on us. Because I know about dogs. I know how they can bite, can sink their teeth deep into your flesh and shake and scar you forever, I remember. And if you're tough, and quick, and you had a lighter in your pocket maybe, then you could get away, but not if you're a baby, not if you're a tiny little girl.

The dog's still slobbering and snarling, its attention full on her now, and I can tell by the way it's crouched that it's just about to spring. I think of the pictures I've seen in the paper, dog attacks on babies, all that blood and torn flesh. I get this big hard rush of adrenaline and fear ripping through me and I run straight for my baby and snatch her up into my arms and squeeze onto her like I'm drowning and she's the only thing that floats. Her blonde hair tickles my nose and her milky sun-cream smell fills my head. *Bethany. My Bethany. I got you back, like I knew I would. I love you, darling, I'm so sorry.*

I grit my teeth and kick out at the dog, thumping its muscly shoulder with my knackered trainers. That pisses it off enough to switch its focus to me, ignoring Bethany. It's growling worse than ever now looking up at me, teeth fully bared, but I've got my baby in my arms now and she's safe and she's mine, and even if the dog takes my leg off, I'm never letting go.

She's safe. Because of me.

'Go on, Dani. It's a dare. You got to.'

I looked out of Richard's patio door and chewed at my lip.

'Can't I do something else?'

Jamie scowled down at me like an angry little prince from a fairy tale. He'd got a good few inches on me, Jamie. He could win a fight between us easy, even if I cheated. We used to be the same height, but things change.

'No. You got dared to do this. You've got to do it.'

I knew when I was beaten, but there was no need to lose face about it. I tilted my chin up and glared at him.

'Or what?'

A grin snaked its way across his face. He gave me a look like, something horrible. I'm going to make something really bad happen to you, *and said—*

'Or something worse.'

I scuffed my toe on the deep red carpet, making a line where I'd pushed it all the wrong way.

'You wouldn't. Mamma and Richard would stop you.'

He was still grinning. His face, normally all butter-wouldn't-melt, looked glinty and mean.

'Would they? Or would they not believe you?'

I glowered at him. They never believed me, and Jamie knew it. Ever since we met, Jamie had been the good one, and I'd been the naughty one, and now it had been going on so long I knew no one would ever take my word over his. Pointless to even try.

Those were the days when me and Jamie were meant to be Bonding and Being Grown Up About Everything, so we got given a lot of little jobs to do. You know, stuff like go to the shops and get some milk. Load the dishwasher. Feed the dog. Jamie wrenched open the patio door and shoved the bowl of dog food into my hand. My fingers closed around the slimy metal.

'Are you going to do it then? Or are you chicken?'

It's funny how long you can miss something. We'd been living with Richard and Jamie for years by then, but there were still some mornings I woke up and, just for a second, wondered why my walls weren't pink any more, why they'd changed to boring off-white. I still didn't think of it as home, there. Richard's home, I suppose, and Jamie's. Maybe even Mamma's. But what about me?

I glared up at Jamie.

'I'm not chicken!'

He tilted his head at the door, like, prove it then. I gave him my worst look, and stepped out into the garden. It wasn't a proper garden, though, like we used to have, with grass to play on and flowers in borders at the edges. This one was all paved over, because Richard said it was more practical, what with no one having time to mess around with flowers, and with the dog.

A massive Alsatian called Bella with black pointy ears and long, sharp teeth. She sat up when she saw me with the bowl and thumped her tail on the floor. The only time I ever saw that dog's tail wag was when someone had food. I took a big, juddery breath. Maybe this wasn't going to be so bad. It was just food, wasn't it?

Jamie slammed the patio door after me.

'Oi!'

I banged on the glass, all panicked.

'I'll open it back up when you've done it!'

I went up to Bella. She'd got her eyes fixed on the bowl of dog food I was carrying, like, locked onto it. Her mouth was open, tongue hanging out and teeth glistening with drool.

I took a step towards her, then another. She didn't bark at me, or growl, or anything.

I put the food on the floor. I bit my lip, so hard I tasted blood, and glared at her.

'Stay.'

I was never that interested in the dog to be honest, but Jamie was obsessed with her. He was always sitting, face pressed to the patio door, just watching as she paced up and down. I'd never understood that about him. It wasn't like we didn't have a telly, was it? And in the evening, when she was allowed in the living room with us, he'd always sit on the floor next to her, leaning back against the sofa as she slumped by his feet. He always said he loved her, and Mamma would coo and say how sweet it was, a big lad like him loving the puppy, but that wasn't it. He didn't love her – he was fascinated by her. I knew the difference even then.

I got down on my hands and knees. I heard a rumble, deep

down in Bella's chest. The very start of a growl. The roughness of the paving slabs bit at my knees.

I could smell the meaty stench of the dog food and it made me gag. The dog growled, louder now, and huffed on me, her breath hot and rank.

If I was that sort of girl, I might have started crying then. But I wasn't, and I'm not.

I leaned down, closer to the food. It looked raw. I'd never eaten raw meat before. To be honest, I didn't like anything that wasn't chips or chicken nuggets. I couldn't even really deal with peas.

'Eat it! Go on. Eat it!'

I looked over my shoulder. Jamie was there, hiding behind the glass, his face all lit up with this, like, glee of making me do something I didn't want to.

But I was there already, wasn't I? And I wasn't chicken.

'I'm gonna, don't get your knickers in a twist.'

I lowered my face. Bella barked, once, low and loud. The kind of bark that means NO. Don't do that. Stop. But I couldn't, then, could I?

I closed my eyes and felt the grit under my hands, the spit already flooding my mouth like I was going to throw up.

Come on, Dani. It's okay.

I tipped the last little bit forward, so my face was right in the food, and I opened my mouth and took a bite. The cold, slimy meatiness of it filled up my mouth and made me want to spit and puke and run but I didn't. I stayed.

And, determined, I started to chew. One, two. I had to swallow, so it'd count. Bella barked again, but I didn't pay her no mind and I didn't open my eyes. I just concentrated, and kept chewing.

Three. Four.

And then my shoulder exploded in hot white light and I was screaming and screaming and screaming. The dog's teeth were lodged into my shoulder, squeezing into me hard and I was sure that she'd never let me go.

When I wake up, my arms reach out for Bethany before I can think, but all they find are sweat-soaked sheets. For a second I panic – *Where is she? What happened?* – but then I come back to myself and my breathing slows down. My pyjamas are drenched, clammy and cold on my skin, and my Bethany's not here. I look up to her photos and have to squeeze my eyes shut hard, so tears don't come out.

Martha's already sitting up in her bed and looking at me.

'Well?'

I think of last night. Her holding my hands and whispering to me and laying me down to sleep. I think of the closeness of her and how much I liked it and I feel awkward and look away.

'Yeah, I saw her.'

'Great!' Martha gives me this massive, told-you-so grin and goes, 'How is she? Everything okay?'

The sick, terror feeling of the dream rises up inside me again and it's all I can do to choke out,

'No.'

And I sit there, trying to breathe, trying not to start bawling over my nightmare like a little baby. This dream isn't doing that thing they normally do, where they dissolve as soon as the sun comes up. This one's sticking around, hard and heavy inside my head.

Martha comes and sits beside me on the bed. She pushes

me over to the wall so she can get in and puts her arms around me and I'm so upset I don't complain, to be honest I'm glad of the comfort. And she says in her soft little voice,

'Oh no! Oh, Dani. Tell me what happened.'

I snatch a big, shaky breath in and I go

'I saw her – I found her. In Brockwell Park. When Kate Middleton was there.'

She nods, and gives me a little squeeze.

'Okay. Then what?'

'There was a dog. A big, horrible one. It was going to attack her. It . . .'

I break off and just gasp for air for a bit. It's like there's nothing that's helping me going into my lungs. I'm sucking away at the air but there's no oxygen at all. Martha just sits there, calm and still.

'Come on. Then what happened?'

Her arm lays heavy on my shoulder. My lungs feel a little bit less tight.

'I saved her. I managed to save her.'

'Okay.'

Martha nods, this little, satisfied nod, like the officers do when they've just finished doing some massive bit of paper-work or something. She smiles at me, like, excited.

'That's great! Fantastic. You got a vision.'

And I have no fucking clue what she's talking about. There's something about the way she says that, though, all quiet but with this proper heft of authority behind it, like she really knows stuff, that makes me scared and hopeful all at once.

'A vision? What do you mean?'

She's not paying attention. She drops her arm from around my shoulder and scoots over to her end of the bed, facing me properly.

'You said it was when Kate Middleton's in Brockwell Park?'

I nod. Martha sits up, dead straight. It's cold without her arm.

'That means we've got two months to prepare. Then, you'll save her.'

I roll my eyes at her because, come on, keep up.

'Yeah, but I'm not going to be in Brockwell Park in two months, am I? My release date's still, like, six months away. I'm going to be here.'

And she stares me dead in the face, all long dark hair and big blue, serious eyes. She's kept a bit of that feeling from last night about her, that air that she knows stuff, that she's doing what she's made for.

'You said, in the vision, that you rescued her? From the dog?'

I swallow, hard. The sight of the dog, its glinting teeth so close to my little girl's face, is still so fresh in my head.

'Martha, what's a vision?'

Her eyes are proper boring into me now, giving me the creeps. My pyjama top's still damp from my sweat and I'm starting to shiver. Martha leans forward and pulls, like, a gentle, sorry-for-me face. I can tell she's trying to be kind.

'A vision's when you see something from the future. Something that will happen, or, will probably happen. One of the options of your future.'

I furrow my brows and stare at her, trying to make myself

understand. I've always been a bit slow to be honest, but this is important.

'So you reckon what I dreamed is what will happen. That's what happens in the future?'

She nods.

'Yes.'

I chew at my bottom lip. I don't like where this is going. I just wanted to hug my little girl again, that's all. I don't want to get mixed up in anything mental.

'So what'll happen if I'm not there?'

She looks at me, straight in my eyes. For the first time since the pool, she's starting to look scared.

'You said you saved her from a dog?'

I nod my head. My mouth's too dry to speak. I can still see the dog in front of me, still smell the sweat and the slobber and dirt of it. That dog's still right in my head, like it's got its dirty fangs deep in my brain.

'If you're not there ... The rest will still happen. You just won't be there.'

And neither of us says anything else. We just sit there, staring at each other. It's still so early the sun's barely up and the prison hasn't heated up yet, and I'm cold. I don't get my hoodie, though. I just sit.

And it's not like I believe her, obviously, about the vision. Obviously. But with the picture of the dog still burned in my brain and the memory of Bethany, solid and heavy in my arms, I don't quite not believe her either.

Chapter Five

Extract from PSO 4800 – Women Prisoners

There are strong links between many women's substance misuse and previous experience of trauma – often sexual abuse in childhood. There is a strong correlation between drug or alcohol misuse, previous abuse and self-harm. We know that many women 'self-medicate' to try to forget.

At least 75% of women entering Holloway were misusing substances at the time of arrest.

'Alright, bitches?' Chris swaggers through our door and stands, feet wide, in the middle of the room. 'Call this a fucking cell? I wouldn't keep a rat in here. Not even a fucking cockroach.'

I look over at Martha, like, *fuck*, but she doesn't meet my eye. she's obviously bricking it too much to even turn her head, she's all frozen up again. *Shit*. What the fuck is Chris doing here?

I swallow. She's between me and the door. It's standard prison racket out there, all clangs and shrieks and Heart FM. If we started screaming the officers wouldn't notice for ages. Martha'll probably be crap at fighting, realistically, nice girls like her can never throw a punch worth shit. So it might as well be one-on-one, and Chris is a lot bigger than me, as well as being a psycho.

Basically, we are fucked.

I swallow down all that scaredy bullshit and give Chris a brisk, I-respect-you-but-don't-fuck-with-me nod.

'Alright, Chris.'

She sits down on Martha's bed. Martha presses herself into the corner, face white and lips trembling. Pathetic. I turn to face Chris, but then I don't let myself move another muscle. If you wriggle about while someone's talking to you, they know they've got you on the back foot, running scared or whatever. People with power stay still.

Chris stretches out across Martha's bunk, lazy and slow as a cat.

'You owe me one for that shit at the pool, you know. I got busted down to basic for that. Lost my telly, and now I can't watch *Corrie*. Fucking inconvenient, is what that is.'

I tense up, ready to take a punch, or leg it – at least she's not blocking the door now – but she's still sprawled over Martha's bed like we're at a sleepover or something. She looks at me, all expectant, but I'm not sure what I'm meant to say so I just go,

'Yeah. Um. Sorry.'

Chris pulls a face at me, lips pouted and head tilted, like she's weighing me up somehow.

'That's nice. Thing is though, Dani, sorry's not really good enough. I'm going to need some ... reparations.'

I look at her, dead blank. I've got no clue what she's talking about. Chris snorts air out of her nose, like I've pissed her off.

'Some compensation, get it?'

I hold myself dead still and upright, but on the inside I'm fucking melting with relief. If all she wants is to cadge a bit of canteen or whatever off me, we're not in nearly such deep shit as I thought.

I pull this regretful, love-to-help-you-but-I-can't face, and go,

'I'm on basic too, I got nothing.'

Chris smiles, what I'd call a nice smile if it was on anyone else's face.

'I'm not after any *stuff* from you, Dani. Just a little favour.'

I narrow my eyes. This is less good. I'd only said that about basic to open up negotiations, you know, start a bit of dialogue. I'd happily give her a couple of bags of sugar or whatever to get her off my back. The thing is, there are favours and favours, and you've got to be really fucking careful round here. It's not difficult at all to get mixed up in someone else's stupid little war, without even meaning to. I crack my knuckles, to buy myself an extra couple of seconds. I'm not sure I'm up for hassle like that.

'What kind of favour?'

'I need a pigeon grabbing for me.'

I blink at her, like I'm a total div. Martha's looking at me like *what the fuck?* and I've not got much more of a clue what's going on. Which is to say, I know what she means, but I've got no idea why she'd want that.

'What?'

'Go on. It's just a pigeon.' Chris leans forward and gives me a matey little wink. 'Tell you what, you can even have a little taste before you hand it over. Can't say fairer than that, now can you?'

She smiles, wide.

I hesitate, because I'm not sure. There has to be a catch here somewhere, this is way too sweet a deal to be proper. Just grab a pigeon, then all's forgiven? My fucking arse, it is.

I look over at Martha. She's giving me this look like, *watch it watch it watch it*. I glare back at her, like, *yeah, I know, I'm not a complete twat, am I?*

I mean, maybe this is the only thing she needs? Maybe she's giving me an easy little favour to do as an out, because she doesn't want to fight with me, so she's just putting on a show of making me do payback. That could be it, couldn't it?

I grab a handful of hoodie and twist it between my fingers. Chris looks at me, steady.

The thing is, I really want to believe her. It'd be so great to have her off my back, just like that. And the idea of that taste she promised is huge in my head. So when she flashes me her sugary-sweet smile, leans forward and says,

'It's either that, or I fucking kill you both.'

All I can do is nod and go,

'Yeah Chris, no problem, sure.'

She smirks at me and nods and hauls herself off Martha's bed. And I breathe out and let myself have a little, tiny smile. Because if this is real, if Chris means it, we have just fallen on our feet in an absolutely massive way. Like, what the actual shit? This is brilliant. I thought she'd want some proper revenge for that whole pool business, not just a little favour.

Chris gets to the door and stops. She turns and stares at Martha.

'Alright, new bitch?'

And I look at Martha, bricking it, like *please please please do not be this stupid again.* But Martha looks up from her hunched little ball and gives Chris a quick, nervous nod and goes,

'Alright, Chris.'

And Chris nods back and leaves.

Seriously, this is all she wants? I do a secret little fist bump to myself and think *bloody YES!*

'Erm ... Dani?'

I look over at Martha, who is looking at me like, *what the fuck was all that about?*

'What was all that about? What's a pigeon?'

'Little grey bird, Martha. Get them a lot, in London.'

She gives me a look, like, *you know what I mean, you twat.*

'You know what I mean. What does Chris want us to do?'

I shrug. My shoulders crunch as they loosen up.

'Don't worry about it, mate. Just a little favour. No hassle.'

She does look worried, still, but she doesn't say anything. I give her a smile, like, reassuring, and lie back. I close my eyes and feel my body relax back down to normal.

Maybe we really are alright.

'Just act natural. We're just going on a little walk, right? Exactly the same as always.'

Martha tugs the sleeves of her hoodie over her hands, even

though it's a boiling hot day, and there's no shade at all out here. It must be like 40 degrees at least. Middle of a heat-wave, they said on the radio. Still, it's nice to be out in it, to feel the sun on your skin. It's pretty nice to be anywhere that isn't the cell.

'Yeah,' Martha goes, staring at the ground. 'Okay.'

I roll my eyes at her.

'And could you try and look a little bit less shifty, maybe? Like you're not out here to do something dodgy?'

And that makes her do a little smile, so at least it looks a bit less like I'm trying to make her walk the plank or whatever.

The exercise yard is packed, full of girls with their tops rolled up to their ribs, trying to get the feel of the sun on their bellies. We're not meant to have cropped stuff, or to mess with our clothes, cut or roll them up, but the officers turn a blind eye in heat like this, which is pretty decent of them, I reckon. They're not monsters, most of the officers, and besides, it's too hot to do anything out here – definitely too hot to give a hundred different women shit about a rolled-up T-shirt. I'm hoping it'll be too hot to pay too much mind to what we're doing, as well.

We loop around the yard in a lazy figure of eight. I'm pretending we're just having a little stroll and a chat, just shooting the shit and killing time out here, but really I've got my eyes peeled, scanning the place over and over for the pigeon. It'll come over the wall, and soon, but I'm not sure where.

My eyes are flick-flick-flicking round the yard the whole time, looking for anything that moves. Wooden benches, all draped in people – no.

Flower beds, all chock-full of cheerful red flowers, the prettiest ones you can get for cheap – no.

Barely used basketball hoop, with girls sprawled out under it, backs leaning against the fence, flesh pushing through the crisis-cross holes the wires leave – no.

Central gate, where the officers hang out, cracking jokes and pulling collars away from sweaty necks – no, thank fuck.

I side-eye Martha, because we're too quiet. Why would you go for a walk with your mate if you didn't want a natter? I'll have to sort this out. I turn to her, but end up just chewing on my lip. It's unusual for me, but I'm not sure what to say.

Normally I'd talk about whatever's on the telly, if I wanted to get some chatter started. Something like *X Factor*'s really good, because you can have your favourites and get some good opinions going, say who should win and then get all outraged when the other person thinks someone else. You can keep up talking about that for hours – that's why it's my favourite pro-gramme. But as we're on basic, we've got no telly and that's not going to happen. I try to think of something else to ask.

'Where you from, Martha?'

She looks up at me, surprised. Pleased a bit, I think, as well.

'Durness.'

'Durwhat?'

'Durness.'

I roll my eyes at her, because fucking obviously I was joking. 'That's in Scotland, yeah?' She nods. 'Is it near Glasgow?'

Glasgow's the one that comes to mind, because Justin went there a couple of years ago. He said it was a bit of a shithole, but the takeaways were really nice.

'No. A lot further north than that. It's on the north coast.'

I shrug. As far as I'm concerned the whole of Scotland's beyond north. I've never really got out of London that much, but I do think about it. Scotland wouldn't be first on my list, though. Maybe I'd go to Italy, as I'm from there. It looks like all pasta, ice cream and sunshine on the telly, and that sounds alright to me.

We take a few more steps around. Easy, normal. Not doing anything wrong. Nothing to see here.

I was put in a prison near Manchester once. It was bloody freezing, and the accents were so different from what I was used to so I couldn't understand people straight away. Everyone thought I was even thicker than I actually am. It all seemed so weird and wrong. It's funny how in Holloway half of us don't even really speak English, but I feel closer to home.

I look at Martha. Maybe that's what she feels like, here.

'What was it like?'

Martha shrugs, and looks at the ground again, but at least it looks like we're chatting now, so it'll just seem like normal ground-looking to anyone with their eye on us.

'I don't know. It's just a little village. One shop, one school, one church, no pub. Nowhere to go. No one to talk to except your mum, and her friends, and . . . '

Martha's still looking at the floor, but I can see the side of her cheeks and they're flushing a very pale pink, like she's got posh blusher on. She's got my attention now. I'm a very nosy person, and I can always smell out a story, if there's one there.

'And . . . ?'

She looks up at me, all defiant.

'And the baker's son. What?'

I smirk at her, like, *ooooh, baker's son, eh?* and I'd normally make her tell me, because I love a proper romance, but there's something else I want to know.

'And how'd you end up here? What made you leave Scotland?'

She looks at me, like she's trying to work out whether she can trust me, which is weird in a way because I thought we were past deciding whether or not to tell each other stuff. Ever since the dream thing we've been mates, and mates don't keep secrets like that, do they? But I don't bother getting offended. Even if she won't tell me, I reckon I can guess, because there's only a handful of reasons to leave a place when you get down to it.

'Baker's son?'

And she looks down. And I know, I *know*, she wants me to ask her again. I really want to hear Martha's story, and she wants to tell me, I just know she does. But right then, something catches my eye, flying over the fence on the other side of the yard and straight into a flower bed. I swallow, hard. Shit. We're on. I grab at Martha's arm.

'Fuck. Come with me. Quick. Don't run, though.'

We hustle over the yard, trying to get there as fast as we can while still giving the impression we have nowhere in particular to go.

This bit is delicate. You don't want another prisoner finding the pigeon before you do, but obviously it'd be worse if it was a guard. The weather's working in our favour here – most of the prison's asleep in the sun, spread out like lizards on the hot tarmac. We pick our way around them, as fast and slow as we can.

We finally get to the right bit of yard and, dead casual, I look down at the flower bed and spot the pigeon, lying among a load of cheap-yet-attractive red blooms. Its little head's lying at a funny angle, like it's been half twisted off, and flesh is bulging out around the big, careless stitches on its breast. In the heat of the day it's already starting to stink.

Poor little thing. I always think, if you're going to kill them, you should at least do it with a bit of dignity. Respect costs nothing. I make myself not look around, not check to see who's watching, and I go,

'Oh, shit, my shoe. Hang on.'

I bend down and hold my breath, more out of nerves than the smell. This is the most dodgy, dangerous bit. If the officers find me near the pigeon, or even looking at it, that could be an accident. I might not know what it is, might be being nosy, or even be just about to report it. But to actually touch a bird is proper incriminating. No one ever picks up a dead thing without being pretty sure why.

I lean forward and, quick as I can, scoop the pigeon up and shove it down the front of my knickers. Its flesh feels loose already, the feathers rubbing against me. I stand up and rub my hand on the side of my trackie bottoms to get the goo off, casual as I can.

Martha's looking at me, pulling her big-eyes face. I thought she'd be all quiet and moody, because it's not a nice business to be fair, but she looks almost excited by it.

'Is that it? Do we go in again now?'

I let out a long, shaky breath and take a step forward. The pigeon shifts in my pants, feathers pricking at me, but this part's nearly over and soon everything'll be fine.

'Yeah. In again now.'

*

Back in the cell, I eyeball the dead pigeon on the table. It's well past its best, puffy and stinking. I don't have a razor, just a pair of little blunt nail scissors, so this is going to be a right mess. I take a deep breath and get to work on the first stitch, working my scissors deep into the rotting flesh.

Martha leans forward to look. I would have thought she'd be practically throwing up, what with this cell being tiny and reeking of dead bird. But instead, she's sitting there, head cocked, staring at the pigeon like we're on a fucking nature documentary or something. Fucking mental, Martha is.

It's proper gross, this bird. There's stuff already starting to leak out of where it was cut and stitched up again. I worry at the stitch with my scissors until it finally snaps, then I set to work on the second one.

Martha sits back on the bed, head in cupped hands, still watching me.

'So ... Is this it, then? This is what Chris wanted you to do?'

The second stitch snaps.

'Yeah.' I wince as I feel around for the third stitch. It's all mushy in the wound, not firm, like meat when you cook it. I remember helping Mamma roast chickens, rubbing oil and salt on the flesh and it not being that bad. Sort of springy. This bird's flesh is really loose and grim. 'This not enough for you?'

She frowns.

'Not really, no.'

The third stitch snaps. Nearly there, *come on Dani, it's fine.* I shrug, but she goes on.

'It just all seems a bit too good to be true, doesn't it? She says she's going to kill us, but then instead she just wants us to do a little job, and then you get some drugs for it? Doesn't make sense.'

I've hacked out a big enough hole in the pigeon now, for what I need. I grit my teeth and ram my fingers into the bird, feeling the hotness of rotting and the squish of innards on them. I swallow, hard, prod further and scoop the little plastic bag out of the bird. I hold it up, slippy between my fingers.

'It's doing a job to say sorry for a diss. Happens all the time.'

The bag's all covered in greyish-red pigeon goo, and the whole cell stinks worse than ever. Even Martha's looking a bit pale now, but I'm too interested in what's inside the bag to really care where it's been. The powder inside glints a gorgeous yellow-brown from under the layer of slime.

'Does it?'

No. Of course it doesn't, it never happens like this. A proper beating's the price of a wronging in prison, no two ways about it. The more public and the more shaming it is the better. Something that leaves a scar, a reminder. It's never just a do-me-a-favour-and-we'll-forget-about-it kind of deal. Either it's for real or it's not, but it seems like at this stage there's nothing I can do.

I ignore Martha and grab some bog roll. She pushes herself right back into the corner of her bed as I carry the gear back to the desk. I wipe off the bag as well as I can, then rummage under my bed. There's a little bit of tinfoil and a lighter I keep on the off chance something like this might happen. My fingers close over them and I scramble up and sit on my bed, baggie and foil and fire in front of me. Martha's still sulking over on her bed, but I can't think of her. I can't think of anything except for the little plastic bag and the beautiful powder inside.

I tap a little bit of powder onto the foil. My hand wants to pour the whole lot on, make enough smoke to swim in, to drown, but I keep a hold on myself. Just one tiny tap. It's been a while since I've had any, my dosage'll be different. I've seen too many people make that mistake. Besides, when Chris says a little taste, she *means* a little taste. I reseal the bag and tuck the rest away safe. I hold my lighter under the foil and flick up a flame.

Over on her bunk Martha's nervously rubbing at her hand.

'Just … be careful, alright, Dani? There's more to this. I don't trust it.'

Martha's concerned face peers over at me. And I'm not stupid – I know deep down she's right. She's right, and there's worse to come, and there's nothing I can do to stop it. Chris is going to get me, and I'm not going to get my parole, and maybe I really won't ever get Bethany back. Maybe I've fucked up everything, forever. As the bad thoughts are swirling inside me, faster and faster, the smoke begins to form on the foil. I breathe in a deep lungful of delicious acrid bliss and I'm gone.

'Do you think she should take it, Dani?'

I was sitting in the living room watching telly with Mamma and Richard and it was a good night, for us. Me and Richard were going through a bit of a good patch – there'd been no rows for a month and a half, now. Not bad at all. I pull a face, like, hmmm, and have a swig of my Coke.

'Nah. She should hold out, I think. Push for a bit more.'

Mamma had a vodka and tonic and Richard had a beer and I had a Coke and Deal or No Deal was on. I liked Deal or No Deal. Gives you something to talk about, you know? Even if you sometimes can't think of a lot to say.

Richard went,

'That's right. You should never take the first offer you get. Bad business.'

It doesn't matter, on Deal or No Deal, if you were never good at school or your dad left when you were little or you never had loads of mates or whatever. It's just luck. Choose a box. See what's inside. You never know, you might win! Not your fault, though, if you get it wrong.

On screen, the woman turned the banker down and me and Richard shared a little grin between us. I nestled back in the sofa that felt a bit more like mine now, and took another drink of my Coke. It fizzed on my tongue, sharp and bright.

There was the noise of slamming doors from the corridor, of a bag dropped by the stairs, and then Jamie barged into the living room. He was so tall by then, and broad, and blond as a Disney prince. Everyone always went on about how handsome Jamie was – his grandparents and family friends and that. Like it's so clever, being blond and big for your age.

'Hey, Dad! Connie! Guess what?'

He grinned around the room and I glared up at him from the sofa. I wished he had football every night, and for longer. Or he went to boarding school. That would be great. Mamma smiled at him and my tummy went all sour and tight.

'What is it, Jamie?'

He held up a brown envelope triumphantly.

'We got our report cards today!'

He handed it over to Richard, who read it, beaming, with Mum looking over his shoulder. I shuffled further back on the sofa and stared down into my can of Coke. I didn't want it, suddenly.

'Gosh, look at this Jamie! All As and Bs ... And you've won the year eight prize for English and maths. Oh, good boy, Jamie. This is great.'

I stared out of the patio window, and then back in. I didn't like looking at the place the kennel used to be, even now. I went back to staring into the can. So dark inside there. Imagine if you were small enough to be able to hide ... On the TV, the woman picked a box. She jumped up and down, grinning and yelling, hugging the bloke who opened it.

Mamma looked over to me, smiling.

'Daniella! Why didn't you tell us it was report card day?'

My heart started beating faster, bang-bang-banging at my chest. We'd been having a nice night. Richard had agreed with me. I'd been having a break from feeling stupid.

'They didn't give my class theirs. Year seven gets them next week.'

Jamie snorted.

'Yeah right! Nice try, liar.'

I glared at him, furious. Bloody goody-goody Jamie. It was so easy for him. Richard was already on his feet and scowling at me.

'Where's your bag?'

He went into the hallway and picked up my rucksack, rummaged through and finally pulled the card out, all crumpled up at the bottom. I couldn't quite bring myself to just chuck it out, is the thing. I knew I should have. Richard read it, face all stony, then handed it over to Mum.

She scanned through my report, her face dropping a little bit with each new line. I watched her and wished and wished we could go back to that time I was six and I'd only got three right on a spelling test. She'd hugged me, and thumbed my tears away and told me not to worry, that everyone's good at different things. She used to say that to me all the time.

'Oh, Daniella. This won't do. You're not in primary school any more. These grades . . . And the rest. What's a demerit?'

Jamie plunked himself down next to her.

'It's something you get for bad behaviour. Talking, or being late, or not doing your homework, that kind of thing. I only got two for the whole year.'

Mamma looked at me, mouth open. Jamie stretched his legs out, taking up the whole living room. I shot him a glare, teeth gritted, but all he did was smirk.

'Daniella. You must try harder. Understand? This won't do.'

My eyes prickled. I do try! It's hard, is all. I try and try, but the stuff won't go in. I open my mouth to explain, but then I look at the three of them, all ranged up on the other sofa. Why can't I do it, if all the other kids can, if Jamie can, that's what they'll say. And I don't know. I just don't know. I went,

'Yeah, yeah. I'll try.'

Richard huffed out his cheeks and went,

'It's just not good enough, Daniella.'

And I could tell, from the look in his eyes, that little bit of peace we'd been having was over. Because it wasn't good enough. I wasn't good enough. I could feel the sick feeling of disappointing them building in my throat, so I glared as hard as I could and said,

'I said, didn't I?'

On TV, the woman picked another box. Her face crumpled up. The game was over.

That night, I waited there until they were all asleep – a good ten minutes after the last little bit of noise. Then I snuck out of bed, and shrugged on my dressing gown. I crept along the hall and down the stairs, into the living room. Then I went over to the sideboard, all quiet, grabbed the vodka bottle and took it back to bed.

The first sip burned at me, all petrol harshness in my mouth. It took a lot to swallow down that mouthful, and the next. But it got easier as I went.

Chapter Six

Extract from PSI 68/2011 – Cell, Area and Vehicle Searching

2.29 *All prisons must carry out intelligence-led searching, as appropriate.* Intelligence-led cell searches may involve full searches of the prisoner and property record checks where this is required.

I crack open an eye. I can see sunlight, and Martha's mug peering down at me. She's pulling that face, that mix of worried and disapproving that people always pull the first time you use in front of them. Except for other junkies, of course. They just grin, like, a mix between *you're proper fucked now, mate* and *nice one, join the club.*

I manage a little smile for her.

'Morning. You alright?' I say, and she doesn't smile back, but she does go,

'Yeah.'

So that's something.

I reach under my pillow and find the little packet. I hold it, feeling the powder solid and slight through the plastic. I like just knowing it's there. Martha says,

'What, are you having more?'

With this harsh edge to her voice I haven't heard before.

For just a moment, I let myself think about it. *More.* Just another little hit, a tiny sip of smoke, to take away the greyness of the world and make everything beautiful again. To make the aches fade into softness and the bleakness of life dissolve into happy nothing. *More.*

I shake my head. My brain gets banged about with the movement.

'Nah. I was only allowed a taste. If I take any more, they'll fuck me up.'

Martha frowns.

'How would they fuck you up?'

I try to lever myself up to sitting. I manage to get halfway, so I'm kind of at a diagonal, and then I run out of steam, but it'll do.

'They'd say I owed them, that it was a debt.' I close my eyes for a second, to have a little rest from the light. 'As soon as I was on the out they'd come after me for the money, with interest, and if I didn't have it, I'd have to work it off.'

I said it straight enough, but the idea of it makes me go all cold and sick and small-feeling, even more than I already am. It's not nice, hustling for the kind of people you end up working for, over gear. That's why I try not to use when I'm inside – it's almost impossible to do it without running up debts, and it's almost impossible to pay off your debts without working for it. I knew one girl who turned herself in to the police, she hated it so much. There's not a lot that's worse than prison, but there are a few things.

Over on her bed Martha's looking a bit less arsey, a little more sympathetic.

'Oh. Right.'

I heave myself up the rest of the way and swallow the wave of sick-feeling that comes with being upright. I hold up the bag to the light.

There's loads of powder left in there, beige-yellow drifts climbing up the sides of the bag. Shitloads left. Would they really notice if I had another tiny little hit? Surely not.

I had such a small bit last night, practically nothing really, half of what I would have had when I was properly using. Less than half. I shake the bag, and as if she can tell what I'm thinking, Martha looks over and glares.

I give her a glare back. I meant it about the debt, I really did, but the fact is, Chris'll probably say I owe them anyway, won't she? I mean, that was probably the trap Martha was talking about, the real payback for it, that she'd say I'd taken like five hundred quid's worth and that now I'd have to work it off. I'm holding the bag that hard my fingers are slipping with sweat, all mixing with bits of pigeon goo I didn't quite wipe off. I mean. If I'm paying that steep anyway, wouldn't it make sense to at least have a decent dose . . . ?

But just then this massive clanging starts up, banging out from down the corridor, the noise of shoes on bars. Then there's a shout of *cell search, cell search, cell search* and I feel a sharp drop somewhere deep in the pit of me. *Oh, fuck.* Me and Martha look at each other, and then at the scrumpled little baggie in my hand. Martha looks fucking horrified, but fair play to her, when she speaks, her voice is steady.

'Down the loo?'

I grip the bag, so hard my nails dig into my hand.

'No! We can't. They'll proper kill us for that. Fuck, oh, *fuck* . . .'

Without the drug in my brain, nothing's working properly. Everything feels foggy and I'm frozen, helpless. All I can think is that I'm ending up in seg for this, and they're going to put at least an extra year on my sentence. And at the end of it all I'll be working for them anyway, cos they'll make me pay off the bag if I get nicked and it gets confiscated. How much is in there? A couple of grand's worth. Maybe as much as five, they'll say. Shit. Another year after, for them, then. *Shit* . . .

Martha sticks out her hand.

'Give me it!'

And she snatches the wrap off me, and stashes it under her sheet where her pillow is, pulling all the bedding back straight afterwards so you can't see. I open my mouth to go *no no no, not there, they'll find it in five seconds*, but Martha's launched herself back onto the bed and is lounging there all innocent and the clanging's still going on around us so loud you can't think and the cell door bangs open and Miss Green's standing there, the mass of her blocking the only way out and the words die in my throat.

'Alright, Grove. Clarke.'

Miss Green steps into the cell. She looks properly knackered, huge bags under her eyes and her skin all grainy and dull. Her tie's all crooked and there's a bit of her shirt at the back that isn't tucked in. I mean, I know I can't be looking a picture myself, but she looks proper rough. That baby must be giving her some right grief.

She turns to me.

'Off the bed, Grove.'

And I get to my feet, trying not to wobble or throw up. She takes the duvet off my bed, and the pillow. There's sweat stains on my sheet, marking out the rough shape of me on the saggy little bed. She lifts the sheet, showing the bare mattress, then flips that over too. I swallow and level up my not-throwing-up efforts.

Fuck fuck fuckfuckfuck . . .

Martha gives Miss Green one of her nervous little smiles.

'What are you looking for, Miss?'

Miss Green ignores her. She's going through my metal cabinet now, taking out all of my things, shuffling through the bits I've pulled out of magazines, looking inside my half-finished jar of coffee and nearly empty sugar bag, uncapping my toothpaste and squinting into it. It's not taking her very long; there really isn't that much stuff. Miss Green nods at the middle of the cell.

'Stand here, Grove.'

And she starts patting me down. First my sides, then the inside of my legs, around the ankles. Both my arms, shoulder blades, the bit between my boobs. Miss scowls at Martha, then back at me.

'We got a tip-off there were drugs coming in on this wing. You two heard anything about that?'

Martha shakes her head, eyes all big, like, concerned, and goes,

'No, Miss. We've heard nothing like that.'

Miss gives us this *yeah, whatever* kind of grunt. She finishes frisking me and starts going through Martha's cabinet, which takes no time at all, she's got even less stuff than me. Martha, who you'd think would be cringing away in a corner, as she's about to be caught with several thousand quid's worth of smack and get a massive whack of time added on her sentence, has hopped off her bed all obliging and held her arms a little bit out to the sides, waiting for her pat down. Miss Green finishes the cabinet and goes to frisk Martha. Sides. Inside of legs. Ankles.

Martha holds herself bolt upright and still. Miss Green hasn't noticed, but Martha's staring down at her, proper hard and scary. Arms. Shoulder blades. Between the boobs. I would have bet you money Martha could never make her face as tough looking as that, if you'd asked me five minutes ago. She's got her hands clenched so hard you can see the muscles in her neck standing out against her manky grey hoodie. Miss Green doesn't seem to think anything of it, but I do. I look at her and I don't see some new girl idiot, a newbie that doesn't know her elbow from her arse. For the first time I see Martha as someone with real power.

When Martha speaks, her voice is syrupy and soft.

'Well, good luck finding them. See you later.'

Miss goes over to the bed. She lifts the pillow, and flicks up the duvet to check underneath. *No no no no no fuck no.* But then, instead of chucking the bedding on the floor, like she did with me, and pulling back the sheet, she just dumps the pillow down again and lets the duvet fall back onto the bed. I watch it, mouth open, as it drifts back down to the mattress, soft and innocent as snow.

Miss Green heaves out a long sigh.

'Alright, you two. Watch yourselves, yeah?'

And she lumbers over to the door. She tugs it closed behind her and, *clang*, it bangs shut and she's gone.

The din of shouting and clanging's still going on outside on the landing, *cell search, cell search, cell search*, but it seems so far away now. I sit on Martha's bunk, legs gone floppy with relief. I just literally can't fucking believe it.

I turn to Martha and grip the soft flesh of her forearm in my hand. I can feel a massive grin splitting my face in two.

'Did you see that? Did you fucking SEE that? She just didn't check under your covers. Like she didn't see them or something. Like it just didn't occur to her to lift up the fucking sheet!'

Martha sits down next to me on the bed. She looks like herself again, now. She unclenches her fists, and I can see white crescents in her palms where her nails have dug in, fading up to red. She flashes me this massive smile, her eyes all glittery and bright. If I didn't know better I'd swear she'd taken something, she looks that high.

'I told you. I can do stuff.'

I banged on the door, bangbangbangbangbangbangbangbang, swallowing down all the panic and the hate that was ballooning up in my chest, threatening to choke me.

'Oi, Jessica. You can let me out now. It's not funny any more, yeah?'

I tried to keep my voice all, like, firm and hard, but there was an unmistakable wobble going on in there. From outside, all I could hear was this cackling and jeering from the rest of the kids.

I swallowed, hard, and tried to keep it together. It never lasted all that long, this kind of stuff. You just had to get through a few minutes, then it was alright.

I banged again, a bit half-hearted.

'Come on . . .'

I looked around the stationery cupboard. At least there was a light in there, I suppose. Nothing else, though, except a load of old textbooks, a few blank exercise books and a box of old geometry crap. I fished out a compass and sat, back to the door, picking at one of the stripes in my tie to give myself something else to think about that wasn't just the cupboard. My tie was three different colours of blue, one deep navy, one so pale it was almost white and a middle one that was a bright royal blue. It was the bright blue I was picking at. I worked the tip of the compass into it and wiggled until the thread snapped. I was so caught up in it, I didn't realise the laughing had stopped.

There was a horrible lurch and I fell backwards, sprawling, into the classroom. Miss Morris glared down at me.

'Daniella Grove. WHAT do you think you're playing at?'

And I could feel myself going red, like my whole head was filling right up with burning hot blood, but I tried to keep my cool and mumbled,

'I got locked in, Miss.'

And she didn't even ask. You'd have thought she'd want to know who, wouldn't you? But she just scowled and went,

'What were you even doing in there in the first place?'

I'd been dared, was the answer to that. I could never resist a dare. I knew enough to know, though, it was no good trying to share the blame with Jessica Fisher. I snuck a look at her. She was smirking at me, eyebrows raised, like, whatcha gonna do, bitch?

'I got mixed up, Miss. Thought it was the way to the toilet.'

The whole class burst out laughing. Jessica, sat on the back row, laughed loudest of all of them. She gave me this look, like, ha! Loser! and all of a sudden I just felt like I could do with a break. I turned to Miss Morris.

'Can I go then, Miss?'

'What? Where?'

'To the loo.'

The laughs started up again, louder. Miss Morris rolled her eyes at me, like she couldn't be arsed with my nonsense.

'Fine. Off you go.'

And I walked off, fast as I could without running, out of the classroom and into the cool of the deserted corridor.

It was only when I got to the loos and locked myself in a cubicle that I looked down and noticed the compass, still clasped tight in my right fist. I stood there and stared at it for a while, the glinty silver point of the end of it.

I pulled my knickers down and sat on the loo, even though I didn't really need to go. I pushed up my skirt, showing the soft white flesh of the top bit of my thigh, the bit that no one would see. I scraped the edge of the spike across myself, watching the thin pink line it left. Again, and again, marking me like a barcode. Then, I took a deep breath and pushed, jamming the compass right into my leg.

And just for a moment, the feeling of the cold metal spike in my thigh was all I could think about. There wasn't room in my head to remember the feeling of being penned in the cupboard, being trapped like an animal, like a thing. The humiliation of being the butt of the joke. I'd actually been excited, when Jessica had dared me. Can you believe that? I thought she might just *think I was a laugh, want to be mates. But there wasn't room to think about that.*

There wasn't even room to think about Mamma. About the look on her face last time she got called in to talk to the head, about my 'behavioural difficulties' and 'inability to pay attention in class'. Or this suspicion I'd got, growing bigger year by year, that she might prefer Jamie to me. Jamie was never picked on, never in trouble, never behind the rest of the class. There wasn't room in my head to remember what Mamma had said when we got home, this look in her eyes, not even angry, but sad. Why couldn't I just be good?

*Just a tiny little bit of metal. Bigger than all my thoughts, at least for a momen*t.

I swagger my way down the landing. The bag of smack stuffed down my bra digs into the side of my tit with every step, but I still give my walk a bit of bounce because the front you put on is important, in here. I make my way up the stairs, stepping down as hard as I can to make them clang.

At the top there's this knot of girls, all from Chris's gang, loitering around the pool table. No one's playing pool, they're just chatting and cackling away with each other about nothing, making some noise and taking up space. When they catch sight of me, though, they all shut up and just stare. All of them except Kerry, who gives me this little hint of a smile, like she's deciding whether to or not.

I have no patience for this kind of shit at the best of times, and, after the morning I've had, I feel fucking invincible. No shitty little gang of suck-ups is going to intimidate me, not today. So I give them the old hard, don't-fuck-with-me eyes,

and lift my top lip in the barest hint of a snarl. Shoulders
hitched up all intimidating, I take a deliberate stomp forwards, like *yeah, you fucking want some of this, you fucking
want some?*

They scatter.

Fucking cowards.

I get to Chris's cell door and wait outside for a couple
of seconds, like, psyching myself up. I'm not sure what I'm
walking into, is the problem. Now her little plan for getting
me busted for dealing's backfired, she'll be working on a new
one. She might be waiting behind the door for me with a
kettle full of sugar water. Not subtle, but effective, that one
is. I knew a girl it happened to. It was five years before I met
her, she got sugared, and the scars had faded into white ridges,
but they still itched every night, drove her mental, she said.
She thought maybe they always would.

Someone did that to her, just for nicking their canteen
stash.

I hear a little gasp from inside, though, and I shove open
the door. I'm far too nosy to resist a peek in, when there's
something going on.

There's no one in the room but Chris, and she's sitting,
curled up on her bed. She's holding this little strip of metal,
a razor blade, it looks like, worked free from a disposable.
As I watch she drags it, slow and deliberate, across the flesh
halfway up her arm. Blood beads then wells up over the cut,
running down over her wrist. The blood's shocking dark
against the pale white of her skin.

For a moment I'm a bit embarrassed. Like, what am I
meant to do now? I don't want to cause any unnecessary

offence, you know? But I'm not going to stand there and just watch her like some weirdo, so I take a step in and clear my throat.

There's a tang of copper in the air. Chris looks up at me and sighs, like, *rude*. She puts the razor blade down on her cabinet without even bothering to wipe it off, picks up some loo roll and tears a load off. She wraps it up, taking her time, and presses the wodge she's made down onto the cut on her arm.

I'm still not sure what to do, so I just reach into my bra and fish out the wrap. I hold it out.

'Here's your stuff. I just took one taste. Like you said.'

Chris smirks.

'Ta.'

I turn around. I'm about to leave, I swear it, but something in me makes me stop. A little tiny part of me can't just leave it like this. I've got a bit of self-respect. I stare, hard, at the bottom of her door and I go,

'I know you grassed to get them to inspect.'

I turn back slowly, wary as fuck. Because that's a massive thing, to call someone a grass. Even if they've obviously just grassed on you. In here, that word carries a lot of disrespect. But Chris doesn't look bothered at all. She shrugs.

'Yeah. And? That was the payback, wasn't it?' She rolls her eyes at me, like, *thick bitch*. 'Didn't work, though, did it? I'll have to think of something else, now you've fucked that up.'

And her words are harsh enough, but there's something about the way she says it, makes me think this isn't proper malice from her, it's more like a . . . business deal. I get the feeling she's not really angry with me – I'm just something she has to sort out. She's still pressing the loo roll into the cut on her arm and gazing past me, into the corridor, her eyes unfocused. She's so different when there aren't people around.

I pull her a sarky, ta-very-much face.

'Yeah, great. I'll look forward to that one.'

She laughs, this great big yell of a laugh, then looks like she's surprised herself. I flash her a quick, tight smile. She just sits there and looks at me, saying nothing. The not-speaking stretches out. I shift from foot to foot and feel the empty space in my bra where the gear used to be.

When I reckon I've stood there long enough to be polite, I give her a quick nod and make to leave, but to my surprise, she leans forward.

'Oi, Dani.'

She's frowning at me, like she's trying to work something out.

'Yeah?'

She sits back on the bed and lets the loo roll drop off her arm. I try not to look at the bright red inside of it.

'That Martha you hang around with.'

'Yeah?'

She fixes me with this proper stare, the kind that makes me know I'm in a lot of trouble. I've seen it many times before from her, but she has never used it on me. Until now. 'She's not normal, you know.'

I shrug, because, yeah, obviously she's not, I know that. But Chris reaches out and grabs me, tight, fingers digging into my bony forearm. I have to concentrate to keep myself still, to not struggle against her.

'Seriously. You've got to make a choice in here. You know

that.' Chris leans in towards me. I can see the greasy tracks her comb's left in her hair. Chris narrows her eyes.

'You used to be so good at keeping your head down, staying out of the way. Are you gonna keep doing that? Or are you gonna change, and be a freak like her?'

I smile and detach her fingers, calm as I can.

'See you later, Chris. Alright?'

She doesn't answer me. She just stares down at her arm. The blood's still flowing, rich and red.

And I don't say it out loud, because I'm not completely stupid, but as I leave her cell, in my head I'm thinking, *freak like Martha. Definitely.*

Chapter Seven

Extract from PSI 06/2012 – Prisoner Employment, Training and Skills

2.3.7   The last months of the sentence must focus on up-to-date vocational skills relevant to the labour market into which the prisoner will be released. Offender managers, advice and guidance services and other relevant interventions will inform the activity identified for offenders.

I trudge back into the cell and flop down on the bed. The bit of my boob the heroin was jammed against feels all naked and exposed without it there. I stare up at the crack, but I don't know if it's changed. I don't care. My eyes flick over to the pictures of Bethany, but the memory of that dog in the dream makes me wince and look away. My arms miss her. They want to hold her again. It felt so real in the dream.

Martha comes and stands by my bed. She leans forwards and her face looms over me.

'Did you get it back okay?'

She looks really weird from this angle, it's not flattering. I can see right up her nose.

'Yeah, fine.'

She throws me a massive, sunny smile, which also looks weird, all sideways and from underneath. It looks a bit creepy, a not-quite smile. Somehow much worse than a frown.

'Good.'

And she's right. I know she is. It's just – it's very, very hard for me to know that there's drugs in the world, and to not take them. Once, one of the times I was in NA, I met this guy who was in for all sorts of shit, anything going he used to take, and he was talking about drinking. He said, every night he'd end with pouring all the beers he had left down the sink. He said otherwise he wouldn't be able to think about anything else, if he knew there was beer in the house. By pouring them away, he could get some sleep. And I remember thinking – fucking brilliant idea! It made me wish a bit I was an alkie, and stopping myself could be that simple. You couldn't just flush smack, it's too valuable, is the problem. But I reckon I could just about pour away a beer.

Martha plonks herself down on her bunk. I roll over and stare at her, all pathetic. Even though, obviously, it's well overfamiliar, I wish she'd sit down next to me. I'd forgotten how shit the day after is, in prison. No cups of tea and crap TV and rolling up in a duvet with a nice warm body to keep the horrors away from you in here. You've got to face the day all on your own once the smack's filtered out of your system and abandoned you. And if you want a story to keep your mind off it, you have to find it yourself.

'Oi, Martha. You were talking about a boy. Baker's son, yeah?'

And she goes bright red and I know I've found my distraction, for a little while, at least.

I smile, a we're-both-girls-together-smile and go,

'What's going on with that then?'

She looks off to the side, face burning bright red, but I know Martha now and I know that doesn't mean, necessarily, that she doesn't want to talk about it. She just needs a little nudge. I sit up on my bed, chin propped in my hands.

'Come on. Sit here, and tell me.'

And I pat the bed, all inviting.

She heaves herself off her bunk and plonks herself down on mine. I lean back and say,

'What was his name?'

And I wait. And after a long, long pause, she says,

'David.'

And the way she said it, I could have sworn she loved him. From the way Martha said his name, she might as well have been saying Romeo.

I get comfy, slouched against the wall.

'Tell me about him.'

'Nothing to tell, really. His dad was the baker. I had to go in there every day. We used to . . . talk.'

I wait, but she doesn't go on. It's like getting blood from a stone, getting Martha to tell you stuff. It'd be proper fucking irritating, any other day, but right now I'm up for the challenge, it's just another thing to keep me occupied, sort of like a word search. I like a word search, now and then.

'So, was he your boyfriend then?'

She doesn't answer me, not really, but she looks off to the side, all, like, lovesick or whatever.

'He used to give me free buns. I'd come in, just enough money for a loaf, and if his dad wasn't around he'd tuck a little cake in the bag. For me.'

As she's safely looking away, I risk rolling my eyes. This is like a fucking kids' TV programme. He used to give her free cake? Justin used to give me free coke. Things are different in Scotland, I suppose.

'That's nice.'

'Butterfly buns, they call them. With the tops cut off and stood back up in the buttercream. They look like little wings.'

I nod. I remember butterfly buns. I prefer chocolate myself, but they're pretty, I'll give her that. She's still looking off to the side, dreamy as a Disney princess.

'I used to sit by the side of the road and eat them. Mother never used to let me have cake.'

Hang on. What? I look over at her.

'What, never?'

She shrugs. I frown at her, because this is weird, even for her.

'She must have, though, sometimes. Like, on your birth-day, even?'

She shakes her head.

'We just never had it. She was ... particular, about food.'

Fucking hell. No wonder she lost her head over a free bun or two.

'What, like, she never fed you?'

'No, she fed me, it's just ... There were a lot of rules, in our house. No sugar. No telly. No music, except for the stuff she wanted. And you had to do your chores.'

'What kind of chores?'

She shrugs, like, uncomfortable. The kind of shrug you give when you're telling someone about a bad boyfriend.

'It takes discipline, the things she did. And time. Concentration. So I had to help out, more than kids in other families. But we weren't like other families.'

I lean towards her. This all sounds a bit familiar.

'Did you get punished, more than kids in other families too?'

She gives me this look, like, a bit reluctant.

'Yes. I did, okay?'

I put my hand on her forearm and give it a little squeeze.

That's really not fucking on. I mean, don't get me wrong, my mamma wasn't a saint. But she wasn't proper mean to me, was she? She was just going along with Richard, I get it. I look up at my photos. I let myself imagine, just for a moment, what it would be like if Bethany was with me. I'd give her cake for pudding every Saturday night. I mean, I will.

I go,

'So what did you and David talk about, then? Just cake?'

And she rewards me with this little smile, and says,

'Everything. We used to go out walking, into the woods and right onto the moors. For miles and miles, just talking. Telling each other the old stories we'd heard about the hills and wondering about what it'd be like to live in a city. David had been to Edinburgh, twice. He used to tell me about it, again and again.'

I want to be polite, so even though that sounds like the most fucking boring thing I can imagine, I say,

'That sounds well nice.'

And she smiles this dreamy smile, and goes,

'I think it was the best time of my life.'

I nod and smile, but sort of tentative, because I think I know what's coming. Martha looks down at her lap, and twists her fingers together. Round and round.

'One day, we were out in this bit of woodland we liked. It was autumn, and the wood was getting damp, but it was just warm enough that you didn't mind. We were . . . '

She breaks off and looks out at me from under her eye-lashes, all shy. I nod to her, like, encouraging. Christ, this is hard work. Has she never talked to her mates about sex before, or what? I suppose, coming from this little nowhere fairytale-type village, she might not have had any mates to tell.

'We were kissing. At the base of this old tree. But I should have known, that was the only place around there that this type of fungus . . . '

She looks down at her hands, and so do I. Her fingers are all interlaced, and dead white, she's clasping so hard.

'That was the only place around there that had this type of fungus Mother needed for the bundles she makes, for protection. And I *knew* that. Such an idiot. And she saw us.'

I'm on the edge of my seat here. I feel like shaking her, I want to know what comes next so badly.

'Then what happened?'

Her head stays down.

'She told me I was never to see him again, and she dragged me home. And . . . '

But she doesn't have to go on. I understand.

'How bad?'

Martha shrugs, again. Then, she lifts up her top. Right across her belly, there's a tight pink line, splitting her in two. I look at it for a moment, not understanding.

'What?'

Her mouth twists up into almost a smile.

'A poker. Five minutes in the fire.'

She pulls her hoodie back down, dragging it over her hips and tucking it under her bum.

'Shit. I'm sorry, mate.'

She shrugs, and stares off at the wall, but I can tell she's seeing nothing.

I lean back on my bed and I feel a kind of sick and sad and shaky that has nothing to do with the comedown. Poor Martha. She shouldn't have had to live her life like that, always looking over her shoulder, waiting for the next punch. No wonder she's so afraid of everything.

I stare up at the crack, but it's like I'm not even seeing it, I'm so upset. And it's not just because of Martha. That's shaken me enough, but it's hardly the first time I've heard a story like that. No, it's because I've thought of something.

When you come down to it, is there a difference between hurting your kid and letting harm come to her? Cos I can't really see any.

I roll over and I look again at my pictures of Bethany. Her soft, sleeping face. Her bright, wide eyes. And, don't get me wrong, I'm still not sure if I believe it. But it's not worth the risk, is it, if there's even the tiniest little chance that it's true. I know, deep down, what a real mum would do.

*

Emma smiles at me, her normal bright, eager smile. Her hair's still all in place in its heap of plaits-in-plaits, her white shirt still crisp even in this heat.

'Daniella. You asked for a meeting. What can I do for you?'

I swallow back the *probably fuck all, like always* that's on the tip of my tongue. I sit up straight, because they told us on one of the jobs courses if you sit up properly people take you more serious. It's weird sitting bolt upright like this in trackie bottoms and an old T-shirt, though. Prison clothes are more made for slouching. I make myself smile. The expression feels tight and weird on my face.

'Yeah, the thing is, Miss, I was thinking about what you've been saying. About the making something of myself, and the courses and that.'

She stares at me, already half frowning like she's expecting me to tell her to go fuck herself with them, which is fair enough, I suppose.

'Yes, Daniella. And what have you decided?'

Emma looks at me, real intense. Makes me feel a bit weird to be stared at like that. I shift my weight from one bum cheek to the other. I really want to slouch back down, but I stay sitting straight up.

'I want to do it. Like, properly give it a go.'

She's still just staring at me, like she's not sure. I stare straight back, and try to make my eyes big and honest looking. I go,

'Look. I want to see my kid again, you know? She's my baby, and she's out there with someone else, and it's not right.'

Which is true, of course. I try to be a grown-up about it, obviously, in here, but it kills me, doesn't it? She's mine. Every moment she's not with me, some moment this other woman gets to be her mum, it's like a tiny little piece of me gets taken.

'Basically, I'll do whatever. I'm getting her back, and I'll do what it takes to make that happen.'

I mean, I'm not going to do it the way she thinks. But still. I give it a last, proper honest look.

'I really mean it this time.'

And I just look at her. That's all I've got, and if she doesn't believe me, I'm fucked. The moment drags on forever, like there's just the two of us looking at each other, with this big ocean of time all around us. I swallow, and wipe at my face. It's roasting in here. Hotter than the cell, even.

And I'm on the edge, literally two seconds away from going, *I was just joking, you silly bitch, you can stick your fucking fresh start up your arse*, when she smiles. Not her normal tight, professional little smile, but a big old real one. It makes her look almost pretty, in a nerdy sort of way.

'Is that right?' she goes. 'Daniella, that's wonderful! I'm so pleased. What a brilliant decision.'

And I nod at her, dead enthusiastic, and secretly relieved. I mean, she does go on a lot about second chances, and doing the courses and that, Emma, but there was always the chance she wouldn't let me, when it came to it. You can't be trusting these probation officers, can you? And most especially not Emma.

'Yeah. Right. And I was just wondering – how do you do it? You know, the courses and that.'

Emma flips her notebook over to a new page. I like the look of it, all clean and white like that, with her pen hovering over it.

'Okay. Well, first thing we've got to do is make sure you've done all the offending behaviour interventions you need. Have you done the drugs course?'

I nod because, yes, I have done the fucking drugs course. About seven times now. The problem with the drugs course is, I know it's not a good idea to take smack. I've worked that one out for myself. They only tell you why you should stop on those courses, though – they never tell you how you're meant to actually do it. Emma goes on. She sounds proper excited about it.

'Okay, we'll send you on a quick refresher. You should be able to do that in a week or so. The other thing is, release planning. We need a proper solid plan of action for you – how you're going to keep your recovery up, what you're going to do for money ... Have you ever had a job on the outside, Daniella?'

And I'd been nodding along, like, *yeah! Makes sense* but at the job thing, my mouth goes all dry. It's hard for me to open it to say,

'Nah.'

Fuck. I'm twenty-three. I rack my brains. Can I *really* have never had a proper job? I mean, obviously, I've worked, one way or another, since I left home at sixteen, but an actual, legal, paycheque-and-go-home-at-five job? I don't think I ever have.

Emma's patting at her hair and squinting at me.

'Are you alright, Daniella?'

'Who the fuck's ever going to give me a job, though?'

I'm fucking horrified that there's this kind of tremble in my voice. For a second I think Emma's going to be sympathetic or something, which I just fucking couldn't deal with, I'd have to kick off rather than have her feel sorry for me, no question, but she just shrugs, like it's no big deal.

'Lots of people. There's all sorts of people who believe in second chances out there.'

I'm chewing on my lip, but she doesn't look worried. She goes on.

'Anyway, first things first. Let's get you trained up, and then worry about that.' And she gives me this little smile, but it's like, a nice smile, not all patronising like usual. 'Now, have you ever wanted to do one of the courses? Is there anything you're especially interested in? A passion of yours?'

I don't say *nah, they all look shit*, which is what I'm thinking. Instead, I look down at the course list she's shoving at me. I scan down. There's a lot there's no way I'd do – industrial cleaning? no fucking thanks – but when I'm halfway down, something jumps out.

'Yeah! This one. Beauty and hair.'

When I was little, and even as a teenager and that, I never liked bath time. I always put it off and put it off and threw tantrums, and fought over it. Because it's embarrassing, you know? Taking your clothes off. Seeing your own body staring back at you, all white in the glare of the bathroom, and the secret parts of you that you cut with their vivid red stripes on display. The thing is, even though I never liked the baths, there's something about the feeling after, all clean and tucked up in pyjamas, that's really nice. I used to like sitting there, getting my hair brushed and put into plaits. There was something soothing about it, about someone caring that you look all neat and pretty. Even now, when my hair's clean and wet, and I brush it, that's when I feel best about myself.

Emma's nodding.

'Brilliant. We'll get you signed up. Very good, Daniella.'

I give her a proper grin.

'And I'll get out by the end of August? For definite, yeah?'

Emma taps her pen on the fresh white page of her notebook, which now has *hair and beauty* written on it in big neat letters. She shakes her head.

'Daniella, I have to be clear with you. There are no guarantees. You may get out in August, or you may not. You can't change your history, and we can't say for sure what the board will decide. But if you do what you say you will, you are giving yourself the very best chance you can of the parole board considering your release.'

I squint at her, sizing her up. She's still smiling a bit.

'But I might get out for August, right? I *might*.'

'That's right. You might.'

And I'm happy with that.

As I walk out, she gives me this nod, like, a respecting nod, and goes,

'This is great progress. Well done, Daniella.'

And even though it's only for Bethany, and I didn't mean half of what I said in there, I'm happy. As I leave the office, I've got this great big bubble of hope inside me, like it's lifting me up from the inside. I get let back onto my landing, and I think, for the first time ever, *Yeah. Maybe. Maybe I can do this.*

I stood there, brand new uniform a bit too big, psyching myself up to go in. It was green, that uniform. At my old school everything was navy, but this one was a deep bottle green, and it didn't even have a tie you could pick apart when you got a bit nervous. I didn't much like it.

All around me there were people swirling round, shoving and running and calling out to their mates, but not me. I was the new girl again that day, and I knew no one. But it would be better here, wouldn't it? A new start, Mamma said.

This girl swanned past me. Her skirt was shorter than the others', so you could tell she was one of the cool ones, top of the tree or whatever. She went around me and into the classroom, and, as she did, she let her lip lift up in this little curl, like she could smell something a bit funny. I gave her a good glare back. Because I had to show her, didn't I, she wouldn't get any sport out of picking on me. This was a new start.

She swished her long blonde ponytail and went to sit down. They always had long blonde ponytails, that kind of girl. You know – princess types that grown-ups think are so sweet, but they'd stab you in the back as soon as there was no one looking. Like a girl version of Jamie.

The bell rang. School bells always ring like there's an emergency, like a fire or something, some big event, when all that's ever happening is that it's time to go to maths and get made to feel like you're the thickest person in the world. I sighed as more people rushed round me, scrambling to get into the form room. I waited until the bell stopped ringing so I was that little bit late before I went in. There's no point lying about what you're like, is there?

I went through to the form room. It was the first time I'd been in that one, but they're all the same. Desks, chairs, some shitty posters about Shakespeare on the walls, and the smell of teenager – Impulse body spray and sweat. There were only two desks left free, both of them on the front row. Typical. I slung down my backpack and dropped into the chair. The backpack was new, because Mamma had said I should have all new stuff for this school, to make a new start. Richard had kicked off a bit at that, but she'd insisted.

The teacher came in. She'd got that look of an art teacher about her – all flowy skirt and hair in a messy bun, the kind of thing you'd get told wasn't smart enough for school if you tried wearing it.

'Hello, class.'

Her voice was all drippy too. Definitely art. Maybe the kind of English teacher who spends a lot of time on poetry.

'Hello, Miss Dickinson.'

Pretty much everyone said it too, all dutiful, like a room full of robots. I snorted to myself. You'd never have got this kind of business at my other school. This place was well posh.

The teacher smiled around, a wet, hippy kind of smile.

'Good morning, everyone. Did you all have a nice half-term?'

There was silence at that. Good. At least they're a little bit normal round here. Hippy Teacher pressed on, though.

'Today we're welcoming a new classmate. Everyone, say hello to Danielle.'

I didn't turn round, but I reckoned about half the class went 'hello' at me. Not very enthusiastic.

'*Danielle, welcome. I'm Miss Dickinson, and I'll be your form tutor until you've finished your GCSEs.*'

I fucking hate being called Danielle. You can always tell, can't you, when people get your name wrong, that you're not worth a lot to them. They're not paying attention.

'*And you won't know yet, because you're new, but when I come into the classroom and say hello to you all, you reply with "Hello, Miss Dickinson". Yes?*'

And she gave me this big smile, like, we're all going to be great friends here, or else. *I shrugged.*

'*Hello, Danielle.*'

And I had this little pop of an idea, of something that might be a laugh.

'*Hello, Miss Dick.*'

For a second, there was silence. Like, proper, hear-yourself-breathe silence. Then the whole room exploded with this big burst of laughing. Miss Dickinson had these two little red patches, high up on her cheeks.

'*That is NOT my name, Danielle. In this school, we respect our teachers.*'

I looked at her, and I almost felt sorry. But the warmness of having made people laugh was still with me, and I couldn't resist.

'*Yeah. Sorry, Miss.*'

She nods, and turns to the board. And I say, just loud enough to carry to the back row,

'*. . . Dick.*'

And, obviously, I got sent to the office for that, and in a whole shit-stack of trouble back at home. But what I also got was Ponytail coming up to me after class. Her name turned out to be Emily. She said that some of them went down the old cemetery

*at lunchtimes, for a smoke and a mess about. Said I could come
if I liked.*

*I suppose it really was a new start. Maybe not quite what
Mamma had in mind, but good enough for me.*

I swagger back onto the landing feeling like the cock of the
walk, as they say. Except I'm not a boy. So maybe I'm the
vadge of the walk. That'd be pretty appropriate. I clock
Martha, sitting on her own on a sofa in the corner, reading a
fucking book. I try to catch her eye, give her a wink, maybe
a cheeky thumbs up, but she's all absorbed in it.

I march up and down the landing, circling the pool tables,
pulling a big smile and waiting for someone to ask me what's
up.

Kerry's the first one to bite. Nosy cow, she is, just like me.

'What's up, Dani?'

I pause a second, just to make sure all eyes are on me, and
everyone's listening. I puff my chest out and I go,

'I'm getting out early, is what's up. My parole's going to be
approved.'

There's this buzz of activity as a load of girls swarm around
me. That's one of the actually alright things about prison.
Nothing ever fucking happens round here, so if you've got
some real news to tell, people'll be a proper appreciative
audience for you.

Over in her corner, Martha looks up. I give her a grin, but
all she's got for me is a frown, like, *what you on about?*

Debs, who's one of Chris's lot but still basically okay,
goes,

'How did you manage that, Dani?'

I turn to face Debs, because I want everyone to think I'm talking to her. But I make sure my voice is loud enough to carry all the way over to Martha.

'I went and had a chat with Emma. Said I'd do the courses she wants, stay out of trouble for a bit, you know. She says if I do all that, the parole board should let me out by the end of August.'

Debs tilts her head in an irritating way and goes,

'So it's not a done deal, then? You just *might* get released.'

I narrow my eyes at her. Maybe I was wrong about her being alright. People are always trying to get you down.

'Yeah, but I *am* going to keep my nose clean and do the course, aren't I? So it is a done deal, isn't it? It just hasn't quite happened yet.'

Debs pulls a face like she's well unconvinced, but she doesn't actually argue back, so I take it that I've won that one. Kerry, who on reflection is a lot more sound than Debs, goes,

'What course are you doing then?'

I flip my hair back off my shoulder, to demonstrate.

'Hair and beauty.'

Kerry laughs.

'You? Hair and beauty?'

I give her a fucking mean look, as hard as I feel knocked.

'Yeah. Something funny about that?'

And she looks like she's about ready to shit herself, and she goes,

'No, Dani, sorry, Dani. I didn't mean it like that, I swear.'

I smile her a little smile, all generous.

'That's alright. Maybe I'll do your hair for you sometime, yeah?'

Which I'm obviously not ever going to do. I only said that for Martha's benefit, to see if I got a reaction. Because, to be fair, she could come over and congratulate me, or something. Wouldn't kill her, would it?

'Yeah, thanks, Dani. That'd be great. Maybe a bit of colour put in . . .'

I look over, and Martha's still pulling this sort of confused, worried little face. I wish she'd chill out and stop wrecking my buzz. I thought she'd be pleased for me, maybe.

I do a big fake smile at Kerry.

'Yeah, whatever you like . . .'

But she's not looking at me. She's staring past me, over my shoulder. I get this feeling, deep inside me, like this sinking feeling that I've fucked something up, even though I don't know quite how yet. I get that kind of feeling a lot.

'What's going on, bitches?'

Chris comes sauntering down the stairs, walking them like she's in a TV show or something. She's smiling at me. Not a nice smile. *Fuck.* I shrug, but Kerry goes,

'Dani's doing one of the courses. She's going to get out early, if she keeps her nose clean and that. Her parole board meets in a few weeks. Just after mine, isn't it, Dani?'

I shrug again, eyes on Chris. Her not-nice smile gets wider.

'Is that right, Dani?'

And like I told you before, I'm not that bright. It's only occurring to me right now that it might have been better if Chris didn't know what I was up to. Maybe it might have been a bit lower profile to not run around shooting my mouth off about how I'm going to get the fuck out of prison before she can really get at me. But it's too late now. Like, what am I going to do, lie to her face?

'Yeah, that's right. Might get out a bit early. You never know.'

Debs goes,

'That's not what you just said! You said it was a sure thing. As long as you keep out of trouble.'

I glare at her and make a mental note to think of something to do to fuck with her, later. Chris leans forward, hanging off the banisters, looming at me.

'So which is it, Dani? You getting out, or not?'

And she looks at me, and I look back, and I think, *yeah. It's that simple, isn't it? Am I getting out, or not?* And I know the answer to that, don't I? I am going to get out. I'm going to save my baby girl. And, anyway, the damage has already been done. I lift my chin.

'I'm getting out.'

She pulls this, like, fake innocent face, and goes,

'Oh right, nice one. Better keep out of trouble, then, hadn't you?'

And she looks at me, like, *whatcha going to do now? You gonna take the bait?*

I look at her. I reckon she wants an apology, you know? For me not letting her fucking drown Martha. Psycho bitch. She wants me to kiss up to her, show her I'll toe the line from now on.

And I wouldn't normally. You know me, I really wouldn't. But this matters now, doesn't it? I can do it. For Bethany. So I swallow my pride and I dip my head, and I go,

'Yeah, Chris, right. I will.'

Chapter Eight

Extract from PSO 1700 – Segregation, Special Accommodation and Body Belts

Measures will be put in place to safeguard the mental health of prisoners who are kept in Cellular Confinement.

I lie on my bunk, waiting for Martha to come back. I stare over at my pictures of Bethany, and feel that familiar sweet ache of looking at her. Purse my lips up at her in a kiss. *I'm coming to save you, little one.* Glance up at my crack. Not bigger. I bounce my shoulders up and down, listening to my mattress creak.

The door clangs over and Martha comes in, holding a book. I bounce up off the bed and right into her face.

'So, I got it then!'

Martha walks into the cell, so slow it does your head in, making a big show of it, and puts her book down on the table. It's *The Seven Habits of Highly Effective People*, which is an odd choice, in prison. Like, what are you going to get more effective at? Hanging around in your cell and doing fuck all?

Martha sits on her bed and looks up at me.

'No.'

I feel my mouth drop open at the fucking cheek of her.

'I fucking did!'

Martha starts unlacing her left trainer. This is one of the many fucking weird little things she does. Like, why unlace your trainers? They pull right off as long as you don't tie them up too tight.

'You can't have got it, your hearing wasn't today. Best-case scenario is, Emma said you were in with a decent shot of it when they do meet. Yes?'

I flump down on my bed and pull a face at her. Because, *yes*, if you *insist*, that is the exact technical version of events, if you want to be a dick about it. I look over at Martha, who's working on the right trainer now. I flash her a grin, because no one can bring me down today.

'They're going to say yes, though.'

She leans over the side of her bed, lining the trainers up next to each other neatly, rather than just kicking them under the bed like a normal person.

'We'll see.'

To be honest, I don't know what her fucking problem is today. Why won't she just admit that I'm right?

'But I fucking will, though!'

Martha shrugs. She goes over to her cupboard and gets a Tesco bag out, bulging with stuff, and her cup. I can't believe what I am seeing – where the fuck did that come from? We've both got so little, I thought I had track of every scrap she had.

Where did she even get the bag? She takes it over and sits at our chair.

'Yeah. If you stay out of trouble. If you stay away from Chris. If the courses go well, if you don't get kicked off . . .'

I lean myself up, making the flimsy springs of the mattress ping about under me.

'Why would you say that?'

I feel myself start to get the anger-finger-tingle thing, but Martha looks at me and her eyes look really kind, like, *sorry, I'm just saying it like it is.*

'Look, sorry. It's just, that's the way it is, isn't it? Things are stacked against us. You can't expect to win against the system if you're always playing by their rules.'

Martha hunches over the bag and takes out this bunch of weird shit – looks like twigs and feathers, mainly.

'What do you fucking suggest then? If you're so clever, what do you think I should do?'

Martha looks up, and flashes me this smile. It's a bit like one of Chris's smiles, though, which is to say, it puts me on edge. She's got that high look about her again.

'We could break you out.'

She's staring at me, still smiling. I take a breath and let it out, slow. Anyone who's ever been in prison, I guarantee you, they've thought about how to escape, same as when you're on the outside you think about winning the lottery. Except it's even less likely to happen, isn't it? You almost never hear about break outs, and, even when you do, they're scooped up and back inside within a couple of days. *But if it was just to save Bethany from that dog, a couple of days would be enough . . .* No. It's impossible, is what it is. I've never known anyone who's escaped. It's basically a fairy tale – nice idea, but no chance in hell of pulling it off. And Emma said I could get out in a couple of months. She *said*.

'Yeah, right. You'll see, when they let me out. It'll be fine.'

Martha shrugs, in an annoying *I know better than you do* way.

'Okay.'

I glare at her. It *will* be okay, though.

As I watch she dips three twigs into her cup. They come out dripping thick yellow goo – honey, I suppose. She counts out seven feathers and sticks them to the twigs, and then gets some string and loops it, round and round and round, until you can't see the feathers any more. She ties it off in a bow and saws at the end with my nail scissors until the last thread of the string snaps, sets it down and gets to work on the next one. Because I don't really want to be having this conversation with her any more and, to be fair, I'm nosy, I go,

'What's that?'

She doesn't even look up.

'Good luck charm. I'm making them for some of the girls.'

I raise my eyebrow, which she can't see, because she's still hunched over the bundles. Since when does Martha talk to 'the girls'? Since when does she have any mates, apart from me?

Does this mean other people know? About the ... stuff she can do?

Do they believe her too?

I don't know why, but that idea makes me a bit twitchy.

'Why's that? They your mates or something?'

I mean, it's not like I want her to have no mates, or be

miserable or anything. But the idea of her having other people that she chats to, shares her secrets with and stuff ... Like, I wouldn't want her telling anyone about Bethany, and the dog. I'm not ashamed of anything, and I'm straight with people about the stuff I done and being a junkie and that, but the Bethany thing ...

Martha doesn't look bothered. She's winding her string about again.

'Not really. It's nice to be owed a favour, though, isn't it? Never know what you might need a bit of leverage for, in here.'

I frown, like, confused.

'What?'

Martha rolls her eyes at me, which is a cheek.

'Leverage. It means, like, a favour.'

'I know what fucking leverage is Martha,' I say, which is a lie. 'It's just, why do you need someone to owe you a favour?'

Martha puts down her bundle of twigs.

'I don't need them to. But then they *owe* you. You've got them.'

And I nod like, *oh, right, of* course, but I don't mean it. Because in here, the way things stand, and with Chris hating her guts, what's she going to do with favours? Maybe I don't understand her at all.

'Daniella. Your turn.'

All around the circle, ten sets of eyes swivel round to look at me. I slouch down low in my chair. It's the first session of the drugs refresher thing, and this one's different to the courses I've done before. Normally you just sit in a room and they tell you that drugs are bad, and they're going to fuck you up and kill you, and it's obviously pretty boring, but it's easy enough. This one, though, they want you to talk about stuff, say what you think about things. It's weird.

The drugs session lady, Karen, smiles at me. She seems pretty nice, to be fair.

'Come on. It's okay. Just say your name and why you're here.'

I stare at a patch of floor.

'My name's Dani. I'm a junkie.'

Karen shakes her head.

'Remember the ground rules.'

I sigh. We're meant to be not labelling ourselves, she said. Whatever. Doesn't stop it being true.

'Okay. I'm Dani. I use heroin sometimes.'

'Great, thank you, Dani. And why do you use heroin, do you think?'

I smirk around the group and raise my eyebrows. And I can't help it, even though I said I was really going to try this time, she's laid it wide open for me. I grin and go,

'Because it's really fucking nice.'

And everyone laughs. To my surprise, even Karen.

'That's a really good point from Daniella there. There are a lot of things in life that can feel frightening, or upsetting, or just not nice. A lot of people use drugs to get away from those things, to find somewhere that's safe. Sometimes we all feel like we just want something nice.'

I stare at her, a bit nonplussed. She smiles back. I really thought she was going to bollock me for that bit of cheek, but she took it proper serious.

I suppose, now I think about it, it was sort of only half cheek, but half real as well.

'So, would you like to stop using heroin?'

I roll my eyes, and there's giggling all round the room. It's not so bad, this drug group thing.

'Um. Yeah?'

She's still smiling at me. Firm. Steady.

'Why?'

And that proper floors me. Because I know it sounds mental or whatever, but no one's ever asked me that before. I'm not sure I've asked myself, even. Why do I want to stop taking heroin, then? I mean, the stuff that they say on the courses, obviously. It's illegal, and expensive, so you'll need to rob stuff, which is also illegal, so it's odds on you'll end up in prison if you're on the smack, sooner or later. And it's dangerous. The overdoses, and the risks you take to get it, and the way it makes you feel like nothing else about you matters apart from a vein to stick it in, they all make it that much more likely you'll end up dead before your time – not just a bit, but a lot. But the thing is, that's not it, not really.

It's just, I want my head back. The way I feel, when I'm around smack, it's like this animal thing, or even like I'm a robot – if it's there, I'll take it, I'll find a way, and that's the end of that. And if it's not there, I'll go and seek it out. No choice for me to make, I just do what I have to, to score. And I didn't used to mind that – it used to be a relief, almost, to not have decisions to make, to have no responsibility for how stuff turned out. But ever since I had Bethany, I've wanted my choices back, so I can make them for her. I want to be in charge of what I do again, because I've got a reason to do it right, haven't I? I want to try and be a good mum for her, and this is how I'll start.

I look Karen dead in the face and I shrug.

'I dunno. It's bad for you, innit?'

She's still smiling.

'Is there anything else you'd like to share, Daniella?'

I shake my head.

'Nah, you're alright.'

Karen nods at me. Not a patronising nod, but the kind of nod you'd get from another one of the girls. Like, a respect kind of nod. Thing is, she said at the beginning, she used to be a junkie too. Maybe she really does get it.

'Okay, thank you for talking to us.'

Karen turns back to face the whole group.

'Tomorrow we're going to be looking at triggers. Who knows what a trigger is?'

One of the girls puts her hand up.

'It's what you get on a gun.'

I roll my eyes at her. I mean, I don't know what she's on about either, but that's pretty fucking obviously not it, is it? Karen smiles, like she does when any of us say anything.

'Yes, just like a gun. A trigger is something that makes you want to take drugs. It might be a place, or a person you often take drugs with, or a situation like being drunk or feeling sad. But it's something in your life that, when it crops up, you'd normally want to take drugs.'

Again, I can't help myself. I go,

'Miss, that's everything, though!'

And everyone laughs, but I'm not even half joking this

time. Like, seriously, unless she means breathing or being awake are my triggers, I'm not sure how I'm ever going to find them. I've wanted to take drugs every second of every day since I was a teenager, practically. The only time I haven't is that moment in the hospital bed, holding Bethany. That's the only time I've felt like I had enough without it.

'Don't worry, Daniella. Everyone's got them. Tomorrow we'll figure out what yours are. Then we can work out how to avoid them.'

And I'm dead sceptical about this, but I'm trying my honest best to do it this time, do it right, do it for Bethany, so I meet Karen's eye and I nod.

Emily took a deep drag on the cigarette and passed it over to me.

'What we gonna do today then? Anything going on?'

I shrugged and took the fag.

'Not heard of nothing.'

I took a puff. I hadn't been smoking long and the taste still made me feel a bit sick, but I kind of liked it as well. Most of my best memories of those few months had been with the sour-acid taste of smoke in my mouth. It sort of tastes of good times as well as chemicals.

'Oi. Don't doggy the end.'

'I won't.'

'You always do. Your mouth's too wet.'

I took another drag, folding my lips in so the end of the cigarette didn't touch any of my spit.

'What you want to do today then? Go into town?'

Nicking stuff, is what I meant. Nail polishes and sweets and hairbands, little treats. I loved going into town.

Emily examined the end of the fag like she could tell her fortune from it.

'Nah. Actually, I'm meeting my cousin. He's a bit older than us.'

She said this, all casual, like it was nothing. I scowled. So she was going to go off and have a nice little family day, was she, and I was just going to be stuck on my own? Fucking perfect.

'You didn't say.'

I scowled down at the floor. I didn't want to go home on my own. Richard kept making these snidey little comments about how much better Jamie's grades were than mine and then Mamma would tell him to shut up and then sometimes they'd fight.

'I'm saying now, aren't I?'

Jamie had been bothering me, too. I'd properly lost it with him, a few weeks ago, and given him a little swipe on the arm with one of the blades I'd worked free from a razor and hidden under the bed. He'd freaked out, and hadn't even really looked at me since. I thought he'd tell on me, but it was worse, somehow, that he hadn't.

She took a drag and blew smoke out of her nose, which she reckoned made her look really cool. I jutted my chin up.

'Well, I'll go into town then. Nice day for it.'

Mamma and Richard had even put a lock on the drinks cabinet. They hadn't said anything either, but it was because of me. I knew.

None of this felt great, obviously. I was trying not to think about it.

Emily tapped the ash on the edge of one of the gravestones.

'I thought you might like to come with me. Say hello to Adam and that. Might be fun.'

I looked up at her, sharp. She wasn't above doing a trick about something like that, wasn't Emily. She'd asked to meet up before and not turned up.

'What, really?'

'Yeah.'

She pulled on the fag again. It was nearly burned down to the end.

'Oi, my go on that.'

She handed it over. I went,

'Thanks.'

And took a breath in of the lovely sour smoke.

A bit later, she nodded to me.

'That's him.'

And pointed to a figure, coming towards us through the gravestones. He was blond, with that floppy curtain hair that they had in boy bands, and he was wearing baggy jeans with one of those belts with studs on. He wasn't tall – maybe only an inch bigger than me, and I was pretty little for my age.

'Oi!'

Emily waved, and he looked up and smiled, this, like, million-watt smile that felt like it was lighting up the whole town. Something about that smile made me feel very aware of myself all of a sudden. My hands. Was the way I was holding my hands a bit weird, somehow? I put them behind my back. But was that worse?

He got to us and punched Emily on the arm. But not hard.

'Alright, Ems? How's it going?'

'Not bad. You get away from my place then?'

'Yeah. Said I was meeting you for a film.'

'Twat! I said I was at homework club.'

He grinned, all lazy.

'Yeah. You're in a bit of shit now. Wouldn't go home for a while if I were you.'

I just stood there, awkward. Mamma and Richard didn't even ask me where I was going when I went out, these days. It was like they were just glad to be rid of me.

Adam nodded at me. My hands felt wrong again. I moved them down to my side, in fists.

'Who's this then?'

'This is Dani. I said she could hang around with us.'

He gave her this look. And I could tell it was a look that meant something, but I couldn't get my head around what.

'Did you now?'

Emily raised her eyebrows at him.

'She's alright. She'll be up for it, she can be proper mental, right, Dani?'

That sounded like a compliment, so I shrugged and went, 'Right.'

Even though I didn't know what the fuck she was on about.

'Alright. Cool. I got enough. She got cash for them?'

Emily raised her eyebrows at me. I did like a shrug-nod. I knew where the housekeeping money was.

'At home, yeah.'

He smiled his best smile in the world.

'Alright, safe. Just a tenner for you two, yeah? As it's family.'

Emily shoved him.

'You're such a dick.'

And I felt this ache. Quite gentle, but deep.

Adam pulled out a little plastic packet from his pocket. There

were a few little white pills inside it. I suddenly got what we were
talking about and felt like a bit of a prick. Of course it was drugs.
What did I reckon we were on about? I tried to make my face
look not surprised. He handed them to me.

'Ladies first.'

I took the bag.

'What, me?'

And he smiled right into my eyes.

'Go on. It'll be fun. We'll have a laugh.'

Back then, that was pretty much all you had to say to get me
to do anything.

I'm walking down the landing, on my way to the second day
of the drugs refresher class, and feeling pretty fucking good,
all told. It's morning, so not too hot, and this has been one
of those days I've managed to actually have breakfast. That's
unusual, for me. They give you these packs for the morning,
you see, like some cereal and fakey milk or if you're lucky a
peanut butter sandwich, but they do it the night before, when
they're locking you up. I'm not good at resisting, that's my
problem, so I always eat it pretty much straight away, and
then I've got a solid eighteen hours without food staring at
me. I know every time I do it that it's a bit stupid, but I can't
normally help myself. I don't know what was different, last
night. I just put it in my cupboard and shut the door. It was
calling to me a bit less, even though it was my favourite –
Crunchy Nut Cornflakes.

I'm also feeling good because, and this is a bit of a first for
me, I'm looking forward to the drugs session. It was alright
yesterday, and I've been thinking about it and I've worked out

a trigger – bloody Justin. I've never been near that boy and not taken something, not since the day we met. And obviously there's more, because I was already a junkie, or 'taking heroin sometimes' when we got together, but that's a decent start, isn't it?

'Alright, Dani?'

I raise my hand in greeting and smile. Like I say, good day.

Thing is, the course might help me, or not. I've tried this kind of shit before, and I don't have massively high hopes for myself. But it's obviously better than just sitting in my cell on my bum all day like I'd normally be doing. And they even fucking pay you for it! £1.50 or, if you like, two and a half Dairy Milks per day.

I turn the corner, and in front of me there's Chris, with her gang of girls all around her. I swallow but I make myself look dead calm and I nod, a little respectful nod to show I don't want any trouble, and I go,

'Alright, Chris?'

And the girls all stop talking and they look at me. I swear, even the racket of the prison goes suddenly quiet and calm. It's like the place is holding its breath. Chris turns towards me and gives me this look, like, proper evil, and goes,

'Alright, Dani?'

I nod again. I go to walk past her, but she moves, dead quick, and plants herself straight in front of me.

'Where you going?'

I take a step sideways, and so does she. I take a deep breath in, and try to keep myself calm, to not lose it at all.

'Just off to my drugs course.'

She puts her face right up in mine. I want to square up to

her, puff myself up and show her I'm not for fucking with, but I stop myself.

'Oh yeah? Busy learning not to be a fucking junkie whore fuck-up, are you?'

I shrug.

'Yeah, that's the plan.'

There's a bit of laughing from the gang about that, but Chris flashes a quick look round her like, *shut the fuck up*. She turns back to me.

'I don't know why you're bothering, Grove. Even if you get out a bit early, you'll be back inside within a month. You know you will.'

I say nothing. Maybe she's right. Maybe not.

Chris narrows her eyes and tilts her head. You can feel the anger coming off her all hot and strong.

'What? You think you're better than us or something? You really think you can change?'

I look her square-on and try to keep my face all smooth and not afraid and I go,

'I can try.'

And for a moment, I think she might let it go. Her face clears – she stops frowning and smiles. But then the smile grows, bigger and madder until she's showing every single one of her brownish teeth, and then she just fucking launches herself forward and before I know it she's on top of me. The noise of the prison comes rushing back, the screaming and the shouting and the whooping are all louder than ever. Chris's gang are all bunched around us in a circle stamping and pounding their fists in the air and shouting.

Fight fight fight fight fight.

My whole world's full of slaps and kicks and pulled hair. She's heavy and hot on top of me, the gone-off biscuit smell of her high and full in the back of my throat. She rakes a clawed hand down the side of my face.

Fight fight fight fight.

And I pull my hands up to my face without thinking, blocking her nails from my cheek and pushing her left hand away. As I do, she hooks her right one round, landing a proper hard clang to the side of my head. There's a sickening thud of bone on skull as her hand connects.

Fight fight fight.

The punch, with the pain and jangle it brought with it, seems to make the world slow down, just for the moment. I can see ahead of me, really clear, that I've got two choices. I can either take this beating, let her kick the shit out of me right here in front of everybody, or I can land her a proper wallop back.

Fight fight.

If I let her pound me, I don't get into trouble. She goes to the seg for a bit, I keep my nose clean and carry on with the plan. But everyone knows that they can shit me up a bit, any time they like, and I'll probably just lie down and take it. If I punch her back, we both get done for violence. That's the way it is in here; once it's a proper fight it doesn't matter who started it, you're both fucking convict thugs as far as they're concerned. We both go to seg, and I don't get my parole. But I do get to keep my chin up, keep my pride, and I don't get fucked with every single day left of my time inside.

Fight.

Even if I do get my parole, I'm still in here for another six weeks. I'm not sure if I can stand six weeks of having people think it's okay to fuck with me. I'm not sure I can stand one.

Fight.

So I let my fist fly up, putting all my anger and panic behind it and sending it crashing right into Chris's mouth. I feel her teeth cut into the tops of my fingers and the hot gush of her blood as it runs down my wrist and in that moment, with the hooting of the crowd and the adrenaline flying through me, it's as if this is what I'm made for. This is what I'm meant to do, and I'm not sorry at all.

Before I can even land another punch, I feel massive hands wrapping round my biceps and wrists and ankles, pulling me off. I'm too far gone to stop myself struggling but they've got me good and tight and I just wriggle about like a fish on the end of a line. As they drag me off, I twist around, trying to get one last look at Chris, to see how much I fucked her up. I don't see her, but I must have done pretty well. There's a puddle of blood on the floor, shining up at me red and slick.

Chapter Nine

Extract from PSI 27–2001 – Prison Discipline
Procedures

2.1   The use of authority in the establishment is
proportionate, lawful and fair. A safe, ordered
and decent prison is maintained. Prisoners
understand the consequences of their behaviour
and consider and address the negative aspects of
their behaviour as a result.

I give Emma a tentative smile through my bruised face. She's standing over me, her hair backlit by the ceiling strip light. There's nowhere for visitors to sit in solitary, which isn't surprising, I suppose. There's a bed and a bog and that's it. I've only been in for three days, but that's so much time to be shut up on your own with just your own thoughts that I'm almost glad to see her, just for the company.

'Oh dear, Daniella,'
she says, and shakes her head. Like I said, *almost* glad to see her.

'Alright, Miss?' I say, and squint up at her through eyes that'll only open halfway.

'No, Daniella, I'm not alright. What do you have to say for yourself?'

I scan the rest of the ceiling for something to look at rather than Emma's face. There's nothing there. This is a boring ceiling, flat and smooth. I miss my pictures of Bethany I had up in my old cell, and even the crack in the ceiling. And Martha, I suppose. There's been nothing to do in here, nothing to distract me from what's going on inside my head, which is nothing but *Bethany Bethany Bethany, you fucked it up again you stupid junkie fuck-up whore, Bethany Bethany Bethany, you're never going to save her now.*

Eventually there's nothing to look at but Emma's pissed-off face.

I shrug, helpless, like, *what do you want from me?*

'Miss, she started it.'

She doesn't soften at all, just keeps glaring down at me.

'Why didn't you call for an officer?'

And I give her a look as if to say *are you serious?* because come the fuck on, everyone knows what happens to grasses in here, even Emma. She seems to work that out, because she goes,

'Or waited for one, at least. Why didn't you?'

And I think about trying to really tell her. I could try to explain properly, about what showing weakness in here would mean, for me, and how the time I had left was too long to bear it. Time moves weird, you can't trust it to just tick along at the same rate, and six weeks of hell is so much longer than five months of just pottering along. I could tell her about the animal instinct of it, of another thing hurting you, and how hard that is to resist, and how you'd never know if you hadn't been in a fight, but I held out for ages, for me. I could tell her that I was actually trying this time, and that I wanted to finish the drugs course even if it didn't count towards parole, because I think it might be working, just a little tiny bit. I reach for the words, but the best I can do is,

'Miss, she disrespected me.'

Emma's face puckers up.

'That is not a valid reason for violence, Daniella! You can't attack everyone you meet in life who hurts you.'

And I know then that I'm never going to be able to explain, because in Emma's world you can sort things out all civilised and friendly like and in mine you can't. In this place, in my life, you not just *can* go after the people who come after you, you've *got* to. If you let someone do something to hurt you, and you don't get them back, the next time they'll just do it more. And, worse, that time it'll be your fault, not theirs, because you should have known better. It'd be nice to live in a world where that wasn't the rule, but it is. If Emma doesn't understand she can't help me. So I shrug at her and I pull my old arsey face and I go,

'Whatever.'

She doesn't like that. Her lips go all tight and I feel a tiny rush of triumph, because even if I can't do anything else, at least I can piss Emma off a bit.

'You realise there's no way I can approve you for early release now?'

And I mean, I did know that, I knew that at the time, but it feels different to have her actually say it to me. No parole.

No getting out. No saving Bethany, no being the hero for once. I close my eyes and see blood, and a little girl lying there, bitten, bleeding out under the roasting London sun. There's this lump in my throat so I can't say anything back. I just shrug and stare up at the boring ceiling and try to look like I'm not bothered.

'I'm disappointed in you. You've let yourself down badly. You know that, don't you?'

I swallow, but my throat's still too tight to tell her to fuck off. I sit and she stands and, for a minute, neither of us saying anything, just ignoring each other even though we're practically touching in this tiny room. I can hear her breathing, even, we're that close together. After what seems like about a million years, she turns and clangs the door to be let out. An officer comes, *stomp stomp stomping* down the corridor, and me and Emma wait for her to be let out and don't look at each other. I've had to turn my head as far as it'll go to the left to find something to look at that isn't her, and I stare furiously at my hoodie, dropped in a puddle at the end of the bed. Nowhere else to put it. Nowhere to put anything.

As well as being tiny, it's too quiet in here. I hate how you can hear everything that goes on. I don't like hearing people have a shit, or a little cry to themselves at night. I'd rather it was drowned out by a hundred catcalls and radios.

We wait some more. I listen to me and Emma breathing and I clench my hands into fists.

The officer opens the door, and Emma takes one last look at me before she goes. She's pulling this sad face, like she's so upset, even though I'm the one who's all smashed up in solitary and lost my early release. She goes,

'I really thought you'd decided to change this time, Daniella. I'm sorry I was wrong.'

And she gets out of the cell and slams the door shut behind her. I thump my fists down into the saggy mattress either side of me and stare up at the ceiling and feel all tight and full and churned up inside, because I had! Not for the reasons she thought, not in the way that she wanted, but, still, I had decided to change. I really fucking had.

I close my eyes and think about Bethany. About the dog, and its teeth ripping into her. She's my baby. Why can't I protect her?

And even though I know people might hear me, I let out a big, choking sob.

Even though it's hours later, when I come back into my normal cell I'm still shaking all over with anger and fear and the unfairness of it. Things get big in your head, when you're down the block. It's a good thing I wasn't there longer, it can drive you fucking mental if you don't watch out. Martha looks up from where she's reading on the bed.

'Are you okay?'

It feels so nice to be spoken to all soft like that, after three days of just guards and the inside of my own head, that I nearly burst into tears. I do a big sniff and try to pull myself together.

'No.' I stare down at my knackered, once-white trainers. 'I'm not getting my parole now. Emma said.'

She gets up and stands next to me, all close in our tiny cell which feels massive to me now.

'Oh ... You poor thing.'

At least Martha isn't being all *I told you so* about it, I'll give her that. I probably would. She reaches out to me, all awkward, with one arm, and it takes me a second to realise she's trying to give me a hug. I freeze a bit. I don't really do hugs, either in here or on the out. Nothing against them, I'm just not that sort of person, I reckon. Still, there's no one around, and I've been a long time alone, so maybe it'll be alright. I stand there, dead still, and let her put her arm around my shoulders and give me a quick squeeze. As she does, she whispers,

'Don't worry. We'll work it out.'

And it feels really nice. I feel sort of safe, and calm, and like someone's properly got my back. All three of those are rare enough feelings in here.

'Yeah?'

She lets her arm drop and sits on her end of my bed.

'Yes. We'll fix it. We'll still get you to Bethany.'

And at the sound of Bethany's name, I have to start stalking around the cell to stop myself from crying or hitting something or slumping on my bed and never getting up again. *Bethany, Bethany, Bethany.* I've been turning it over and over in my head but I just can't find a way. How am I going to save her now?

She puts a hand out, reaching for my arm, but I just shrug it off and keep walking. She stays sitting and looks up at me, all calm, and goes,

'Really. We will.'

I run my hand through my hair. My palm comes away oily from it. I can't remember when I last had a shower. Five days? Six?

'How, though? How can we? It's all fucked up, there's no way.'

'There's one way.' And she looks at me, head tilted and a twinkle in her eye like she's waiting for me to get it. But I don't, until she says, 'You'll have to escape.'

I collapse on my end of the bed, suddenly too knackered to keep standing.

'You can't just escape from prison, Martha. That's not a real thing.'

She shrugs.

'Of course you can. People do it all the time.'

I give her a stern look, like, *are you fucking mental?*

'All the time?'

She looks a little bit chastened at that, but her eyes are still bright.

'Okay, maybe not all the time. Sometimes, though. There was that thing last year.'

'What? Pentonville?'

'That's right.'

'Martha. They had a fucking *helicopter.*'

It was massive news at the time. We all pissed ourselves, the thought of a helicopter landing in the yard in the middle of exercise period, and this guy just hopping into it and flying off. It must have been fucking hilarious, the look on the officers' faces, they'd be all like *Oh shit, how are we going to C&R this one then?* Brilliant. But that doesn't help us, does it? That bloke was a proper gangster, like a drug lord or something, and we're just a couple of bottom-of-the-pile slags with no help at all.

But Martha doesn't look bothered in the slightest.

'Maybe. But maybe we don't need one. We've got something better.'

I feel like I'm really missing something. Her smug little know-it-all face is starting to really piss me off.

'What the fuck are you talking about?'

She leans forwards, hair swinging down by her face, and smiles.

'I can help. I can *do stuff* to help.'

And suddenly I get it. And that feeling that someone had my back, that maybe there was a chance, just melts away and all that's left is anger. Because the Mars bars and the drugs not getting found and the seeing Bethany is all great and everything, but come on.

'What, you think I'm stupid? Are you having a fucking joke? You can't use shit like that to get out of fucking prison!'

I'm shouting right in her face, but Martha doesn't even flinch.

'Why not?'

'Well, what the fuck are you still doing here, if you can?'

Her eyes are proper boring into me, hard and steady and not easy to look away from.

'I didn't say it'd be easy. It won't. It'll be hard, and take a lot of planning, a lot of risks. But we can do it, just. And we need to, don't we?'

I shrug and look away. I'm really not sure about this. She grabs me by the shoulder and turns me to face her and in this gentle, urgent voice, goes,

'Look, you've seen yourself there. You've had a vision, haven't you, of yourself on the outside. So you must be able to escape, mustn't you? It must be possible. Otherwise how could you have seen yourself there?'

And I shrug again. I'm confused. I mean, it doesn't properly make sense in my head, but maybe there's something in what she's saying. There might be. I don't know.

'But that was just a dream, Martha. Just a stupid dream.'

She looks at me. Long and hard.

'You know that's not true.'

And if I'm honest, I do.

The thing is, if there's any chance I can save Bethany, any tiny little chance at all, then I have to try. I owe it to her, after what I did.

So I take a big deep breath and I look Martha in the eye and I go,

'Okay.'

Martha gives me a nod, and a tight, hard little smile. I have this weird feeling about me. Like I've just said something bigger than I meant to. Martha goes,

'For this to work, we'll need a distraction. Something big.'

She's staring off into middle distance like she can't even see me, she can only see her plan taking shape. I shift so I'm at least sitting in the space she's looking through.

'What, like, we start a fight or something?'

Martha shakes her head. Her fingers are still drumming away, making her look like she's vibrating all over.

'No, bigger than that, much bigger. And not involving us. We need their eyes on someone else.'

She looks at me, this assessing sort of a look, like she's weighing me up, or asking herself a question. There's a moment she says nothing, she just stares, and then she seems to work out what her answer is, because she goes on.

'We'll have to use someone. It's quite a . . . deep thing to make happen. Quite dark. It might . . . hurt a bit.'

I frown at her. Hurt a bit?

'What would happen to them?'

Martha shrugs.

'Not too much. Nothing . . . lasting. But it might not be that nice.'

I swallow. I mean, I've hit people before, of course. But if you're in a fight, or in a panic that someone might hurt you, or so angry you don't know what you're doing, that's different, isn't it?

'Who would we use?'

And Martha looks at me, hard and deep, and whispers,

'An enemy.'

And we look at each other, and say nothing. For a moment, it's really fucking heavy, scary almost, seeing her sitting there all serious, chatting about enemies, and pain. And then, at exactly the same time we go,

'Chris!'

And it breaks the spell and we both burst out laughing. It hurts my bruised-up face, to laugh like this, but I don't care. I don't know if it's the relief of it, or how nice it is not to be lonely after my holiday in the seg, but as we laugh together I get this flash of what it might be like to have a proper friend.

'Of course, we'll need some of her hair for it,' Martha goes, dead casual. 'And some other things. Tissue. Eggshells.'

I look at her, like, sharp.

'What? Her hair? Like fuck.'

She just nods. I think of Chris and her tiny stubby ponytail and her terrifying arms. I put on my most reasonable voice and go,

'Ah no, Martha, come on. She'll kill us before that happens. We want to be staying as far away from Chris as we can, it's a fucking miracle she hasn't got us already.'

Martha smiles.

'We're not going to fight her though, Dani. You've already solved that problem.'

I look at her all blank. Like, seriously, *what*? Martha pulls this face, little bit patronising, I'd think it was, if she wasn't being so good to me.

'All you've got to do is keep that place on the hairdressing course you got.'

I suck in a breath, through my teeth. Martha's all grinning away. And don't get me wrong – I want to believe her. I want there to be something we can do.

'This hurting thing. Not lasting you said? Not nice, but not that bad?'

Martha nods and gives me her *trust me* face.

'You just need to get the hair. For Bethany. Trust me.'

And I do trust her. So I nod.

Fate throws you a funny hand, and you've just got to deal with what you have, especially in here. Your cellie is pretty much going to be a well good mate or the bane of your fucking life, and it's all random, like everything is. Good job this time I pulled out such a clever one. A little bit of luck, for once.

'The thing is, Miss, I've been thinking. I really do want to better myself, in here. I want to try to make this my last time inside.'

I make my eyes go all innocent and round and I look as honest as I can as I stare down at Emma. I haven't sat down in the chair I normally sprawl across when I go to see her. It seemed more respectful to stand – repentant, if you like. It takes her a while to answer me.

'You messed it up, Daniella,' she goes, and her face says, *again.*

'Yeah, I know, and I'm sorry,' I say, and I make my face look really sorry. And then I just wait for her to come back with something. One thing I've learned off Martha is, there's power in silence. Eventually Emma rolls her eyes, and her face softens, and she goes,

'Okay, fine. If you want to. You can still finish the drugs course, if you were finding it helpful. Karen said you made a lot of progress, even in one session.'

And for a moment there's so many different feelings sloshing around inside me that I can't speak. Karen said I was making progress? No one's ever said that. Does that mean I was good at it? Shit. And, yeah, I *was* finding it helpful. It made me feel like maybe, perhaps, I could get out of here and not use. I thought they could maybe teach me, anyway.

The thing is, though, that's not what I'm here for. It's a nice idea, finishing the drugs course, but I need the hair, and if I put it off for a week, sod's law that'd be the week that Chris came in. I can't risk it.

'No, Miss, I've done the drugs course before, that's okay. But I thought what might really help me on the out is the hairdressing course. I thought it might be, like, a good opportunity for me.'

'Places are limited, Daniella. It's a good opportunity for a lot of other people as well. Someone who's kept themselves out of trouble, who's being released imminently.' She leans forward and gives me the old earnest eyes. 'Look, are you sure you don't want to finish up the drugs refresher?'

I ignore her and press on.

'The thing is, I need to learn a trade, don't I? I need to get a life, find something to do out there that isn't just drugs and hanging out with fucking Justin and his loser mates. Get a bit of purpose.'

I'm getting a lot more wound up about this than I thought I would, but she's looking a bit sympathetic so I decide to just go with it.

'There's a reason they make you do that course to get out early, though, isn't there, Miss? It lowers your risk and that. Isn't that still worth doing, even with parole out of the picture?'

And she does this weird combination of a smile and a sigh and I know I've got her. It's weird, but I feel a little bit sad, as well as that big ball of happiness I always have when I get my own way. I think about Karen. I never got to tell her, did I? That I found my trigger. Never got to ask how you stop yourself from going off, once you know.

'Well . . . They haven't actually given your place away yet.'

I pull a face, like, *I am proper excited about doing hairdressing and learning a trade.*

'So I can still do it then?'

Emma lets out this big sigh and puts her pen down and looks at me, like, sort of cross but not really, like a mum on an advert. And I have to do this really difficult thing, which is to have my face looking nice as pie, but remind myself to hate her. Emma's sweet like this sometimes, and I've always got to remind myself that she can't be fucking trusted. I have to make myself keep the walls up. You only get to fuck me over once, that's the rule, and I'm not breaking it for her.

'I'm putting my neck on the line for you here, Dani. You have to promise me you'll try and do this properly, yes?'

I keep my hating-Emma wall in place and give her the biggest fucking grin ever, and I go,

'I will, Miss!' And I think of exactly what she might want to hear, and I go, 'I'll make the absolute most I can out of this opportunity, Miss.'

And I have this weird feeling, like I've won something but lost something all at once.

'So I was thinking, right, that I'd do Drama, Art and Photography, but then Mum was like, Art and Photography are actually quite similar? Which is right actually. And apparently a lot of unis don't take Photography as, like, a really academic subject?'

I nodded at Emily in time to the music. Nod. Nod. Nod. Nod. I wondered if it'd go louder.

'Yeah, yeah. You want to drop again?'

Emily looked a bit pissed off, which is rude as I was asking her a nice question, wasn't I?

'I've only got one left. I'll have it later.'

Shit. Only one left.

'We can get more, though. Maybe some coke?'

She shook her head, like, dismissive, and went,

'So I was thinking, like English or History instead of Photography. Or maybe Psychology. Which one do you reckon's easiest?'

I shrugged.

'They all sound shit to me.'

She pulled her arsey face. There was a time when it scared the shit out of me, that did, but I'd grown up a lot since I first met Ems and she couldn't shit me up so easy by then.

'Alright, Dani. Just because you got kicked out. Some of us still have to do A levels.'

I gave her a smirk, like, I'm so happy I don't have to do A levels. *Which, don't get me wrong, was true, wasn't it? I would have hated all that shit, never could stand school. I'm glad I got such shit marks in my GCSEs, in a way. And that the school said they wouldn't keep me on. Which is good. I would only have fucked A levels up, wouldn't I? No point.*

'Yeah, yeah. Some of us never got to worry about school ever again, or no one telling them what to do!'

I held up my WKD in the air and she clinked it.

'Yeah, yeah, very lucky.'

I grinned.

'Next week it is, I move out.'

Emily frowned a little bit.

'Richard still not letting you stay then?'

No, he wasn't. He said that if I couldn't keep my shit together enough to stay in school, I couldn't stay in his house. I was distracting Jamie, apparently. He had his A levels to think about. Everyone had their A levels to think about.

'I just want to move out, that's all. I'm not a little kid any more.'

Emily shrugged.

'You got a flat yet?'

I rolled my eyes. She kept saying shit like this. I'd thought once she'd finished her stupid exams I'd get her back but all she'd been doing was going on about uni this and jobs that. I dunno why she couldn't just have some fun.

'Look, do you want me to find us a line, or not?'

She shrugged, sipped. I gave her one of my grins.

'Come on . . . you're celebrating, aren't you? No more exams!'

She threw her head back and laughed, all blonde hair falling down her back. And I caught, just out of the corner of my eye, this man clocking her. Older than any of us. What was he doing at a house party with a load of kids, eh?

'Alright. You know who to pick up from?'

'Nah, I thought I'd just ask around a bit.'

She nodded at me, her eyes flicking round the room.

'Darren's usually got some.'

I winced. I owed Darren for three lots. He wouldn't sell to me any more.

'Yeah yeah. You go and grab it and bring it back, though, yeah?'

She narrowed her eyes.

'What, and pay as well, yeah?'

And I felt, like, wriggly about that. It'd been harder and harder to get into Mamma's purse lately. She hadn't said anything. But when she'd asked if I'd got a flat and I said yes, she didn't push it. Didn't even ask where it was. Almost like she knew I was lying. She's not a bad mum. She just likes the quiet life, that's all. I don't blame her. I know how much trouble I've been.

'I'll get you back, though, won't I? I can get Jobseeker's in, like, two weeks.'

She just looked off to the side, like, annoyed, and didn't answer. The sleazy guy popped up between us, like he'd been summoned by her arsey mood or something.

'Alright, girls?'

He gave me a grin. He was definitely too old to be there. Must have been twenty-five, at least. Emily glared at him.

'Fuck off, creep.'

And I gave her a look and went,

'Yeah. Fuck off.'

And she gave me a little smile. So maybe it actually was good timing.

He shrugged and smiled a bit wider.

'What, don't you ladies want to have a good time tonight?'

And Emily went,

'Not with you.'

And smirked to herself, like she's said something really funny. But I was paying attention.

'Whatcha mean?'

'With me. And this.'

And he put his hand into the front pocket of his jeans, which were way tighter than anyone normal wore them, and fished out a little bit of baggie, so I could just see the top.

Emily didn't let her fuck off mate *look slip, but I could tell she was interested.*

'What's that then? Pills or coke?'

He was grinning too much. It was, like, unsettling.

'Something better than that . . . '

Emily grabbed me by the hand.

'Come on, Dani, let's get another drink.'

She tugged, but I stood my ground.

'How much?'

'First time's always free. Call it a public service, eh?'

Even though he was older than us, and wearing too-tight jeans, he wasn't that bad looking, the bloke. He hadn't got Adam's boyish good looks, but, then, he wasn't a boy, was he?

'Come ON, Dani.'

I turned to Emily and looked her up and down, with her swingy blonde ponytail and her smug little about-to-do-A-levels face.

'What? You scared?'

The man leered at her.

'Nothing to be scared of, princess.'

She tugged on my hand again.

'He means heroin, Dani. Let's get out of here.'

I tilted my head to the side and gave her a patronising little smile.

'No shit.'

She dropped her hand.

'Seriously?'

'Just because you're chicken. No need for me to have a bad time, is it?'

Emily pursed her lips at me, in that come on, Dani, don't be stupid *way she always had.*

'Come on, Dani. You're not serious.'

I bit my lip and shrugged.

'Why not? It's free, isn't it? Might as well give it a go.'

Emily glared at the man, who smiled back at her. Like nothing could touch him. Maybe I'd like a bit of that.

'Smack's for losers. Everyone knows that.'

I felt a tingle in my arms. Emily had always thought I was a loser, hadn't she? Everyone did.

'You think you're so fucking clever, Emily, but you don't know everything. You're not the boss of me.'

And maybe they were right, even. But I couldn't be Emily, I couldn't be Jamie. Couldn't make Mamma proud. So it was time to try something else.

Emily looked like I'd slapped her.

'Dani . . .'

I jutted out my chin.

'You all think I'm such a fuck-up, don't you?'

She shook her head at me, all slow.

'Don't do it, Dani.'

I grinned. It felt good, being the one who got to make the choice for once.

'Fuck off, Emily.'

She flashed me this look, just for a second, all angry and hurt. And I thought, you know, maybe she'd say something more. Maybe she wouldn't give up on me, like the school, or even Mamma had. Maybe she wouldn't leave.

She turned and left. I watched her ponytail as it went swish, swish, swishing away through the crowd.

I come strutting back into the cell and give Martha one of my best grins.

'We're on! I got back on the course.'

She gives me a little nod, like, approving.

'Great! Very good.'

I nod back. Nice to get a bit of recognition round here. I look up at my pictures of Bethany and give them a little wink. *Hold on, baby. I'm on my way.*

'Yeah! Nice one, wasn't it? That bitch didn't want to give it to me, but I convinced her.'

Martha puts a bookmark into her book, all careful, and sets it down on the table. She frowns over at me.

'Why do you hate Emma so much? She's so nice to you.'

I frown right back, because, *what*?

'What? She's not. She's a bitch.'

Martha keeps looking at me. It's creepy when she goes all still like this.

'No, she isn't. What happened?'

I sling myself down on the bed and stare up at the crack. Not bigger.

'Nothing happened. She's a dick to me, that's all.'

'Come on. Don't bullshit me.'

I look over, almost laughing, but she's giving me a little bit of a glare now, so I stay schtum. The word sounds weird in her mouth, though. She's starting to talk like a prisoner now, a little bit, but her accent still makes it sound like she's inviting you for a walk to pick flowers up a mountain or some shit.

'I ain't bullshitting you.'

She ramps up the glaring.

'What happened?'

I mean. It's not like it's a secret, is it? I don't like to talk about it much, but this is Martha. I take a deep breath in, and go,

'She took my baby away. Okay? She was the one that took Bethany.'

Martha at least has the manners to look fucking appalled. She gapes at me

'God, really?'

I nod.

'Why did she take your baby?' Martha's eyes narrow. 'Why would a probation officer be doing that? Wouldn't it be a social worker or something?'

I roll my eyes, because, keep up. I'm doing deep emotional sharing here, the ins and outs of it aren't that important, are they?

'Right. Yeah, no, she didn't like, snatch her. She just told me I wasn't getting her back.'

Which is the same thing, yeah? Clearly.

Martha's nodding. If I was being picky, I'd say that she seems more thoughtful than sympathetic.

'So what happened?'

I feel sick. It's always like this, when the bad memories come. They don't fall into your head all gentle, they punch you right in the guts and force their way in.

'Like I said. I arrived at prison. First meeting I got, I said, will I get her back? And she said yes, when I'd done their courses, and been assessed, and . . . I said, no, she's mine, when I finish my time, do I get her back straight away? But I don't. Only when they think I'm ready. So I did the courses, I . . . '

And I squeeze my eyes shut hard, because they're prickling suddenly. They're never going to think I'm ready.

'But that doesn't make sense, though. That she'd be the one who told you. Surely the social worker who took her in for fostering would have explained . . . '

I glare at Martha so she knows I am thinking *fuck off or I will seriously fuck you up*.

'No. It was her. She said I wasn't getting her back. Nothing else you need to know.'

She gives me this little frown, like, *yes but that doesn't quite make sense*.

'Yes, but . . . '

'LEAVE it, Martha.'

I'm shaking. The thoughts are getting stronger and stronger and I look around the cell, hunting for something to distract me. There's nothing there. I sink my head in my hands and try to breathe through the bad thoughts and the remembering.

I feel the mattress next to me sink down, and Martha's hand on my arm.

'Hey. You want to hear about what happened next? With me and David, after Mother found us?'

I do a big deep sniff and give her a smile, like, *thanks, mate*.

'Yeah. What happened?'

Martha gives me a sad, twisted-up-mouth look, and shrugs.

'She dragged me home, screaming at me all the way, that I was a slut, a whore . . . And then she locked me in my room for two days. She didn't let me out of the house for a week. But in the end, she let me out to go and get the bread again. Someone had to, and she wasn't going to do it for more than a couple of days running. They were beneath her, those kinds of errands. So I saw David again.'

And she smiles this soft smile, like, remembering.

I lean against the wall, getting comfy. I'm only feeling a little bit shaky, now.

'So, did you get to talk to him, then? You worked out a way to sneak off and see each other?'

It's romantic, a bit, all this sneaking about. I've never been in a situation where anyone's given much of a shit about where I'm going and who I'm seeing, to be honest. No point hiding what you're up to if no one really cares.

'Not at first. It was too risky. But we could pass notes, him with the cakes, and me on scraps of paper, folded up with the money.'

God. Her life. Just like a story. I am desperate to know what happened next.

'But Mother would always sleep late on a Sunday morning. Her friends would come over, on Saturdays, and they'd ... Anyway. The bakery wasn't open then either, so David was free. So we'd meet, back at the tree—'

'Back at the tree where she found you?'

The story-telling dreaminess fades out of Martha's eyes a bit as she focuses on me.

'Yes. That tree. Why?'

I shrug. I dunno. You don't go back to the scene, though, in real life, do you? That's a story thing. Surely there's more than one tree in this place?

'I just ...' She's still glaring. I mean, it doesn't matter, though, does it? Not enough to piss her off. 'Nothing. So you met up at the tree ...?'

She gives me a smile, like, *thank you. Don't interrupt though.*

'Yes. We met up by the tree. OUR tree. And I hatched a plan.'

I shift about a bit. These mattresses really hurt your bum after a while.

'What was the plan?'

Martha rolls her eyes at me, like, *come on, Dani, keep up.*

'There was only one thing we could do, wasn't there? We had to escape. And soon. Mother had become ... even more difficult. Life was getting harder and harder for me, and David and I wanted to be together. So, David would take some money out of the till, enough to get us to London. I'd work out the way.'

'And did you?'

She goes on, ignoring me.

'We were to do it the next Sunday, early as we could. The bus out of the village ran once an hour, on Sundays, and the trains from the town every two, so we'd have a good head start before anyone noticed we were gone.'

I'm sitting there, almost bouncing, I'm that impatient.

'So did you do it? Did you get away?'

Martha looks at me and sighs. She sweeps an arm around our cell – our two cupboards and one chair and table and sink and bog. Our radio. Her bunk, and mine.

'What do you think? Yes. I did it. I escaped.'

Chapter Ten

Extract from PSO 2300 – Resettlement

5.21   *Activities and programmes such as education,
        training and prison work must be co-ordinated
        for resettlement purposes, with the ultimate aim of
        reducing reoffending. Work to improve prisoners'
        skills must focus on increasing the likelihood of their
        gaining employment on release.*

Martha's scratching at the wall above my bed with the nail scissors. *Scratch, scratch, scratch.* That'd be well annoying, if I had to put up with it all day.

'What time is it?'

Martha looks at her watch, slower than is really called for, I think. I don't have one of my own, I never have. I don't normally care what time it is.

'Three minutes to nine. Two minutes later than the last time you asked.'

I roll my eyes at her. Sarky cow. It's not my fault she's got a shitty day hanging round here doing nothing ahead of her. Should have done a course, shouldn't she?

Martha's still in the big T-shirt she sleeps in. As she kneels up on my bed, *scratch scratch scratching* at the wall around my photos, it rides up and shows the smooth white of the bit of thigh under her bum. I've already got my shoes on. She looks back at me, like, amused.

'You doing something new today then?'

I'm standing next to the cell door, bouncing up and down on the soles of my feet. My trainers make this satisfying *squeak squeak squeak* noise on the cell floor.

'Yep. First time on the colour station.'

I've been looking forward to this one. I get my hair bleached once in a while, when I can con someone into giving me a hand and scrape together the money for the dye, and I've always loved it. The smell, and the sitting still and not having to do anything when it's on your head. Then, the moment you take the foil off and rinse and look at yourself in the mirror for the first time.

I still remember the first time I ever dyed my hair. I was fourteen, and I'd wanted to have it done for absolutely ages. I'd been asking like every week but Mamma wouldn't let me, said I was too young. But over the months, she sounded less and less bothered, until one day when I asked she snapped and said I could do what I wanted, so I was ready for my first dye job. I'd gone into town with Emily especially to nick a box of Nice n' Easy from Superdrug, and I was that excited about it I didn't even bother taking a nail varnish or anything along with it. I just wanted to get back and get it on my hair.

If I'm honest it was a pretty fucking shoddy job – full of

orangey streaks and blocks where it was dead white – hardly the 'honeyed golden tresses' the packet had promised. But that moment, of looking in the mirror and for the very first time, seeing a different girl looking back at me – that was like magic.

The thing is, you can transform yourself, with a bottle of dye. There's something special about that – you can choose who you're going to be.

Martha stops scratching for a moment and leans back, like, admiring her work.

'You finish reading the book?'

I nod. I was so excited about doing colour, I even went to the library and got out this book on art and colour and that. It's fucking massive, takes up like half of our table. To be honest, it wasn't really that helpful. There wasn't anything practical about how long to leave the dye on or whatever, like I'd been hoping. It was all, like, theory of what goes well together, colour wheels and that. Still, it passed the time.

Martha smiles at me, a bit of a funny smile to be honest, not actually nice.

'Look at you, waiting early for them to let you out. You're really into it, aren't you?'

I do a shrug and pull a not-bothered kind of face.

'Better than hanging round here all day, isn't it? Something to do.'

She looks at me. This hard look.

'Are you sure that's all it is?'

I do a little snort.

'Yeah. What else would it be? What, am I going to get out and, like, be a hairdresser or something?'

And I make myself laugh, like that's a really funny idea, me making something of myself. Even though I'm not that thick, not really. I mean, I did just read a book.

'Right. Just remember the plan, okay?'

She taps at the wall. It's a little calendar she's been making up there, underneath Bethany's pictures. A countdown of the twenty-one days until we do it, until I escape and save her. She can scratch it as much as she likes, it doesn't make it feel more real. But I give her a big fake smile and go,

'Yeah! Course I do.'

And she doesn't look convinced, and if I'm honest, she shouldn't be. Because it's more than that, the hairdressing course, for me. It's only been two weeks so far, but already it's something I can really see myself doing. Not just in here, but on the outside as well. Being in the salon, even the grotty prison one, it's ... not quite what you'd call *fun*, exactly. It's mostly sweeping up and washing dirty heads, and there's only a little bit of actual cutting so far. But it's ... absorbing, I suppose is the word. It's like the opposite feeling of boring, which is not quite exciting, having a whale of a time, but a more gentle kind of happy. Time goes fast in the hairdresser's, I suppose is what I mean, and I love the chat and snip and sweep and wipe rhythm of the place.

It's the first time I've seen another kind of life I think I could maybe have.

The cell door opens. I turn to Martha and go,

'See you later then.'

And make myself do a slow swagger down the hallway, even though all I want to do is run like a little kid, excited for the day.

*

I'm standing at the colour station, which is actually just a bit of table if we're being totally honest about it, and trying to find something to do. It's hot in here – so hot I wouldn't mind a turn at the sinks, where you can run your wrists under a cold tap whenever you like, and there's two of you, so you've got someone to chat to. Colour's a one-person job. I've already sorted out all the bottles of dye so that they're in rainbow order, and put all my foils in a nice neat stack. It's been a bit of a slow morning so far. I'm thinking about giving myself a red streak or something, just to pass the time, but I kind of thought it might be better to practise on someone else first, get my eye in a bit.

'Oi!'

I look up to see Kerry come stomping in, with a knitted hat on her head despite the heat, which is weird. She was only in last Thursday, getting a head of highlights done. Our tutor, Vicky, her name is, looks Kerry up and down, all nervous.

'Erm ... Hello?'

She doesn't know any of our names, not even on the course, let alone girls that come in to get their hair done. Kerry stares at Vicky with psycho eyes. Vicky takes a step back and Kerry pulls off her hat. There's this gasp goes up from all the girls in the room – under the hat, Kerry's hair's bright green.

'What have you fuckers done to me? Is this someone's idea of a joke?'

And she's so upset she's practically crying, but the look of her with her bright green hair and face all red's so funny, the whole lot of us crack up. Over on the other side of the room the girls on hair-wash duty are leaning on sinks for support, they're laughing that much. It's pandemonium in here, everyone's getting closer to have a look, and pissing themselves at Kerry and shouting,

'Nice colour that, Kerry!'

'You a punk now or something?'

'You fuck off, you—'

'Shut UP!'

That last one's from Miss Green, who's the one who's supervising us today. We all go quiet and pull our *yes, Miss, sorry, Miss, don't discipline me, yeah?* faces. Kerry turns to Vicky and goes,

'What happened?'

And Vicky looks terrified that a prisoner's spoken to her. Vicky's a bit useless to be honest, she's the least good thing about hairdressing. The problem is, it's pretty obvious she's scared of us and doesn't want to be there. I do sympathise. It must be the short straw, having to teach a load of criminals in this shithole, all running around with scissors and kicking off all the time, when you could be tucked up in some nice little college somewhere. No wonder she's a bit miserable. She says,

'Have you been swimming?'

Kerry, who's basically crying now, says,

'Yeah, yesterday afternoon.'

Vicky puffs her cheeks out and nods, all wise.

'Yes. That can happen sometimes.'

And everyone, girls and Kerry and Miss Green and me all look at her, waiting for her to add anything useful to that pearl of wisdom, but no. What a fucking idiot. I'm going to have to do a proper apprenticeship, when I get out of here, ain't no way Vicky's going to teach me enough to get by in a real salon. It might be easier to get a lower-down position than a stylist job as an ex-con, anyway, so it doesn't matter to me, but that's not helping poor Kerry. She's looking like she wants to punch Vicky, which is fair enough really, and she goes,

'I've got a probation review panel meeting tomorrow.'

And the mood of the salon changes dead quick. It's not funny any more, because actually, that's proper serious. You definitely don't want to be going in and seeing the board with green hair. Probation will use any old shit against you, anything they can think of. Something tiny and not your fault, like someone starting a fight with you and you just doing some self-defence. Fucking bastards.

Even Miss Green looks a bit uneasy. She turns to Vicky.

'Can't you bleach it again?'

Vicky shakes her head.

'It doesn't work like that. It'll just be lighter green.'

A tear works its way down Kerry's bright-red face. Her skin clashes with her hair and she looks a right state and I feel for her, I really do. I've been where she is loads of times.

Hang on. Clashing.

I take a big deep breath and try to concentrate. There's this thing prodding at me, right at the back of my mind, wanting to be remembered.

The colour wheel.

I reach out and grab Kerry by the wrist. She looks up at me, dead startled, but she doesn't pull her arm back. I give her a smile, much more cheery than I feel, and I go,

'Come with me.' And give her a little tug. She doesn't come. I pull at her arm again. 'I've got an idea.'

Kerry gives me a *don't you fucking dare fucking fuck with me today* kind of look.

'If you're going to fuck me over just because Chris has been hassling you, you can—'

'No! No, I . . . I just know what it's like, yeah?'

She scowls at me.

'No shit? Cos Chris'll get you worse next time. I can get her to.'

My heart's going, banging round my chest well hard, but I keep my cool and look Kerry dead in the face.

'No shit. Honest.'

I drag her over to my colouring table and reach for a dye bottle about three in from the left of my rainbow scale. A really bright orangey red – they call it Sunset. I thought about using this one for my red streak, but I decided on Cherry in the end, because Sunset really is a bit obnoxious, but this is the colour that's least like her hair.

'So, the idea is, we put this colour on over your green, but because red is, like, opposite, they cancel each other out. Because of the colour wheel.'

Kerry looks well suspicious, like I'm taking the piss out of her.

'What the fuck?'

I make myself look all trustworthy. I really want to do this. As well as wanting to help her out, I'm interested now.

'No, look. It'll work. I read it in a book. It *neutralises* it. So you won't see, especially if you put your hair up, yeah?'

Kerry looks pretty unconvinced by all of this, and I can't say I blame her, but she gives me a reluctant nod.

'Yeah, okay. It can't look a lot worse.'

I look at Vicky and go,

'This is alright, Miss, isn't it?'

But I'm not really asking, I'm telling. Assertive, that was, but not aggressive. Just like they say to do on the behaviour courses. Vicky gives me a nervous little nod. I uncap the dye, the familiar, chemically tang of it all up in my face, and I really hope I'm right.

The whole room is all crowded round the sink, where I'm standing over Kerry, and her possibly-blonde-again hair. I look around the room and everyone in there's staring back at me. One of them is halfway through a cut, with hair in long straggles down past her shoulder on one side, but a neat little bob on the other, all soaking wet. Everyone's stopped what they're doing to watch.

I force a cheery smile.

'Alright! Should be done by now.'

I'm that fucking nervous, my hands are shaking inside their see-through plastic gloves as I start rinsing the colour off. You could hear a scissor snip in here if there was one, but everyone is as still as a statue. It's like the whole room's holding its breath. I shrug my shoulders and roll my neck around a bit. I'm so tense I can barely move my head, but there's no need for that. I'm right. I have to be. I turn the water on.

Like it always does when you wash out red dye, the sink looks like Kerry's head's having the worst period ever. The bright-red water flows through Kerry's hair and swirls down the plughole. I point the water stream onto one bit of hair at the front and rub at it with my fingers to help it along. The dye's still lying too thick on her head for me to tell if it's worked.

Come on, come on, come on . . .

And after what seems like hours of rubbing, I see a bit of blonde peeking through. I let out a sigh I didn't know I was holding. It fucking worked.

I rinse off the rest as fast as I can, making sure it's not just that bit. But her hair's all fine. Not the nicest blonde colour in the world, perhaps, not quite as nice as it was when it was done, but hair-coloured. No green in there at all.

Kerry opens her eyes and looks up at me.

'Is it working?'

And I do a big grin back at her. She goes,

'YES!'

And rushes over to the mirror, dripping water and the last little bits of hair dye all over the place. I saunter after, dead casual.

'There you go. Fixed it.'

'Fucking brilliant!' She runs a hand through, which comes out a bit reddish, but she's still smiling. 'I can't believe it worked!'

And to be honest, I can't believe it worked either. It was a fucking mad plan, really. But I give her a big, cocky smile and go,

'Told you so!'

Like it was no big deal, and I always knew it'd be fine, because I'm a fucking pro. Kerry pulls herself away from the mirror and looks at me, proper full on.

'Seriously, thanks, Dani. I owe you one now, okay?'

And I just shrug, like, *no big deal, whatever,* but inside I'm going *yes yes yes!!!* Kerry gets her hair back to normal, and I get back in Chris's gang's good books. Win, win, fucking win.

Everything's sorted again, and for the first time since Martha first showed her face round here I can relax.

Just then, the bell goes to get back to cells, which is maybe a bit of a shame for the girl who only has half a bob, but suits me just fine – I feel like a cuppa and a sit down after all that. And the atmosphere as we all leave is proper nice, cos it's like if today was a story, then we've had a happy ending, all of us. A couple of the girls I'm not that friendly with smile at me and give me a quick nod and an 'Alright, Dani' as they leave, and I've got a smile and an 'alright' for everyone.

As I'm on my way out, Miss Green takes me aside.

'That was good work today, Dani. You really helped her. Nice one.'

And she gives me this really quick squeeze on the arm. I can't help grinning all over my face. The whole of me feels warm, and kind of fizzy. It's a bit like the feeling that you get from gear, but it's just come from me and what I've done.

I stepped off the bus onto Brixton High Street and tried to look normal. To my left there was a young black guy in a nice suit, holding up a handful of pamphlets and shouting about being saved from eternal damnation, and to my right, a couple of old Rastas banging out calypso on steel drums. I took a deep breath in, the popcorn-and-spicy-chicken smell of the place filling up my lungs, and I stopped myself touching my backpack. It's okay. We're fine. *I turned left, which isn't the quickest way to Coldharbour Lane if I'm honest, but the police station's off to the right and besides, it was a nice enough day. I could do with the fresh air.*

I hadn't been out a lot, the last few weeks. Don't get me wrong,

*it was nice enough of Tony to offer me a spare room and that, he'd
always been well generous, but there was a lot of sitting about
there. I'd sort of thought living on my own would be more about
going out – pubs and clubs and even just hanging round town,
I didn't mind. But all we did was sit on the sofa watching telly
and taking stuff. Cider on a bad day, smack on a good one. The
odd trip out to sign on or lift a couple of essentials from a shop.
And like I said – it wasn't a bad life. Don't get me wrong. But it
was nice to be out in the sun.*

*I overtook a couple of girls in front of me. They were about
my age, but clacking along on high heels, piles of hair on top of
their heads and faces carefully painted on. They looked great. I
couldn't remember the last time I wore make-up. A month ago?
Two? As I walked past them they gave me snotty,* what we got
here then *kinds of looks. I could feel their eyes on my tatty trainers, my stained T-shirt. I gave them a glare, and decided their
hair wasn't that nice.*

*I let myself touch my backpack, feeling the solid shape of the
package through the flimsy canvas. I took a breath.* It's okay.
Just look normal.

*Up ahead of me there was a junction. I was nearly there. Just
past that bridge, then another two minutes, tops, and then I'd be
done. Fine.* Sorted. *I hit the button on the crossing and waited
for the lights to change.*

Okay. Tony was right. This isn't a big deal. *And he was
right, wasn't he? I mean, I gave him bits of my Jobseeker's, when I
could, but I was hardly paying market rates for a flat in London.
I dunno how anyone can ever afford to live around there. I went
to look at one place, you know, to make an effort. It was totally
shit, like, the kind of place you wouldn't keep a dog. A tiny room,*

filthy, and the door broken, sharing with six other people I'd never met in this cramped little flat. And I couldn't even afford that one. So he was doing me a big favour, Tony. It was only right that I did him a little something in return.

The crossing beep beep beeped and I headed across. When I got to the middle, though, I looked up and my body flooded with panic. Two policemen, with their radios and stupid hats, had just come out from under the bridge and they were heading straight for me. Fuckfuckfuck. I felt like I couldn't breathe, but I didn't dare stop walking so I just kept going, my feet carrying me closer to the coppers. I clutched at the rucksack and tried not to throw up.

I was on the other side by then and the police were only a few feet away. I swallowed and thought about what the head had said when she told me I couldn't stay on for sixth form. Prison, next, she'd said. If you don't change your ways, you're bound to end up there eventually.

One of them met my eyes, and frowned.

'S'cuse me, love.'

Everything in me was screaming, but I couldn't run. That'd make me look so fucking guilty I might as well have just handed the bag over then.

'Yeah?'

'Shouldn't you be at school?'

This big wave of relief went through me. I felt that good about it, I even gave him a grin.

'Nah, mate! I'm seventeen, not been to school for ages.'

I've always been little for my age. He nodded and I pretty much skipped past him. Fucking yes!

I was that buoyed up, I forgot to be nervous when I buzzed to be let in the flat.

Tony was right. This was just a little favour. No need to be worried at all. I was just pulling my weight, wasn't I? And now I reckoned I didn't need to feel bad for not paying for my smack for, like, a week, at least. No need to be extra nice to Tony, or any of his mates, for seven whole days.

I was still grinning as I opened the door into their grubby little flat. Like the police are worse than the dealers. Idiot.

'And she's just standing there, yeah? With green hair. GREEN.'

I'm so into telling the story that I'm bouncing up and down on the bed, making the knackered old springs creak so much you'd think they were about to break.

'So then I grab Kerry, and I go, "Oi, come with me, I can fix that", and we go over to the dyes together, but she's like, "what?", she doesn't know what I'm doing, no one does.'

I'm laying this on proper thick for Martha – with actions and different voices and everything. If you've got a really decent story, I always think you should try to do it justice, make it as fun as you can for whatever audience you've found. But Martha doesn't look that impressed. She's just sitting bolt upright on her bunk, arms crossed and left foot tap-tap-tapping at the floor. I don't know what her problem is. I keep going, bigging it up even more.

'They're all looking at me like I'm proper mental, like, *whaaaaaaaaaat?* but I know exactly what I'm doing, I've got everything well under control, and—'

Martha cuts across me, proper rude, and goes,

'But have you got Chris's hair yet?'

I roll my eyes because, *hello*, I was obviously in the middle of a story. I'm in a really good mood, though, so I'm still pretty friendly when I say,

'No. She hasn't come in yet, has she? I can't have got the hair if she hasn't come in.'

Which is totally reasonable, I reckon. Martha tightens the cross of her arms though, and glares.

'This is important, Dani. We've only got three weeks left. We can't do it without the hair.'

And I just shrug because . . . I dunno.

'Yeah. I know. But . . . '

Martha gives me one of her piercing looks with those big blue eyes and goes,

'What? But what?'

I give her another shrug. The truth is, this whole thing, with the vision, and the escape, and the making stuff happen . . . It all feels a lot less real now, than it did when I had the dream. If I'm honest, it's started to feel a bit silly.

'Well . . . What if we just sort of . . . Didn't do it, though?'

Her nostrils flare out and her mouth screws up, all tight and like, disgusted.

'What do you mean, didn't do it? You can't give up now. You had the vision. Bethany needs you.'

And the sound of her name, *Bethany*, it gets to me, a little bit. I look at up at her pictures, and our countdown. But I'm surprised how little it hurts.

'The thing is, Martha, it might not have been a vision. Like, what if it wasn't? She might be fine.'

She glares at me. She looks proper pissed off, like she wants to turn me to stone or some shit.

'It WAS a vision.'

'It's just ...'

I'm struggling here. The thing is, I'm not great at saying I won't do stuff. Because it's never mattered before, has it? I'll go get your package, keep hold of something for you, nip out to drop something off for your mate, sure, what's the worst that can happen? Get into trouble for you. Prison, maybe, but that's normal. I've never had anything to give up before now. I take a deep breath and try to explain.

'I just have a lot to lose, if we're wrong about this, don't I?'

Martha's all quiet, over on her side of the room, just giving me silence and glare. The beds seem a lot further apart than normal. I have another go at explaining.

'I mean, I have a real chance, this time. I'll be out in a few more months. I could do a hairdressing apprenticeship. Sort myself out.'

Martha's face goes all hard and mean.

'What? Like you've done every other time, when you've got out?'

'Yeah, but ...'

I stop. I can't really explain it. Obviously, she's right. It's not like I've ever managed to actually keep my shit together on the out, for more than a few weeks. I know that there's no reason to think this time's different. But still, there's this voice in the back of my head telling me to give it a go. I just reckon I might be able to actually do it this time. And then maybe I'd get Bethany back again for real, wouldn't I? My little girl, back with me again for good. Not this stuff, that's started to feel a bit pretend.

Martha's sticking her jaw out. Her face looks all square. If I didn't know better, I'd say she looked pretty hard.

'But nothing. You're abandoning us, your plan, your own little girl. And for what? Because you think some stupid piece of shit little prison course is the same as a shot at an actual job. But it's not. How could it be? No one's ever going to give a job to a junkie fuck-up like you. Are you really so stupid you can't see that?'

And for a second I can't even speak. The trueness of what she said stabs into me deep because, of course, she's right, and it really fucking hurts. But right behind the hurt, only a second behind, is the anger.

I jump to my feet, getting right up in her face, and I go,

'Fuck you! You don't know. New bitch. You don't know anything.'

She just sits there, bolt upright on her bed.

'And you do? I know more than you do. At least I lived a normal life for a fair bit out there. You've barely lived in the real world at all. Always living in some junkie nest, or in prison again. What could you know about anything?'

There's a lump in my throat now but I can still choke out words around it.

'I know you can't tell me what to do. I know ... I know that you can fuck off!'

Her face twists up, and the hate and disdain in it is that strong it takes my breath away. When her voice comes out, all the softness in it's gone, just leaving behind this hiss.

'You're nothing without me, Dani Grove. Nothing. At all.'

And it's like those words just hang in the air, thick and heavy as the smells lie here in summer with no breeze to blow them away. And I sling myself down on my bunk and I turn my back on her, because she's just a stupid fucking first-timer and she doesn't know shit. I'm the one who knows what's going on in here, and that's the way it's going to stay. I pull up my knees, and hug them tight to my chest. I have to be the one who knows shit in here – without drugs, that's all I've really got.

I stare at the wall ahead of me. I've got no idea how to block out feelings like this without a bit of smack. I've never been this upset before, this angry and hurt and guilty, and not taken something to make me forget it. All I can do is lie as still as I can while the feelings slosh around me, making me feel seasick. I wait for them to die down, but they just get worse and worse.

That night, I dream the dream again. It's all the same stuff happening, but things seem different somehow. Kate Middleton's there, still smiling away, but there's something weird about her dress. I'm sure last time it was lemon yellow, pale and pretty and nice, but this time the yellow looks different. This is the yellow of pus, of the stuff you cough up when you've had a bad chest for weeks, of things that aren't quite right.

She's still waving, but I can barely see her past the glare of the sun. It's bright out here, far too bright for England, even in August. I look up but I can't see the sky without it hurting my eyes. This is a sun that wants to burn.

The people are pressing in, so many of them and so close that I'm starting to feel that itchy panic of crowds closing in on me. I look for Bethany, calling out to her again, but there are so many people I have to push and shove my way through, each of their faces turning to me as I push past. Their faces are either hard, all disdainful of me, like I'm nothing, worse than nothing to them, or they're smiling. The smiling's worse. These aren't nice smiles, the kind of smile a mate would give you. These are smiles that say, *I know something you don't, and you're not going to like it at all.*

Finally a gap opens in the people and I see her, *Bethany, Bethany, Bethany,* with her blonde curls and her pink dress, the only thing here that doesn't look scary and wrong. I look at her and I smile and rush forwards, but then I hear a low growl off to my left and I remember. I turn away from Bethany to look at the dog.

It growls, drool hanging from its mouth, and barks at me. Big, and loud, and hard.

And it's like I fall out of time.

I blink and I'm back there in the yard, rank raw meat in my mouth, the smell of dog shit in my nose and the sound of growling all around me, so loud it shakes my chest. I feel the bite. Teeth ripping, tearing flesh, searing down into the very core of me.

Like it'll never not hurt again.

I'm back in the park.

The dog jumps towards Bethany and sinks its teeth into my baby girl. I'm frozen to the spot as I watch the dog shake her and Bethany screams and screams and screams.

I wake up and for a moment I'm not sure where I am. Then it comes back to me, bit by bit, what's real and what's not. I'm trembling and soaked in sweat. I turn over, to tell Martha about it, but then I remember. We're not speaking any more, because I wouldn't believe her, because I wouldn't take a bit of fucking responsibility to stop something bad happening again.

Get it together, Dani. I squeeze my eyes tight shut and pinch my thigh under the covers, so hard I have to bite my lip to stop me gasping.

The problem is, my whole life, I've fucked things up. Every little thing that came under my nose, if there was a way for me to make it go bad, that's what I did. School and work and friends and boyfriends – everything. I just fucked it all up.

And I thought, right, I honestly thought that me taking the hairdressing thing serious and building a plan for the future and that, I thought that was me not fucking it up for once. But what if I was wrong? What if it was Bethany that was the one thing that I wasn't meant to take my eye off. That'd make sense, wouldn't it? My little girl. Of course she's more important than a crack at a job on the outside for me. It's obvious.

I stare up at my photos. Her asleep, so trusting. Smiling the best smile in the world.

It was just so nice to imagine a life outside that was different to how it used to be. I let that idea get me all distracted, and I didn't know what to do.

And that's my problem, at the end of the day, isn't it? I'm too thick. I never know what to do.

I glance over to Martha again.

I can see her really clearly – they never turn the landing lights off and it comes in through our door hatch. She's holding herself dead still, but I can tell by her breathing that she's not asleep. I say nothing to her, though, because I can't. I can't even look at my Bethany pictures, because I'm ashamed to look her in the eye. All I can do is just sit and shiver in my own sweat, and stare at the crack in the ceiling until the sun comes up, and count down the seconds until I can get out of this cell and, for once, take a bit of action. Actually get something right.

Chapter Eleven

Extract from PSO 4800 – Women Prisoners

The 2003 resettlement survey showed that half of all women prisoners had dependent children (including stepchildren) under 18.

There is evidence to suggest a link between the maintenance of supportive families and reduction in re-offending.

In Emma's office, I'm sweating already, and I haven't even said anything yet. It's a bloody hot day, one of those ones that make you feel mad with the heat, like if you could rip your skin off to feel cooler, you would. If you'd asked me three weeks ago, I'd have said it couldn't possibly get any hotter than it already was. I should have known better, though – there's always room for things to get worse. I scuff my trainer on the floor and watch the ruck it makes in the cheap prison carpet, but then I force myself to look up, because that's respectful, and I want to do this right.

'Miss, I've got a question. Like, an information request kind of thing.'

Emma already has her arsey face on. When I came in, she was scowling at her phone, like it had done something to piss her off.

'What is it, Daniella?'

I take a deep breath and go,

'I'm worried about my little girl.'

Emma frowns at me.

'She's perfectly safe. The foster parents are taking good care of her.'

And I can see in her face she wants to say, *much better than a useless junkie fuck-up like you could do.* And I have to bite at the inside of my lip 'til I taste blood to stop myself from kicking off and starting screaming at her.

'Yeah, but I have a message for the foster mum. I'm allowed to do that, aren't I? Give messages?'

And Emma's still frowning at me, but she's also nodding, pen poised over her notepad.

'Yes, you can have a message passed on. But, Daniella, is everything okay? You've never asked for a message to be delivered before.'

Her face says *because you don't even give a shit about her, which shows what a shit mum you would have made, so it's good I'm never going to give her back.* I think of all the times I've tried to write Bethany a letter, all the scrunched-up sheets of paper that I'd swapped good biscuits for, but I could never make the words go right, never make them say what they should. I make fists with my hands and jam them into the tops of my thighs. Talking to her like this hurts a lot more than the thigh jab and the lip bite. I wouldn't be doing this if I wasn't really fucking desperate.

'The message is, be careful on the bank holiday weekend. Don't go to Brockwell Park.'

Emma stops writing and reaches up to pat at her hair. I can see the glint of sweat on her forehead as it creases up into a frown.

'Why? What's happening in Brockwell Park?'

I look down at the notepad. From what I can make out upside down, she's barely written any of my message down. She's just staring at me and frowning. So I answer,

'It's the royal visit that day, the opening and that. I heard on the news, it's Prince George's first ever public opening thing, isn't it?'

Emma shakes her head slightly. She still looks confused.

'What's wrong with Prince George?'

A drop of sweat falls from my forehead straight into my eye, stinging me. I run a palm over my face to get rid of it.

'There's nothing wrong with Prince George! He's a little stunner. You'd be mad not to want a kid like that. It's not him, it's what's going to happen there.'

Emma looks at me funny, then flicks to a new page of her notepad and starts scribbling, keeping it covered so I can't see. *Shit*. That's going straight in my file now. I should know better than to open up to stuff like that with them, even a little bit. Emma stops scribbling and leans forward.

'What do you think's going to happen, Daniella?'

But no fucking chance am I telling her absolutely fucking anything about the vision, or the dog, or Martha. They'll have you carted straight off to high security for crap like that. Puts a shitload of points on your risk factors, being a fucking nutter does. I pretend she didn't say anything and go,

'Are you going to tell them, or what?'

'You know, if you're worried about something, it's always best to talk about it, don't you? If you're spending a lot of time worrying about things . . .'

'Miss, no. I'm fine. But will you just send them the note, yeah?'

Emma sighs, and pulls the collar of her shirt away from her neck. She looks well uncomfortable in those prissy office clothes. At least I've only got a T-shirt to sweat through.

'I'll follow procedure to pass it on, of course. But you know it can't arrive in time?'

I go dead cold in the stuffy little office.

'What?'

'Messages to foster parents take two months to get through, at least. We have to contact the social worker, she gets in touch with the family, asks their permission to contact them, then your message needs to be vetted . . . It can take a long time.'

I stare at her, mouth open. I'm so desperate I'm willing to beg her for it, even if she is the evil bitch who took my baby away. I'll forgive her that now, if she can do this for me.

'Can't you do anything to hurry it up a bit, Miss?'

She pulls this face, like, *I'd love to help you on this, but I can't*, which is clearly a lie of a face if ever I saw one.

'Even if I send it now, and phone them every day to hurry them up, there's no way it'll get to them in under three weeks.'

I stare down at the grubby floor and try to keep it together.

Bethany Bethany Bethany. No no no no no. How can it take two months?

'Dani . . . Trust me on this. Bethany is safe. She's well. You did a good thing for her, and now you don't have to worry about her any more. She's in good hands.'

And I hear the bit she doesn't say as well. *You can't just think you can get in touch with her whenever you want. You're fucking scum, and you don't deserve that. You want to count yourself lucky for what you have. That little girl's way better off without you in her life, because you're a worthless junkie fuck-up and you can't do anything. You're nothing at all.*

You'd think her eyes looked kind, if you didn't know, but I can tell what she really thinks.

When I talk again, my voice has gone croaky, like I've got a bad cold.

'You're sure there's no chance?'

But Emma's already shaking her head, and I think I knew this wouldn't work, deep down. They can't forgive you for the kind of stuff like I did. They can't, and they shouldn't.

I don't really want to face Martha right away, so when I leave Emma I don't go straight back to the cell. There's still half an hour of association left, I reckon. Instead, I climb up to the third floor, where I almost never go, because who can be arsed to leave their nice little second-floor cell to come up here?

When I get to the top I'm drenched in sweat. I've got to lift up my T-shirt and do a proper wipe down of my whole head, neck and stuff as well as my face. I've even sweated so much it's made my hair wet. It's a new kind of hot on the wing today, worse than it has been all summer, even. On the outside, you don't get hot like this, where there's windows that open more than an inch, and showers whenever you want them and fridges. The hot of being locked up is different to the lazy hot of summer in the park and cans of Stella – this hot isn't nice at all, it's like another set of bars.

I lean over the edge of the landing, clinging to the rail. The nets criss-cross beneath me, but I still get that lurch in the pit of me that you get too close to an edge. Two floors below, I see the other girls going about their business, chattering and laughing and swaggering about, far enough away that they don't seem real. I see Martha, plain as day even from up here, going up to a couple of girls and handing them something, surreptitious like. It's obvious to any idiot that she's up to something. Selling her honey twigs, I suppose. She'll get caught straight away if she keeps looking that shifty, but see if I care. She says something to them and they throw their heads back and do the sucking-up hyena laugh, the noise of it carrying all the way up to me.

I push back against the railing and stare out along the landing. Fuck. What am I going to do about all this, though? Every time I even blink I see the dog lunging at Bethany, tearing at her. I've never been one for nerves or whatever, I've always taken pride in not making a fuss about silly shit I can't change, but to be honest I'm not looking forward to going to sleep tonight.

From across the wing, this bright blonde head catches my eye. It's Kerry, so that's my bright blonde, that I made happen. I smile at the idea of that. At least one person in here doesn't think I'm a total shit. She's climbing up the stairs, which is weird because her cell's on the second floor too, I'm fairly

sure. Well, maybe she wants to be alone, like me. She's still
here, so that'll mean her parole was knocked back after all,
which is as good a reason to sulk as I can think of. I catch her
eye and try to flash her a grin, but she looks well pissed off,
all clenchy fists and staring at the floor. Must be the parole
thing then. Fair enough.

Maybe there's some way I can get out without having to
go and kiss Martha's arse? You hear about it, people do do it
sometimes. There was a lad in Brixton who, they say, swapped
clothes with his brother on a visit. When they came to take
everyone back to their cells, the wrong brother went. Easy.
Except, I don't have a sister, of course. I don't have anyone.
Don't know Mamma's address any more, even if she'd want
me to get in touch, which she wouldn't.

Martha leaves the two girls. One of them waves as she
walks away. *Waves*. Like a fucking five-year-old.

Kerry's over the other side of the landing now and pacing
back and forth like some sort of caged thing, like you'd see
at the zoo or whatever. I've only been to the zoo once, but
I remember, and I know from being a caged thing myself.
There's something comforting about moving around when
you feel most trapped. It reminds you that you can still
move, at least a little bit. Kerry doesn't want to be doing
it in the open like that, though, because it does make you
look a bit mental, makes people nervous. Also, it's hot as
the devil's arsehole up here, and if she's not careful she
might pass out.

Down on the ground floor, Martha goes over to another
girl. They nod at each other, just like you're meant to.

I lean back against the painted brick wall. The cool of it

chills the sweat on my back. It's clammy, but it's nicer than the heat so I stay.

I mean. Could I just ... not go? Leave Bethany and her new mum to it. That would be, like, the 'right' thing to do, wouldn't it? The option they'd want you to pick in all the courses. You tried your best, now trust the system, don't be mental, keep your head down and don't be a pain. That's what you're meant to do, isn't it? That's what they say. Who breaks out of prison because of a thing they saw in a dream? A nutter, that's who, who's going to be stuck in high security for a very fucking long time, and definitely not be allowed near baby girls and hairdressing scissors again in a hurry, that's for sure.

Already, the wall underneath my back's lost its cool and turned hot again. I peel myself off it and lean on the landing railing.

The girl Martha's with slips her a little package, all stealthy, into her hand. What's she up to? She dealing in here now? It's like I don't know her at all.

I can't leave it, though. I know it's not just a dream now, and I can't go back and I can't pretend. I have to check to see if Bethany's okay, to see her with my own eyes, to make sure that dog doesn't get her. To save her if I can. There's no way for me to get a warning to whoever's looking after her now. There's no way I can leave her, either. I owe her this much, don't I? At least this much.

I let a long, shuddery breath out of me. I suppose there's only one thing I can do, then. And I'm just about to shove off the railings and traipse back to my cell, when a glimpse of that bright blonde head catches my eye and stops me. Kerry's stopped pacing. She's standing still, right by the railing. As I watch, she puts first one foot up on the lower rail, then the other, then hops up so her bum's resting on the top bar. She spins, clambering over onto the other side. She stands on the edge and grips the rail, holding herself over a three-storey drop. My mouth goes dry, so when I scream out,

'Kerry!' my voice is all croaky and weak.

She doesn't look up, but everyone else does. One by one, girls and guards all along the landings shut up their chatting and lift their heads, looking at her. There's a movement on the stairs below, an officer lumbering up to her, but she'll be far too late.

'Kerry?'

She lifts her head and stares at me, and gives me the ghost of a half-smile. Maybe she'll talk to me, maybe I can talk her . . .

'Bye, Dani.'

And with that, she jumps. She hangs in the air for what seems like way too long, her skinny figure and bright hair suspended over the emptiness of the drop, and then she falls.

She plummets, falling through the air, until the net catches her. It stretches beneath her, down and down and down, but it doesn't break. I lean over to look. She's rolled over to the middle and the net's gently bouncing up and down. Kerry's just lying there, like she's in a hammock, eyes closed and this peaceful look all over her face.

I'm in the cell already when Martha comes in. She doesn't look at me and I don't look at her, except for that one peek to see if she was looking at me or not. I just lie back and stare, switching between the crack (bigger, definitely bigger) and my photos of Bethany, with the countdown Martha scratched beneath them. Not many days to go.

It's fucking pandemonium outside on the landing. Officers and girls alike all screeching at each other, making a right fuss. The *clang clang clang* of the doors keeps coming. Every bang gives you a little jolt – you can't help it, no matter how tough you are.

Martha goes to her bunk and sits there, just staring into space. She looks a bit wobbly, and I can't tell if that's because this is her first ever lockdown, or she feels weird about her and me or what. I'm really not sure. I think I'll let her be the first to speak.

I'm not waiting long. Straight away, she turns to me.

'What's happening?'

Her voice is kind of flat. It's like she's not quite taken in what's happened yet, maybe. I decide to assume she means it like that, believe in the old, clueless Martha for a bit.

'Kerry jumped off the landing.'

She blinks at me, once, then again. I really can't tell if her face is saying *what? what the fuck's happening?* or *yeah, I fucking know that Dani, fucking* obviously *she jumped*. Like, is she the stupid one, or me? She keeps that steady looking at me going, and says,

'But why are we in here?'

I sit myself up a bit, so I can look at her properly. It looks like we're talking again, now.

'When someone gets on the nets, they have to lock us down. They're only built for one person, so if someone else got on, they'd both fall. So the officers lock us all up so we can't chuck each other off the landings or whatever, then they try and talk the jumper back to the ledge.'

'What if they can't talk them back?'

I shrug.

'I dunno. You've got to get down eventually, don't you? Unless you went on there to starve yourself to death or something . . .'

There's a long silence, or, rather, a long time of clanging and yelling, but me and Martha not talking. I wipe the sweat off my forehead, just for something to do with my hands, and go,

'You okay?'

Martha shrugs, like, *what do you care if I'm okay?*

'I thought they'd just pull you straight off them. I didn't know they were fragile.'

There's another load of *clang clang clang* and O*I get in your CELL* as neither of us speak.

And she looks at me, long and steady, like she's waiting for something. The quiet between us draws out and I think about Emily. That was another thing I fucked up, wasn't it? But maybe I can learn. Maybe I don't have to make the same mistakes again.

I take a deep breath. I'm not great at this kind of stuff. I put on a proper sorry face now and I go,

'I'm really sorry, okay? About yesterday.'

Her eyes snap back to mine. She sits there, perfectly still, just staring at me. I go,

'You were right. I shouldn't have said that, I . . .'

She's still just staring, not saying anything. I keep talking, because I don't know what else to do.

'Emma won't let me send a message and she won't even tell me if she's okay or anything and I'm really scared about it and I need you. Okay? I need you. Please help me save Bethany.'

And I look at her, and for one horrible second I think she's not going to take it. Because she might not. I can almost see her face splitting into a big, spiteful grin, almost hear her going *oooooooh, scared are we? Not so grand now, are you Dani Grove?* But after a second she gives me a little smile and when she speaks her voice is back to being soft and nice again. And she gives me a nod, and she just goes,

'Okay.'

I hadn't noticed how hard it had got recently. Now I think about it, I've missed that soft Scottishness of it. For a couple of weeks now, it's got tougher. Hard edges and loudness where there used to just be a murmur.

And we smile across the cell at each other, a bit awkward. I sort of remember this, from the days when I actually had mates, rather than people I'd just hang about and use with. Your first fight, and your first making up again, is sort of a big deal. That's what means you're proper friends.

She looks up at me, from behind her hair, all shy. I like it a lot more than those stares I can't see behind.

'I got the eggshells today.'

She reaches into her pocket and pulls out these two broken eggs. The four halves are stacked up into each other, the top one with a puddle of congealing clear slime resting in the middle.

'Um. Cool?'

'I traded them. You can get anything round here, can't you? If you know who to ask.'

She separates the bits of shell, bends down and puts them on the floor, laying them out in a neat little line.

'They're for the amplifiers.' She grins at me, well pleased with herself. 'When they're finished, they can bend people to your will a little bit. Just a tiny nudge.'

I look at the eggshells. All of them have got that slime stuff inside them. The white, it is.

'Nice.'

And I'm not sure about making spells. It seems really baby-ish and dangerous, both at once. Martha sits on the floor and pats the ground next to her.

'Come on then! Give me a hand.'

The thing is, though, I still feel like I should be in apology mode, a bit. I've made up my mind to try and save Bethany now, and Martha's the only one who can help me. I suppose I have to do whatever she says. For a while, at least.

I sit. And, actually, the floor's nice and cool under my bum. The shouts and clangs are still going on outside, but there's something about sitting low down on the floor that makes the outside noise seem more distant, less like it matters.

'Spit on this.'

Martha passes me a bit of bog roll. I stare at it.

'What?'

She rolls her eyes, like, *you heard*, and just looks at me. Whatever. I spit. She hands me another bit.

'Now touch this to your eye. Get it wet.'

I lean back, away from her and the bit of tissue. Put it in my *eye*?

'Urgh, what? What are you talking about? Get my eye juice on it? Why?'

She looks proper calm, though.

'Well, I can do it, but it'll be a lot stronger if it's you. If we use mine instead, it might not work.'

She just looks at me, dead in the eye. Then, she reaches up to her face with the tissue, and—

'No.' I snatch it out of her hand. 'Fine. I'll do it.'

'Press it in deep. Your eye has to water, it has to be wet.'

Without letting myself think about it too much, I wrap the tissue around my finger and squish it straight into my eye. The cheap prison bog roll feels like I've just stuck sandpaper in there. I keep it in, though, for a good count of three, because I'm not soft, obviously.

I pull the tissue away and look at it. It's all wet with eye juice. I blink my eye, carefully. I'm surprised it's not blood. Fucking raw, it is.

'Great, thanks.'

Martha's not even looking at me. She's got some dried leaves, and she's counting them into two of the eggshells. I watch her, she's all careful, precise. Seven leaves in each.

'So did you use these amplifiers in your escape, then?'

She doesn't even look up.

'No. I needed a lot more than this for mine.'

She shreds some of my spit and eye juice tissue and adds it to the eggs. They're getting quite full now.

'So how did it happen? How did you get away?'

She stands up, hauling herself to her feet. I just sit on the floor and watch her. It seems so unlikely. She doesn't seem the type to do stuff like run away. But, then, people will do almost anything, when they're really pushed.

'We woke up early on the Sunday, just like we planned. But David didn't have the money.'

She gets her cup of honey out from the cupboard, and sits back on the floor.

'Why not?'

She narrows her eyes off into the corner, like, pissed off about it again.

'He didn't want to steal. Even though that was the plan. And he'd done enough unpaid hours at that place, it wasn't really stealing anyway, I told him . . . Anyway. Mum had a bit of cash she kept in the bedroom. Normally a few hundred, money she charged for the charms and things. So we had to take that.'

I'm fucking gripped by this, but Martha just spoons a bit of honey into the first egg, calm as you like.

'So what happened? Did you get it? Did she wake up?'

It's weird the way honey always clings to the spoon like that. Like it doesn't want to leave you, or maybe it's scared of falling. Martha's watching it too.

'Yes.'

I feel like fucking screaming, and shaking her.

'Yes to which?'

She puts the honey spoon down, leaving a sticky golden trail between the egg and the mug, which isn't like her at all.

'Yes to both. I got the money. But she woke up.'

Martha looks up at me and the look in her face is, like, scared and sorry and defiant all at once. I know that look.

'She wasn't happy.'

Martha looks down again and puts the two empty eggshell halves on top of the full ones, like little hats. She hands one to me, and I hold it in my hand, all fragile feeling, and sticky.

I can barely breathe over here, but Martha's hardly looking

bothered. She's measured off a big piece of string, sawing at it with my little nail scissors. It finally releases, and she hands a length to me.

'Wind this round the egg. Nice and tight, then tie it neatly. We want it so it'll only break when you squeeze.'

I stare at her like she's mental, because she's being really mental.

'Martha. What happened?'

She frowns and starts winding the string around her egg. I do the same, waiting for her to start. Because, fucking *hell*, like anyone takes this long to get to the good bit. I try to be all patient and nice about it, though, because I know how the past can hurt you, even if it seems so far away. After about a million years, she goes,

'We were in her room. I was taking the money. I actually had my hand in the box. It's like me touching it was what woke her. And she came at me, screaming and punching, shouting things about me, stupid slut, whore, the same things as always. But I was ready this time. I had the poker. The same poker . . . I knew this would be the one day I stood up to her, the one day I didn't let her push me around, because I was going to be free.'

I finish wrapping the egg and tie it, not even looking at it. Poor fucking Martha. This is awful. She goes,

'So I hit her. I whacked her with the poker, as hard as I could. And even when she went down, I kept hitting her, again and again and again. Until she stopped moving. Until well after that.'

She looks down. I feel like giving her a hug, and I don't stand for hugs and stuff normally. Fucking hell, though. I know what it's like, to find yourself with a little bit of power over someone who's hurt you, and to snap. To pay them back. It's almost irresistible, the wanting to do that. No one could stop themselves. And she got five years for it? Poor cow.

'You didn't have a choice, mate. You had to.'

She shrugs, but looks, like, grateful. I change the subject, to give her a bit of space on it. I go,

'What exactly is an amplifier, then?'

She gives me a smile. My first proper one in days. I've missed her, if I'm honest.

'So. The amplifiers help you, with the nudging. If you want someone to say something, or do something, you concentrate really hard on what you want to happen, and then you break the egg. That'll let the energy out.'

I frown. I'm not going to lie, this all seems pretty unlikely.

'And then they do whatever you want?'

'If it was something they might have done anyway, yes. They'll do whatever you want.'

Martha's still winding her string. Carefully, slowly, round and round. I watch her. I mean, if that's true . . . That's amazing, isn't it?

'And they really work, do they?'

She gives me one of her angry looks.

'I *keep* telling you. It's not about working, or not. It's much more subtle than that.'

I really don't want to be in another fight with Martha, so I just shrug, and go,

'Yeah, yeah. Right. Of course.'

I sit back on my heels. This feeling of good concentration isn't as strong as it was before, when we were doing the vision.

It isn't even as good as the hairdressing. These little eggshells make me uneasy. It seems like it might be more worthwhile to give people decent highlights, than to force them to do stuff they don't want. But the feeling of doing something with Martha, of being on a team with her again, is brilliant.

And, anyway. *Bethany.* I've got a plan now, don't I? I've got to save her. Don't have to understand it to make it work.

Martha finishes tying the strings on her egg and holds it up, smiling.

'There we go! Perfect.'

And I try to grin back, but this niceness is making me uneasy as well, if I'm honest.

I've never been happy with someone for long, and not had it all go wrong.

Tony leaned into the circle and held up his can of K.

'Ladies and gentlemen. We are gathered here today to welcome back our much-missed friend . . . Dani!'

There were whoops and cheers from all around the group and I grinned all round.

'Thanks, guys.'

Tony gave me a smile and a nod.

'Only six months, eh? Flies by in no time.'

I shrugged, and put on a cocky, tough-bitch smile.

'Yeah, course.'

Although that's not how I would have put it, exactly. But it didn't matter. I was out by then.

I took a long swig of my cider and tipped my head back, star-ing into the sky. I'd got everyone to come to Hyde Park with me, because I'd been thinking about it a lot, inside. It wasn't our usual spot, but sometimes it's fun to hop on the bus and go where the tourists are. Seemed nice enough.

Katie, who was new in our gang since I came out, turned to me.

'Heya. You okay?'

I gave her a grin.

'Yeah, I'm GREAT, mate.'

She laughed. She looked well pretty in the sunlight. Her hair was red. Strands of fire in the sun.

'Well, you watch out. Your tolerance will be fucked after six months.'

'Yeah, lucky me!'

And she laughed again. I liked Katie loads.

It was a fucking beautiful day, as well. Nothing will make you appreciate the sky like only being able to see it out of a sliver of window for half a year. And the people, as well! I loved looking at people as they went past, seeing their different clothes and trying to think of their life stories and that. Prison's shit for people-watching. You look around and just think, junkie, junkie, prozzie, murderer, junkie. Very bloody boring. But Hyde Park's a treasure trove. I gave Katie a nudge and pointed to a young bloke, early twenties with long dirty-blond hair, rolling past on a unicycle.

'Where do you reckon he's come from?'

She narrowed her eyes at him and swigged her cider.

'Meeting with Daddy about how much money he's going to get for his trip to India, I reckon.'

I shook my head.

'Nah. Escaped from the circus, hasn't he? Sick of having to just ride round in the circle all the time. Wanted his freedom.'

She gave me a look like, you okay? and I forced myself to laugh and went,

'Yeah yeah. Probably the daddy thing, though, haha.'

'What about that blonde bit over there?'

I looked over to see a girl about my age. She was wearing leggings and a vest top that said Exeter Uni *on it. A boy with floppy brown hair had his arm around her. Her hair was caught back in a swishy blonde ponytail.*

'I reckon she's doing psychology at uni. She's on the lacrosse team and she only drinks apple sours . . . '

'Fuck,' I went, my mouth suddenly dry. 'I know her.'

Just for a second, I thought about turning away. Legging it, even. But the cushion of the smack I'd had earlier swooped under me. Why be bothered, just because we haven't seen each other in a while? It still might be nice to say hello.

I held my hand up in the air.

'Emily! Oi! Emily! You alright?'

She carried on walking, squinting at me, her mouth open a little bit.

' . . . Dani?'

I gave a little laugh.

'Yeah, alright. Don't you recognise me?'

She gave me a smile, but it wasn't a proper smile. It was more like a not-really-sure, humouring me sort of smile.

'No. Yeah. Course I did. You look . . . Well.'

And I gave her a glare, because I knew full well that was a lie. But, still, I'd rather have a tatty T-shirt and my roots all showing than be a stuck-up bitch like her.

'Yeah, well we can't all get our mums to buy our clothes for us, can we?'

She gave me this, like, very quick smile, and then looked away. And it hit me, nice as any rush – she's frightened of me. I gestured to the bloke.

'Who's this then? Boyfriend?'

Emily nodded.

'Yeah, this is Craig. Craig, this is Dani. She's ... We went to school together.'

Even the smack couldn't cushion that one.

'What, seriously? That's it?'

She took a step back.

'Dani ...'

'What, just because you don't like what my life looks like now, cos I've been inside, means we were never mates?'

She looked at me like I was scum.

'You've been in prison?'

I shrugged, *like,* I'm not bothered what you think, Emily.

'Yeah. And?'

'Does your mum know?'

The anger at that, at hearing her talk about my mamma, and at the disgust on her face, picked me up onto my feet.

'You know what, fuck you, you little fucking princess. You ain't all that. I know, I know you. Think you're so clever. You're not! You're nothing special. Yeah, you BETTER fucking run!'

And Emily and the boyfriend were doing this double-time fast walking away from me and all the people in the park were staring and Tony was eyeing me like, watch it love, *and Katie was looking all worried and suddenly the only thing I wanted in the world was to go back to Tony's and do another bump and not have to think about any of this shit.*

Katie got up too.

'You alright, babes?'

I breathed in deep through my nose and made myself smile.

'Yeah, yeah. Just some bitch from school, that's all.'

Tony smirked up at us.

'You ever get off with her?'

And normally, obviously, I'd have told him to fuck off with a comment like that. But right then . . .

'Maybe. Why don't we go back to your flat, have another little hit and I'll tell you all about it?'

He stopped leering a second and looks me right in the eye.

'You got more cash?'

But my discharge grant had only covered the first dose. And I could already feel the fingers of feeling normal creeping back into me, and I couldn't have that. I dug deep inside myself and gave him my very best smile.

'Can I owe you?'

Chapter Twelve

Extract from PSO 1600 – Use of Force

4.22.   Staff arriving as the 'first on the scene' at an
        incident involving violence (e.g. a fight between
        two prisoners) must act in a common sense
        manner. An individual officer must not put
        themselves in grave danger and it may be
        prudent for them to await the arrival of other
        staff in such a situation.

'So my mate Katie, she just goes, fuck it, they can't just sell
them like that, for two hundred quid, who do they think they
are? We're having one. So she just reaches right into their
little box thing.'

I do the actions properly, miming reaching into a box.

'And she pulls out one of the kittens. This really cute little
grey one. And then, quick as anything, she just sticks it in
her handbag.'

One of my audience screws up her face.

'No way.'

I nod, all emphatic. I'm proper milking this story, and I know it. They're such a good crowd, though. It's a slow day up on the hairdresser's, dead quiet, and half the course has bugger all better to do than listen to me. I'm meant to be on sweeping up, but there's no hairs to be swept around here. I've always got a story, though, if folks want entertaining.

'Seriously. Right in her handbag. So her and me, we're just casually walking out through this shop, sauntering, like you do, cos we're home free, right? There aren't any security tags on a kitten, are there? But just when we get to the front of the shop, just by the tills, Katie sort of flinches and holds her bag away from her.'

I pull a face, holding my broom out away from me, like it's my handbag.

'And I see that the side of her top's all wet. The kitten's done a wee, right in her handbag.'

There's squeals from the whole lot of them, and screams of laughing. No one's bothering to keep their voices down – even Miss Green lets out a bit of a snort at my ending. I look around the laughing faces, all entertained because of what I've said. I lean on my broom and get a hit of happiness.

But then, just like you'd get in some crappy Western, the laughing stops all at once. The place goes all quiet, the only sound the hairdryers, all whirring away, but held in still hands. I whip my head around to the door, trying to see what's what, and there's Chris standing there, regal almost in her tatty grey tracksuit.

My heart does that thing where it beats so fast it makes time feel slow. This is it. She's finally come in.

Miss Green looks at her list.

'Christine Donaldson. You were down for eleven, it's only ten now.'

Chris shrugs.

'I can come back later, Miss. Thought you might not be busy.'

Miss looks at Vicky. I don't know whether I want her to just piss off or not. I mean, I was meant to be waiting for this, wasn't I? Got a job to do. The sight of her, though, makes me want to just fucking leg it. But I force myself to stay dead still, and hold my casual kind of pose, leaning on the broom. It was the most natural way to stand a few seconds ago, but I feel dead weird now.

Vicky shrugs.

'We're not busy, really. In you go. Hair wash first. Ladies, new customer.'

Everyone scrambles back to where they were meant to be. Chris swaggers around the room, an unnecessarily long way round to get to the sinks. She's got a nod and grunts,

'Alright?'

to everyone except for me. When she walks past where I'm standing, she just gives me this long blank stare. My mouth fills up with spit, like I'm going to be sick, but I gulp it down and go,

'Alright, Chris?'

She just keeps staring, and then walks on over to the sinks.

I swallow again. This isn't good, not good at all, but it's not the worst it could be. At least I'm not on washes or cuts. I sweep away at a patch of floor. It doesn't have a single hair on it, just the stains of twenty years' worth of hair dye and filth.

Maybe she'll just get a haircut and leave. Maybe she won't

give me any hassle at all and I'll be forgiven and we'll just never talk about it again. Or maybe she's planning something really big – some massive bit of psycho revenge, in front of everyone, but I am not scared. In eight days' time with luck and a fair wind, I'll be gone.

Chris takes the band out of her tight little ponytail. The hair stays pulled back, held with dried sweat and grease, looking as if it wasn't the band keeping it there, that's just where it likes to sit. She sits at the sinks and lays her head back. The girl who's working them looks like she's about to shit herself. She turns on the tap, holding her hand under the shower attacher thing to make sure it's an okay temperature, like we've been taught to. Normally you'd just wave your hand in front of the shower head, just to make sure it wasn't actually going to burn the customer or freeze them to death, but this one's doing it really properly.

Chris doesn't look round, but she goes,

'You going to wash my hair sometime before I'm released, or what?'

There's a bit of nervous giggling going around the room, but not too much. After all, she's got her eyes closed. The girl turns the tap on her. She wets the hair and squeezes the shampoo into her hand, just like we're taught to, and puts it on her head real quick with these sort of pats of her hand. I roll my eyes. Don't get me wrong, I'm not saying I'm the expert in not pissing Chris off or anything, obviously I'm not doing great on that front at the moment, but even I know that there's no quicker way to wind up someone who likes to scare people than to act like you're fucking terrified of them before they even get going. If you're such a fucking wimp you can't even use shampoo without wetting yourself, what chance do you have of getting the respect of someone who's killed people?

The room's just starting to relax a bit, go back to its normal snip-sweep-chatter, when Chris's hair's done and she sits up. It's not holding its shape any more, the water's dragged it down around her face and she doesn't look like her. Framed like that, her face looks softer, almost pretty.

Vicky spots her, and cranes around the room.

'Right, and for your cut, we'll give you ... Erm ...'

I look up, a bit half-hearted if I'm honest. I mean, obviously if I'm picked then it'll be easier to get the hair, but I'm not sure I want the hassle. I'm sure floor hair'll work just as well, and it won't come with a side of twenty minutes of being called a useless bitch. But I needn't have worried. Chris swivels her eyes to meet mine and points at me.

'NOT her.'

And Vicky doesn't even pretend to ignore her. She just goes,

'Um, Michelle for your cut, I think. Michelle, station three.'

Michelle puffs out her cheeks, but she doesn't look completely terrified as she stands behind Chris, which is a decent enough start.

'Same again, just a bit shorter, yeah?'

Chris nods.

'Yeah. Don't fuck it up.'

Michelle holds it together pretty well. She even manages a bit of a smile.

'Yeah, alright, Chris, that's the plan.'

And she gets out the scissors and starts snipping.

Realistically, it's only about five minutes – it doesn't take long to cut a boring style like that, I could already do it in my sleep. Watching her, though, leaning on my broom and trying to pretend I'm just bored, looking about randomly, it seems like it's taking a million years. I edge a bit closer, looking in the other direction. I have to be the first one in there with the broom.

Michelle does a last snip and puts down the scissors. I let out a big puff of air, but keep myself held up straight. Not long to go, now. She turns to get some spray for the blow dry and nearly crashes into me.

'God, Dani, get out the way. Why are you standing so close?'

And I'm just on the verge of making some crack, like, *oooh, I just want to be close to you, Michelle, I fancy you so much*, cos a joke's the best way to hide what you were really doing, but then there's this flash of silver right in front of me and Chris's grinning face and my whole head explodes in pain.

I suck in a breath and clutch at my face and my hand comes away bright red. The pain resolves into a line of burning below my right eye. I look at the glint in Chris's hand. A pair of hairdressing scissors.

I roar and launch myself right at Chris, pulling and scratching and punching and biting. There's something about the sight of my own blood that always works on me like a whip – no time for thinking, just straight in and do what you need to. This time she smells of the cheap shampoo we use, and clean soft hair. My rage has made me stupid, but through it I remember to reach up and grab a handful of her hair.

Before the guards can stop me, I yank at it hard and I grip on tight tight tight and don't let go as she kicks and punches and slashes.

'Leave it, Dani, come on.'

Katie had her hands on her hips, her eyebrows pulled together so deep they almost touched. She looked like she'd rather be anywhere else than out here. I took in a lungful of London night air, spicy and sweet with the smell of curry and weed. I disagreed. I'd always loved that pub, and the thought of the fight just made the night all the sweeter for me. I jutted my chin forward, pulled my toughest tough-bitch face and glared at the girl.

'You don't want to mess with me, you fucking bitch. I've been inside, I'll fucking have you.'

Katie put her hand on my arm but I shook it off and chucked a grin at her.

'Won't I, Katie? You tell her, you fucking tell her, I've been inside, I can fucking sort her out quick as you like, can't I? CAN'T I?'

The girl looked really angsty about all this. She was biting her lip so hard it was like she was going to slice it in two, she was proper in bits. I'd almost have felt sorry for her about it, if I hadn't heard what she just said about me. Thought I heard, anyway. Probably heard.

Katie kept looking between me, the girl and the gate. Proper angsty as well. Why was I the only one who was still keeping my cool, eh? When I was the one who'd been fucking slagged off by this little fucker.

'Dani, come on. The bouncers'll hear you. Just leave it.'

But I knew they wouldn't hear. It was a Saturday night, a proper, going-for-it Saturday night at that, and the music was coming out of the Hootenanny that loud you could have heard it from Buckingham Palace, I reckon, or Battersea at least. It was a cool, crisp night, one of those nights where you're either too hot from dancing or too cold from standing outside smoking fags in just a vest top, but either way it's like that good kind of too hot or too cold. Sometimes being uncomfortable just makes you feel more awake, you know?

The girl swallowed. She was one of those girls that gets really, really done up. Face painted on like it was a work of art.

'I din't disrespect you.'

I don't go in for all that, myself. Bit of mascara, or nothing much at all is what I go for. But I think it looks nice, don't get me wrong. I spit on the ground, right close in front of her.

'Oh, you did, love. I know what I heard.'

'I didn't say nothing, you fucking mad junkie bitch!'

And let's be honest, that was what I was waiting for all along. I grinned and swung a punch, hard and clumsy, but she leaned back and my fist just swooped through air. She looked at me, gorgeous painted face all cunning, and darted forward, hooking her foot around my calf and bringing me down, hard. I just about managed to get my hands out in front of me before my nose hit the beer-washed ground.

The weed and the booze and the little bit of smack still in me from the morning all acted like a cushion, so it didn't hurt me at all. When I looked down at my palms and saw blood I was so surprised I laughed out loud. They didn't look like my hands. Those ones were all gravelly and soaked in bright red, but my hands were fine, I felt fine, I felt on top of the world.

Katie crouched down next to me. She looked like she was about to cry or something.

'Dani! Get up. Fucking hell.'

The girl was staring down at me, and I looked right back up, defiant like, because you can take me down but you need to know I'm never gonna just roll over to you, you know? And I was thinking, I don't know, maybe she'd be a bit triumphant or whatever. She'd just won a fight with someone who was proper tough and aggro with her, you'd think she'd be a little bit chuffed at least. But she wasn't. She was staring down at me, mouth open, white as a sheet. Proper shitting it, it looked like. She stared down at me for just a second. Then,

'Come on. Fucking come on!'

And her and her mates turned and scarpered.

'Yeah that's right!' I shouted at her from the floor. 'You better run!'

But I was laughing so hard I'm not sure she took me that serious.

'Dani!' Katie went. 'Get up! I'm not fucking kidding. You'll get banned for this. Maybe searched. Come ON.'

I stopped laughing. Searched. I didn't like the sound of that. I tried to get up, pressing my hands down into the floor, but I'd forgotten about the graze. Even with my cushion of drugs and booze, the pain made me suck my teeth with the shock of it and crumple back down.

Katie was proper crying by then. The tears were making her eyeliner run thick black lines down her face.

'Come ON can you please just fucking . . .'

And then I felt strong arms lock around my waist.

'Oi!'

There was a smell of fags and expensive cologne and sweat and the arms scooped me up as if I was nothing. I staggered as I took my own weight again and I turned.

There in front of me was a man. A fair bit taller than me, with muscled arms all covered in tattoos, those spiky, black ones that I always liked. And big dark eyes you could fall into forever.

'Hey hey,' he said. 'You okay there, babe?'

I just stared up at him, saying nothing, just staring at him. The most beautiful man I ever saw.

'What's the matter, babe?' he said, a slow smile sliding all across his face. 'Cat got your tongue?'

'God. What happened?'

Martha jumps up from her bunk and I just stand there in front of her, all bloodied and shaking. I've just been escorted back to the cell. They don't do that, normally. Unless you get carted off to seg, they'll just leave you in your session after a fight until it's time to move you with everyone else. I must have looked well fucked up.

I hold out my fist towards her and force my fingers to relax open. In my hand there's a chunk of mousy brown hair, matted together with my blood. On one end there's some kind of gross skin stuff, follicles maybe, still hanging off of the hairs. There's quite a lot of it. I hope I made that bitch bleed.

Martha stares at me, eyes wide.

'Shit. Well *done*, Dani.'

Martha and me look at the hair lying in my hand and then at each other. She leans over and gives me this little squeeze on the upper arm, but I can tell it's not a squeeze to make me feel better, like an *it's going to be okay* kind of squeeze. What she means is, *fucking respect, mate. Job well done.* She gives me a little nod and this understanding kind of flashes between us, and just for a moment I don't feel like a beaten little junkie fuck-up. I feel like a warrior.

The door handle turns. Martha moves mega quick. She snatches the hair chunk out of my hand and hides it deep in the pocket of her trackie bottoms.

Clang.

'Dani! Are you okay?'

It's Miss Green. She's a bit out of breath and I can see a prickle of sweat on her forehead. She must have run to get here. I file that away, in the back of my head, like, *noted*.

'Yeah, I'm fine.'

Miss Green frowns, and leans heavy on the back of our little chair.

'Have you been to the medical block?'

I shake my head, because it's not like they ever do fuck all in the medical block. Junkies aren't allowed any decent painkillers, so all they'll do is wash it. I trust Martha to do that a lot more than those snotty bitch nurses.

'I'm alright, Miss. I've had worse.'

Miss Green stares at the spot under my right eye, then away again dead quick, like it's hurting her to look at it. It must look a total fucking state. I won't find out for a while – there's no mirror in here for me to check it. I could have had a look in one of the big ones up in hairdressing after they dragged Chris off, but what's the point? I know blades, and a cut that deep'll scar pretty bad. It doesn't matter, though. It won't be the ugliest thing about me.

Miss Green makes herself look back to my eyes, and nods at me, like, professional.

'Okay. Well, I hope it feels better soon. And don't you worry about Chris coming back for you. She'll get at least a week in seg for this. More like two, probably. She's got previous for inmate violence, that one.' Her scowl deepens a little. 'And staff.'

I catch Martha's eye. She looks fucking horrified, pulling a *fuckfuckfuck* face at me behind Miss's back. She nods to Bethany's picture, and our little countdown. Only eight days left until Princess Kate's visit to the park. And Bethany's.

I swallow, hard, and summon up every bit of lying that I have. I give Miss Green my biggest, most Martha-y eyes, and I go,

'Aw, Miss, get them to go easy on her. I know what it's like, all cooped up for this long, you go a bit mental, she can't help it. Tell them I've forgiven her. They don't need to chuck her in seg forever on my account, do they?'

Miss raises her eyebrows, like, *really, Dani?*

I shrug and concentrate on keeping my breathing really slow and steady. It makes you look well trustworthy, if your breathing's all slow, cos people aren't calm when they're lying.

'The thing is, Miss, I'll be out of here soon. She's in for ages, and it's proper bad for your mental health, seg. I don't think it'll make her less likely to do it again.'

Miss Green nods, like, *fair enough.* Behind her, Martha looks dead impressed. Miss heaves herself back off the chair and upright.

'Alright. I'll put a word in.'

She goes to leave, but at the door she turns back.

'I'm impressed with you, Dani. You've come a long way this sentence, it's good to see. You keep it up on the outside, and I think you can really make this work.'

And she looks down at me, all proud like a parent might be, I suppose. Behind her there's Martha, with exactly the same look on her face.

My mouth goes dry. I manage a weak smile.

'Yeah, Miss. Thanks.'

And the door clangs shut.

Without me having to ask her, Martha goes over to the corner and wodges up some bog roll. She wets it in the sink and brings it over to me, along with the rest of the roll. She pulls over the chair and parks it square in front of my bed.

'That was clever.'

She folds over some dry bog roll and presses it onto my face, under my eye. I talk around it.

'Thanks.'

She pulls the tissue paper off. It's bright crimson, and properly wet. I have to pull my breath in fast to not freak out, that way you always do when you see something that's meant to be inside of you. Chris must have cut me deep.

'It was clever of you about Kerry, too.'

Martha dabs at me with the wet tissue. My face feels cold, apart from the red-hot line right across it where she cut me.

'What?'

Martha tilts her head and half smiles at me, like, *what do you mean, what?*

'You know. Sorting out Kerry's hair like that. Making a play to one of her gang. Nice way to give Chris a challenge, but still be able to deny it. To provoke her into coming for you. It was clever.'

Bloody water drips off my face and onto my lap. I don't try and stop it. I'm covered in blood anyway, a little more won't hurt.

'I didn't mean to do that.'

Martha frowns at me, then smiles.

'It still worked, though.'

She replaces the wet tissue with dry again, and holds it there. I try to smile with the side of my face that isn't cut up.

'Yeah. Still worked. Got what we needed, didn't we?'

Martha's still holding the tissue to my face. My blood's soaked right through it, though, and it's dripping down her arm. I swallow, hard, and look away.

'Would you want to run Chris's gang, Dani?'

Martha's not looking at the wound any more, she's looking dead in my eyes. Like she's trying to read me.

'I . . . I've never thought about it.'

Martha gives me a look, like, *fucking bullshit*.

'Come on. You must have.'

My blood's still dripping down her. It's halfway down her forearm, now.

'No, I haven't. It's not good, having that responsibility, you know? Makes you a target.'

Martha snorts through her nose, like, *nah, mate*.

'Not if you play it right. Only if you're all up in everyone's faces all the time, like Chris.'

'How else would you keep control, though?'

She raises up her eyebrows at me.

'There are ways.'

I shrug, gently, so as not to move my face and jolt her hand on the cut.

'Anyway. I'm not a leader. No initiative, that's my problem. I can't plan ahead.'

Martha doesn't say anything to that. She just smiles herself a little smile, as if she knows things. The blood reaches her elbow, and drips on the floor, but she hasn't noticed. Hopefully the bleeding will stop soon.

Chapter Thirteen

Extract from PSI 10/2011 – Residential Services

2.21 <u>Prisoners are afforded a minimum of 30 minutes
in the open air daily, as defined in the SLA/
Contract.</u>

*This provision is mandatory subject to weather conditions
and the need to maintain good order and discipline.*

'We'll need some of your blood, of course.'

Martha holds out a bit of blade ripped off a disposable
razor, like she's offering me a cake or something. I scooch
away from her, shoulders scraping against the painted brick
wall.

'Like fuck.'

Because of the short-staffing, we've missed out on morning
association for the second day running, which Martha said
was good, actually, because we'd get a chance to do some
planning, make another of her charm things. Myself, I'd
rather have a wander about than be cooped up with Martha

and her little bit of razor. She smiles at me, all encouraging.

'It won't work properly without the blood, though. We need a bit of you, a bit of her. It's just a little scratch.'

Fucking hell. The eye juice was bad enough, and now this? Why does all this type of stuff have to be so disgusting, is what I want to know.

'You can have a bit of my hair then, yeah? Take a bit from the back, go on.'

Martha shakes her head, all calm.

'No. Her hair, but from you it has to be more. A cut for a cut, blood for blood. That's the way it works.'

Hang on a minute. I thought we were just making a bit of a distraction, right? Wasn't that the plan? I didn't sign up for going round stabbing psycho fucking murderers.

'Who said anything about blood? Is Chris going to bleed? Are we going to cut her?'

Martha gives me a patronising look like, *come on, keep up.*

'No, we're not going to cut her.'

'But is she going to bleed, though?'

Martha shrugs. The calmness of her is frightening me, a bit.

'The thing is, Dani, it's your choice. I can't make you, no one can. But it's between causing a little bit of harm to Chris and preventing a lot of harm to Bethany, or not. You're getting hurt too, aren't you? You're paying for it. What happens to her will be barely worse than this little cut. Nothing lasting.'

She's still holding out the bit of razor. It glints at me under the light strip.

And this feels like a new step for me, and not a good one. Because I have hurt people in my time, and I know it, but it's never what I've set out to do. Protecting yourself, or a straight-up fight – even just losing your head, those are different somehow. Things happen, plans go bad, it happens all the time, but . . . This would be the first time I've ever meant to do harm.

Nothing lasting, though.

'You promise?'

She nods. And I mean. What choice have I got? I'd stab another toddler for Bethany, never mind slightly hurting a murderer. Of course I'm going to. I snatch at the razor.

'Alright. Let me do the cut, though.'

Martha shrugs, like, *makes no odds to me.* I put the edge of the razor to my arm, and make myself not pause.

I scratch, hard, at the side of my wrist. My blood comes to the surface real quick, welling up into a kind of black slug shape around the cut. Martha takes one edge of tissue paper and presses it, very delicate, into the little blood puddle on my arm. It sucks up the blood really well, making this crimson blotch on the edge. I stare down at the cut. It's different, doing it in front of someone.

'Okay. Good.'

She lays the chunk of Chris's hair right over my blood. I stare at them. They look really gross, together like that. Somehow, I don't want the bits of us touching each other. It feels wrong.

'How does this one work, then? Is it like the eggshells?'

Martha reaches into her pockets and pulls out another little wadded-up bit of loo roll.

'So, we need to be close to Chris. Within a few feet, really. That's the first bit, it has to be during association.'

I nod. Makes sense. Martha takes some dried-up herb things out of her twist. They look a bit like really shit weed.

She starts sprinkling them all over my blood and Chris's hair.

'The way we activate this one isn't breaking it. We just set it alight.'

'What, on fire?'

Fucking hell. Blood and fire. All very swords and castles, this kind of stuff.

She nods and starts rolling the blood and hair and herb all up together in the bog roll. She's making a massive bundle out of it.

'Yes. So there's our distraction. Do you remember what to do then?'

I nod.

'Yes.'

Martha squints at me.

'You're sure? You don't want to go through it again?'

Fucking no. The amount of times . . .

'No. I know it.'

Martha tucks the loo roll into the end of the wodge. She's made a surprisingly neat package.

'Okay. Remember, though. Remember, if we don't do this . . .'

Martha nods to our calendar beneath Bethany's pictures, with its days nearly all crossed out now and its *Bethany Bethany Bethanys* scratched all round the outside. She added those last week. Ages, she sat there, carving them into the wall with my nail scissors. *Scratch scratch scratch.*

I think of dogs and teeth and little girls screaming and I feel sick.

'Alright! Alright. Let's run through one more time.'

*

I sit, head in my hands, sweat dampening my T-shirt all down the back. I look up at Martha and give her a glare.

'Fucking boring, in here.'

For the third day running, we're stuck, no association, no courses, just trapped here. It's doing my fucking head in. Not as bad as the seg, obviously, because I've got Martha, but still.

She doesn't seem bothered at all.

'Mmmm. I know.'

I tap my feet on the ground. *Taptaptaptaptaptaptap*, like I'm running on the spot.

'They can't just keep us locked up like this, can they? Days and days. They treat us like animals round here. It's not right.'

Martha's reading her fucking stupid effective people habit book again.

'Yes. You've said.'

I'm not going to lie, I'm a little bit jealous. She's all like, serene, not having her head done in at all. I wish I could put up with being bored that easily.

'I just mean. Seriously. Why can't they get enough fucking staff to cover the holidays? I know they're not meant to be spending money on us or whatever, but they've got to let us out sometime, haven't they?'

Mamma used to say sometimes *only boring people get bored*. Which I always thought was obviously bullshit, right? Because boring people are happy just sitting, not doing anything, which is boring. It's the interesting ones who go *fuck this shit* and get up and find something to do. Isn't it?

'Mmmm.'

As sad as the end was, I wish Martha still had some story to tell me. That's the only thing that'll keep your mind off something, when you're feeling all twitchy and crazy and like you want to climb out of your own skin. A decent story, to keep your brain busy.

'I've missed two of my hairdressing sessions this week. I was meant to start cutting.'

And she doesn't even reply. She just sits there, nose in her book. She looks like she's well into it. I sling myself back on the bed.

Once I got so desperate I tried to read a novel in here, to try and get the same feeling as someone telling you about their life, like a film can sometimes. It didn't really work out, though. My brain wondering about the story went a lot quicker than my eyes could read the words. I just ended up half bored, half feeling thick as fucking shit, so I stopped.

'Yes. Oh dear.'

I glare at her. I bet Martha's never felt thick in her life. I bet she's never sat in an exam, staring all helpless at the page because she didn't even understand the question, let alone know the answer. I bet she never had to put up with fucking Jamie and his fucking GCSE results, stuck up on the fridge for a whole year, like he was a little kid who'd done a picture. None of that.

Come to think of it, though, there's something that's been niggling me, a little bit, about Martha's story. Something that's making me think that maybe there's a little bit left still to go.

'So Martha. You know with your mum and that? And the arrest.'

She looks at me over the top of her book.

'Yes.'

'Well, I'm not being funny, but why are you here? If you got arrested in Scotland, what are you doing in an English prison?'

She looks at me, all patient.

'I didn't get arrested in Scotland. I got arrested in London.'

I look at her, like, *what*?

'WHAT?'

'Yes. Covent Garden. Near the opera house.'

And then she just looks back down at her book, like nothing's happened.

I, on the other hand, am well fucking confused about this.

'Hang on. Why did you get arrested in London? You got away, but the police followed you, all the way from Scotland?'

She sighs, like it's very silly of me to have not already realised all this, and finally puts the fucking book down.

'No, I was never charged for what happened with Mother. I don't think she would have pressed charges.'

Hang on.

'What, so you don't know? Do you even know if she was okay after that poker thing?'

And she just looks at me. Stone cold.

'No. I don't know.'

And I stare back at her. I'll be honest, she's really surprised me. I never had her down as the type that wouldn't feel guilty about stuff. And don't get me wrong – I don't think she should be. Someone that does bad shit to kids deserves all they get, in my book, and Martha's mum seems to have been a proper nasty piece of work. But, still, a lot of people would be tearing themselves up inside about that. Their own mum. Not even knowing if she was okay in the end. Not knowing if she'd lived. It bothers me, enough, not knowing where my mamma's moved to, but to not know if you'd killed her? Most people would go to pieces. I'm so surprised Martha's not one of them.

'So what happened?

I prop myself up, chin on cupped hand, and listen to my bonus story.

'David and I got away. I got the money, I found the right train – I did everything. And we set off to London.'

Martha scowls into the middle distance, remembering.

'We weren't even at Stirling before David started complaining about it, saying he felt guilty, he was homesick, he wanted to go back.'

I nod, like, sympathetic. I could have told her he'd do that.

'The toughest lads go soft like that, sometimes. When there's no one about.'

She nods, vigorous.

'Exactly. Baby. Anyway, we got to London, in the end. And when we got there . . . It was so big. You wouldn't understand, but when you grow up in a village . . . '

'Nah, I get it.'

I mean, we all know no one grows up in Hyde Park. Everyone's got a moment when they first realise how massive London is, or they come across a chunk of it that seems like a whole world, but that you never knew was there. Martha's leaning forward now. Getting into the story, enjoying telling it. Maybe she wasn't as lost in that stupid book as she made out.

'Anyway, it was perfect. A perfect place to get lost, and start again. But David didn't see it like that. He kept

whining about it, over and over, saying that we should go
to the police.'

Her lip curls up, all disgusted, like he's there with us.

'And as well as that, we weren't coping. I hadn't realised
how useless David was, before. Good enough for baking buns
and talking sweet, but pathetic in the real world. We were
sleeping on the streets, because there was nowhere else to
go, and he was crying and crying about it, like a little kid.
So useless.' This sort of proud look comes into her eyes. She
looks, like, pleased with herself, and angry but in a good
way. I've sort of never seen her look more alive than she is
remembering this, other than the spells. She jabs her finger
into the air, marking her words. '*I* was the one who found us
some food, *I* was the one who got us a Swiss Army knife. But
I got no thanks for that. All he could talk about was that it
was cold, he was wet, he was scared ... But he'd never come
up with any answers himself. Anyway, it was the third night
of sleeping rough. It's a hard thing to do.'

I nod. I know. Honest, I know.

'And he was saying over and over that we had to go to the
police, that it was wrong what we'd done, that he was going
to go first thing, that he was going now. And I was so sick of
him, I lost my temper and told him to go if he wanted to. And
I thought he was just being a little baby again, but he actually
stood up, he made to go. Terrible timing, for him to suddenly
grow a pair of balls.'

She scowls at an imaginary David in the corner, like,
vicious.

I'm proper on the edge of my bunk now. This is the best
bit of Martha's story, no contest at all.

'And then what?'

And she looks at me and it's like she's only just remembered I'm still in the room. For a second she looks uncertain, but then it's like she makes a decision, and she laughs. The noise bounces around the cell, not in a nice way.

'What do you think? I stabbed him. I stabbed him five years' worth of times.'

I stare at her, mouth open like a fish. Martha picks up her book. Her face has gone back to normal. Cool, icy calm.

'Don't look like that. Haven't I told you? He deserved it.'

'Babe?'

I walked into the lounge and flashed him this smile, like, nervous, because you never knew what kind of mood Justin was going to be in, those days. He could be right moody. I said to him sometimes, what, you on your period or something? Because I always knew how to make him laugh. Most of the time, anyway.

He looked up and grinned.

'Alright, Kittycat?'

And I felt my smile go proper and let myself breathe out. Nice one. It was a happy Justin day.

'Yeah, alright.' I picked up the cat and tipped her onto the floor so I could sit down next to Justin on the sofa. I curled my feet up under me and gave him a big grin. I was that excited I was almost fizzing with it. 'I got some news, actually.'

'What's that then? You been down the bank? Got yourself approved for a small business loan, is that it?'

I winced. One time, that's all I'd ever said to him, one single time, months ago, I said I quite fancied running a shop. I didn't even mean it, I was off my face, but I'd seen one of those little corner shops standing empty, and now he wouldn't let it go. Justin never just drops things. That's one of the things we've got in common.

'No, it's not that. It's—'

'You won the lottery then? You going to take me away, Kittycat, buy me a Porsche and finally pay me back for all that gear you borrowed, yeah?'

He laughed, not a nice laugh. I bit my tongue and did my best to give him a decent smile. I couldn't have his mood turning on me now. This had to go right.

'No. Justin, I—'

'Cos I need that money back, Kittycat.' He gave me a glare. 'It's a bit tight at the moment. I've got a couple of blokes lined up for tonight . . . '

I grabbed his hand to get him to pay attention.

'I'm pregnant.'

He stared at me, and for a second I'd managed to stop him talking. His mouth was slack, dropped open in this little o of surprise. I grinned. It was a nice feeling, giving news that can just shut people up like that. And in the silence, I let myself imagine how things might turn out. Me, pushing a little blonde toddler on a swing, while Justin goes to get ice cream. Tea at McDonald's and then a Disney film, the three of us snuggled up on the sofa. It's not that much to ask, is it?

Justin laughed. Louder than he normally would.

'Well, that's a bit of a fix, isn't it, Kittycat? Bet you don't even have the first clue who the dad is. Bit of a mess you've got yourself in there, isn't it?'

That hurt so much it was like it knocked the breath out of me. I went,

'No, I do know who the dad is, Justin. Of course I do.'

And I gave him this look, like, please. Come on. Please.

He rolled his eyes like, yeah, right.

'Yeah, right, course you do. You've been on the game this last six months, but of course you know whose kid it is. Yeah. Of course.'

I swallowed. We'd never called it that before. On the game. Sounds really sleazy, doesn't it? All I'd done was earn a bit of cash, through mates of his mates. He was the one setting it up, he was the one who said it was the easiest way to pay him back. But favours is what we'd always called it. Nothing heavy. Just favours.

'I use condoms, with them. Every time. You're the only one I don't use them with, I swear.'

Because it was a way to make it special with him, that's why. I know I can talk tough sometimes, but deep down I'm a romantic, and he knew that.

'Well, yeah, you say that, don't you?' *He was using his most reasonable voice, the one he uses to explain that of course, stands to reason he had to add interest, so he's afraid you still owe him.* 'But I've seen the state of you when you're working. Smacked off your face, half the time, aren't you? No way you'd be able to make sure you were using them properly, every single time, is there?'

'I did, Justin, I swear. Every time. You calling me a liar or what?'

But it was like he couldn't even hear me. His voice had changed, it had got harder, and louder, and his eyes had got that mad look in them, the way they did when he was about to hit something.

'I suppose you'll still want to keep working for me, living off my cash and taking my gear? Knocked up with some other bloke's kid, but that mug Justin'll help, yeah? Is that what you think?'

I shrank back into my bit of sofa. My head was spinning, like I couldn't keep up with what was going on. This was meant to be good news, you know? I'd thought this might be a nice day.

'I didn't ... I just thought ...'

He looked at me, and gave me a little smile. Just a little one, just a shadow of his normal smile.

'Don't worry, though, Kittycat. We'll sort you out. Get you down the clinic in no time, they can have it done in a couple of hours now. Just take a pill or something these days, don't you?'

I looked at him, not understanding for a second, because those hormones had made me even thicker than normal I reckon, and then I twigged. I fought the urge to cradle my arms round my belly, round my baby, to protect it from the thought of ...

'It's too late for that.'

'What? How do you know? Have you been to the doctor? You'd better not have been to the doctor, Dani, if they tell the social, if they turn up here, I'll be properly fucked, you understand?'

I shook my head.

'No doctors. But I took the test because I felt it move.'

Justin looked at me, steady and still. I waited, staring back. And out of nowhere he caught me a slap, right around the face. It was that hard it made my ears buzz.

'You stupid FUCKING junkie whore. How could you not have known? Too fucking thick to realise you were pregnant? Jesus CHRIST.'

Something about the shock of the slap, and the hormones, made me start bawling. And, if I'm honest, the shame of it. Because he wasn't wrong, was he? What sort of mum doesn't even know she's pregnant for that long? Through sobs I said,

'I'm sorry, alright? I'm sorry! I didn't know, I don't ...'

And it was almost like he just wanted to see me cry. As soon as I broke down, he softened, and looked normal again, like my Justin. Like the one I like.

'Don't worry, Kittycat. I'll still look out for you.' He slung his arm round my shoulders, or, if I'm being picky, my neck, and pulled me in close to him. 'Lucky for you I'm such a nice bloke, isn't it?'

After what seems like a million hours, the familiar *clang clank slam* of the cells being opened starts up and me and Martha grin at each other. Fucking *yes*, at last.

By the time the noises get to our cell, I've already got my trainers on. I can't fucking wait to get out of this shitty little box.

Miss Green creaks open our door and stands in the doorway. Blocking it. She looks all flustered and sweaty, and no wonder. The weather's still roasting hot. I give her a big, happy smile.

'Can we do swimming? Miss, it's boiling . . . '

She pulls a weary, *you're not going to like this but don't give me shit about it, okay?* face and goes,

'Sorry, ladies. No association today. Staffing cuts.'

All my muscles, like, tense themselves up at that. Even my arms and legs feel like they're angry on their own, without me even doing anything. It's all I can do to stop myself from kicking off. I go,

'MISS, this is the fourth day . . . '

Martha cuts across me.

'What's the maximum you're meant to put us on reduced hours, Miss Green? Before it becomes a human rights issue?'

Miss Green looks a little bit uncomfortable at that, to be fair.

'Look, I've seen the rota for next week. Starting tomor-row, you'll be on full hours for at least a week before there's another disruption, okay? A full week.'

She leaves and Martha nods, satisfied.

'Brilliant.'

I tear off a trainer. Fucksake. I hate feeling disappointed about shit like this. Makes you feel like a stupid kid. It's pathetic, how much I wanted to go and lean against a pool table and not even play pool.

'Why's it brilliant? We've still got to put up with today.'

Martha gives me a *come on now* look and goes,

'The plan, Dani.'

Ah, yes. The plan. Mustn't forget the fucking plan. I flop back down on my bed. Martha sits down all ladylike on her bunk, and picks up her sodding book again, but I ain't got no book. I've got nothing.

There's this weird thing, about being bored – it makes you really knackered. You'd think that if you just lay still all day, you'd have loads of extra energy, all fizzing around inside you, so you could sniff out things to do, whatever was going on. You could, like, teach yourself to draw, or practise your reading until you were good enough to actually enjoy it or something, you'd think. But real boredom doesn't work like that. It's more like shit sleeping pills. Your brain and body just give up, it's like, *if we're not getting out of the cell today, we might as well not even get out of bed* and before you know it you've got to spend twenty minutes psyching yourself up just to have a wee.

And I've already had my disappointment for today. That's why, when there's the *clang clank clatter* of something going on, I can't even be bothered to get up to have a nose. I just lie there, like a fucking slug or something. I can't even be arsed to be nosy. This is bad.

Martha stands up, though. Fucking perfect Martha. She's been keeping herself occupied, of course. With her fucking *book*. Not even bothered about not being let out today. She presses her face to the little window on the door. I don't even raise my head, but I do go,

'What's going on then?'

And she turns to me, big shit-eating grin, and goes,

'Chris is back.'

'WHAT?'

And it's like a load of energy rushes into me.

'Let's have a look.'

I give her a shove, but, like, a gentle one, and put my eye to the window.

If Martha hadn't just said, it would have taken me a fair while to place her. The way she walks is totally different – all the old Chris swagger gone. Instead, she's shuffling down the halls, head hung, not looking up at anyone, not answering the calls and shouts and *alrights*. There's even a couple of jeers. People are brave, behind their doors. But Chris has got no threats or glares for them. She's got nothing at all.

I frown at her.

'Fuck. What did they do to her in seg?'

'What do you mean?'

'She looks all broken, doesn't she? It's creepy.'

Martha gives me an elbowing in the side. Not gentle. I glare at her and move out of the way. She sticks her face back to the window.

'She's fine. Look at her! She's walking. She's okay.'

I sit on the edge of my bed again, cos there's not really room for us both to be standing up. I'm not sure why seeing Chris like that has made me feel so weird.

'There's more than one way to be not okay, though, isn't there? Walking doesn't prove anything.'

She turns away from the window and flops herself down on her bed.

'Well, she shouldn't go round drowning people and cutting up their faces, should she?'

I give Martha a bit of a glare.

'I wasn't, like feeling sorry for her or anything. But it looks like seg's fucked her up a bit, and I know what it's like.'

She head-tilts at me.

'*Sounds* like you're feeling sorry for her.'

'Nah.'

I get a little mini-glare off her, like, *watch it, sunshine*. And it's crazy of me, because it's only Martha, isn't it? But I get a little rush of fear at that. My old Martha could have never looked like that.

'Okay. I believe you. But don't fuck it up now. We're so close.'

I twist round on the bed and I look at the photos and the little calendar, with just two days left on it. Her name sings out to me from the wall. *Bethany Bethany Bethany*. I clench my teeth, like, determined.

'Don't worry. I won't.'

Chapter Fourteen

Extract from PSO 4800 – Women Prisoners

2.3   Women in prison bring with them a considerable
amount of vulnerability: one in 10 will
have attempted suicide, half say they have
experienced domestic violence and a third sexual
assault. Nearly half of all incidents of self-harm
in prisons will be committed by a woman even
though women represent only 6% of the total
prison population.

Me and Martha stand behind our door, staring at each
other all big, excited eyes and clutching hands, like kids.
Today's the day – the big fucking day! – and we're waiting
to get let out on morning association. I'm dressed in the
very clothes I saw myself wearing in the dream – grey
trackie bottoms and a faded green T-shirt. My hoodie's
round my waist, in spite of the heat. Martha didn't tell me
to do that, I thought of it all by myself. I just really don't
want anything to go wrong. If I don't manage to get out,

to save her ... But I push that thought away. I *will* get out. I *will* save her. I have to.

The *clang clang clang* of doors is getting louder and louder; the officer unlocking, nearer and nearer to ours. Martha gives me this big grin and whispers,

'Ready?'

and I nod. I mean, I'm not really ready. This is some fucked-up shit we're talking about. But I want it to be over, which I think is pretty much the same thing. I look over at the picture. One last look at her face, before I see the real thing.

As our door's unlocked, I let go of Martha's hands and squash my face back into its normal can't-be-arsed-with-anything-ever expression. I take a step towards the door, but where there should be empty space there's Miss Green, barring the way. She's looking extra fucking knackered today. The smudges under her eyes are a bruised-looking grey-black.

'Dani. Wait in your cell a minute, okay? Emma's coming to see you today.'

I exchange a look with Martha, that says *fuck fuck fuck fuck fuck*. We can't stay in the cell. We need to be within a few feet of Chris when we use our little bundle, Martha said, or it won't work. *Fucking* Emma.

'Why? What does she want?'

Miss Green sighs, and rubs at her eyes, hard. You can see the bright red rims of them coming away from her eyeball.

'I don't know, Dani,' she says, even more bolshie than she usually is. 'I can't be expected to keep track of every little thing going on around here. Just stay in your cell.'

I want to give her a fucking death glare for that bit of disrespect, but I've got a mission today. Today I don't do what I want, I do what needs to be done. So I make myself give her a nice little smile.

'Okay, Miss. Thanks for telling me.'

She squints at me, like, a bit suspicious. She's obviously got shit to be doing, though, cos all she does is heave a heavy, put-upon sigh and push off. Martha turns to me.

'Well, we can wait five minutes.'

But I've got the prickle now, the same feeling I have every time I know I'm coming out. There's something about the promise of air that hasn't been filtered through bars or a load of other women's lungs, of choosing what you want to eat, of fucking *freedom*, that calls to you once it's close, that won't let you sit still. Besides, this is Emma. She might have said she wanted a quick chat, but probation are never fucking straight with you. It might be she wants to do some paperwork that'll take hours, or that I've got a last-minute appointment with someone, or even a surprise move or something – they do that sometimes. Twenty minutes to pack a bag and then start again from scratch somewhere no one knows you. I look up at the wall. *Bethany, Bethany, Bethany.* There's no way it's worth the risk.

'Nah. Come on. We have to do it now.'

Martha gives me a little nod, and we catch each other's eye. I get that proper friend feeling again. We walk out of the cell.

I take two steps out there and my insides, like, drop. Out on the landing, the first thing I catch sight of is bloody Emma, way over on the ground floor at the other end of the strip. She hasn't spotted me yet because it's totally rammed in here, a sea of girls' heads clogging up the landing. She'll clock me soon enough, though. I breathe through the shock of seeing her. Even though my skin feels like it's fizzing, I grab Martha and head off in the other direction. We keep our heads down, weaving through the other girls as fast as we can, and not looking back.

We get down to the floor below easy enough. I stop and scan the level above, near our cell. I can't see Emma, which is both good, and not, because it's not like the out of sight, out of mind thing's stood me well over the years. We sneak, hugging the wall, over to Chris's cell. I let myself take a breath before I peek in. Even though I'm not afraid of Chris or anything, I can't shake the idea that when I look around the corner she'll be standing there with the knife again, ready to get the other cheek and even me up. I touch the puffy, split skin of my face. I'm not scared, though.

I swallow, and lean over to look into her cell. She doesn't have a knife, of course. She's not waiting to cut me. She's not doing anything at all. She's just sat on the edge of her bed, staring at the wall, but you can tell from her face she's not really seeing it. Her face is just blank, like she's empty or something.

Martha pulls me back out into the hubbub of the main wing, and leans over to whisper,

'Okay, great. Have you got the lighter?'

She's reaching into her pocket, and I have a quick crane about, just to make sure there's no trouble going on.

There is.

At the other end of the wing, there's Emma. She's moving, prowling around, looking in every face as she makes her way towards us. She's not just wandering, I reckon. She'll have found our empty cell by now – she's proper looking for us.

'Martha. *Fuck.*'

Martha follows my gaze over her shoulder, but she doesn't do that frozen-up silent thing she normally does when she seems frightened. Instead, she grabs my hand and pulls me sideways, so hard I almost go over. Her fingers, which I've always thought of as soft, are strong and tight on my wrist.

'It's alright. Here.'

I follow Martha, stumbling into a cell. The one next to Chris's. Two girls, sprawled on their beds, stare up at us, like, *fucking what?* I roll my shoulders and jut my jaw out at them, like, *yeah?* I can take both of them out, if I have to. I can have a go, anyway. Martha just stands there, cool as you like, staring back. She goes,

'Go on then. Get out.'

I stare at her like she's totally lost it, because she obviously has. She's going to get her fucking head kicked in if she goes on like this. But the girls aren't doing anything. They're just looking at each other weighing something up. One of them goes,

'You'll do the . . . the looking thing again? Right?'

Martha glares at them.

'I said, didn't I?'

They get up. The one who's on *my* bed, the one against the left-hand wall, pulls this expectant little face at Martha and goes,

'On both of us, yeah?'

Martha rolls her eyes. Since when does Martha roll her eyes? Since when does she boss people about like this?

If I think about it, she's been doing it for a couple of weeks

now. Martha's changed, right under my nose. If I was brighter
I'd have noticed.

She puffs out a sigh.

'We'll see. I need your cell *now*, though. You know what
to do.'

And the girls scurry out. As they get to the door, each of
them gives her a little nod. I turn to Martha.

'Wait, where are they going? What are they going to do?'

But the two girls just slink off. I've got this bad feeling
bubbling up inside me, and I jump as they bang the cell door
shut behind them. If this is part of the plan, why didn't she
tell me?

'Martha? What's going on?'

But she doesn't answer me. She's already sitting on the
floor. She's got the parcel out, and she's turning it over in
her hands, examining it from every angle, all her attention
laser-focused on this one thing. Seeing her like that's kind of
unsettling but there's something about it I like. It's not often
in here that you really feel like anything could happen, but
today it doesn't just feel like we might break the rules. It feels
like we might shatter them completely, change them into
something new. For the first time in months and months, I
don't know how today's going to end.

While I'm watching her, she looks up, spearing me with
her concentrating look.

'Ready?'

My heart's going dead fast, my chest doing that *boom boom
boom* shaking-me-up thing it does whenever I'm about to
take the first hit of something in a while, or steal something
really expensive. I feel a bit sick, that special sick feeling that

means dares and pushing your luck. I clench my hands into fists, because fists is better than shaking.

'Yeah.'

I sit down next to her on the floor. She grabs my hand and puts it on the loo roll parcel along with her own.

'Hold tight.'

I squash down the disgusted, sick feeling that's coming up my throat – there's bits of Chris's scalp in there, mixed up with my days-old blood – and do what Martha says. I grip the tissue paper as tight as I can, even though something gives under my finger, squishing around, making me think of the pigeon. I look at Martha. She seems almost like a queen, sitting on this grubby cell floor and holding on to a bit of bog roll with a murderer's hair in it. She looks like this is the thing she was born to do.

'What now?'

She smiles at me, this scary smile, all narrowed eyes and nostrils flared, and goes,

'Think about how much you hate her.'

I blink at her.

'You what?'

Her smile widens.

'Really concentrate. Give your whole self over to the hating.'

And on any other day, of course, I would have thought that was completely mental, and getting on the way to creepy as fuck. Think about how much I hate her? That's never going to fucking work, is it? Not in a million years.

And anyway, I'm not that kind of person, cheers. I'm not bad, not really – I just fuck things up. Planning like this, wanting to cause hurt like this, feels a bit over the line. Say it does work. If we can change things, but we do it based on hate, is that just a distraction any more? Or does that make it a curse?

But this isn't any other day. Today, I'll do whatever it takes to get out; I'll do whatever Martha tells me. She hasn't been wrong yet, has she?

I think of Bethany. The dog, biting into her flesh.

I close my eyes.

And I think about how much I hate Chris. Because I really do. Those scissors, slicing across my face. Martha, thrashing and held under the water like a kitten, back when she couldn't defend herself. The little things I've seen her do, even to her own gang. Hurting and cruelness, all the time. I think about all the prison bullies I've known, and the ones in schools and on the streets before them. From Chris right back to Jamie, a catalogue of faces. The ones on the outside, who give you drugs and cuddles like it's a kindness, and then use them to trap you. Every time I've been locked in a cupboard, bruised in places the world won't see, had every little scrap of what was mine stolen. I let the hate wash over and through me like lava, burning all the other thoughts away.

The package is tugged from my hands, and my eyes blink open. Martha's got it in one hand, and in the other, the lighter. She flicks the top and sets it on fire. The little package catches straight away, big yellow flames licking up towards the ceiling. The flames slide down to Martha's fingers and she drops it on the floor. The whole cell stinks of burning hair and something else, some kind of musty herby thing I can't place. The two of us stand there and watch the package fizzle down to ash, glowing bright at first and then fading. It burns itself out to just black scraps on the painted, mucky cell floor.

I sit on the floor and stare, hard, at the ashes. Martha gives me a bright smile and a hand squeeze and goes,

'Great. Well done.'

She gets to her feet, brushing at her jeans and T-shirt to get any stray bits of soot off them. I look up at her. I'm still sat on the floor. I feel really small somehow, like a kid. I sort of want to stay on this dirty cell floor, and never see what we've done.

'How do we know that it's worked?'

She flashes me a smile and grabs my hand, pulling me up to my feet.

'We'll know.'

Martha shoves me out of the cell.

'Go on.'

She looks as happy as I've ever seen her, today. She always looks thrilled when we do stuff like this. For someone who seems so quiet and easy to boss about, she really thrives on being in charge.

'Where are we going?'

The landing's still bustling, all full of women milling in different directions and leaning chatting all over the place. A nice sight, normally. Martha gives me a little push.

'You go. Look normal. I'll be there in a bit.'

I swallow, the bad-feeling back, and stronger than ever.

'But . . .'

She gives me a proper, tough-bitch glare, and it's so at home on her face, for a moment it's like I don't even know her.

'GO, Dani.'

I turn left and walk away from Chris's cell, quick but casual steps. The burning hair smell clings to me. It seems to be getting stronger, even. My mind's racing as I walk away. What's Martha gone to do? Some final part, I suppose. But why's she suddenly not telling me stuff? I shake the thought out of my head and walk. I'm about half the length of the landing away when there's a shout from above me, up on the second-floor landing,

'Oi, look. Look!'

and a couple of screams. I look round, to see one of the girls pointing straight at Chris's cell.

There's smoke coming out of her door.

I stare at it, dumb and fucking useless, just for a second. Then, all hell breaks loose. There's officers coming out of nowhere, and the sound of alarms bouncing all over the big, echoey space of the landings and wherever you look, screaming girls, all running from the cell and the smoke pouring out of it.

But not me. I lurch forward, back towards the cell. I can't explain it. I need to see. I shove my way past the girls running in all directions around me, stumbling and weaving through the crowd. I push my way right to the edge of the crowd, getting close to Chris's doorway until I'm stopped by the heat.

I look in and see flames, jumping and flailing and forming the shape of a body on the bed. For a far too long moment, all I can do is stare at the Chris-shaped fire, my head empty and numb.

'MOVE! Everybody back.'

Miss Green and another officer barge past me with their little fire extinguishers and break my spell. I turn away, coughing and gagging on the bitter smoke and the image of her still burned in my head no matter where I make my eyes look.

Her shape, picked out in flames.

I've seen this before. Back in young offenders, years ago, I had this mate, Cat. She stopped taking the pills they gave her, and a month later, wrapped herself in a sheet and set it on fire. Nicked my lighter to do it, as well. They let me visit her in the hospital wing, as it was still young offenders and we were such good mates. She was all muffled with bandages, darkness seeping under the edges of the snow white. Even though her skin healed over in time, she was never the same after that. You wouldn't be, would you?

Imagine. Your whole self, on fire. Totally consumed.

Martha's next to me again, right at the front of the crowd. I turn to her, to share a look of *oh fuck, is this what we did?* It was just meant to be a little distraction, wasn't it? I want her to help bear the guilt of it, reflect it back at me. But her face is dead calm.

'Break these when you need them.'

She reaches into her pocket and holds out the two eggshell charms we made a couple of weeks ago. I just gawp at them. The burned-hair smell has changed now. There's a kind of sick, delicious smell coming in under it. Like roast pork. I wipe my mouth with my hand, hard.

'Where've you been?'

Her eyes are bright, like she's taken something.

'Here. Take them.'

I look at her. Like, *really* look at her. But no. She couldn't have. She didn't have time.

'Martha ...'

She places the eggshells in my hand, and closes my fingers around them. Then she gives me this patient, *come on, sweetie* smile, like a teacher might give you back in primary school, and a little push on the arm.

'Go on. Run.'

Chapter Fifteen

Extract from PSI 55/2011 – Management and Security
of Keys and Locks

3. <u>BEHAVIOUR TO MAINTAIN KEY AND
    LOCK SECURITY</u>

General – All Staff

3.1   *Keys must not be exposed during filming or close-up
      photography.*

3.2   *No prisoner must be allowed to handle or examine
      any key or lock.*

3.3   *Keys must be kept concealed when about the person.*

As much as I can, I run. The crowd of girls swirls around the
wing, no direction to them at all. Half of them are pushing
against me, wanting to get closer to the scene, have a peek.
Even though that's what I just did, that idea makes me proper
pissed off with them. Like, you know what's going on now,
why do you need to look? The rest of the girls are flowing

with me, away from the heat and the smoke and the smell. More girls pour down the stairs, three landings' worth of women all scrabbling around the ground floor. It's a combination of the weather, bodies and the fire, means it's getting hot. Panicky hot.

My eyes are watering loads, from the smoke and the shock, I think. I want to sit down. I want Martha. Why did I have to do this bit on my own again? She's better than me, at this kind of thing, at talking, keeping it together. I'm not sure when that started being true, but all I know is, now, I need her.

There's a big gaggle of girls in front of me, blocking the way. All they're doing is chatting and gawking, craning their heads about to try and get a peek into Chris's cell.

'Get out the WAY.'

They scatter and I feel a little better.

Part of me can't believe we've done this. Set someone on fire. I look back. I can see flames, now, from here, and the screaming's building, up and up and up.

Maybe they got her out, though? They must have got her out.

The burning meat smell's getting worse. What kind of state will she be in? Will she live, even? I press on through the crowd. Probably. You do hear of it happening, a lot, around prisons. People normally survive. They *do*.

The other part of me, like, actually can't believe we've done this. Mars bars and hidden drugs is all very well, but this? If we had the power to do this – what else can we make happen? The two eggshells nestle in my loosely clasped hand, and for a second I think about lobbing them up into space, hurling them against a wall and watching them shatter. An end to this. I never have to find out what else I'll do. But of course, *Bethany Bethany Bethany*, I don't.

If we really did do that to Chris ... It's better that it isn't all for nothing. Right?

I press on. *Just get to the gate*, I think. *Get them to open the door. Out to the car park. Sorted.* I run one last dodge around a clump of girls and, breathing hard and dripping sweat, I'm at the gate.

In front of me, there's Emma. Her normal elegant composure is dishevelled. There's a film of anxious sweat over her face and her white shirt's all rumpled. Even her baby hairs are sticking up all frizzy. I've never seen her looking like this before. Normally, no matter what else you want to say about Emma, she's properly got her shit together.

'Daniella! Where have you been?'

I swallow. I thought it'd be an officer, minding the door. One of the ones I don't know that well, maybe, one of the jobsworth ones who don't give a fuck about us, or protocol. Easy to trick. Not Emma, someone who knows me, who, like, gives a shit about me, even if it is just to hate me and try and fuck me over.

But Emma's got keys, I can see them, shining silver on her belt. And I proper hate her anyway, don't I? So really, this is better. I feel the eggshells, sitting light and fragile in my hand.

'What do you mean, where've I been?'

She's clutching this little radio. Holding it up to her ear.

'You weren't in your cell.'

She looks really lost and small. I tell myself that's a good thing. I've got stuff to do. I give her a look, a *you're not being sensible* look.

'Miss, there's a fire. Aren't you going to let us out?'

She looks to the gate behind her, hands on her keys, then back at me.

'Where were you?'

There's no officers with her. Miss Green and the other one who ran into the cell must have been the only two on duty. *Cutbacks*.

'I'm here now. Miss, the door.'

She cranes past me to look over at Chris's cell. I turn and look as well. From here, all we can see is a mass of girls, pressing and swirling round. I can see uniformed arms gesturing them back and hear a

'Get back, could you get BACK, please, give us some space,' from Miss Green. There are still flames, flickering inside the cell. Where did Chris find so much stuff to burn?

Emma's mouth is this hard little line. She holds up her radio, to her mouth,

'Come in, come in,'

and then her ear. There's nothing coming out, though, that I can hear, not that I can hear much. The whole wing's a fucking chaos of noise, running, screaming. I have to yell to make myself heard.

'Miss. You have to take us to the new fire meeting point.'

She blinks at me.

'What?'

The screaming and confusion of the landing's actually getting to me now. There's a big part of me that wants to join in with it. I could do it. Punch out Emma, take her keys, leg it away from the burning and the noise. But then, of course, that's instant lockdown. No way out, if they're looking for me, if I've just thumped a probation officer. I need to get Emma to let me out. I take a deep breath and slip one of the little eggshell charms into my pocket. I cradle the other one, all gentle in my hand.

'Miss, they changed the meeting point, for the fire. Last month. It's the car park. We need to get down there.'

'Not the wing yard? It used to be the wing yard. I'm sure it's the wing yard, here.'

She looks confused. There's this little pop of understanding inside me, lighting me up. Of course. She goes into loads of prisons. She might get mixed up between them. I nod, all authority.

'It was. Now it's the car park. When the building's on fire, when the normal meeting point's a danger.'

She looks at the gate again, then the officers again, then her radio.

'My radio's down. I should wait, get an officer, I should . . .'

She looks around her and I can see how close to tears she is, and for a second, I waver. But I cried, when she told me I couldn't have Bethany back, didn't I? Crying changes nothing. I squeeze hard, and crunch the eggshell in my fist.

'Miss, the smoke's getting thicker, we're gonna suffocate in here! You've got to take us somewhere.'

And I give her some big, *I don't want to suffocate here in fucking Holloway Prison* eyes. The thing is, the smoke actually is getting a bit thicker, or maybe drifting a bit towards us. The screaming's still as strong as ever, or maybe that's worse too.

Emma doesn't look sure. A little voice inside me goes, *you're fine. Push her harder.* I take a step towards her.

'Miss. There's only three of you here. Everyone's scared.

You're gonna have a riot on your hands if you don't do something. A riot, and a fire. Open the door.'

I turn my head back around me, making Emma look too. Girls screaming, shoving, fighting. I go,

'You don't want to be in here, if it really kicks off.'

Emma looks at me and I look right back at her, and you know what, in that moment I even believe it. There might be a riot. She has to let us out. The pressure's been building up, day by boiling hot day, all summer. You can feel it pressing in on your every side. After the longest second ever, she gives me this little nod. She doesn't say anything, just turns and starts unlocking the door.

The rush of it hits me like a car. I've never felt anything like it.

Emma clips her radio back to her waist, and yells,

'Everyone over here! Come on, follow me . . . '

And I hang back, over to the side, waiting for Martha. I want us to go through the door together.

The screaming calms down a bit as we walk out to the car park. Everyone's still upset, I can feel the tension fizzing about in the air, but when you're in prison there's something just about the action of going outside that can make everything okay, at least for a little while. Smelling fresh air and seeing the sky above you makes you feel a bit better, no matter how bad things are.

We make our way through the corridors made out of chain-link fence, round corners, about buildings. Emma's at the front, leading us towards the car park, and Miss Green's bringing up the back. The other guard's not here. I think of her, back on the landing, with Chris. The flames will have stopped by now. Surely they'll have stopped. Now that I'm outside, and the smell and smoke have gone, it's easier to think about it.

I've got this giddy, school trip type of feeling. I can't believe we're getting away with this. We round the final corner and get let into the car park, and Martha elbows me in the side, but I'm already looking.

Sitting on the tarmac at the edge of the fenced-in yard, as if I'd wished it into being there, is a lorry. Massive, the kind they use to bring in big stuff like furniture, or enough food for a whole city. You almost never see them in London. They're a motorway kind of a thing. Loads of cover behind it, loads of room underneath. Me and Martha swap a look, like, *fucking YES*.

Miss Green slams the gate shut behind us and yells,

'RIGHT. Head count. In lines!'

Me and Martha shuffle into lines and stand there. Trying not to be noticed, not to make any kind of fuss.

Martha leans into me, close, and goes,

'There's one last bit of the plan. Here.'

And I feel her shove something into my hand. Paper, and string.

'What? What's that?'

She gives me this big-eye look, like she's trying to hypnotise me. Around her, people shuffle and fuss, but she stays dead still.

'Take it to the address. Coldharbour Lane, not far from the park. Hand it over, and they'll give you something you need.'

I swallow down the sick feeling rising up my throat.

'Yeah, but I don't need anything else, though, do I? I need to get to Bethany, don't I? Fast as I can.'

Her eyes flash, like, *do what I say, you junkie piece of shit.*

'This is important, Dani. You won't be able to do it without her help.'

'But—'

'Don't you trust me?'

I look at her. Deep in her eyes, all wild and huge. I push the package into my pocket and nod, and try not to think about whether that's a lie.

Now we've stopped moving, now we're shut in again, everyone's getting twitchy. Someone next to me gets pushed, and steps on my foot, but I bite back the yell-and-shove I'd normally do. *Don't get noticed, Dani. Don't make a fuss.*

Emma's just hovering at the side, not far from where I'm standing. Miss Green gives us all a glare, like, *stay STILL!* and goes over to her.

'Right. Fifty-nine, all accounted for.'

Emma nods. She looks well rough, like she might throw up.

'What happens now?'

Miss Green's jaw is set, hard.

'We wait 'til the radios come back on. Then we get them to a temporary wing.'

Emma nods, but says nothing. Miss Green rolls her shoulders. I've never seen her look as pissed off as this before, no matter what kind of shit us girls have got up to.

'Why are we out here? We're meant to be on the wing yard. This isn't the meeting point.'

Poor Emma looks fucking horrified by that.

'What? No ... They changed it, didn't they? I heard they changed it, if there's a fire.'

Miss Green shakes her head, but keeps eye contact with Emma the whole time, scowling.

'No. Always the same. We shouldn't be here. Shouldn't have left the wing, even, without clearance.'

Emma pats at her hair. She's getting nervous now, which is exactly where I need her to be. I smile myself a little smile, like, triumphant.

'But the radios weren't ... Why didn't you stop me?'

'I was at the back, making sure none of the prisoners escaped. Why didn't you just take them to the right place? Why did you even think it had changed?'

And Emma's eyes comb the lines for me and meet mine and I'm like *fuck*. We are rumbled. I turn to Martha. Getting busted for making us come to the wrong place wasn't in the plan. What the fuck do we do now? She just glances at me, gives me a tiny little smile, and then calm as you like, turns and punches the girl next to her full in the face.

And the thing about this prison, these women, is, all summer we've been like a tinderbox just waiting for a spark. Summers are hard here, the grind of being too hot and cooped up, it drives you mad, bit by bit. Like any other time it's too hot for too long, we're all begging for a storm.

The girl Martha hits punches back, but Martha dodges and the fist hits someone else, who roars and launches herself into the crowd, knocking people flying. And just like that, it's chaos. Shrieking, fist-flying, kicking, biting chaos. The crowd presses and swells around me, and Miss Green and Emma are yelling, but it's too much, far too much for the two of them to have a hope to contain.

The crowd surges and pushes me and Martha together, and I feel something on my cheek that might be a kiss or might just be her head getting shoved against mine, and I hear a whispered,

'Good luck.'

And I'm off. Under cover of the heaving mass of bodies, I scamper round the back of Emma and Miss Green and slip behind the lorry. I drop to the ground, not minding the filth of the floor or the roughness of the tarmac on my arms. I lie on my back and I breathe.

Under here, I can still hear the fighting, but it's like it's in a world that's not quite my own any more. Here it's just darkness, the smell of petrol and the merciful cool of the shade.

I look around. It's as good as I'd hoped. There's a couple of feet under here to wriggle about in, and, by one of the wheels, an area of denser dark, like a kind of metal cave. I crawl over on my elbows, bum down close to the ground, and stick my head up there. There's a space – a ledge kind of thing, just about big enough for me, I reckon. I haul myself up. My back just fits on the ledge, as if the little space had been made for me. I twist a bit, and my hands find a solid bit of metal jutting out to brace against.

I hold tight, waiting to fall, to be found, to be somehow stopped. I can feel my heart thudding inside me. Nothing happens.

This might actually work.

*

I wait there a good long while. I wait while the screams and sounds of fighting happen around me, for what seems like hours. I hear the radios clicking back on. I hear the other officers come rushing in, and I hear the screams and thuds of the women who won't stop punching. It's hard to stop, once you start, I know. I wait for someone to do the head-count again, to notice I'm missing, to find me. I imagine Miss Green, crouching under the lorry and spotting me, her furious face, or Emma's smug *wouldn't I have guessed it* one. I wait for arms to reach in and grab me back. But no one's noticed.

Eventually, the thuds and screams and clangs are all gone and all that's left is silence.

There's a funny thing about silence – in here, you crave it. There's noise all the time, every second of the day, tellies, radios, the chatting and the yelling and the *clang clang clang*. But as soon as you get it, you don't want it any more. The constant noise is soothing somehow, and when all you can hear is your own breath, rasping in and out, it makes you think. There's space for your brain to start going too fast, coming up with all kinds of shit. Imagining things. Remembering. Most people don't want to be left in the silence, alone in their own heads. It can be a lot noisier than a rave in there.

I wait for a long time.

In all my years, I don't think I've ever done something as bad as this. Even if it was just a nudge, we shouldn't have. I do know right from wrong, deep down, no matter how many times I've been inside.

I try to breathe.

I don't know when this thing at the park is, of course. It might have started already. Bethany might be there, right now, eating an ice cream, standing in the sun. The ceremony might already be over. The dog got her, the scene played out, and me not there to save her, to do anything at all.

I squeeze my eyes shut against the dark, trying to push out the image of her little broken body, lying there, blood soaking into the grass . . .

Breathe.

I keep waiting.

In the darkness down here, I see things. I see the image of Chris, again and again, outlined in flames and flailing in her room. In my head she becomes a fire monster, coming at me, running, going to burn me up . . .

No. Breathe.

I struggle to remember what Martha said about Chris before. I knew it would be bad. I knew it would hurt. I didn't think she'd go that far, though, I didn't know . . . I'm sure she didn't say. Would I have gone ahead with it, if she had? What about if it had killed her? Her life, for Bethany's? That sounds like a fair enough trade, put like that.

I don't know. I wait.

Finally, when my arms and legs are cramped to fuck, and my back's screaming at me to stop twisting, to lie flat, and the smell of the petrol and oil's got me feeling like I'll throw up at any second, and I've made up my mind that Bethany's already dead, I hear a rumble. Or, rather, I feel it, getting into the heart of me and shaking up my bones. For one second, as the engine roars into life and the lorry pulls away, the panic is replaced by a feeling of freedom. I can't believe it. This is actually going to work!

And then it hits me. I'M UNDER A FUCKING LORRY. The shaking picks up, and I'm sure I'm going to get shaken right off my ledge, pitched right onto the road and then crushed to death on the filthy prison tarmac. I think of the times I've seen roadkill. Crows and squirrels, flattened, their shapes blurred on the sides of the roads. That'll be me. Just an old, dead crow. That's how I'll end. But then I think, *Bethany*. I have to keep it together, for her. I use all my concentration and I manage to not totally lose it, breathing in and out, deep and slow. *Bethany, I'm coming.*

I clench my teeth together and I brace myself harder because I can do it. I am.

As the lorry rolls along, I tell myself over and over again that I'm nearly there. We've maybe gone twenty metres. Soon, the lorry comes to a stop again, and I hold myself, tense and taut and dead still. There's a glint to my left and I twist my head round to see. A mirror on a stick is shoved under the lorry, and, as it tilts, it's like it's winking at me. I take one of my hands away from where it's bracing me, and for one sick-making moment I'm not sure the other one can hold me on its own, but I manage to steady myself, just. Desperate, I slap at my leg, once, twice, three times before I find the place where the eggshell is lodged in my pocket. The shell gives way under my palm, and I feel the crunch, little shards of egg pressing themselves into the side of my thigh. *Please please please work please please please.*

There's a shout. I hold myself still, too afraid to even breathe. But then the mirror goes, and the lorry jolts forwards.

And, just like that, we're moving again and the rumble of the lorry's juddering my bones. And right then I feel like I'm riding on top of the lorry, like I'm soaring among the clouds. I've done it. Despite being squashed in under a lorry, scared shitless and clinging on for dear life, I'm free.

I waddled back from the loo, because I needed to go to the loo every five minutes in those days, and plopped myself down on the sofa. Justin looked over to me, a big lazy smile all over his face.

'Go and get the fixings, yeah, Kittycat?'

I heaved a big sigh.

'Aw, Justin, come on, I only just sat down.'

'Well, you should have got them when you were up, shouldn't you?'

I shifted on the sofa, trying to get comfy. I was never comfy, then. I'd never been big before and hauling around the baby was killing my back.

'I'm not even using them.'

Katie shot Justin a shitty look.

'I'll get them.'

And she stood up. I tried to catch her eye, to shoot her a cheers, nice one mate *look, but she just turned and went in the kitchen. Justin laughed.*

'What's up her arse then?'

And Tony shrugged. I shifted some more on the sofa. We hadn't seen Tony and Katie for ages. The rest of the old gang had drifted off, and it was only those two we ever saw, and even then just to use together. Since I found out about the baby we were down to once a month or so, at that. And me and

Katie, we used to be in and out of each other's places all the
time, every day practically. Not that I was at my place that
often. But still.

Katie came back and dumped the syringe, the needles and
tubing all on the coffee table, and plopped back down on the floor.
Justin gave her a big grin.

'Cheers, darling. You know how to earn your keep round here.
Not like this one.' And he jerked his head towards me. 'She never
gets off her fat arse these days. Do you, Kitty?'

I gave him a glare.

'I'm pregnant, Justin. What am I meant to do, go get a job on
a building site or something?'

Which I thought was pretty funny, as it goes, but no one
laughed.

Katie lit a fag and turned to me.

'You found out if it's a boy or girl yet, Dani?'

I rested my hand on my tummy.

'I reckon it's a girl.'

She frowned.

'You didn't find out?'

Justin leaned over me to cut into our chat. His hand was prop-
ping him up on my thigh, leaning hard enough to hurt.

'She hasn't been to any scans. Doesn't want them to make you
give up the smack, do you, Dani?'

He sat back, pleased with himself. I look at him like, fuck
you, Justin because that's not it and he knows it. We've had that
many rows about me going to the doctor's. I wanted to just go, to
take whatever they had to say to me and get it over with. They
don't arrest you, do they? Not if it's, like, a medical thing. And
I know people who've had kids and not even got them taken off

*them when they were junkie mums. One person, anyway. Who
my mate knows. But Justin kicked up that much of a fuss about
it, all worried they'd ask who was supplying me and that, he said
I shouldn't go, said it wasn't worth it anyway. He was probably
right, I suppose. But it wasn't because of giving up smack.*

Katie gave me this look, like, a cold look.

'You still using then?'

*I didn't answer, but Justin reached over and handed me my
lighter, and the little scrunch of tinfoil with the powder measured
out on it. She turned her head away like I was disgusting, which
was pretty fucking rich, wasn't it? When that was the only reason
she was there, to get some herself.*

*I glared at her and held the tinfoil by its edge. I flicked the
lighter and stared at the heart of the flame.*

Justin went,

*'She can't stop now, can she? The baby'll have to withdraw
as well, won't it? It'll just die inside her. Got to wait till it comes
out, now.'*

*I chucked Katie a quick glance. She hadn't tapped the ash off
her fag and it was hanging off the end in a crumbling tube, about
to drop any second. I said, dead quiet,*

*'I'm smoking, though. Not injecting. Haven't injected since I
found out.'*

Tony laughed, and said to Justin, like, mocking,

'Sweet. Seeing you looking out for your kid like that.'

Justin narrowed his eyes and went,

'Not my fucking kid, mate.'

*And I flicked the lighter again, under the foil this time, and
watched the smoke start to form above it. Katie leaned forward
and hissed,*

'Still, though. Still.'

And the guilt and fear swirled around inside me, faster and faster, until I breathed the smoke deep into my lungs and held it until everything went calm again. I rested my hand on the bump and felt everything except the baby and me just melt and flow away.

Chapter Sixteen

Extract from PSI 25/2011 – Discharge

2.23 *All eligible prisoners must be given a discharge grant of £46.00. See Annex B.*

2.26 Those prisoners who need adequate clothing for release will be given it.

After what must be at least a hundred are-we-there-yet-is-this-it stops at red lights, and a thousand times thinking I was falling to the road, we finally roll to rest. The engine stops. This isn't another red light – it feels like a proper pause. I count to ten, and listen hard for traffic noise, but there isn't any. Right. Go time. I unlock my arms and let myself roll off the ledge and on to the floor. I land, really heavy, on the palms of my hands, and my nose fills with the smell of hot road. The flesh on them stings enough to make me dizzy, but I drag myself out from under the lorry, quick as I can before it starts up again with me still underneath it.

For a second, all I can do is stare at the sky, so bright and huge above me. After so long in the dark, it's dazzling. I just lie there for a moment, and enjoy not being under a lorry any more, not grimly clinging at hot metal and thinking that any second I'm going to die. I just lie there, alive.

Then I stand up on shaky legs, and try to get my shit together a bit.

I look around. I'm by a long, red brick wall, crowned at the top with barbed wire. There's not many people about; it's a road, but there's no other lorries or cars or anything. There's a navy sign with white lettering over to the left, and I crane to see. It says HMP Brixton.

Fucking YES.

I know where I am. Brixton prison's only round the corner from Brockwell Park, and Coldharbour Lane. I know it round here like the back of my hand. Then it dawns on me. I am at a fucking prison, the last place I want to be. I look round, all frantic. I clock two officers, up front near the cab, both in their uniforms, standing in that *alright then, what's going on here* way that police and officers have. Sweat prickles the back of my neck. I'm not sure they've seen me. I turn and take a step. My legs wobble under me. *Fuck.*

If I can't leg it, fast and right now, there's no way those officers aren't going to see me. They'll have to check the lorry contents before it goes in the prison. They'll come round the side, and see me, and be all like, *oi, love, what you doing here, aren't you the one that escaped from Holloway?* and I will be. *We bin waiting for you,* they'll say. They'll grab me and cuff me and send me back and there'll be no one to save Bethany and that dog will get her and she'll die.

Fuck fuck fuck. Hopefully they'll think I'm just some

random nutter. Maybe I could hide my face? No, that's worse, that's way more suspicious. Will my picture be all over the news, yet? Surely they've noticed I've gone by now. Surely it's too much to hope that they won't twig until bang up.

I take another step. And another. Still wobbly as fuck, but the blood's flowing back into my legs, I'm starting to be able to feel them again. *Come on, hold me up, help me get away, just for a little bit, let me get away.* It doesn't matter, really, if they get me straight back in tonight. I'm expecting they will, if I'm honest, and I don't care. As long as I can make it to the park, and I can save Bethany, they can do what they want with me. It's not like I have to stay out, for it to count. I just have to save her.

I take two more steps. *Come on, come on, faster.* I'm getting to the end of the red brick wall. I'll be able to dodge round the corner, soon. Nearly there. Nearly . . .

'Oi!'

There's running steps, coming up, fast and hard behind me. I freeze, waiting for the baton, the grab. *Oh God, Bethany, Bethany, Bethany, please no. Not yet.* But all I get is a hand on my shoulder. It wheels me round to face one of the officers. He's young, this one, shaven-headed and proper stacked. He looks like he could snap me in half like a twig. He glares at me with this evil scowl. His hand's still on my shoulder, heavy and solid, pressing down on me.

'Oi, love, this area's restricted.'

I look up at him, mouth hanging open for a second before I manage to say,

'Right . . . Yeah. Sorry.'

He juts his jaw at me and furrows his brows.

'You can't be hanging round here, right? S'not permitted.'

He lets go of my shoulder, though. I'm that relieved, I feel like I might fall over without the support of it. Thank fuck I'm not a man, so I'm not in uniform for being on basic. With my trackie bottoms and T-shirt on, I'm not going to get into a club or anything, but I look normal at least.

'Yeah ...'

He jerks his head to the side, like, *fuck off, then*.

'Off you go then.'

And it's not like I believe in God or anything, but as I hobble away I flick my eyes up and go *thanks thanks thanks* in my head. Maybe something up there's looking out for me, wanting this to work. Maybe. I head out, quick as I can on my weak, cramping legs.

Pounding down the pavement, blood back in my legs and head up high again, I get my bearings quick. I pop out at the base of Brixton Hill and breathe in the curry-traffic-chicken-pot-smoke smell of one of my bits of London. I never lived round here, but my Justin did. Still does, as it goes. Second on the left up ahead, then follow the road all the way down to the right. My feet could walk it on their own, I know it that well.

I let myself think for a second about Justin, and his flat, and him, and his drink and his drugs. Any other day at all, that's where I'd be headed, no matter that I'm fucked off with him at the moment, no matter that it's only ever a week of good times with him before he starts up again with his bullshit. Normally, I can't help it, I'm drawn there like a cat'll come to tuna, even if it knows you're going to take it to the vet. But not today. Today, I've got a mission. I'm going to be better than that, for her.

I look left and right, and run across the road. A car honks its horn at me, and I give it a quick flash of middle finger. I had loads of room there, what, you think I can't cross a road or something?

I push through this little bit of park by a flat block and cut down the side of it. Not far, now, not far. I come out on this road lined with the kind of shops I've never known anyone to go to. Not even a little McDonald's or something to spice it up – a boring, pointless sort of street. I feel this burning pain in my palms and look down. They're a mess of blood and bashed-up skin. I must have grazed them when I got out from under the lorry, and only just noticed. I wipe them on my trackie bottoms, on the sides where they won't show as much, and hold them up to my face.

There's only a little bit of dirt in there. Nothing to really worry about, I reckon. But this close, I catch a whiff of that same roast-pork smell there was back on the wing, and it makes me drop my hands to my sides, and wipe them again, no matter how much it makes them sting.

Whatever. I start to speed up.

I look down at the package, to check it again. Flat 12, 242 Coldharbour Lane. Janie. That's all it says. And it's sealed round the sides, folded over and over and then tied up so there's no way I could open it up and have a little nose without anyone knowing, even if I had time.

I squint up, looking at the sun, high up in the sky. What

time is it? We get let out for association at 9.30, and then there was, what, an hour between then and now? Fuck.

I reach out and buzz flat 12.

It had occurred to me, of course it had, that I could just . . . not do this bit. I mean, Martha's been good to me, fair play, but of course Bethany's more important – she's my world. I'll be honest; I was pretty much planning to go straight to the park. But I can't get out of my head, the way the eggshells worked. Emma, all confused, opening the gate for me. The mirror not seeing me, slipping away.

I'm still not saying I believe in it all. Course not. But it didn't seem like it was quite worth the risk, you know?

I snort and buzz the door again. Fucksake. I've got stuff to be doing. Also, and I know this is stupid or whatever, but I hate it round here. Bad memories, you know? Not my favourite bit of Brixton.

I have my hand raised to buzz again, when there's a crackle from the intercom, and a voice croaks out,

'What?'

I lean in.

'Got a message for Janie.'

Another crackle.

'Yeah, what is it?'

I sigh. Fucksake.

'I dunno, do I? It's in a letter.'

I shift from one foot to the other. It's bloody hot out here. Everything feels like it'd be sticky if you touched it, even the air, you know?

'What, you a postman or something? Can't you stick it in the box?'

'I'm dropping it off for a friend. Martha.'

The voice sounds suspicious of me, like I'm trying to trick it.

'Don't know a Martha.'

'Martha Clark? I was—' I look round the street, and lower my voice, as much as you can when you're yelling into an intercom. 'We lived together. In Holloway. She said you were expecting me?'

There's a long buzz, and it takes me by surprise so much I almost miss the door.

At the top of the dark, winding staircase, there's a woman waiting for me. She's wearing pink pyjama bottoms with clouds on them, and a vest top. Kind of thing you'd see in a sleepover on a film, you know? Doesn't go with her dingy flat and cold, hard stare.

I barely get to the top of the stairs before she goes,

'Give it, then.'

I hold out Martha's package and she snatches it from my hand. She rips off the string and peels the pages open, staring down hard at Martha's neat rows of writing. She reads the whole thing, then folds it back up, careful careful, and puts it in her pocket. She gets out her phone and starts jabbing away at it, like it's pissed her off. She glances up at me.

'What you still doing here?'

I jut my chin out at her. I know how to do this. Tough-bitch stare. *Come on Dani.*

'She said you had something for me. Something I need. Should say in the letter, yeah?'

She laughs, a big, open laugh, like I'm joking. But I keep staring her out, calm and level so she knows I'm not fucking about, and her laughing slows down and comes to a stop. Now, she almost looks sorry for me. I ramp up my glaring. Pisses me *right* off when people look sorry for me.

She looks around her dingy hall, then unhooks a little string of beads from a nail by her door. They're blue, with darker blue circles and a white blob in the middle of each one. They're barely long enough to fit over my head. She presses them into my hand and smiles.

'To keep you safe, yeah?'

And the smile fades out of her face completely as she goes, 'Good luck.'

Back out in the blazing sun, I clutch the beads tight in my hand, and I feel uneasy. I try not to think about what all that was about. I try not to think about Martha, or the officers, who'll definitely know I'm gone now, or even about Bethany. I just put one foot in front of the other. Fast as I can.

I head back down the street and towards Brockwell Park. Fast fast fast. If I thought I could get away with it, I'd run. Running's suspicious, though, and I couldn't keep it up, I know that. Back when I was a kid I was fast enough, fairly nippy. After so much in-out of prison and drugs, though, my body's fucked. I'm already starting to hurt.

My lungs are bursting, that kind of hurting dizziness you only get when you're running scared or getting chased. I have no idea what time it is. There's no clocks anywhere around, and I haven't even passed one of those new-type bus stops that tell you the time. Although, to be fair, it doesn't matter – it's not like I've got any idea when the thing in the park starts, so it really makes no odds. It's not a comforting thought.

Up ahead of me, I see a familiar shape of a building up to the left, and I let myself smile. The Hootenanny.

From the look of the sun, blazing high above me, and the feel of the heat on my back, it can't be that far off midday. Please let the opening be in the afternoon, and let it be midday.

I draw level with the pub, looking all weird in the daylight with no bouncers on the door and no music pumping out all round it. Me and Justin met here. We used to come here a lot, with other mates as well, when I'd been having the kind of good patches where I'd be having other mates. We used to hang out in the garden, smoking and getting pissed and ignoring whatever bands were on, because we were obviously more interesting than the fucking bands. Good times. Nice to remember them.

This means I'm nearly there.

I do a not-suspicious, not-knackered fast kind of walk over, past the posh houses and through the last couple of streets to the park. This part of town's like a different world from the kind of bits me and the people I know live in, though it's only half a mile from here to Justin's, if that. I used to like to look at them, though – used to slow down when I was walking round here, and take a peek in every window. All their pastel sofas and dining tables and kids' toys made out of wood. And I mean, I've had sofas, and tables, and toys, but it's completely different somehow, in houses like that. You can never put your finger on exactly why, but you know that the people in there live different lives to yours, and there's far more than just a door that's stopping you from going in.

No time for that today, though. *Keep it together, Dani. Focus.*

And then I'm standing in front of the main gates of Brock-well Park, breathing hard and sweating, but feeling suddenly like I could run a hundred miles, I'm that happy and nervous and excited. Because I've done it. I'm here.

I stand at the gate and gape into the park. I barely recognise it – my sleepy sunny park for drinking Stella in has been trans-formed. There's crowds of people, thousands and thousands of them, all swirling around the lawns. It makes me uneasy, the familiar-but-differentness of it. I take a deep breath, though, and try to hold it together. It's always like this, after you come outside. Everything looks weird for a bit, because it *is* weird. While you've been banged up the world's kept changing, and you've been locked in a box, left behind. It always takes a little while to catch back up.

As well as normal people, folks sauntering about with their ice creams and sunglasses, there's police everywhere, all bun-dled up in their black uniforms. The more I look, the more I see them, like beetles, crawling all over the park. Will they have my face yet? That prison officer at Brixton didn't, but, then, you'd hardly expect an escaped con to rock straight up to another prison. The police, though . . . there's tons of them, millions, and they're guarding the gates. They're ahead of me now, forcing this bottleneck by the gates, making you walk past them, far too close. I don't want to be paranoid or what-ever, but it's almost like they knew that I need to get here.

I'm still standing there like a dick, lurking by the gates. There's two coppers stood just inside it, and they seem to be looking hard at every face. Looking for me? I feel my breaths go all ragged and I get that lightheaded feeling I get sometimes, when things aren't going right, and a voice in my head screams *run run run run run*.

There's a whirring noise above me, and I look straight up. *Fuck*. Fucking *helicopter*. I take a few steps back, away from the gate, and it's all I can do not to scream and hit the ground. They've got a helicopter out looking for me. But how do they know I'm here? Am I being tracked, or what? Have they put something in me while I was inside, like, a chip under my skin or something? *How do they know?* The sweat's running off me and I feel like I might throw up and the brightness of the day is, like, pulsing in front of me, closing in on me, far too bright, too loud, too much. My whole world's dissolved into a soupy mess of panic. *Fuck fuck fuck fuck fuck. They're going to get me.* A little girl wearing a plastic crown skips past me, all happy, as if everything's fine, as if my world's not falling to shit around me.

She laughs, a cute laugh. I stare at her. A happy little girl. In a crown.

And then, all at once, I twig. *Kate bloody Middleton*. Of course, that was the whole point of today, wasn't it? It's a royal visit. The police and stuff are all here for her, not me.

I'm that wound up, I actually let out a bit of a laugh, out of relief. They're not here for me! It's for the duchess, and the little prince. I make myself take some deep breaths, one, two, three of them, to get some of the panic and stress out of my system and let me think a bit. *The police aren't there for me. They're not there for me*. I mutter it out loud a bit, to try and make it real.

'You're fine. They're not here for you. Okay? You're fine, totally fine, yeah?'

It makes people look at me funny, but that's okay. Better to be a random nutter than an escaped convict, isn't it? I catch the eye of some snotty bitch having a good gawp at me and give her a big, mad grin. She rears back, like I'm a wasp that's flying at her face or something, and my smile turns proper and I feel like myself again.

I take one last deep, calm-down breath, and I walk through the gates, past the policeman guarding them. They don't give me a second glance.

Inside the park, it's fucking rammed. There's people everywhere, all milling about the place in their shorts and sundresses. I wish I was wearing shorts. My trackie bottoms are thick, designed for winter really, and I'm soaked in sweat. The sun's beating down on me, hard. I'd forgotten that feeling you get when you're out too long without shade. It's been a while since I've been free in the summer. Funny what you miss so much when you're inside, but how quickly you forget anything bad. It's fucking roasting in prison, but you never get sunburn, and there's no wasps. And you always know what's going to happen next.

I push myself deeper in the throng, keeping up my nutter muttering.

'Shhhhhhh. Fine, we're fine. Nice walk in the park on a nice day, isn't it?'

It makes me feel better, and, besides, it gets people out of the way. I walk more, head craning about on my neck, scanning the crowd again and again. If I'm going to find Bethany, I need people to get out of the way. She'll only be little. How tall are two-and-a-half-year-olds? Three feet? Two? Little, anyway.

I push past a group of teenage girls, all crop tops and dead straight hair. They stare at me, horrified, but I don't care. I looked like that too, not long ago at all. Their time'll come. One minute you're sixteen and everything's a laugh, the whole world's ahead of you and everybody wants to snort lines off your toned little tummy, the next you're banged up in a cell, all stretch marks and sag from the baby you didn't even get to keep.

'Enjoy it while you can, loves.'

They pull disgusted faces at me and stalk off. *What's their problem? Snotty little bitches*, but then after a second I realise I said that out loud. *Fuck.* Better rein in the muttering, at least a little bit. I take a few more steps and try to look as normal as I can.

This must be where Kate and little George are going to be, because the crowd's getting denser and denser. A woman wearing posh clothes gets pushed against me and bumps into me. Her hands go straight to her handbag, like, *Oi, I'm watching you, junkie.* She obviously wants to walk off, get away from me and my grabby little hands, but she can't, the crowd's too thick. There are people crushing in on all sides, and police everywhere. I take a deep breath, to remind myself that I can, and look around me a bit, floor level where I can. *Where the fuck is Bethany?*

I clock this one policeman, about twenty feet away, who's looking at me. He catches my eye, and doesn't let it go again. *What you looking at, eh?* I think, but I'm frozen there, trapped by his staring and pushed in by the crowds all round me anyway. I'm as stuck as if I'd been C&R'd. Still looking at me, he lifts up his radio, and presses a button on the side. He says something into it. He's still looking at me.

And, suddenly, I don't feel good any more, I feel bad, really bad. These thoughts keep chasing round and round my head, and I can't control them. I keep thinking things, like that I'm shit, and I can't cope with anything, and I've fucked everything up because I just can't keep my shit together for more than five minutes, ever, and I'm pathetic and worthless and Bethany's going to die because of me. I'm her mamma, but I'm the shittest mum in the world, I can't even do this one little thing for her, *Bethany Bethany Bethany I'm sorry*, *Bethany no no no*. And now I'm going to get arrested again and they're going to cart me back to prison and I've fucked it all up again, again, again, again, again. I can feel myself getting properly sucked into the old spiral of panic and hate and horror, just on the verge of letting go, surrendering to it. And even as I'm shaking and I start to cry, there's a little tiny part of me that's relieved. In my head I'm already tracing the route back to Justin's house, already thinking about the hit I can get there, the blissful nothing that can drown all these feelings out, that can mean I don't have to live in my own head, at least for a little while.

But then I hear a bark. A big, angry bark, booming out all over the park. It's coming from behind me.

I whip round and I fucking run.

Chapter Seventeen

Extract from PSO 2300 – Resettlement

5.13   The effects that imprisonment can have on
        family relationships and community ties is
        acknowledged. For many prisoners, particularly
        women, the return to the role of primary carer
        will be a significant aspect of their resettlement,
        as may seeking the return of their children from
        local authority care.

When I spot her, the sweat of the day freezes to my skin. A little blonde toddler, absolute stunner, just like I knew she would be, wearing a pink sundress with white polka dots on it. She's smiling, this lovely little smile, brighter than the sun, and her hair's pulled up in two curly pigtails on either side of her head. She's got an ice cream, clouds of it piled up on a cone. Across the park, raised up on a little hill, thick crowds still between us.

Bethany. My Bethany. I've found her.

And next to her, the dog. Just like it was in my dream, a

massive Staffie, just two feet away from her and stood in that way that dogs do, that shouts danger all over it.

Bethany scooches a little closer to him. She waves her ice cream in front of the dog, and he snaps at it, but misses. She reaches out a pink little hand.

In real life the dog's even bigger and more muscly and vicious than I'd thought. Its face is scrunched up in a snarl, lips back from its teeth like it wants to taste her, like it's thinking of sinking its teeth right in.

Bethany, not knowing any better, licks the ice cream. Like she hasn't got anything to be afraid of in the world.

I'm full with feelings, happiness and anger and fear and regret all swirling around inside of me, crashing into each other, and I use them as, like, fuel, to help me get one last burst of strength. I ram my way through the crowd, all of them just standing there gawping, not noticing or caring about the little girl and the massive wild dog next to her. I shove people out of my way and push forward, not minding the 'ExCUSE me' and 'Oi's of the crowd. Nothing matters except Bethany.

Gasping for breath and dripping with sweat, I push through the last few people and run to my baby. I can hear from here that the dog's growling, low and threatening. As I get close, I can feel the rumble in my chest. The dog takes a step closer. Every muscle of it looks tensed. Ready to jump, to bite, to tear.

The dog's filthy mouth is almost on her when I get there. Its drool-slicked teeth are shining in the sun, and it lets out a bark, big and deep, a warning. There's a rumbling from the crowd. People are starting to notice that things aren't right.

There's faces all round me, not looking pissed off, any more. Concerned. No one moves a muscle, though.

I get there just in time. I fling myself at Bethany and the dog and reach for her, snatching her up into my arms, just as the dog snaps at the space where she was a moment before. I hold my baby, safe and warm and back with me at last.

I hug her to me, breathing in the smell of her by the lungful and feeling her skin, so soft and pressed against me. I'm full of a feeling I've been craving for years, that everything's where it should be. She's with me. She's safe. She's mine.

From my left there's a scream. A man's voice, deep and posh, shouts out,

'Who's dog is that?'

The dog's still got its eyes on her. It's still growling its deep growl, staring right at my Bethany. It squats back on its hind legs, as if it's getting ready to jump.

'Somebody! Stop that dog!'

I glare at the dog. *Not my baby, you don't hurt my Bethany.* I reach out with a foot and kick the dog, firm and precise, right on its shoulder. It looks up at me, like *ow, what you do that for?* and stops growling. I twist Bethany away from the dog, squeezing her tight. I'm not going to let anything bad happen to her, ever, while she's with me.

'Should we get a policeman . . . ?'

I stare into Bethany's face. She smiles up at me, trusting and sweet. I smile back and go,

'Hello, lovely. My little girl. Hello.'

This woman comes out of the crowd and grabs the dog around its belly, clipping a lead to its collar and pulling it back. The dog chokes itself, trying to get to us, rearing up on its hind legs but held back by its throat. I cling to Bethany, hugging her close close close to my chest. *Thank fuck for that.* Her ice-cream cone drops, splatting softly on the ground, and I'm not sure she even notices.

'Did you just KICK my DOG? That's animal cruelty, that is. I should report you.'

I give her my worst look, my *I've been in prison, I've seen stuff, don't you think for a moment about crossing me* look.

'Oi. Your fucking dog nearly attacked the little girl. He was just about to bite her face off or something. I only just got here in time.'

The woman looks at Bethany. I can tell she's thinking about feeling guilty. I dip my face to Bethany's hair and drink in the smell. I don't want the woman looking at her, even.

'Shit. Sorry if the dog scared the baby. He never bites, though.'

The man calls out,

'It looked like he was going to bite!'

I nod over my shoulder at him and bristle, puffing myself up at this stupid bitch. How fucking dare she act like everything's fine, when her dog just nearly ripped my little girl in half?

'What the FUCK are you doing letting that thing off the lead somewhere like here? With kids about the place?'

I can tell by the set of her mouth that she's scared of me, this stupid bitch in her tiny little shorts and pastel pink vest. I could take her, easy as anything, and we both know it. But she holds her ground and goes,

'He's not dangerous. He didn't bite her, did he? No need to overreact.'

And she leans down and ruffles at the horrible dog's brindley fur, like it's some sort of harmless toy rather than a massive brute of a mutt that could have killed my Bethany. She could be lying in front of me, right now, bleeding out of her little body where it'd ripped and torn her flesh. I squeeze my baby and glare at the woman. I can feel the other glares of the people around me, all backing me up like we're in a gang. Which is what being a mum might be like, at its best, I suppose. A kind of gang.

'It could have fucking KILLED her. Filthy beast should be put down.'

I can tell that got to her. She looks down her nose at me, all scared and pissed off.

'Excuse me. There's nothing wrong with my dog's behaviour.'

I let out this laugh, like, *are you joking or what?* and square up to her, as much as I can with Bethany still in my arms. But she goes on,

'What were you doing leaving the baby on her own, anyway?'

And it feels like she's kicked the legs out from under me, for a second. Because that's not what she means, she doesn't know the story, but, yeah. I did leave her on her own, didn't I? I chew my lip, so hard I taste blood. *Bethany, I'm sorry.*

The crowd are staring at me, all curious, now. Even the shouting man's quiet. You can almost hear them all thinking, *yeah, good point. Why did she leave her?*

And why did I? Could I really not have kept her? Would it have been impossible? If I'd worked harder, if I'd done better, if I'd have been better . . . The guilt bit of the emotions going around me pushes up bigger, so big that for a moment all I can do is stand there and breathe in Bethany's sun-cream-and-ice-cream smell and try to keep it together. But I manage to snap back to myself and go,

'*Filthy* beast. I'll report it next time.'

And I give her my best confident, *I know what's going on and I always get my own way so don't try any shit on me* look. For a moment, I'm not sure what she'll do. I can tell she doesn't want me to have the last word, but she doesn't really want to fuck with me either. I think about how I must look to her – blood-stained trackie bottoms, greasy hair and a fresh scar all across my face. I must look rough as all fuck, like someone who's escaped from a loony bin or something. But that's good, right? If she's scared, she'll fuck off.

My mate the shouty man finds his voice again and goes,

'Shouldn't be allowed. Vicious dogs like that. It's not safe.'

We glare at each other, her and me. For what feels like hours.

There's mumbling from the crowd. For the first time in my life, ever, I hope a policeman looks over at us. I'm that angry, and that right, I'd report her myself if I could.

She fucks off. Gives me one last mucky look, and then turns on her heel and stalks off as fast as she can through the crowd, dragging her dog along behind her. It strains, turning back to look at us, but she's tugging on its lead, really pretty hard.

I just stand there, legs wobbly with relief and arms full of Bethany. All I can think is, *YES!!! Fucking yes. I did it. I DID it. She's saved.*

*

I shuffled my weight off the too-high hospital bed, wincing a bit as I got to my feet. They'd told me to rest, said I should try and get some sleep, but I couldn't. It was like it's Christmas morning that day, back when there was nothing more magic than Santa and a brand new doll.

I waddled over to Bethany's little see-through cot and peered in. She was sleeping, her lips pursed up into a pretty little pout, her eyelashes making perfect half-circles on her cheeks. Who even knew babies were born with eyelashes?

I reached down and stroked her soft little cheek with just the tip of my finger. She blinked her eyes open and looked up at me. They were a deep, bright blue – shocking in such a tiny little face. I looked around, like, looking for someone to ask what to do, but then I remembered. It was okay. She was mine. And even though it had only been a few hours, I could barely remember what life was like without her, you know? My baby. The other part of me. I gave her a smile and picked her up.

'Hello there, little one, Mamma's got you, it's okay, shhh shhh . . . '

And she closed her eyes again. I took her back to the bed and sat back against the pillows, laying her on my chest. I could feel her breathing against me, her little chest coming out like bellows beneath my hand. So perfect.

And in that moment I was glad of all the crap luck I ever had in my life. Every time my plans had gone wrong, every time I'd been stung for something not my fault, all those times I just got the shitty end of the stick for some reason. Because if all the luck was saved up, was just kept for this, then that was worth it. Because Bethany was fine.

And I hadn't even dared think it. But it's not like I haven't talked to people, you know? I'd heard all the stories, the babies born addicted, the social snatching them straight out of your arms. I thought about what withdrawing could do to me, how it could tear me up and make me feel worse than dead, and the idea of Bethany going through that, and I felt sick.

I looked down. Her sweet little face, clear and fresh and new and asleep again now. Nothing wrong with her at all. All she was was right.

For once, for this one time, I got away with it. The nurses were nice, and Bethany was perfect, and everything was going to be just fine. Not just fine. Brilliant.

I look down at Bethany. Little blonde curls tumbling either side of her face, and still smiling up at me, bless her, despite the shock of the dog. Brave little thing. I've been brave today too. Maybe she gets it from me. I give her a kiss on her soft little head, and breathe in the still-babyish smell of her. This is my happiest moment ever, I think.

'Hey, you. You okay?'

She nods at me, little bit shy and cute as anything. I hug her close, and grin a massive grin to myself. I did it! I saved her. Her bitch of a foster mum is going to be fucking devastated she never listened to my message. Because I was right, wasn't I? People want to pay a bit more attention.

Shouting man comes over and goes to me,

'Is the little one alright?'

And I smile at him and hug her close and go,

'Yeah. Cheers.'

And he gives us a big smile as he walks away. And I grin back, nuzzling into Bethany's hair.

Just because I used to take heroin sometimes, doesn't mean I'm thick. I know what's what. And I know not to leave little toddlers on their own so they can get attacked by dogs. I'm going to give the foster mum a right bollocking for letting her out of her sight like this, just you wait. I crane about a bit. Where is she?

'Bethany? Where's ...' The word makes me feel sick, but I make myself say it. 'Mummy?'

She looks up at me like she doesn't quite get it. She doesn't answer. Oh. I would have thought she was old enough for a question like that. Ah, well, she's had a shock, I suppose. But it shouldn't be too hard to find her foster mum. I look about the place, searching for a panicking woman looking for her kid, but there's no one acting out of the ordinary at all. I suck in a breath and use my best pay-attention-to-me-you-twats yell.

'Oi! Has anyone lost a baby?'

Nothing. All the people who were around with the dog have peeled off, and I don't recognise a single face now. Everyone's just staring off any other way, trying to not look me in the eye. Rude. I nudge Bethany.

'Hey, love, say "Mummy". Shout it out.'

She looks at me all big eyes. Reminds me a bit of Martha, this one.

'Mummy?'

I give her a smile, all patient, like.

'Little bit louder, love.'

'MUMMY!'

I look about again. No. Nothing. Just people swarming about, same as usual, and the police buzzing around, listening to their radios and eyeing us all up like they know stuff. I feel sick, partly with the after-wash of the adrenaline and partly because – *fuck* – now I'm going to have to report Bethany lost, aren't I? Which means going up to a policeman, and pretending to be normal, and giving a fake name, and then handing her over to some random bastard copper and hoping they'll look after her okay. And then they'll only give her back to her foster mum, who was the one who lost her in the first place, wasn't she, and put her in danger? And who isn't her *real* mum, after all . . .

I look down at her. She's so perfect. Even though she's heavy, it's like my arms want to keep holding her. They don't want to let her go.

No. I mean. I know I have to give her back. I can't just keep her, not like this. I know that. I can do it.

I crane around for a policeman. Which isn't hard, to be fair, they're bloody everywhere. Still with the radios, talking and listening, every single one of them. I pick a policeman, quite close to me, because he looks young and his eyes aren't all hard-edged and closed down, the way people's are who aren't going to listen to you. I go up to him. He's playing with his radio, but I go,

'S'cuse me.'

Like, polite. He looks at me and little Bethany with this kind of not-really-paying-attention half-smile.

'Miss, if you could head to the exit of the park now, please.'

I scooch Bethany up on my hip a little bit. I don't like this, at all. I can see other policemen around the place, getting into the crowd, all *move along now, come on, if you could move along please* and herding people to the gates with their arms.

'What?'

My young policeman looks down at me. He seems a bit pissed off now.

'We have to evacuate the park, Miss. If you could head towards the exit for me now. Please.'

And he turns away. And every fibre of me's going *go go go go go go go*. You don't want to be arguing the toss with policemen, do you, when you've just busted out of prison? But . . . if it's not dangerous or whatever, I should really get Bethany back where she belongs first. It'll be a nightmare trying to find her foster mum if we end up leaving from different gates, they're all spread out and the streets'll be packed. I do a bit of a swallow and summon up my last little bit of braveness, and I go after the policeman.

'Sorry, but—'

He turns and rolls his eyes at me, well exasperated now.

'Didn't I tell you to evacuate the park, please, Miss?'

I shift Bethany from one hip to the other. She's being really good, as it goes. Must have good genes.

'It's just . . . Why are we evacuating?'

He shrugs.

'There's an alert on.'

I frown at him. *Come on, that could mean anything.* I need to know if we need to get out or not, to make sure the baby's safe. That's reasonable, isn't it?

'Yeah, but what's the alert for? Is it a bomb or what?'

He looks like he's going to just tell me to fuck off, but then he kind of glances at Bethany. Gives her a nice little smile, like, *alright kiddo.* When I look down at her, she's smiling at him, her shy, seriously-fucking-cute little toddler grin.

Nice one, Bethany. Good girl.

The copper gives in.

'Some nutter's escaped from prison. The little prince might be a target apparently. Kidnap risk.'

I can feel the blood draining out of my face. My heart's pounding, *BOOM BOOM BOOM*, so hard it's shaking me. It's all I can do to keep standing there, pretending everything's normal. Inside my head all I can hear is a voice going *nooooo ooooooooooooooooooooooooooooooooooooooooo*.

The policeman smiles at me.

'So don't worry, okay? Not a bomb. You get along home.'

I make myself smile a smile that's like, *phew, that's a relief!* but it's not a fucking relief. I give him a friendly nod and let myself be herded along towards the gates. I go slow as I can stand, willing myself to not start running. Do they mean me? They must mean me. They can't mean me. Can they?

It'd be a big fucking coincidence if they didn't.

In my head I'm replaying that moment, ages ago, when I tried to get a message to Bethany's foster mum. Emma asked me about Prince George, and I said he was great, and she wrote something down. I see her, over and over and over again, writing something down.

That's always how they get you.

I said I'd do anything to have a baby like him.

Fuck.

We head to the gates, me walking, carrying Bethany, in, like, a daze. There's a policeman up ahead. I could hand her over, right now. I should hand her over right now.

Except, I can't just report Bethany missing, can I? Now Emma's told everyone I'm a fucking baby stealer. I can't even

risk hanging around and waiting for the foster mum. If I get
found out, they'll rip me to pieces. I know what people are
like, about anything to do with kids. And they should be,
don't get me wrong, it's just ... Breaking out of prison, to
steal a baby. If people believed I'd done that, they'd bring
back hanging, just for me. And they'd definitely believe I'd
done it. Who'd take the word of some low-life junkie prisoner
fuck-up like me?

People are staring at us now, I can feel their eyes hot
on my skin. Do they all recognise me? Is that why everyone's looking? I can feel that thud-thud-thud in my chest I
always get when I don't know how I'm going to get out of
something.

I look past a group of mini-shorted teenagers, who I swear
are nudging and giggling to each other about me, and see a
copper under a withered old tree. He isn't like your normal
kind of London copper, not like the ones on the gate. This
one's standing stock still, holding himself all awkward and
upright. He's wearing sunglasses, so I can't see his eyes. I don't
like it when I can't see people's eyes.

A helicopter drones overhead. I lean back and look up at it.
The sun hurts my eyes, but I still look.

I swallow and stare back to the tree. There's a glint of something tucked under the copper's arm. A sick feeling slimes up
the back of my throat as I realise he's holding a gun.

I force myself to take a deep breath and hold my daughter
close, give her a kiss on her soft little head.

'Look, Bethany! Helicopter.' I keep my voice as sweet and
nice as I can, but inside I feel all scrunched-up like a fist. The
sight of a weapon will do that to you. My body tenses up all

over as I get ready to run, or kick. Anything I have to. The only thing that matters is keeping Bethany safe.

Because I've got her now, back in my arms, and I'm not about to fuck this up again.

As we leave the park, pushing our way through the swarm of people filtered through the narrow metal gates, I spot one of the policemen looking at me. It's the *eh up, what's going on here, then?* look. I know that look. I try to head away from him, stay out of his way, but I'm being swept towards him by the crowd. Even as I push against the flow, aiming for the left, someone will step in front of me, shoving me over to the right again, closer and closer to him. His radio buzzes and he holds it up to his ear, squinting at me the whole time. I make myself keep walking, normal, normal, calm.

Bethany squirms around in my arms and goes,

'Where we going?'

And I'll be honest with you, I have no fucking clue where we're going. I never thought this far ahead – the plan was, get out of Holloway, save her from the dog, give her back to her mum. There was never any going anywhere. I'm just going to have to improvise.

I ignore the copper staring at us, so close to us now, so close, and the push of the crowds and the sweltering heat of the day, and I look down at my little girl. I give her my best smile, the one I've been waiting years to give her, and I go,

'We're on a day out, Bethany. It's a treat. We're going to find something fun to do. Do you like the sound of that?'

And she smiles back up at me and laughs, this lovely little laugh that sounds like how Mars bars taste.

The squinty copper smiles at the two of us, and looks away.

'You're silly.'

I decide not to ask her why I'm silly while we're still quite so close by all these police. I mean, I wouldn't call taking a toddler on a walkabout with no idea what you're going to do with her, while being looked for by the police, a 'silly' thing to do, but then I'm not a two-year-old. There's a junction up ahead, and the crowd's thinning out now. I turn down the street with the least people on it, and walk. I've got no clue where, I just walk.

I mean, how am I meant to know what I'm doing? It's Martha who makes the plans, not me. And she didn't plan for this bit, because Bethany's foster mum was supposed to just come and take her off me, all smiles and reunited. So where is she? We haven't seen hide nor fucking hair of her, this entire time. She's the one to blame here, really, even more than that bitch with the dog. Who leaves a toddler just wandering around a park on their own?

I shift her onto my other hip. Bethany's not light, she's a healthy, sturdy little thing. I give her a kiss on her little blonde head and smile down at her.

'You alright there, Bethany?'

She laughs.

'Who's Bethany?'

I laugh back. Funny kid.

'I'm Dani. Nice to meet you, yeah? I'm your . . . ' The word sticks in my throat. 'Friend.'

She nods at me, like, shy and solemn.

'We're going for a walk together, yeah? Going to have a nice time.'

She nods again. I keep walking, feeling a bit uneasy. How much can toddlers actually talk? I can't remember when kids learn. Isn't it littler than this?

Fuck. I've got no idea what I'm going to do with her.

I keep walking. There's another turning. I choose at random. I still don't know where we're going. We do more walking. Turn again. A strange street now. Fuck. And then this little voice pipes up,

'What's your favourite film?'

I look down at her, all surprised. She blinks up at me.

'What is it?'

I mean, *Fight Club* is my favourite film, as it goes. Might not be appropriate, though. I wind back to when I was a kid.

'*Sleeping Beauty*. You seen it?'

She nods, hard, like *you fucking betcha I have*. I turn another corner.

'I seen all the princesses.'

I widen my eyes at her.

'What, all the Disney ones?'

We pass an oak tree, all massive and ancient, its roots pushing up the pavement around its base. I'm sure I've seen this tree before.

'ALL the princesses.'

I pull a kind of jokey, *nah, you haven't* kind of face.

'Have you seen *Cinderella*?'

She nods.

'YES.'

We pass a shop, with a load of old pipes in the window, and I've *definitely* been there before. I remember me and Justin thinking about buying one, to smoke weed with, real classy.

I think I might know where we are. If we just turn left, up ahead here . . .

'Have you seen *Snow White*?'

She wriggles around in my arms, all excited.

'YES.'

'Have you seen . . . ' Not going to lie, I'm running out of princesses. 'What's your favourite one?'

Up ahead, I spy a playground. *Yes!* I knew it was here somewhere. I head towards it.

'*Frozen*! Anna and Elsa.'

I smile down at her. She's so cute. What was her foster mum playing at, leaving her like that? I'm getting angrier and angrier at the thought of her.

'I ain't seen that one. What do they do?'

Her little eyes light up.

'Elsa has magic ice in her hands but Anna goes off with a reindeer and a snowman who can sing and Elsa gets sad and builds a castle.'

Kids are bloody mental. I pull an interested, *oh, yeah?* face for her.

'Is that right?'

I mean, what's the point of giving your kid up so it can have a better mamma than a smacked-out, fuck-up junkie, when the new one just abandons her in a park to get eaten by dogs anyway? I swallow, hard. Kids deserve better than this.

'YES and they sing the song . . . Let it go . . . Let it GOOOooooo . . . '

Something about her reedy little toddler's voice and her proud smile as she sings makes it the best song I've ever heard, better than any tune any DJ could ever drop in any club in the world.

'That's a nice song.'

She grins up at me.

'YES!'

She doesn't deserve a little girl as lovely as Bethany, if she can't even keep her safe.

We're at the playground now. It's not much – just a couple of rusty swings and a knackered looking roundabout – but you don't need much, do you, with family? Just each other.

'Hey, look at this! Do you want a go on the swings, yeah? Woooo!'

I load her into the swings. This is one of the things I'd always thought about doing, when I was locked up. Just a little, normal mamma thing. There's a massive grin on my face, splitting it in half. She's going to love this.

'Do you want me to push you, Bethany? Push you big and high?'

She laughs at me, her happy little face smiling into mine.

'Who's Bethany?'

And I laugh too and go,

'You are, silly! Ready? Let's gooooo!'

And I give her a massive shove and launch her up, high, high, high, into the bright blue sky. Right now, this weather isn't too hot, too sticky, close – it's glorious. It's a sunny day, and I'm in a park with my baby girl. Watching her soar like that, it hits me – maybe I'm not a junkie fuck-up any more. I mean, I set out to save her, and I did it, didn't I? I didn't get distracted, or chicken out, or give up. I didn't fuck it up. I did it.

'Higher!'

I push her again. I feel myself moving the weight of her

sturdy little body and I think – well, things change. I changed. Look at me. Maybe . . . Maybe I can just keep her.

'You want to go higher? Wheeeeee!'

Her foster parents can't be that great, can they? They lost her, after all. She's not safe with them. Maybe I can dye my hair to disguise myself and do a proper hairdressing course out here and get a flat and look after her myself. Bethany was never hers to begin with. She was always mine.

I shove her on the swing again, and watch her fly.

Chapter Eighteen

**Extract from PSI 04/2015 – Rehabilitation Services
Specification – Custody**

4.14   Structured interventions are most effective if
        participants have the opportunity to practise
        new skills with support whilst in and when they
        leave custody. Custody is a good place to initiate
        personal goals and it is important that momentum
        and progress towards achievement is not lost at
        the point of release back into the community.

'I'm hungryyyyyy.'

I tug at Bethany's hand. She's trailing along behind me, and she's going bloody slow. I mean, I know kids do go slow, but this is ridiculous.

'Stay still. Just a sec, don't go anywhere.'

I pull the hoodie from around my waist and put it on. From being the kind of day where it's too hot to breathe, it's getting nippy now. I pop up my head through the neck hole to see Bethany, glaring at me.

'I'm HUNGRYYY.'

Yeah. I'm hungry too. Don't hear me whining about it, though. I take her hand again, and give her a little tug down the street.

'I know, Bethany. I'm gonna get us some food in a bit.'

She pulls at my hand, leaning away from me, but I've got her good and tight.

'No! Not Bethany! No!'

And she bursts into tears. Well, she was already kind of half crying, to be honest. She has been for ages now. But a few more tears streak themselves down her mucky little face and the worm of snot hanging out of her nose glistens at me, and I think *fuck. Fuck fuck fuck.*

'Look, alright, yeah? Alright. I'll get us some food soon. Promise.'

I pull on her arm, but she won't budge, and I don't want to yank it out of its socket. I wish she'd get a move on, though. I can't carry her any more.

'I need a weeeeeeee.'

I look about us. We're on some road and there's just houses around, no public toilets or cafés, nothing. I'm not too sure where we are, if I'm honest. I thought I knew it pretty well round here, but ... I dunno. It seemed important to keep moving. To be doing something, at least.

'You'll just have to wait for a bit. We'll keep our eyes out, yeah?'

I've got to get back onto a main road, get my bearings. Surely, whichever way I walk, I'll hit some shops or a tube or a bus stop eventually, right? It's London. My London. Don't feel much like it's mine, though, at the moment.

'Noooooooooo. Now. Please.'

And my heart breaks, looking at her. There's something about her trusting, snot-covered little face that makes me want to do better. I need to set things right with her. I have to look after her, I can't just give up. I look around again, and this time I see a bin. I scoop her up and pull her knickers down, holding her over the ledge.

'Sorry, love, best I can do. Go in here. Go on.'

She looks up at me, a bit doubtful, but I make myself smile, like, *come on, sweetie, it's okay*. And she wees, pretty neatly really, into the bin. I grin, and feel like I've won something.

'Good girl!'

There's nothing to wipe her with, but beggars can't be choosers. Slightly damp pants is better than soaking wet pants, isn't it? I pull them back up over her, a bit awkwardly, her standing on the edge of the bin. As I pull her dress back down, I notice she's shivering.

'Hey, are you cold?'

She nods, but in a sort of confused, distracted sort of way.

'I'm hungry!'

I see goosebumps all over her and feel well guilty. If I was getting cold, she was bound to be worse, wasn't she? *Fucksake, Dani. Get it together, you twat.*

I set her on the ground and take off my hoodie to put on her. It practically comes down to her feet, but she looks well cute in it, even if she is all tear-stained. I pick her up and give her a cuddle. I feel like joining in with her and crying along, but I fight it.

'I know, love. Me too.'

*

'ExCUSE me.'

Some snotty bitch is standing in front of me, giving me some proper fucking evils. In fairness, I'm blocking the doorway to M&S a bit, but, fucksake. Just go round. Can't she see I've got my hands full here?

I've finally found our way back to somewhere familiar – Brixton centre. There's more police around here than I'd like, but I'm hardly the most dodgy looking person about the place, and it's good to be back in somewhere I know, at least.

I give the snotty bitch a decent look of my own back.

'What, you want to start something, eh? EH?'

And she rushes past me and into the shop.

I'm getting to the end of my tether a bit, if I'm honest. It's getting dark, and I'm freezing cold and I have no clue where we're going to sleep tonight. I'm not going to lie to you, I'm getting scared. But first things first. Bethany's hungry, and I know how to sort that out.

'Just act natural, okay, Bethany?'

Her eyes well up again. How's there even any water left in her to do that? She's already been crying for hours.

'No! Nonono . . . ' She starts proper sobbing again. I clench my teeth together, really hard, and focus on not losing my rag with her. *She's only a baby, she's only a baby, she's only a baby.*

'Alright, whatever. Just stay quiet, then. We're going to get us some food.'

I push through the door with her and into the clean, bright-lit spread of the shop. There's people bustling all about, buying their knick-knacks and clothes and insanely expensive ready meals and that. They're staring at us, some of them, and I do my best to glare back. We do stick out a bit to be fair, the pair of us all dirty and smelling slightly of wee. But this was the only place I could think of that'd sell a little girl's jumper, and chocolate. If we can just get those, everything might be okay for a bit.

'Stay close, yeah?'

And to be fair to Bethany, she walks obediently next to me, staring at all the stuff in the shop with her sad little eyes. She's even stopped crying, for now.

'Good girl.'

I've done this a million times. Back when I was a teenager, I used to lift things a few times a week, just for something to do. I spent the years from when I was five until I moved out pretty much permanently in Mamma and Richard's bad books, so while I had pocket money in theory I never actually got my hands on it, it was always stopped for one thing or another. I wanted a nail polish or some crisps, I had to sort it out myself.

I swagger up to this big display, all confident. Like, *oh, look at me, I'm such a lovely mamma. I'm just looking at these nice chocolates, maybe I'll buy some as a present for my friend ...* While my face is looking at these massive boxes of posh chocolates, like, considering them, my hand shoots out and grabs these three smaller bars and stuffs them in my trackie bottoms, quick as anything.

I pick up Bethany, and smile at her. *See, poppet? Easy. Mamma'll look after you.*

But, just then, I sense someone behind me. I freeze. I stand there, staring straight ahead at the chocolate, the sugary smell of it catching in my nose.

Shit.

'Miss. If you put that back, there'll be no need for me to take you to the office.'

Slowly, I turn to face the guard. I remember how to do this. There's only one of him, no back-up. He looks kind-faced, a bit fat. Not nearly as fast as me, I reckon. And my muscles remember. They know just how to shove, and grab more stuff, and run run run run run like hell. They're braced for it.

But I have Bethany now. She's on me, stuck like a limpet on my hip. What am I going to do, run still carrying her? And let her head get knocked, have her squashed if I trip, if they catch me and tackle me? I could fall on her, all my weight and hers crushing her soft baby head on the scuffed beige floor . . . Anyway, she'd slow me down. With Bethany, my legging it days are over.

I look up to the guard, into his kind, fat face, and give him a nice smile. I pull one of the chocolate bars back out of my pocket.

'I'm really sorry, sir. She's hungry, you see, and I've come out without my purse, so I was just going to . . . '

He keeps his hand out.

'Come on. And the rest.'

Saying all sorts of shit to him in my head, but keeping my smile on, sweet and sorry, I pull the other two chocolate bars out of my pocket and dump them into his hand. He looks me up and down, and nods.

'Out you go, then.'

I turn and start to march out. The guard is just behind me, right up my bum, the entire way out. I walk all through the shop and out of the door, head held up and Bethany balanced on my hip. It's ridiculous, and totally not like me, but I can feel a prickling behind my eyes like I'm going to cry. Which is stupid. I mean, this has happened loads of times and I've never been shamed by it before.

It's been a long day, though.

Out on the pavement, it's suddenly got properly dark. I stare around Brixton High Street, all neon and nutters, now. *Fuck*. How am I meant to feed us, if I can't steal? There's only one thing left that I can think of to do. But no. No.

I switch Bethany to my other hip. She wriggles on me, and pulls this proper tragic little face, downturned mouth and everything. She doesn't look like the sweet kid from my photos any more. She's just like any toddler, hungry and dirty and had enough.

'I'm HUNGRY!'

I look her right in the eyes and take a deep breath, but it comes out as a sob. I do a couple of big sighs, calming myself down. Everyone's staring at me, but whatever, let them stare. My face is wet with tears, but I can't let go of Bethany to wipe them away, so fuck it. Poor little thing. This isn't fair on her. She shouldn't be hungry. I've got to sort this out.

'I know, love. I know.'

I trudge up the High Street and cuddle Bethany close to me and I try really hard, desperate, to have another idea. Any other idea.

The baby screamed and screamed and screamed and I bounced her in my arms, tears running down my cheeks too.

'Shush shush, sweetie. Shush shush.'

But she kept screaming. Her little body arched away from me like she hated me, and her face was a red scrunch of disgust. I dug my tit out of my bra and tried to stuff it in her mouth.

'Hey, sweetie. Bethany. Are you hungry?'

But she just writhed and screamed and ignored my cracked, red nipple waving in her face. From the flat next door there was a banging. Bang-bang-bang, right by the end of the bed. They'd been doing it since I brought her home. Like I wanted her to make this fucking racket all the time. Like they were the only ones who were being put out by the fact she never fucking shut up for long enough for you to get your head together, not for a single fucking moment.

'Shush shush, baby. Shush shush.'

She screamed. I gave her another smile, another bounce.

'You need a nappy change, yeah? Shall we check?'

I lay her down on the bed and reach out to get a new nappy. There weren't many left, but I decided I'd worry about that later. If it stopped her crying, even for a second, she could have had a hundred nappies, and I wouldn't eat till she was potty-trained, I didn't care. I opened up her nappy, but it was clean and dry. Just a pink little bottom staring back at me. I looked down into little Bethany's scrunched-up face.

'What's wrong with you? What do you want, eh? What do you want?'

And, just then, a plume of liquid shit shot out of her, soaking the bed and hitting me right in the chest.

'Oh fuckSAKE!'

I ripped off my T-shirt and stuffed it into a bag, tying the top up and chucked it over into the corner with the rest of the shit- and piss-filled clothes. The house didn't have a washing machine. I had to go the launderette, with her screaming like

*that, and sit and wait for the stuff to wash, with her screaming
like that, tomorrow, maybe today. The idea of it made me want
to punch myself in the face.*

*I left her screaming in the puddle of shit on the bed, and went
ferreting around at the back of my cupboard. Surely there must
be something there, that couldn't be my last top. It had only been
four days for fuck's sake . . .*

*I found some screwed-up black cotton, stuffed right into the
back corner, and tugged it out. One of Justin's T-shirts, not mine.
Fine. It's not like I was on my way out to impress anyone, was it?*

*I pulled on the T-shirt, and for a second I was lost in the smell
of him. Fags and expensive cologne and booze and gear and . . .
Fuck.*

*He'd come round once. One single time. Stood there, all awk-
ward, and when I gave him her to hold, handed her right back.
Hadn't seen him since. Hadn't seen him, or Katie or Tony. No
one.*

*I looked at Bethany. Her little arms and legs were drawn into
her body like she was trying to disappear into herself. She was
still screaming. And screaming and screaming.*

*I braced myself. I took a deep, slow breath. And I picked her
back up.*

'Look over there, love! Birdie!'

I point to this pigeon, pecking around outside McDonald's.
It's a mangy old thing, grey and diseased looking. But it keeps
her attention for a second or so, before it gets too nervous
of the crowds and flaps off. It was a grim thing to show her
anyway – it's hardly Disneyland round here. But I'm trying.

We're trudging up the High Street. Slow, because I've still

got no clue where we're going or what we're doing or how we're going to eat or where we're going to sleep tonight, or anything at all. I'm carrying her, even though it's hurting my arms and my feet and my everything and I'm trying to think of anything, any old nonsense at all, to keep her occupied, to keep her from thinking about how shit stuff is. But I've run out of things to point at. We've already done car, car, car, shop, cinema, doggie, and all that's left is drunk, tramp, McDonald's we don't have the money to go in.

I lean in close to Bethany, and whisper,

'Hey! Remember Cinderella?'

She looks up at me from her perch on my hip. She doesn't look sure. She's frowning, a way I've never seen my Bethany frown before. And, I mean, she's smiling in my photos. But still, I've proper pored over those pictures – I've imagined her face every way it could go. I didn't think she'd look quite like this.

I shake the thought out of my head. No time for that.

'Remember? Cinderelly? With the little mice and stuff?'

She nods, maybe a bit hesitant, but back on side. I should have known. It's stories, that's the thing I do best, the reason people like me. The one thing I can always give.

'Remember, she had a really bad time. She had to do all the washing and cooking, and she wasn't never allowed to have anything for herself, because her parents were gone and there was no one left to care for her.'

I feel tears welling up in my eyes, which would have been embarrassing normally, but who cares? What, is Bethany going to take the piss out of me for it on the landings?

She's looking up at me, giving me full-on attention and not

looking like she's thinking about crying, which is pretty good going for us. I go on,

'But that was when her Fairy Godmother came and saved her, wasn't it? And Cinderella got her dress, and she got to the ball, and she met her Prince. And everything was alright for her then, wasn't it? What was it? Happy . . .'

Bethany joins in and we say it together, smiling,

'Ever after!'

I give her a little squeeze.

'Good girl. But we have to remember about Cinderella, when something bad happens. That the bad thing's not just happening on its own, it's just a part of your story, and you'll get through it. It's always darkest before the dawn, isn't it?'

She looks a bit confused by that. It's something people say, isn't it? But I'm not sure. I've been up till dawn loads of times, but never in much of a state to be monitoring the light levels, if I'm honest. I try again.

'After the bad stuff, you get your happy ever after. That's how it works. You've just got to believe.'

She smiles up at me and I smile back. I don't know if I think it's true, all that stuff I just said. Maybe I used to. But a story isn't for you, is it? It's for your audience. Like I've been saying, it doesn't matter what happens to me. My story's already mostly written, and I know deep down there's only so many ways it can end. This little one, though, she's more important. She's still got a chance.

I shift her over onto my other hip and reach into my pocket. I pull out the beads Janie gave me earlier. Protect you, don't they?

'And if you ever get scared during the bad stuff, all you've got to do is remember you're wearing these beads. They'll keep you safe.'

I mean. No harm in trying.

She smiles.

I feel something drop on my head, once, then again. I reach up to feel, but it's just water, not bird poo or spit or whatever. I look up.

It's raining. Not just a little bit of drizzle or whatever. This is one of those summer storms where it feels like it'll never stop raining – they always come after a couple of weeks where you thought it'd never rain again.

Fucking perfect.

I pull her hood up and look around the street, for somewhere to shelter from it. People are running in all directions, holding free papers up over their heads and staring up now and then, all disapproving at the sky, like, *oi, what you doing that for?* Up ahead there's a club or something – shut up as it's still early, but with these big deep shelter things out the front of it. There's already crowds starting to form under them. I make for it, sharpish.

My skin's wet and chilled through. It feels weird, kind of slimy, not clean like after you actually wash. I just feel like I've been covered in more dirt. Thinking about it, it's a long time since I've felt rain on my skin. Inside, all you ever see is pretty okay weather, because they'd never let you out if it was pissing down.

As it goes I can't say I've much missed it.

I get to the shelter and take my place among the rest of the hacked off, damp Londoners. Most of them don't look at me twice, but there's this old bloke, with a posh suit and a takeaway coffee, who gives me a little glare down his nose. I give him my worst look back. *It's public property, mate. I've got as much right to standing here as you have.*

I peer out from behind the heads and shoulders in front of me. There's still people running around the street, looking for somewhere to hide from the rain, but there aren't as many now. Most people have found their little roost to wait it out in. There's only a couple of them dashing about, and one woman who's just walking normally. She's actually got an umbrella – who carries an umbrella in August? – and she's wandering about, not looking like she's going anywhere. As I watch her she goes up to some man in a tatty-looking hoodie on the street, and seems to ask him a question. As she does, she lifts up her umbrella so there's room for him under it too, and I get a glimpse of long black braids, woven back into a French plait.

No.

I must be imagining it. I mean, I'm cold, hungry, had a long day and that, the mind does play tricks.

I push my way, gently, politely, to the front of the shelter. I have to jostle some of the people out of my way a bit. They glare, but say nothing. Can't be helped. I need to see.

I get to the front and see the woman more clearly. She's wearing a boring businessy type suit. I can't see her face because of the umbrella, but the woman's wearing these clumpy shoes. Lesbian social worker shoes.

It's her it's her it's her. *Shitting hell.* What's she doing here? It can't be her. Can it?

I lean out of the shelter, trying to keep the baby at least still in the dry. The umbrella's covering the woman's head again now. I stand there, holding my breath. On the one hand I want her to lift the umbrella up, so I can see for sure, so I can know one way or another. But there's another big part of me wants to stay in the safeness of not knowing.

She finishes her chat with the man and lifts the umbrella and I see that, no question about it, it is Emma after all.

She's not my normal, cool-as-a-cucumber Emma today. Her forehead's wrinkled up into a worried looking frown and she's got this air about her, like, flustered. As I watch, she goes up to someone huddling in a bus stop. Her posh, annoying voice floats over to me, despite the noise of the rain.

'Excuse me, sir . . .'

She leans in and I can't hear the rest, but I can see her showing him something in her hand. A picture? I stroke Bethany's hair, trying to keep her quiet, and calm myself down as well, if I'm honest. A picture of me?

There's something about the way she's showing the picture – kind of quick, kind of nervy – that makes me wonder if this is a completely legit probation move. It sort of looks like this might be something she's doing off her own back – a bit of a rogue manoeuvre.

I narrow my eyes at her. Why the fuck would she do that, though? I know I'm a dick to her and that, but does she really hate me that much? Enough to come out searching, just so she gets to be the one who gets the pleasure of chucking me back inside?

Not today, mate. I'm staying out, till the baby's safe.

I take a couple of steps along the outer edge of the alcove, away from her. There's a decent chance that when it starts raining on her again, Bethany's going to bawl, so I want to be as far away from Emma as I can be before I break cover. I take a couple more steps to the side, eyes glued to Emma, on tiptoes and trying to not even breathe too hard.

And as I do, I knock against the old posh bloke, the one with the coffee, and a bit slops over the lip of the cup and onto his hand. He tuts and sighs and rolls his eyes like I'm the worst thing that's ever happened to him, and he goes,

'EXCUSE me.'

In this huge voice like a foghorn and Emma turns to look. Our eyes meet, and for a second we just stand there, staring at each other. I can't do anything else. I'm stuck to the floor, like in a dream.

She takes a step forward, nervous, faltering. And the spell breaks.

I shove the man with his fucking coffee as hard as I can away from me, and I run. As fast as I can, as hard as I can, rain soaking me and the little girl bouncing up and down on my hip and me clinging onto her tight. She's screaming and my chest's bursting and Emma's just behind us so I don't slow down, I keep running. Pounding down the street, and then a sharp right turn and then a left and then another. I still know the streets round here well enough to get lost, if I need to.

And now that I'm flat out of choices, I know exactly where I'm going.

Chapter Nineteen

Extract from PSO 4800 – Women Prisoners

Some women living in abusive and exploitative
relationships may need long-term support and
assistance to break free.

Justin opens the door and smiles his same old smile at me.
The one that means good times and sex and sunshine and
smack.

'Alright, kitten? Long time no see.'

I arrange my own face into a scrunched-up little *fuck you
mate* scowl, because he can lay off with the fucking kitten
shit. I've got stuff with Justin that hasn't been dealt with.

'Yeah, well, I've been in prison. Got busted, didn't I? For
having a load of drugs in my flat. Remember?'

And I give him a long hard glare, because it was his fucking
drugs they found in my flat, and he knows it. *Just keep them
overnight, babe*, he said, but they were there three fucking
weeks and then I got raided. And the rest. So I reckon he owes
me, which is good because I'm here for a favour.

He just shrugs and goes,

'Yeah. Sorry about that,'

and doesn't look it at all. He reaches over and gives one of the baby's pigtails a little tug. It straightens out, then bounces back up into its curls. Her hair's the only part of her left not covered in dirt or snot.

'Cute kid.'

And she, to give her her due, isn't stupid. She takes one look at Justin, leaning against the side of his door with that old *oh hey there baby* face on him, and she sucks in a lungful of air and lets out a massive wailing scream. She sounds like one of those alarms in old films about the war. I shush and jiggle her a bit, but she's having none of it. She just keeps screaming. Justin looks horrified, and for half a second I think he's going to slam the door in my face, but then he looks right and left down the landing, all quick and shifty, and goes,

'Fuck, come on in then.'

I step into the flat, and she immediately downgrades from her nuclear-type screaming to just, like, a kind of plaintive wailing. The dark of the hall seems to be soothing her a bit, and thank fuck for that. I give her a little squeeze.

'Come on, love. Here we are.'

I head through to the living room, which is probably on balance the living room I've got the happiest of all my memories in, the one where I've always felt most like I'm at home. I mean, I was totally fucking out of it most of those times, but still. I'm fond of the place. With a kid on my hip, though, I see stuff I haven't noticed before. Like, old takeaway boxes and random plastic bags, just lying there. I step around them, and see a hardened old cat crap by the bathroom door. It's all dried up and gone sort of crispy, must have been there for months. Maybe it was even there last time I was round. I'd have been too fucked up to notice.

There's a load of dirty spoons on the sofa. I eyeball them. No needles, though. Justin's got standards, he's always had his shit together a little bit about things like that. Still, I don't really want her playing with them or whatever, so I shove the cat off the knackered armchair and plop her down there. I feel a bit weird and unbalanced without the weight on my hip. Much lighter, too.

Justin slinks into the room, lights a fag and smirks at me like something's funny.

'What do you want then, eh? Damsel and mini-damsel in distress. Turning up at my door, looking to get rescued. What's the story?'

He always talks like that, like he's just waiting for the punchline of a joke. Always, no matter how bad stuff seems. I nod to her and go,

'This is . . .' And I look at her. And I can't say the name. Because, if I'm honest, I know. I was that excited to have her back, and I wanted it so much . . . But life's not a fairy tale, is it? I close my eyes to squeeze the tears back in. 'We need a hand.'

And he looks at me, for the longest second ever. I hold my breath.

The little one starts up screaming again. Her screams are a bit thinner now than they were earlier, a little less loud. I reckon she's getting tired. A big part of me wants to go to her. Pick her up, give her a cuddle and try to do the mamma bit, just for a little while more. But all I can do is stare at her.

I just can't. I feel like I've been used up, and now I'm empty.

Justin steps across me, stubs his fag out and scoops her up.

'Alright, kiddo. Shhh shhh. You're okay.'

He bounces her about a bit. Her screaming dies down to quiet little sobs, and she rests her snotty little face on his chest. Justin looks at me. He really looks at me, like he can see through me. I'll give him one thing – Justin can be a right shit, but when he gives you all his attention, it's like no one else exists in the world.

'Okay, Kitty. Whatcha need?'

I'm that grateful that just for a moment I forgive him for the bust. I forgive him everything, for the feeling of having someone properly on my side. There's something really important about that. Sometimes, it doesn't even matter who they are, but I'm one of those people who need people about me all the time. That's the worst thing about being outside. There's not always someone there.

'Just like ... a tenner. Enough for some warm clothes for her, a bit to eat.'

He laughs.

'A tenner? How long you been inside for?'

Fucker. I'd punch him if he wasn't still holding the baby.

'Nine fucking months. How long were you inside for your gear getting raided, Justin?'

He shrugs, and gives me a cheeky, *you got me* smile.

'Fair point, Kitty. Not a good phrase. But what I mean is, you'll need a lot more than that for you and the mini-damsel. Tenner'll do you for food, for tonight, maybe. The shops are shut for clothes, though. And where are you going to sleep, eh?'

For a moment, I'm just paralysed by the question, like,

completely frozen by it. Then I take in a big, deep lungful of air and start really fucking screaming.

'I don't FUCKING know, alright? You're right! You win! We're TOTALLY FUCKED.'

Him and the kid both stare at me, wearing the same mouth-a-bit-open, *what-the-fuck-are-you-doing* expression. They look so alike, pulling that same face, it makes my chest ache with all the might-have-beens. It feels bloody good to scream, though.

'I know that too, though! You're not so clever. I know that I can't feed her, can't get her warm enough, nowhere to sleep, no money, no . . .'

And I let the sobs rip through me. You'd think they'd shake me apart. I cry and cry and gasp and snort and bloody howl at the fucking awfulness of everything.

How am I back here, again?

Justin looks concerned.

'Hey now. Come on, Kitty. Shhh.'

He comes over and gives me this awkward one-armed hug, with the little one still on his other hip. He's going to get covered in snot from both of us if he's not careful.

He tilts my chin up with his fingers.

'Here. You've had a pretty long day, haven't you, Kitty? You want something to help you relax?'

That stops me crying. I can't help it, it's like a switch has been thrown or something. And I know, I said things would be different this time. But I say a lot of things.

He goes to the coffee table and opens a little box. He pulls out a clear bag full of powder, holding it out and waggling it at me the way he does with the cat and her toys.

'Go and get the stuff. Come on.' He gives the baby a couple of bounces on his hip. 'The kid can have some chips, and you can have a bit of gear, on me. Think about tomorrow tomorrow. Right? You can pay me back later. We'll work it out.'

All I can do is stare at the bag, watch it sway in front of me. It's hypnotised me. Justin bobs his head towards the kitchen.

'Go on. You know where it is.'

I turn and walk towards the kitchen in a daze. My hip still feels weird and light. My feet throb like you wouldn't believe from all the walking, and every bone in me aches. I'm hungry, and cold, and I still don't know what the fuck we're going to do. Now I've stopped running, all of these bad feelings pile on top of me, so heavy I can barely stand.

I go to the drawer Justin keeps the stuff in and pull it out. I look down at the equipment, glinting up at me all grubby under the fluorescent light.

The thing is, that I have to consider, is that if I do this, Justin will let us sleep here. At least for tonight. If I'm fun, if I do this, and if the baby doesn't kick off too much, then we'll be worth keeping about to him. I'll have a chance to take a breather, get my head together a bit, she'll be out of the cold, we'll both have a bit of kip and I can sort everything out in the morning.

Actually, this is the only sensible thing to do. It's the thing that a good mum would do.

Just one hit. I'll sort everything else out in the morning.

And where the fuck else are we going to go?

I pick up the fistful of metal, rubber and glass and I head back into the living room.

*

Justin's got kiddo on his knee and he's sort of jiggling her around, chatting nonsense to her, like,

'Hello, then. Yes, that's right. Hello. Hi there, little one. You're a nice little girl, aren't you? Yes. Yes, you are. That's right.'

For a moment, I let myself hope. Maybe we can stay here more than one night. Maybe he'll look after me and her, and we'll be almost like a little family, the three of us. He had a go, didn't he? Back in the day. I know he wasn't that much help, but he didn't leave me, at least, did he? He came to visit our baby once.

So maybe it'll all work out?

He sees me, and gives me one of his best smiles, the kind that make you feel like you're the only person in the world. Still smiling at me, he slides her off his knee and onto the floor. I want to scoop her up, because it's not clean in here, and while she's not exactly neat herself any more I don't want her actually playing with cat shit or whatever. The problem is, I'm still holding the works. I kind of feel like I don't want to touch her while I'm carrying this stuff, like that would be dirtier, somehow, than the floor.

I meet Justin's smile and nod to the baby.

'Oi, Justin, are we going to get her some chips first, yeah?'

Justin's still grinning and slapping his knees with his hands. Waiting for a treat.

'What?' He looks down, like he'd forgotten she was there. *She was sitting on your lap about ten seconds ago, you prick.* 'Yeah, sure, Kittycat. Let's just do this, then we'll sort her out.'

I shake my head, because I know me and I know Justin and I know junkies. That little girl's been through a lot today, and she's getting a decent dinner, no matter what.

'Nah, we need to do her first, don't we? Otherwise we won't bother.'

His grin starts looking a bit forced now.

'We will. Come on.'

And he pats the sofa next to him, all inviting. And at that moment, after the day I've had, that crappy sofa looks like the softest most comfy thing ever, but I stay standing up.

'You said you'd get her some chips.'

Justin rubs his head with his hands. I've pissed him off, I can tell. But he promised.

'Look. Don't be stupid. She doesn't even want chips. Do you?'

And he gives her a nudge with his foot. A bit harder, I think, than he really needed too. Almost like a little kick, I would say. She looks back at him, and then straight up into my eyes. Her hand goes up to her neck and she clutches at those little blue beads.

'I want Mummy.'

And I look at her, her tear- and snot-smeared face, and her grubby little dress and her big sad eyes, and I feel her words cut right through me.

Justin ruffles her hair. Too hard, again.

'See? She doesn't want chips. Give me that.'

He reaches out and snatches the fixings from my hand. He taps some powder onto the spoon, and flicks the lighter underneath it. Normally, I watch this bit. I proper gaze at it – it's like the opening credits of the night you're going to have.

You don't want to miss the build-up, the anticipation. But this time all I can look at is this kid I thought was Bethany.

And I know now, I'm not this baby's mamma. She's not my Bethany. I didn't get my baby back, I didn't hold her in my arms. This one's not mine. She's someone else's everything.

Justin drops the cotton wool onto the melted powder. Slides the needle under. Sucks the liquid up. Just a little bit of liquid. A tiny needle. A prick on the skin, and then I don't have to be a shit mum any more. I don't have to be an anything.

He smiles at me.

'Go on. You can go first.'

And I pick up the needle. The syringe is solid, reassuring in my hand. Same old needle.

It's not fair on me. That I can't have her, that I can't do what any other woman does without even thinking. I can't be a decent mum, the one thing I want to be more than anything else, and that's really fucking shit.

And Justin smiles at me. That same old smile.

But it doesn't matter what's fair on me, does it? She's a baby. It only matters what's fair on her. That she's happy, and safe. Like my Bethany's happy and safe, I hope. I can't give my Bethany a family right now. I can't give her a home. But I can do this one thing, for another little girl who needs saving.

I put down the needle. It lies on the coffee table, glinting so beautiful under the flat's electric strip lights.

I pick Not-Bethany up, and hold her close to me. I say,

'I'm sorry, love. I'm sorry.'

I don't really know which of them I'm talking to. Then I

turn on my heel and do something I never thought I would,
or could.

I walk away.

*I know, deep down, I can't blame Emma for me not having
Bethany. I know that. It was only ever me.*

*It was February. The coldest we'd ever had, I reckon, though
don't they all feel like that, at the time? Cold, though. I clutched
Bethany to me, and walked up the hill. It wasn't raining, at least.
Every day since she'd been born there'd been the same heavy,
freezing rain, halfway to sleet really, but that day was dry. There
was even a bit of watery sun filtering down. I gave myself a half-
smile. Nice day for it.*

*Bethany was sleeping in my arms. It felt like the first time
she'd slept since she was born. Maybe it was the flat she didn't
like, or the feeling of nothing happening. Maybe she liked the
cold, clean air.*

*I held her close against Justin's T-shirt, crusted with milk and
sick now, but still smelling of him a bit. I tried to take in the way
she felt, the weight of her, the softness. So I'd remember.*

*I struggled on up. She was killing my back, but I didn't have
a pushchair, a carrycot. Nothing. I didn't even have nappies, by
then. I caught a man's eye on the other side of the street and he
smiled at me. That was something I'd noticed, having her with
me. Strangers smiling at me. I'd miss that.*

I didn't smile back. I just walked on.

*Until I was there. I crossed the car park and looked up at the
sign. The Lambeth Hospital. Bethany stayed asleep in my arms.
Her head lolled against my chest, trusting as anything.*

I nearly went to a church, but me and God have never got on

*all that well. I thought she'd be safe in a hospital. That's where
you go to be safe, isn't it? And they were nice to me, when I had
her. It had felt like home.*

*I went into the waiting room and looked around. Pretty quiet.
There was a dodgy looking bloke with a split lip, a girl about my
age, looking miserable and holding her wrist, and an older lady.
She had a posh handbag sitting on the seat next to her, and her
make-up done really nice. Her nose was in a book. I headed over
to her and sat a few rows away, right in her line of sight.*

*I held Bethany up close to my face and breathed in the smell
of her head, one last time. A tear dripped off my nose and fell
onto her face, but she didn't wake up. Part of me wanted to give
her a little jiggle, get her to open her eyes for a last look, but I
didn't. I hadn't been able to do much for her, had I? I could at
least let her sleep.*

*I laid her down, gentle, on the seat beside me, and pulled the
note I'd brought with me out of my pocket. I tucked it into the
front of her blanket and stroked her cheek. So, so soft.*

*You might ask me why I did it, why I'd left her at the hospital
rather than handing her in to the social properly. The thing is, I
know they say you can go to them, get help when you're struggling. But I also know that you can't just hand in a baby, and
then walk away. They'll want to ask you questions, won't they?
They'll want to find out why you can't cope. And you can't say,
can you, that you haven't had any gear for getting on for a week
now, and during that time you've been nearly ripped apart by
this thing that they handed you, that keeps looking at you like
you're trustworthy, like she trusts you not to get in the kind of
state where you can't look after her any more, but that's the only
thing you want to do, to go and get in that kind of state, to give*

up responsibility for yourself, even, let alone her. And you know, you just know, that you'll probably crack. You won't be strong enough, no matter how much you love her. And you do love her, that's the thing, you really fucking do.

So you have to give her up. No matter how much it hurts you, you're just not as important. She has to be safe, even if you have to break yourself into bits to get her there.

If you went to the social, they might talk you out of it. They might give you another chance, and you might be weak enough to take it.

I took one last look. Stared at her, hard, until my eyes went wobbly with tears.

I stood up and walked, fast as I could, out of the waiting room. I kept my eyes on the floor. I knew, if anyone said anything to me at all, that'd be it, I'd just lose it. But no one said anything. Without a baby, I was invisible again.

I went outside, and crouched behind a big bin, peering out and round. I could just see the lady through the automatic doors. She was still just sitting there reading her book. Come on, come on. Go and get a Coke or something. Have a look.

Then, Bethany's cry. My tits got damp at the sound of it, but I smiled. That's right, Bethany. No one can ignore that.

The lady looked up from her book, her lips this perfect red circle of surprise. I saw her get up and run over to where my Bethany was. She was out of range, so I didn't see her pick her up, but I heard her cry out, all startled,

'Nurse!'

And I sniffed, hard, and swallowed down the guilt and the sadness and the feeling of wanting her back in my arms.

I forced myself not to think about any of it. I just walked away.

Chapter Twenty

Extract from PSO 1600 – Use of Force

1.1.   The use of force by one person on another
        without consent is unlawful unless it is justified.

My first time in prison, I wasn't even that scared. Not when they took me from the court, not when they handcuffed me, not when they threw me in the van. The strip search was a bit of a surprise, not that nice, but once I'd worked out they did it to everyone, that wasn't that bad either. And I was surprised that it was so easy. I was nineteen, and just been done for assault. I could never keep my shit together for more than ten minutes in those days, you might not believe it to look at me, but I've really calmed down. All my life, people had been threatening me with getting locked up, that was always the ultimate thing, the thing I was getting one last chance to avoid. And when I got there, when they slammed the door of my first ever cell and left me there ... It was just like a cross between getting sent to your room and detention, you know? No big deal at all. Not at first glance.

The thing is, it's not the one night inside that'll break you. Anyone can do one night, no problem. Two nights, three nights as well. Easy. The hard thing is, it gets in your head, and becomes where you're from. Prison isn't just a thing that happens to you – it becomes who you are.

The second time, of course, it's even easier. Been there, done that, three more months, no problem. And the third. Little by little, the years built up, the sentences built up, and I started to spend more time inside than out.

I used to be a Londoner, and now I'm a prisoner, and that's hard to change. But perhaps it's not impossible. You can move to France if you want, and you're still a Londoner. But at least you're in France. And maybe in five years, ten years, whatever, someone asks you where you're from and, without thinking, you go, *Paris*.

That's what I think, anyway. I hope I'm right.

I stand on the steps of Brixton Police Station and breathe in what might be one of my last breaths of outside air for a while. It's hardly the cool, crisp scent that you think of when you wonder what freedom smells like, but the fumes and fried chicken of London smell pretty good to me. I drink it in.

Cuddling the little girl tight to me, one last time, it occurs to me, of course it does, that the old me would just dump her down here and bugger off. I could set her down, and give her a little push through the door. Even watch her go in through the window, if I wanted, to make sure she was safe. Then a hop, skip and jump straight back to Justin's. A fix, some McDonald's later, if that's what I want, and not back to prison. At least for a little bit. At least for a night.

But as I squeeze her tight, hugging her sturdy little body

against mine, I plant a kiss on the soft little top of her head, and I think, *nah*. Let's say goodbye properly this time. Let's do it right. I shove open the door with my free hand, I brace myself, and step inside.

They're always so bright, police stations. I march up to the desk, blinking a bit in the light. I recognise one of the guys on the desk. Dave, I think it is. Most of them know me in here. He looks pretty surprised to see me, and fair play. I imagine most people on the run don't just mooch into the local cop shop. But before he can open his mouth to start having a go at me for escaping or whatever, I cut him off and go,

'I found this little girl. She's missing, in't she? Her name's ... um ...'

'Olivia Parker!'

The guy on the desk next to Dave gives me a massive grin.

'Oi! Everyone! Someone's found the little girl! She's here.'

And all of a sudden there's a load of police around, all smiling and talking all at once and looking at me, like, *nice one*.

'Great!'

'Aw, you found her.'

'Where was she, eh?'

But I'm just looking at Dave. A look goes between us, like, we both know what's happening next. He looks a bit sorry, even. He says,

'She needs taking down the cells, lads. This is the APB from Holloway.'

And the way everyone looks at me changes in a second. I know I don't have long, so I hug the baby to me, extra tight, and I go, so quiet that no one but her can hear,

'Bye bye. I'm so sorry.'

And I try to make a memory. What it's like to hold a little child in your arms, to be a mum to them, to feel that love between you, strong and bright. To feel the magic of a piece of yourself, back close to you at last.

Next time it'll be for real. I swear.

Dave's come out from behind the desk, and does the actual talking bit himself. That's pretty decent of him. It's like, a little bit of respect.

'Daniella Grove,'

Not-Bethany's snatched out of my arms. She starts wailing as soon as she leaves them. Maybe she did know I was trying to take care of her, after all.

'I am arresting you for escape. You do not have to say anything, but it may harm your defence . . . '

The officers grab me. Their massive hands grip tight around my arms and twist them back and I let myself go limp. It hurts less if you go with it. They lift me, just by the arms, and the sockets in my armpits pop and groan. It always feels like they're going to dislocate them, at this bit, or pull them clean off, but it's alright. They never do.

' . . . if you do not mention when questioned something which you later rely on in court.'

There's a click and pinch as I'm cuffed. The metal's cold against my skin.

'Anything you do say may be given in evidence.'

I don't struggle against them at all. I just look at the baby one last time, and I try really hard to give her a smile.

I sit in the cell of Brixton nick, slumped against the wall. The beds, which are shit enough in Holloway, are even worse in here – just ledges, really. There's just the bed ledge and a loo and that's it. Pretty fucking grim. I expect I'll be back to the comforts of my own little cell soon enough, though.

There's this big empty kind of feeling inside me. It's like having Bethany back with me, even if it was just pretend, had filled a hole in me, like it had made me more solid. Now it's gone, and I'm all hollow. Like I had been, these last two and a half years, but had learned not to notice.

It's bloody quiet, in here. All I can hear is some drunk snoring a few cells down. There's no racket like in Holloway, no hustle and bustle and feeling of stuff going on. There's just me and my ledge and the smells of piss and disinfectant you get in all fresh cells. And then, another noise. There's footsteps, coming along the corridor and heading towards my door.

I prick my ears up. Someone coming to see me? I'd expected to be left to rot until morning if I'm honest, so this is a bit of a surprise. I don't lift up from my slump, though. I mean, who's it going to be? Justin, with some Mars bars and smack for me? Nah. It'll just be some fucking official from somewhere, here to have a go at me and tell me how fucked I am. Not really worth lifting my head up for that.

The door clangs open. A pair of sensible, lesbian social worker-type shoes step into the room and then the door clangs shut again. I flick my eyes up to see who it is.

Fucking Emma. Of course. Just to make sure my day is completely crap, front to finish.

I jerk my head up, to give her a proper, full-blooded glare. Who was it told the police I was a fucking baby snatcher, eh? I could have found her mum if it wasn't for that. And who came fucking looking for me, chasing me all over London, because she couldn't fucking wait to see me back inside again? Fucking Emma. That's who.

I sit there and glare and keep schtum, waiting for her to start having a go at me. Emma's getting nothing out of me tonight. I'm that broken I can't be arsed to kick off at her. If she's looking to pick a fight, she's going to have to look somewhere else.

'Daniella. Are you okay?'

There's something about the tone she takes that makes me look at her again, eye contact and everything. She's looking actually worried. Like, not worried for her own arse or whatever, because one of her prisoners did a bunk, but actually worried about me.

'Can I sit down?'

I nod. I'm not going to lie, I'm that surprised that for a moment I can't speak. Then I go,

'Did they find her mum? Is she back home now?'

Emma looks more knackered than I've ever seen her.

'Olivia. Her name is Olivia. And she is back home now, yes.'

We sit there together, not speaking. And Emma says in this little, gentle voice,

'Daniella, do you know why I was looking for you this morning?'

I blink. *This morning.* Christ, that feels like a while ago. I shake my head.

'I wanted to tell you that I hadn't been able to get hold of your daughter's foster parents. They're away for a few weeks. France, I believe.'

I smile to myself. *France.*

And she gives me this significant look, like, *come on Dani, do you get what I'm saying?*

I give her a look, like, *yeah Miss, I get it.* And, obviously, I don't feel great about it. But that dog would have got her if I hadn't been there. That's still something I did, something I didn't fuck up, and you can't take that away.

She doesn't push it. She just sits down next to me, sharing my bed-ledge, and leans her head back against the wall.

And there's something about the soft silence between us that makes me feel like it's okay to ask her,

'Miss, why were you out looking for me earlier? Did they make you do that?'

Emma clears her throat. She looks well shifty.

'You must be mistaken, Daniella. Probation officers don't go out looking for escaped prisoners. That would be a police matter.'

I narrow my eyes at her, like, *come on, Miss, we both know that's bullshit.*

'Yeah. Why, though?

She shifts around next to me on the ledge, uncomfortable.

'As I said, you must be mistaken.' And she gives me this look. Like she's weighing me up. 'But if I *were* to have gone out looking for you – which I *definitely wasn't* – it would have been because I was worried about you. Because I want you to be safe.'

I don't say anything to that, but inside, I think, *oh.* I didn't know that. After a bit of a pause, she goes,

'You'll be heading back to Holloway tomorrow, Daniella. They'll give you a bit more time for the escape—'

I'm already nodding, like, *yeah, yeah, I know,* but she's not done talking.

'But not that much more. You have a lot of mitigating factors. No violence, no other offences, and you turned yourself in . . . So it'll be a very short sentence for that one. How many will that make now?'

I have a go at giving her my old, chirpy, *I don't give a fuck about nothing* smile.

'Eleven. And this one'll be my last.'

And she gives me this tired little grin. I think I'm due another lecture, but instead she just gives me a squeeze on the arm, so light you'd barely feel it, and goes,

'Yes. I hope so.'

And I give her a smile, my first proper one ever, I reckon. And I make us a promise, her and me, in my head. *Don't worry. It will be.*

Miss Green's *clang clang clanging* me through the prison and back to the wing, and, so far, she's said nothing to me. I haven't said much either. I'm still drinking it in. It's weird, coming back in. I can't believe it was only twenty-three hours ago I was in here. It feels like it might have been a million years, or maybe that I didn't leave at all, and it was all a dream. I know it was real, though, partly because I'm not fucking mental, thanks, and partly because the hoodie's gone from around my waist. I didn't have the heart to take it back off the baby, poor little thing, and, anyway, I don't care. It's still summer.

As me and Miss Green are walking down the last outside corridor before we're back on my landing, I go,

'Miss, you got a new photo of the little one for me to see? He must be, like, six months old now, mustn't he?'

And, I mean, it is still summer, obviously. But there's something about the feeling of the prison that's changed. That stifling hotness, pressure-cooker air of the place has cooled off a little. Must have been the rain.

Miss Green's face stays tight. She just says,

'I don't think that's appropriate, Grove.'

And she won't look me in the eye. We walk the rest of the distance to the gate in silence, the two of us. It's that, far more than the shit at the police station or the things they said on intake, that makes me really feel like I've been nicked.

One last *clang*. She opens the door for me, and nods me in. And what can I do? I go.

Stepping back on the landing, the burning hair smell's still there. It's fainter now, but it'll be lingering around for days, I'd think. Things do, in here. I tilt my chin up and try to put it out of my mind, though. This next bit's important.

I clear my throat, and stand there, shoulders square and a cocky smile on my face, waiting to be noticed.

It doesn't take long.

'Wooooo! Dani!'

'Alright, Dani?'

'You're back then? That wasn't long!'

And I concentrate. I meet every eye, give out nods, and little grins and a *yeah, alright? You?* to everyone I see. It's like being a celebrity, almost, and I smile back at their cheers and grins. They don't even know how much I deserve a cheer, today. How much I've got to be proud about, and how much I'm still going to do.

But all the while I'm doing it, there's only one person I'm looking for.

When I see her, she's sprawled out on the sofas, with a knot of girls all around her. There aren't enough seats for everyone; some of them are sitting on the floor, some leaning awkwardly, bums perched on the pool table. But Martha's reclined on the tatty blue sofa, taking up enough space for at least two. She's not hidden in a corner, or crouched over a book, or looking like she's trying to disappear. She looks like a queen or something. Like she's exactly where she's supposed to be.

Martha gives me this massive flash of smile, eyes and mouth all wide, and like something's really funny, she goes,

'Alright, new bitch?'

And I can't tell, right then, what she means by that. I really don't know if she's taking the piss out of me, or if that's an in joke just for the two of us, or if I should take it at face value or what. Her smile could mean anything, from *I'll fucking knife you later, junkie* to *well done, mate. I'm so proud of you.* I just don't know.

And the thing is, it just doesn't matter, does it? She'll think what she'll think and she'll do what she'll do. Everyone will. But I can do what I want as well.

Who gives a shit that I'm back here, really? What would be the point of hanging round Justin's for a few days and then getting picked up again? And what would have been the point of just bobbing along, like I was before, inside, outside, do drugs, do crime, get caught, inside, outside, again and again and again? Same shit, different shoe, every day forever.

Maybe I don't have to do that any more. Because I've said

no to smack now. I've broken out of prison, and I've saved a baby, and I've given myself up to make sure she was safe. Maybe I can do all sorts of things I never thought I could.

Martha's got what she wanted, I can see that now – she's the new boss. Well, fine. Let her be. There was a time I would have kicked against it. A time I would have shoved her against the wall and asked her what was in that letter she had me deliver, made her say if the whole thing was just a trick. A time I would have really, really cared.

But things have changed. I've changed. Now, I know what I'm going to do, and who I'm going to be. I'm going to get out of this place, and I'm going to get my little girl back. I'm going to be her mum. You watch me.

I don't have to keep being what I was before. I can choose now. I'm free.

So I meet Martha's eyes and I smile at her, a full, proper smile. I nod to her and I go,

'Yeah. Alright.'

And it is.

Acknowledgements

A huge and heartfelt thanks to the woman I met at the Holloway Mother and Baby Unit who, when I asked her if she ever took her son swimming, asked if I would put *my* baby in a prison pool. You were right that I would not. To all the prisoners and the prison officers I've met, for being so generous with your stories and your time. To everyone at the Prison Phoenix Trust, for the work that you do, for the inspiration and for your kindness.

Thanks to my agent Laetitia Rutherford for your tireless work and for getting what I was trying to do. To my editor Sharmaine Lovegrove, for creating such an incredible imprint and for loving Dani like I do. To both of you for making this the best book it could possibly be.

Thanks to Tina Sederholm for reading a million versions of this book, and for all the years of coffee and feedback. Also to George and Nikki Lewkowicz, for the huge help with plot, and for giving me so many excuses to go to Brixton.

Thanks to all my early readers – Jen Thomas, Dan Holloway, Kimberley Atkins, Harry Man, and most particularly to Becky Allen and Claire Trévien. Your enthusiasm and advice were invaluable. To the organisers of the Exeter

Novel Prize – being shortlisted was a boost to my confidence when I most needed it. To Kiran Millwood Hargrave and Daisy Johnson for explaining to me what was going on, and for being excited with me.

Thanks to Bristi Chowdhury, for letting me write the entire first draft in your sewing room, and for making me coffee while I whined about how hard it was. To Orlagh McGrath for your essential assistance in my research into Bethany. To all my friends, who have provided relentless support. There are far too many to name, so here are just a few – James Webster, Dawn Lynch, Mike and Dorothy Fitchett.

Thanks to Henry Ayrton and Anne Cooper, of course, for everything. Most particularly for your fierce enthusiasm about this book at every stage, and for always believing that I could do anything.

And thanks to Paul Fitchett, for the reassurance, the read-throughs, the rounds of tea, and the household tasks when it was definitely my turn. I still can't believe I was right about the commas.

Bringing a book from manuscript to what you are reading is a team effort.

Dialogue Books would like to thank everyone at Little, Brown who helped to publish *One More Chance* in the UK.

Editorial
Sharmaine Lovegrove
Jennie Rothwell
Zoe Gullen
Simon Osunsade

Contracts
Stephanie Cockburn

Sales
Sara Talbot
Ben Green
Rachael Hum
Viki Cheung

Design
Helen Bergh
Duncan Spilling
Hannah Wood

Production
Nick Ross
Narges Nojoumi
Mike Young

Publicity
Ella Bowman
Millie Seaward
Grace Vincent

Marketing
Jonny Keyworth
Kimberley Nyamhondera

Copyeditor
Richard Collins

Proofreader
Sue Phillpott

Also from Dialogue Books

When Rosie and Jules discover a ground-breaking clinical trial that enables two women to have a female baby, they jump at the chance to make history.

Fear-mongering politicians and right-wing movements are quick to latch on to the controversies surrounding Ovum-to-Ovum (o-o) technology and stoke the fears of the public. What will happen to the numbers of little boys born? Is there a sinister conspiracy to eradicate men at play?

In this toxic political climate, Jules and Rosie try to hide their baby from scrutiny. But when the news of Rosie's pregnancy is leaked to the media, their relationship is put under a microscope and they're forced to question the loyalty of those closest to them, and battle against a tirade of hate that threatens to split them apart...

A Sikh girl on the run. A Muslim ex-con who has to find her. A whole heap of trouble.

Southall, West London. After being released from prison, Zaq Khan is lucky to land a dead-end job at a builders' yard. All he wants to do is keep his head down and put the past behind him.

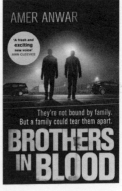

But when Zaq is forced to search for his boss's runaway daughter, he quickly finds himself caught up in a deadly web of deception, murder and revenge.

With time running out and pressure mounting, can he find the missing girl before it's too late? And if he does, can he keep her – and himself – alive long enough to deal with the people who want them both dead?